Nicola Thorne was born in Cape Town, South Africa. Her father was English and her mother a New Zealander, and she was brought up and educated in England. She graduated in Sociology at the London School of Economics, but always wanted to pursue a literary career. She worked as a reader and editor while writing her first novels. Now she writes full time, and lives in Dorset.

By the same author

The Girls
In Love
Bridie Climbing
A Woman Like Us
The Perfect Wife and Mother
The Daughters of the House
Where the Rivers Meet
Affairs of Love
The Enchantress Saga
Champagne

THE ASKHAM CHRONICLES
Never Such Innocence
Yesterday's Promises
Bright Morning
A Place in the Sun

NICOLA THORNE

Pride of Place

Grafton Books

A Division of HarperCollins*Publishers*

GraftonBooks
A Division of HarperCollins*Publishers*
77-85 Fulham Palace Road,
Hammersmith, London W6 8JB

Published in paperback by GraftonBooks 1990
9 8 7 6 5 4 3 2

First published in Great Britain by
GraftonBooks 1989

Printed and bound in Great Britain by
Mackays of Chatham plc, Chatham, Kent

Set in Garamond

Contents

Prologue
1948

There had been Prynnes at Aylestone since the time of the Conqueror, when the warlike Gervase de Prynne had built a fortification on the banks of the Thames.

Over the centuries the rough, stone-walled fortification had turned into a dwelling, a castle, a mansion and, by the eighteenth century, a large and gracious stately home with ivy clinging to its mellow stone walls. It wasn't called Aylestone Manor, or Grange or Place or anything like that. It was simply known by the name of the little village that had at one time clustered around its walls and which by now had been reduced to a few outbuildings and a cottage or two: Aylestone.

Now, as the men from the ministry began to depart, it looked rather bedraggled; its curtainless windows like sightless eyes, the gardens unkempt and the once gracious lawn a mud-covered bog criss-crossed with the thousand tyre marks of heavy lorries.

The Prynne family was, by disposition, cheerful; years of good breeding had taught them that it was bad form to show discontent, disappointment, even tears. But it was hard not to cry as one looked at those venerable walls and remembered it as it had been.

A wing of Aylestone had been preserved during the war as a home for the family. Old Lady Prynne had lived there for the duration, fearful for her safety, pressing a pillow over her head as the planes droned inwards to bomb London, or as they droned out again, sometimes scattering their bombs on the innocent citizenry beneath. Aylestone was on a promontory that jutted out into the Thames just as it bent for that final stretch downstream towards

London and the sea. During the war the work of those who had taken it over was vital: decoding enemy messages, secret information that would turn the tide of the war, defeat into victory.

Now they had all gone; the final boxes were carted away; the final thick coat of paint carelessly applied by the decorators from the Ministry. The drive and the boggy lawn looked as though a battle had been fought there and the house, empty and forlorn, awaited the return of the rest of the family: those descendants of those Prynnes – the offspring of Gervase – who had been part of the fabric of England for centuries past.

PART ONE
A Crisis in the Family
1951–1960

Chapter 1

Judith Prynne sat by the great bay window in the drawing room contemplating the lowering clouds that swept across the sky, harbingers of rain. The house still looked bare, but was no longer derelict. Yet the years since the war had not been easy. The Prynnes were not used to hardship, to the scrimping and saving that were now the lot of a family down on its luck. The gardens were forlorn, but they were tidy.

The door opened and her mother came in, pulled her cardigan closer over her shoulders and rapidly crossed the room to poke the fire.

'Can't stand the cold,' she said. 'I don't think I'll ever get used to it.'

Her daughter turned from her seat in the window and looked at her mother's thin figure bent over the fire, a cigarette in her fingers from which she nervously flicked ash into the grate.

Judith had spent the war years in England and knew all about the cold. Her mother remained in India to which she hoped she and her husband would return after the war and resume their pleasant colonial life. But both Greville Prynne's injury in the war and India's independence afterwards changed everything. Reluctantly they'd come home to Aylestone, a large, neglected stately home in which they had never really lived.

When Angela Prynne had got the fire burning to her satisfaction she sat back on her heels and threw her finished cigarette into the flames.

'Mr Williams is still with your father. I'm afraid it's not too good.'

'Is it about money?' Judith came over to her mother and stood by her side.

'I just say thank goodness your education is finished, *and* Doug's . . . almost, anyway. Moira hates school, so she won't mind leaving it.'

'Are things as bad as that?' Tentatively Judith put a hand on her mother's shoulder.

She was taller than Angela; a tall, slim girl with russet-coloured hair that hung in a long, thick plait down her back. Her hand slid from her mother's shoulder to rest comfortingly around her waist.

Angela gazed despairingly up at her elder daughter before replying.

Judith Prynne in fact knew nothing – about money, about her family and about life. Now aged eighteen, a girls' boarding school had been her lot since she was nine. Holidays had been spent in a wing of the house with Gran. Of her parents she, in reality, knew very little.

'Of course we've got money tied up, you know how it is. No, I suppose you don't. You see we always thought we'd stay in India.' Angela made herself comfortable on the rug in front of the fire. 'When Daddy retired from the Army we planned to grow tea. We bought a little plantation in the hills in Assam and Daddy put a manager in to run it. That's where all our money went, well, most of it anyway.'

'And is it still there?'

'As far as I know,' Angela replied cautiously. 'Of course the Indians *hated* the British. They bundled us out of India and they took all they could get. Personally I don't think we'll ever see a penny again; but Dad is hopeful.'

'Is that why the lawyer's here?'

'Partly . . . partly, well,' Angela shrugged and groped in the pocket of her cardigan for another cigarette, 'we can't *really* afford to keep up the house.'

'You mean we might have to *sell* Aylestone?'

'We'll see. It may not be as bad as that.'

Just then they heard voices in the hall and shortly after the sound of Mr Williams's vintage Bentley backfiring as it began to wend its arthritic way down the drive.

Both Judith and her mother were silent as they waited. Judith went to the door and looked out into the hall to find her father still standing by the open front door, leaning heavily on his stick.

'Perhaps you'd get us some tea, Judith darling,' her mother called out brightly. 'Cheer us all up.'

Before the war Aylestone had three resident maids. By the standards of a great country house that was very little. Before the First World War, in the days Gran always used to reminisce about, there had been a posse of servants, too numerous to count, both for indoors and outdoors.

Now, six years after the end of the war, there was a daily woman who came at nine and left at three always grumbling about the amount of work there was to do. Even then she seemed to make very little inroad into any of it; to regard it as a hopeless task.

'Tea would be a very good thing.' Her father thumped his stick on the floor as if disturbed from a reverie and firmly shut the door. 'Gosh it's cold.'

Judith crossed the hall and went through the green baize door that led into the kitchens. They had been modernized by the Ministry during the war; but the upkeep of the many stoves was too costly and unnecessary for a small family. What had once been the scullery was now the kitchen and even here Judith froze as she filled the kettle, put it on the stove and lit the gas.

Outside the damp hung from the skeletal, forlorn trees and suddenly a wind rose and whipped round the house while under the kettle the gas flickered. The walls of the kitchen were damp; there was no doubt about that. The walls of her bedroom were damp too. The whole house seemed to be falling to pieces about them.

13

Yet, to her, it was home and Prynnes, after all, had been here since the time of the Conqueror.

As Judith brewed the tea she thought about the plantation in India whose existence was only occasionally referred to, like some dark family secret: some moment of indiscretion that had cost them dear. When her parents had returned after the war it was almost as strangers to herself, her brother and sister and even now she realized she knew very little either about them or the present circumstances of the family.

Up in her warm room in the wing, Gran would have made her own tea. The first thing the daily did in the morning was to light Gran's fire and the last thing Judith did at night was to build it up with fresh coal. Gran's room was the warmest in the house and, not surprisingly, she spent most of her time there.

When Judith returned to the lounge with the tea her father was standing with his back to the fire filling his pipe, his stick hanging over one arm. He was a tall, handsome man with grizzled, closely cropped sandy hair and an unmistakably military moustache. When he stood upright his bearing was that of one used to parade-grounds – to ceremonials and to giving and receiving commands.

Her parents had obviously been deep in some kind of animated, perhaps acrimonious, conversation and stopped when she came in.

'Ah good,' her father said loudly. 'I hear Mummy's been telling you about our plans in India that went awry.'

'Yes.' Judith glanced up at him as she carefully put the tray on the table by the chair in which her mother was now sitting. 'I was just thinking about it as I made the tea.'

'Well, Williams said that we shall get very little in the way of compensation from the Indian government. The Indians, of course, were perfectly unfit to govern themselves, as everyone is now finding out. Mountbatten sold us all up the river, Mountbatten and Attlee between them.'

Her father paused to grind his teeth as if he knew quite well at whose door to lay the blame for the circumstances in which the Prynne family now found itself.

'Mr Williams thinks we really ought to sell the house,' her mother said as carefully, daintily, as if she were still at home in the Raj passing a pleasant afternoon taking tea and playing bridge with the Service wives, she poured the tea, added milk and passed a cup to her husband.

Involuntarily Judith shuddered.

'Trouble *is*, he thinks we won't get much for it,' her father grunted. 'He says it's really only worth the land it's standing on. The house itself is worthless. Too far gone to do much about it.'

'But it – it's *historical*,' Judith burst out.

'Can't make money out of history,' her father shook his head and, putting his pipe to his mouth, began vigorously to puff at it. 'He says some developer will probably build blocks of flats.'

'But what will *we* do? What will Gran do? It's Gran's home.'

'It's our home too, dear,' her mother said, a note of reproach in her voice.

'Oh no it's not!' Judith banged the cup her mother had passed her on the table. 'You've really never lived here, Mummy. Aylestone means absolutely nothing to you. It means an awful lot to us, to the children and to Gran. Gran's lived here all her life. What will happen to her?'

'Now then, there's no need to get emotional, Judith,' her father said gruffly. 'With the money we get we shall be able to buy quite a comfortable but smaller house, maybe not too far away. There will be plenty of room for Gran, and you and everyone. The last thing we need is a display of temperament from you, my dear.'

'That's the very last thing,' her mother echoed, abhorring the forwardness of modern youth. 'And don't you go stirring up Gran, please. We just have to convince her that it's the very best thing for us all.'

Marcia Prynne, widow of Greville's father Sir Jasper, had first come to Aylestone as a young bride in 1902. Now she was a spry, slightly eccentric old lady of seventy-six, who disliked taking orders and was used to having her own way. She sat looking at her favourite granddaughter who stood with her back to her, her nose pressed against the window pane of the tower room.

'Mummy says it is the very best thing that can happen, Gran,' Judith said mournfully. In the distance she could see the outline of the round tower of Windsor Castle and this was only possible in the depths of winter when the trees were bare.

'They will pull down Aylestone over my dead body.' Gran reached for a ginger biscuit which she delicately bit into after soaking it for some time in her tea. Gran knew that it was not at all the done thing to dip biscuits into one's tea but, in the confines of her own room, she felt she could do pretty well what she liked.

'Daddy says we haven't got any money.'

'Nonsense! Your mother has money. That's why he married her.'

Judith's eyes opened as round as saucers as she turned to face her grandmother.

'Oh, she was a pretty gal,' Gran said. 'I daresay he was in love with her. But the Prynnes *never* had any money. Even when I came into the family your great-grandfather was always gloomily talking about selling the house. You see,' Gran loftily waved her soggy biscuit in the air, 'the Prynnes have for centuries been devoted to the service of their country; they have always been soldiers or sailors or,' Gran looked as though she was thinking hard, 'diplomats. No money there either.'

'Did *you* have money, Gran?' Judith enquired ingenuously.

'I had a *bit*,' Gran replied guardedly. 'But Jasper didn't know it when he married me. We married for love, my dear, as one could in those days and did; but your mother had money. The Mores were a very successful banking family and her father was a judge. You can't go wrong with commerce and the law. I suspect what has happened to your mother's money is that they've blown it all on that plantation in India. What a stupid thing to do, go into a business you know nothing about! If your father had been in tea all his life it would have been understandable; but he hadn't. Serve him right!'

Gran, Judith thought, looked rather pleased, even if it had meant the house being pulled down about her ears.

Between Gran and her mother little love was lost. Greville was an only son and Gran blamed Angela for taking him away. Of her two daughters one had died in childhood and one had married a Canadian farmer and drifted, inevitably, out of her life.

Gran seldom left her room in the winter. Like some animals, she hibernated until the coming of the spring made it safe for her to venture forth again.

Marcia Prynne was not an invalid; she was just someone who looked after herself. She knew that the cold was bad for old people and the best way to ensure good health and independence of her relations was to stay indoors. Whenever she emerged from her room she was attired as if for the outdoors, seldom removed her thick fur coat until half-way through her meal, and always wore a hat.

It was thus with some surprise that the family saw her descend in time for lunch the following Sunday and take her seat close to the fire for the sherry that preceded it.

Also there were Douglas, the only son and heir to the Prynnes, and a girl whom he introduced as Rosalind, a fellow student at Cambridge.

Gran eyed Douglas and his new girlfriend as they were introduced.

'Rosalind what?' Gran said, cupping one hand behind her ear.

'Drake, Gran,' Douglas said. 'Rosalind Drake.'

'Good. I like a plain name,' Gran said approvingly, accepting a glass of sherry from her son. 'And what does Rosalind do?'

'She's a student at Cambridge. History, like me.' Douglas was very tall and had to lean down quite a long way to be sure his grandmother heard.

'Student?' Gran said, looking surprised. 'Brainy, I suppose?'

'Very.' Douglas looked at Rosalind with some pride.

'Can't say I thought brains any use to a woman,' Gran said tartly. 'Not brains in *that* way, I mean. A woman has to have brains to manage a family.'

'I hope you don't mind me saying so, but that's rather an old-fashioned view, Lady Prynne,' Rosalind said. 'There are a lot of women at Cambridge and there will be a lot more. The days of "a woman's place is in the home" are past.'

'Oh, are they?' Gran eyed Rosalind keenly. 'You've heard we're supposed to sell this house?'

'Yes, Lady Prynne. Douglas told me.'

Rosalind found Douglas's grandmother rather awesome and she groped behind her for the comfort of his hand.

'Well, what do your brains make of *that*?'

'I don't know what you mean.'

'I mean, child,' Gran said thumping her stick on the floor, 'that Prynnes have lived here since the Conqueror. Don't tell me you'd rather see a block of flats?'

'Gran, it's really none of Rosalind's business,' Douglas murmured uncomfortably. 'It's strictly a family matter.'

'Do *you* approve of it?' Marcia Prynne looked at him sharply.

'Of course. I'm sorry, Gran, but the old place has been going downhill for years. It would cost a fortune to do it up. There's simply not the money that there was around before the war.'

'It's a beautiful house,' Rosalind said. 'It does seem a shame.'

'Time for lunch!' Angela popped her head round the door, carelessly mopping her forehead with the back of her hand. 'Sorry, Rosalind, I know it's a bit early; but we have no staff. Judith and I are terrible when it comes to timing. Either too early or much much too late. Not much experience, have we dear?'

'No, Mummy.' Judith dutifully paused behind her mother on her way to the dining room, pushing a trolley which contained the lunch although by the time it reached the dining room from the kitchen, it was usually half-cold.

Douglas escorted his grandmother out of the drawing room into the dining room while Rosalind followed behind, her eyes on the threadbare carpet. There was an air of must, of decayed grandeur about the house, that to a modern mind was depressing. There was something sad and rather woebegone about the Prynnes, being brave, trying to keep up appearances. Her footsteps echoed around the ancient walls as she walked slowly across the parquet floor of the cavernous hall, as though reawakening the ghosts of Prynnes from long ago.

The dining room was even colder than the drawing room. Rosalind's hands, brushing against the central-heating pipes, confirmed they were stone cold. Major Prynne noticed her gesture.

'Costs a bomb to heat the place.'

'I can imagine.' Rosalind felt embarrassed.

'Besides,' he went on, 'you can't get the coal, so we save it for the fires.'

At the far end of the huge room a tiny fire glowed disconsolately in the grate. At one end of the room was a minstrels' gallery and Rosalind stopped, catching her breath.

'How beautiful!' she gasped.

Greville Prynne also stopped and followed her gaze.

'This room is Jacobean.' He proudly pointed to the black beams across the ceiling. 'It is the oldest part of the house. Unfortunately the door in the minstrels' gallery leads nowhere. It had to be blocked up when that part of the house was demolished in the eighteenth century to make way for the new building.'

'It does seem a terrible pity to pull it down,' Rosalind said. 'There *must* be something you can do to save it.'

Already, as they took their seats, Angela Prynne was putting thin slices of beef on the plates in front of her while, to her side, Judith ladled out the vegetables. There were plenty of these. The only full-time member of staff retained by the family was the gardener, Jim Burroughs, who had been a boy in the First World War and too old for it in the Second: one of the lucky ones who got away.

Two bottles of wine, uncorked, stood in the centre of the table and, grasping one, Greville said:

'At least we can still get good burgundy. We really have a very fine cellar here.'

'Had,' Douglas corrected him, tucking his napkin into his collar.

'Oh come, we've still got a few hundred bottles left. No one occupied *us* during the war!'

'What do you mean, Dad?' Douglas looked at him curiously.

'I mean that when I was in France most of the grand houses and châteaux had been occupied by the Germans who stripped the cellars bare. They also took all the paintings and any furniture of value. If you think we're unlucky you should see the state of some of those marvellous old houses in France. Their owners are having to turn them into hotels . . .'

'Why don't you?' Rosalind enquired abruptly, and immediately blushed as she became aware of the eyes of the family upon her.

'A *what*?' Gran said, once again ostentatiously cupping her hand to her ear.

'I said why don't you turn this into a hotel? It would make a marvellous one. The view is spectacular. That minstrels' gallery would be wonderful.'

'A *hotel*?' Gran echoed unbelievingly. 'Did I hear right?'

'A *hotel*?' Angela said, face flushed, and burst out laughing.

'Sorry, it was just a thought,' Rosalind mumbled, surreptitiously taking up her knife and fork as she became aware that Douglas was staring at her.

'A *hotel*,' he said. 'What a good idea. Why didn't *we* think of that?'

'Because we don't know anything about hotels,' his father said, carefully, and economically, pouring the wine. 'You have to learn the business.'

'Well, we could.'

'Not soon enough. Don't be silly.' Greville sounded irritable and put his glass to his lips. 'What would *we* do with a hotel?'

'Before the war there were some beautiful hotels,' Gran said, a wistful look in her eyes. 'I mean the First World War, of course. Oh, the *places* we used to stay at in Germany, *and* in France. It is quite true that Aylestone would make a lovely hotel, Greville; but one does have to have money, doesn't one?' Appealingly she looked around. 'I mean, a *lot* of it?'

'A lot of it, Gran,' Doug said, but he looked thoughtful. 'However, I don't think it's out of the question.'

'I thought *you* wanted to go into the Army,' his father said aggressively.

'Well I did, yes. I don't mean *I* would run the hotel; but it *is* a thought.'

'I think my father might be a good person to talk to,' Rosalind said. 'I mean seriously, if you'd like to.'

'I thought your father was in steel?' Doug looked at her.

'He is, but in other things too. He thinks that steel is going to be nationalized and he wants to diversify.'

'Has your father got a lot of money?' Angela enquired with almost too casual an air of nonchalance. 'I mean is he *stinking* rich?'

'He's quite wealthy, I think.'

'Not in the war of course,' Greville muttered.

'*Someone* had to run the factories.' Rosalind's tone was defensive.

'Of course they did, and steel was very important. Well, we're always open to ideas, aren't we, dears?' Greville seemed determined to put a cheerful front on his woes.

'I should absolutely hate to have anything to do with it, darling. I say take the money we get for the place and run.'

'But you might get a lot more if it was a going concern, Mother, don't you *see*?' Eagerly Judith leaned forward. 'I mean I know absolutely nothing about money and commerce; but people do these things, as Daddy said. Châteaux are turned into hotels in France, why not here? We might even like it. Personally I think it would be fun!'

'You're not serious?' Her mother looked at her, aghast.

'Well, now that we have the idea . . . why not? Why not *try* something like that? You and Daddy and me and Doug . . .'

'Doug is going to be a soldier,' Greville said firmly.

'Only because you want him to,' Lady Prynne butted in. 'All the Prynnes have been expected to go into the Army or Navy and I think it's time that practice stopped. It's old-fashioned; out of date. Do you actually *want* to be a soldier, Doug?'

'Never thought about it.' Douglas avoided her eyes. 'As good a career as any, I suppose.'

'Not in the day of the atom bomb,' Rosalind said.

'Armies will become superfluous. I don't think anyone has quite realized what future wars will be like. I should absolutely *hate* it if Doug went into the Army.'

Rosalind stopped abruptly, aware once more that the eyes of the family rested on her. Greville and Angela exchanged meaningful glances and Judith grinned.

'You're not *engaged*, are you?' Gran enquired.

'Oh nothing like that,' Rosalind said hurriedly. 'I didn't mean that . . . I just, well . . .'

'She doesn't actually want me to go into the Army,' Doug said, smiling. 'Maybe she's right.'

Much later Rosalind snuggled up to Doug, aware of their warm bodies surrounded by the palpable cold of the house.

'I'm sorry. I put my foot in it today, didn't I?'

'Two feet,' Doug said, pressing her close. 'The hotel and the Army. Frankly I welcomed them.'

'You're not serious?'

'I am. I don't really want to go into the Army; but there have been Prynnes in the armed forces since the Conk. I've just never thought in a very original way until I met you.'

'Oh . . .'

'And you *are* original. I think Gran has more respect for brains in women now than she did.'

'I liked your grandmother. I like all your family. A bit frightening though . . .'

'My family . . . frightening?' She felt Doug draw away from her and look at her, although the only illumination in the room came from the moonlight streaming through the window.

'I don't think you realize quite how frightening. I mean, here they are, surrounded by all this decayed splendour, quite unaware of the chasm opening beneath their feet.'

'Oh, I think they are. Very aware. More than you realize.'

Rosalind disagreed. 'I don't. I don't think they could

23

really visualize what it is to be actually poor. Where I come from, though we aren't poor, there is a lot of poverty about. You see it in the streets, around you, everywhere. You see it now, but you saw it much more before the war. I think your father thinks he'll get millions for this place but he won't. He'll make the same mistake as he made about India. I can see that. I know what sort of man he is. He's proud and he's stubborn and not very practical. I tell you, Doug, you can't afford to go into the Army, not if you want this family to survive. Besides,' she said, after a pause, 'I should hate to be an Army wife.'

'A what?' Doug jerked his head back in the dark.

'You heard. You don't think I'd go to bed with a man if he wasn't going to make an honest woman of me, do you? Daddy wouldn't like it at all.'

'You conniving little . . .' Doug began, but Rosalind abruptly closed his mouth with a kiss.

Chapter 2

George Drake was a self-made man and he was proud of it. He enjoyed the appurtenances of wealth, and displayed them fully: the large cars, the obsequious staff and the trappings of power. He was one of those men who always managed to be in the right place at the right time and he had made a lot of money from the war. He had married a girl with a similar background to his, and now he rejoiced in the fact that his beloved only child had been privately educated and had enjoyed all the advantages that money could bring; that had been lacking in his own early life.

As the Drake Rolls turned into the gates of Aylestone, George gave a whistle and glanced at his daughter who was sitting thoughtfully beside him. The gables, towers and turrets of the historic house towered over the trees through which they could see the broad winding river of water as it wound inexorably on its way.

'I see what you mean,' George said in a deep voice which had never quite lost its broad, northern vowels.

'When you get nearer you see how run down it is.' Rosalind leaned forward. 'But you can see the potential, can't you, Dad?'

'You certainly can.' George took her hand and squeezed it. 'Though I'm not committing myself, you know, love, until I've had people look the place over.'

'Of course not.' Rosalind leaned back. 'I think you'll find that the Prynnes will take a lot of convincing. The only one who is really for it is Judith, the elder daughter.'

'And Douglas?' George looked closely at his daughter.

'Douglas is ambivalent.' Rosalind nervously fluttered her

fingers. 'There's something that the family have about going into trade, as they call it.'

'The downfall of many a great house.' George nodded smugly. 'They don't like to soil their hands. That sort of attitude is the making of men like me.' He sat back with a satisfied smile on his face.

Aylestone stood on a promontory above the river and was approached from the road by a mile-long drive which led to a semi-circle in front of the massive, pillared portico of the house.

From the outside it was quite awesome, and the absence of any sign of welcome seemed to reinforce the impression that the occupants of this magnificent stately home were not the kind of people who waited out in the cold to greet their guests.

However, as soon as the car stopped in front of the door it opened and Judith ran down the stairs just as George's chauffeur got out to open the rear door.

'How do you do?' she said, extending a hand. 'I'm Judith Prynne.'

'My daughter has told me a lot about you,' George said, taking her hand. 'The only one who's really keen on the idea.'

'Well,' Judith looked past him to Rosalind who was emerging from the other side. 'It does take a bit of getting used to. I think in many ways they'd rather sell up.'

'Well, we'll see if we can think of something.' George tucked his arm through that of his daughter and followed Judith up the steps and into the great stone hall hung with portraits of Prynne ancestors going back to the sixteenth century. From this they passed into an inner hall which ran from the front of the house to the side which faced the river. The construction, inside and out, back and front, was identical so that each end of the house was harmonious with the other.

The Prynnes had grouped themselves round the fire in

the drawing room to receive a visitor whom they regarded rather as a predator; someone out to grab their inheritance. Even Gran was less well disposed to the idea than she had been, as Angela had convinced her it would mean her moving out of her beloved room in the wing.

Gran sat on one side of the fire attired in her fur coat, her toque swathed with a veil, both hands firmly on the top of the silver-headed cane in front of her. Next to her stood Greville, his face flushed, and on his other side was Angela, whose features remained immobile as the door opened and the procession led by Judith came towards them. Douglas, hands clasped behind his back, stood beside his mother. On the sofa sat the younger daughter Moira, her feet neatly tucked under her legs, her fluffy blonde hair sedately secured by a velvet band and her large blue eyes unable to conceal her boredom about what was happening.

Whereas Judith was the firm, positive member of the family, Moira was understated, refusing to be committed. She resembled her mother not only in looks but in temperament. She was vague, pretty, popular, someone with many friends but few real intimates. She was too self-centred, too frivolous, to be really interested in the affairs of others. Just now she would much rather be staying with the friends she had been forced to leave in London than attending a family conference about something in which she felt she had no concern. She would soon be off, away, abroad, anywhere but in large, draughty Aylestone with its problems: an inheritance of dubious value to the family.

George Drake had taken off his coat in the hall and his portly figure, encased in a well-cut grey-striped suit, seemed at once decorous and slightly comical to the company. Moira's lips twitched in a smile as she rose to be introduced after her grandmother, her mother and her father.

George Drake had a bland face, a bulbous nose and a receding hairline. He was the sort of person whom people

27

like the Prynnes made jokes about behind their hands, treating him with the ingrained arrogance of the landed gentry towards those they considered their social inferiors. Even Rosalind felt a bit ashamed of him as she saw the haughty stares of the Prynnes levelled first at her father then, knowingly, at each other.

'How do you do?'

'My son Douglas.'

'How do you do, sir?'

The 'sir' was a nice touch, making up for Gran's unsmiling stare as she frigidly touched the tips of his fingers.

'Do sit down,' Angela said with forced unctuousness, pointing to the chair opposite Gran. 'I have asked our daily help to bring in coffee. I imagine you're famished on a cold day like this.' She rubbed her hands together and looked over George's head towards the door.

'Yes it is cold,' George Drake said, wishing he'd left his coat on. 'I imagine *this* is a very difficult place to heat.'

'Fiendish.' Angela vigorously nodded her head.

'And *ruinously* expensive,' Greville moved away from the fire, realizing that most of its heat was lost to their guest. 'We don't consider it worth it just for the family.'

'You mean you never have central heating on at all?'

'Only when it's very, very cold,' Angela said crisply.

'Six inches of snow on the ground at least,' Douglas smiled nervously. 'My parents, of course, lived most of their lives in India and feel the cold very keenly.'

'*Do* let me give you coffee.' Angela moved briskly forward as the daily came in with a tray which she put on the table next to Gran. 'Black or white?'

'White please, Mrs Prynne.'

'Rosalind?'

'The same please, Mrs Prynne.'

There was a pause while Angela poured the coffee and

28

Rosalind went to stand next to Douglas and tried surreptitiously to take his hand; but his eyes slid round towards her, as if in warning, and he didn't move.

Greville offered George Drake a cigarette, which his guest declined. Then, lighting one himself and tossing the match into the fire, he threw back his head and cleared his throat.

'I'm afraid you've come on a fruitless journey, Mr Drake,' he said. 'The family have discussed this proposal ever since it was mooted and I must tell you that we've decided against it. We're simply not interested in turning Aylestone into a hotel. We would rather see it razed to the ground and rebuilt as flats or houses, or something quite different. We couldn't entertain the idea.'

George Drake said nothing, quietly sipping his coffee and frowning into the fire. Slowly, however, a flush spread across Rosalind's face as, once again, she tried unsuccessfully to get some tactile response from Douglas standing stiffly next to her.

'So you see your journey is pointless,' Angela said kindly.

'We *do* hope, however, you'll stay to luncheon.' She smiled at Drake, as if trying to make amends.

George said nothing until he'd finished his coffee. Then he cleared his throat, took some papers from his inside pocket and glanced at them with the help of half-moon spectacles. All this took a little time and caused more unease among the group, who started to shift in their places. Gran once or twice thumped her cane on the floor and, finally, George looked up and glanced round the group.

'Sorry, I was trying to digest what you just said and I was also looking at some figures I jotted down in the car on our way here. Naturally I'd never seen the place, though I had some idea of its scale and position from what Rosalind told me. It is, indeed, magnificent and, although

I've not seen round it, has the potential for a hotel that could compare with anything similar in Europe. As you're no doubt aware, a lot of French châteaux and German baronial castles have been transformed into just the sort of project we had in mind here. However . . .' he cleared his throat again, 'I see that as far as you're concerned it's gone off the boil.'

'Quite, quite off the boil.' Angela tilted her chin.

'But you still wish to sell it?'

'To a developer,' Greville said.

'Then I'll buy it from you, lock, stock and barrel. What could be simpler?'

'You mean you'll buy the house and *then* turn it into a hotel?'

'Or raze it to the ground and build luxurious apartments or houses. I haven't decided which; whichever is most profitable. In fact it makes it a lot simpler if you sell outright to me. My impression from Ros was that you were looking for finance to develop the project. Now this is quite a different kettle of fish.'

George solemnly removed his spectacles, put them in a case and snapped it shut. 'Shall we discuss it over lunch, Mrs Prynne, after I've looked around?'

The tour of the house was conducted by Angela and Judith, the latter saying very little. There were thirty-two bedrooms, vast servants' quarters and several reception rooms, besides the huge dining rooms and the kitchens, so it took quite a long time. But in every room the same impression was of neglect: damp patches on the walls, broken hasps to the windows and, occasionally, a broken window which had been boarded up. The roof was clearly in poor repair and there were large areas of damp, and plaster hanging from the ceilings. Everywhere there was the all-pervading smell of mildew, with its attendant atmosphere of decay and neglect.

In some rooms there were the remnants of wartime occupation. In one there were still desks and a blackboard on the wall, and in another a collection of plugs and wires still remained in their sockets, giving rise to speculation as to their purpose.

An exception was the wing into which the family had moved. The roof there was in good repair and in each of the bedrooms there were traces of recent fires in the grates.

The wing had an air of old-world charm. There was pretty wallpaper, chintzy covers and the atmosphere of a cosy country cottage. Yet here too the walls were damp and ill-fitting windows indicated that, on wintry nights, they would admit a bitter wind blowing from the north-east.

George Drake said very little during the tour, though Angela kept up a non-stop prattle in which there was a good deal of family history. She was knowledgeable about the house and its history, what had been added to what, by whom and when, and one could sense in her an air of nostalgia and regret. Finally they came to rest in the drawing room where Gran and Greville were having coffee.

'Well!' Angela said, accepting a cup. 'That is that.'

'What do you think, Mr Drake?' Gran enquired.

'I can't understand how the Ministry were allowed to leave it in such poor repair. I thought they had to do the place up.'

'Oh, we received compensation,' Greville murmured. 'Unfortunately there were more pressing financial needs elsewhere.'

'We had a tea plantation in India. We hoped . . .' Angela shrugged. 'Well we, Grev and I, actually wanted to retire there. We were going to let the old place go anyway.'

'So the money went to India?' Drake enquired, and Greville nodded.

'Sort of.'

Drake could sense that he wouldn't get much out of this

31

family, and their patronizing manner and disdainful airs were beginning to irritate him.

'It wasn't nearly enough anyway.' Greville sensed his guest's displeasure. 'You know what these ministries are. They never give you adequate compensation.'

'They said the house had to be restored to what it was when they took it over,' Gran murmured, 'and, unfortunately, it was none too good then, to be perfectly honest.' She gave him a disarming smile.

'And you lived here all during the war, Lady Prynne?' Drake courteously turned his attention to Gran.

'The grandchildren came here in the holidays from school. My husband, Admiral Sir Jasper Prynne, died before the war.'

Gran's eyes misted over and Greville hastily refilled her cup.

'Do you still want to buy it, Mr Drake, after what you've seen?'

'More than ever,' Drake said. 'I think I can give you a very good price.'

By the time George Drake and his daughter left at four o'clock the family had unbent enough to stand at the top of the steps and see him off, even to give him rather regal waves, hands fluttering about their heads. The Rolls glided smoothly down the drive as both Drake and Rosalind turned to smile from the window.

'Quite a decent chap really.' Greville put an arm lightly round his wife's waist. 'Couldn't say I took to him personally, but there you are. Not a gentleman.'

'What a prig you are, Father,' Doug called after his parents as he followed them into the house.

'Your father is absolutely right, darling,' Angela chided gently, turning round. 'He's a rather common little man and that's the sort of thing *you* should be thinking about.'

'I don't know what you mean, Mother,' Doug replied, but his face changed colour.

'I think you do, Douglas. *If* you marry Rosalind, or a girl like Rosalind, that's the sort of man you'll have for a father-in-law and, doubtless, somewhere he has a wife just like him.'

'I think you're insufferable.'

'And unfair.' Judith had said little in the course of the day; but she had listened. Listened and watched, taken everything in; noticed the patronizing manner of her parents, the disdain in the eyes of Gran; the sideways glances, the half-smile on Moira's lips as George Drake had held his knife like a pencil at lunch. Doug had remained silent too; embarrassed and ill at ease, and this was matched by Rosalind who gave him owl-like, anxious glances.

The family now turned its attention collectively to Judith.

'*Unfair?*' cried her mother.

'He's a very clever man, I understand, entirely self-made and proud of it. He made a big contribution to the war effort. If you despised him, Mummy, you can be sure *he* despised us.'

'Despised *us?*' Gran cried indignantly as they came into earshot where she sat by the side of the fire. 'How could someone like *that* possibly despise *us?* Why, generations of Prynnes . . .'

'And possibly generations of Drakes too,' Judith interrupted heatedly. 'Only they climbed upwards. They worked hard and jostled for position, maybe in the factory line, I don't know. Mr Drake's father was a steelworker and Mr Drake's greatest moment was when he bought the firm where his father had worked on the shop floor. He thinks he's achieved a lot and he has. He's become a millionaire while we, the Prynnes, whose family go back to the Conquest, have gone steadily down until we live in a house that is almost a ruin and nearly die of cold because we can't afford to heat it. How he must despise *us* and, do you know, I despise us too! Don't think Mr Drake didn't

33

notice the smirk on Moira's face, or the look in Gran's eyes or the ever so "gracious" way Mummy was trying to patronize him or Daddy to talk down to him. Now we're going to let him have our house and land and all for a song . . .'

'We don't know that, Judith,' her mother interrupted. 'We never mentioned money.'

'Because it's not ladylike is it, Mummy? Oh no, no one would ever mention *money*. So sordid!'

'Well it *is* sordid, Judith, and if you were any younger I'd send you to your room. I can't think when I was last spoken to like that!'

'Probably behind your back, Mummy, by the Indian servants. Don't you realize that this is a new age? The Indians you thought inferior kicked you out, and the *nouveaux riches*, who *you* try and patronize, pity you. Don't *you* realize that you, and Dad, and Gran have outworn ideas that people now laugh at? I should think Mr Drake will bear all this in mind when he makes his offer simply because you are too embarrassed to mention money and consider bargaining bad form. He will probably take you for a ride and enjoy doing it.'

'Well our lawyers won't let him,' Greville said angrily. 'And I say what your mother should have said. Go to your room at once, Judith, and don't dare show your face to us again until you can maintain a civil tongue in your head *and* apologize.'

Theatrically, arm outstretched, Greville pointed towards the door and, as Judith stood her ground, Doug rose from his seat and took her by the hand.

'I'll go too, Dad. But don't think we'll go to our rooms. I'll take Judith back to Cambridge with me and leave *you* to think over what she's said because I heartily agree with every word. Personally I feel ashamed of you.'

'Oh don't be *silly*,' Moira said, stamping her foot. 'Everyone don't be *silly*. This is a very serious situation

34

and no one is considering it for a moment as it should be considered. Personally I wouldn't talk to Mum and Dad the way Judith did, but I think a lot of what she says makes sense. Maybe it's because we're the younger generation and there's been a war; but I know what she means even if I don't like the way she puts it. I honestly don't see why you don't want to turn this place into a grand hotel and keep a piece of the action. I mean we don't have to live in it. We can't live in it, anyway, if it's demolished; but if it's a great success, what then?'

'I don't know what you're talking about.' Angela looked bewildered, reproachful at this third defection. Doug, however, looked excited.

'Moira means, Mother, that if we accept cash that is that. How do we know land values, house values, won't soar in the years ahead and what we get now might mean very little? If we go in with Drake – and I'm not sure he'll want to after today – then we can protect our investment. Personally I would love to see this house restored, become one of the grand hotels of Europe. Why not? We can lease it to Drake, but still remain owners of the house and the land.'

'But what will happen to *us*?' Angela wailed. 'Oh I can't believe what I'm hearing. And where will *we* go?'

'Where would we go anyway? You and Dad probably definitely want to go back to India, but where will Gran go? If we come to terms with Drake we can negotiate, a flat or a house nearby for Gran, somewhere for us. I think Judith's right and I'm glad Moira thinks so too . . .'

'Oh don't mind me, I shall be *miles* away,' Moira pretended to shudder. 'I was just teasing. I mean I'm not the teeniest weeniest bit interested in trade, in work of any kind. *My* intention is to find some nice rich man who will support me.'

* * *

At the height of the bombing during the war, George Drake moved his headquarters to London from Sheffield. He bought two houses in Mayfair for far less than their pre-war price, knocked down the walls between them and made them the centre of his operations. These continued to expand after the war, when he started buying up stock surplus to the requirements of the various services and ministries, and hoarding it in warehouses, often in aeroplane hangars, scattered throughout the countryside.

But George Drake, an entrepreneur, decided that the real future lay in real estate; in property, particularly in London, and he began acquiring war-damaged houses or bombed sites, mainly in the City: the square mile that remained the life-blood of the business world. Drake was in no hurry, no rush. Most of his bombed sites still remained undeveloped, with no plans, but he knew that one day the City of London would inevitably rise phoenix-like from the ashes and he and speculators like him would come into their own.

Like her continental neighbours, England found the going hard in the immediate post-war years. The dreams of the Socialist government elected in 1945 had proved too elusive to capture. The reorganization of the country was difficult and, inevitably, encouragement was given to people like Drake who wanted to inject some life into the economy.

From his many activities, as well as his profits from the war, George Drake had a plentiful supply of cash reserves. He was always on the lookout for some interesting proposition such as the one brought to him by his daughter, Rosalind.

Rosalind, his treasure, was blessed with brains but not much beauty, except in the eyes of her father. Yet she was not spoiled as a child but encouraged to achieve; and, when she did, she was rewarded. Her place at Cambridge confirmed her place in her father's esteem; now the world, anything she wanted, was hers for the asking.

Douglas Prynne, with his languid air, his classical good looks, his family background, soon found a place in the susceptible heart of a girl not over-endowed with beauty. He seemed to find her amusing, adoring and useful: she let him crib her essays, borrow her notes. She became indispensable to him, and in time he saw more to this studious young woman than had at first met the eye. She was pale with straight black hair; but she made the best of herself and although she may not have had class she had money and knew where to spend it: on clothes, hairdressers, attractive spectacle frames.

She was brainy and brains had their own particular beauty, especially when put at the service of another.

Douglas Prynne had not been aware of her intentions when they became lovers: but the more he thought about them the more normal, the more natural, they seemed to him to be. He was a man, as he had been a lover, who was easily led.

George gazed with satisfaction at his daughter, and also at the young man by her side smoking a cigarette and gazing at the ceiling with contemplative eyes. Douglas Prynne; good family, good stock and just needy enough to be useful.

'Your father, of course, knows you are here.' George leaned back in the leather chair behind his large desk.

'No, but my sister does.'

'That would be Judith?'

Douglas nodded. 'Moira is for it too, but she would be for anything that she thought would bring in a bit of money. She hates being poor.'

'Oh come, you aren't *poor*!'

George knew little about the actual family circumstances but he knew enough. From what he'd seen at Aylestone he'd guessed even more; but appearances could be deceptive, particularly among the upper classes who rejoiced in oddities and eccentric behaviour.

'We are actually pretty poor,' Douglas said with a rueful smile. 'You see, my parents spent the years between the wars in India. Dad was in the Indian Army. They liked the place and wanted to settle there. All the money they had they left there, as they told you, and quite honestly I think the Ministry diddled them about the compensation money for Aylestone. Anyhow it was a pretty paltry sum. They were just glad to take what they could get. You must understand that people like my parents didn't really know a lot about money. Even now they can hardly believe what's happened. Then, of course, you turned up and they were prepared to stretch out their hands and take what they could get . . .'

'And you're not?' Drake gazed at him shrewdly.

'I don't want to settle for a lump sum. I think property and land will go up. Just now it's depressed. I would like to see Aylestone developed along the lines we first suggested, as a hotel. It has amazing possibilities. The vast lawns could be turned into a golf course; horses in the paddock; boating on the lake. To sell it for a few thousand . . .'

'Oh it would be more than a few thousand. Quite a large sum. Are you actually saying that you're now advising your parents not to sell? That they will be looking for capital to do up the property and expand?'

'As first suggested,' Rosalind said. 'I think Doug's right.'

'No doubt you've been advising him.' Drake smiled approvingly at his daughter. 'Rosalind is a very clever lass, you know, young man. I hope she is going to come into my business one day.'

'Is she?' Douglas looked surprised. 'I thought she was going to stay on at Girton and do research?'

'I said *one* day. When she's ready. There's no hurry. What about you? What do you intend to do with yourself when you get your degree?'

'I'm supposed to go into the Army.'

'Supposed?'

'That was the plan.' Douglas paused and lit a fresh cigarette. 'However I am quite taken by this hotel plan, so is my sister. Judith would like to go to Switzerland and study hotel management. We'd all be in it together. I've talked it over with Rosalind and she thinks it's a great idea. I must say we'd all be very grateful if you could advise . . . and help.'

The wind whistled through the cracked pane and Angela got up once more and went across to make sure that the piece of cardboard Greville had put over it to secure it was in place. Then, still shivering, she crossed to the grate and poked the fire. There was no more coal and a few of the embers glowed fiercely prior to expiring. She had left it too late.

'Dash it,' she said and, going over to her bed, put on her warm gown and, opening the door, crept across the corridor to her husband's room. It was many years since they'd shared a bedroom, and then only out of necessity.

Angela tapped on Greville's door and softly opened it in case he was asleep, but his light was on and he was propped up in bed reading.

'Oh goody,' Angela cried, running across to the large fire leaping in the grate. 'Could I have a shovelful of hot coals for mine, darling? It's gone out.'

'Of course.' Greville glanced at her over his spectacles. 'Shall I do it for you, dear?'

'I'll do it.' Angela leaned towards the grate and, gingerly picking up some hot coals with a pair of tongs, dropped them onto the small shovel. 'Shan't be a tick.'

'Careful, dear.'

Greville gazed anxiously after her as she scuttled across the room, the hot coals smouldering in the shovel. Then she returned for more coal and went back again to her room to build up her fire.

When she'd finished she brushed her hands, washed them in the basin in the corner of her room before returning to Greville's room and perching on the edge of his bed.

'Can't sleep, dear?'

''Fraid not,' Greville said, removing his spectacles. 'I keep on thinking of this business of the house. Been in the family for centuries.'

'Me too. It's terribly difficult to know what to do for the best.'

'I must say Douglas's letter rather shook me. Drake is offering him a job. Fancy preferring commerce to a life in the Army! Hardly the thing for a gentleman, is it? Besides, that Drake . . . well,' Greville screwed up his nose. 'Not out of the top drawer.'

Angela gave her well-bred laugh.

'Does it matter, Grev? Times have changed. We forget.'

'The war changed everything,' Greville nodded gloomily. 'I believe Drake's buying up a lot of land in Mayfair. The Sandersons sold out to someone like him and went to live in South Africa. Can't blame them. A better life and plenty of servants.'

'But he's not the sort of person we really want our son to be involved with, is he, Grev?'

'Not really. But Doug is of age. We don't have much choice. Besides he likes the girl.'

'Oh surely he can't!' Angela gave a mirthless laugh and took a cigarette from the box by her husband's bedside. 'She's such a plain little thing!'

'Then why did he bring her here?'

'Because of her father, of course.'

'I think he quite likes her.'

'Out of the question, dear. Doug has got much too much taste for that. Remember the Lister girl? She was absolutely stunning. They were practically engaged.'

'But then she got engaged to a chap with more money.'

40

'Doug was too young. Women at that age are more mature. No, they're simply friends and colleagues at Cambridge. He says she does all his research for him. If you ask me he uses her. No romance there.'

'I hope you're right.' Greville glanced at the clock. 'Half-past one. Good Lord!' He put his book on the table beside him and placed his spectacles on top of it.

'*And* your mother's against it. That's another thing.' Angela threw her cigarette end in the fire.

'Against what?'

'Moving.'

'She'll have to move, whatever happens.'

'Doug thinks she may be able to stay on. He even th we might retain this wing for the family. He was a optimistic.'

'What, and have a lot of oiks running round us thank you.'

'They won't be oiks, Grev. They will have to be rich to afford this place. What Doug says about Dra plans are true. Frankly, I'm becoming reconciled to idea.'

'Angela, you can't be!' Greville stared at her, a glass water in his hand. 'It's not possible.'

'My dear, it would be fun, in a *way*. I mean we'd live luxury, all our bills paid, plenty to eat and drink and what would we have to do?' Angela raised her eyebrows knowingly. 'Nothing, except keep an eye on things. You're used to ordering people about, darling. It would be the same thing. As for me,' Angela looked across at herself in the mirror of her husband's dressing table, 'I'm not getting any younger.' She put a finger to her face and slowly trailed it along her cheek, past her nose, around her mouth to the chin. 'I'm getting lines that won't go away. I'd be able to go up to town as often as I wanted; perhaps we might have a little *pied-à-terre* there. We've always wanted one.'

'I can't think what's got into you.' Greville put down

41

his glass with a thump. 'I never heard such rot. The bones of my ancestors would turn in their graves.'

'They would turn even more if you had a common block of flats here. That Drake person intends to *restore* it to its ancient glory. He has plans to refurbish it completely to what it used to be like in the days your mother came here as a bride. Imagine *that*! I think your ancestors, and mine if it comes to that, might be rather pleased.'

'Rot,' Greville said gruffly and, turning his back on his wife, put out the light. 'Go to bed, Angela. You'll feel very different in the morning.'

Chapter 3

The vast kitchens of the Hotel Daniel hummed with life, with energy but, especially, with noise: shouted commands, queries, laughter and sometimes voices raised in argument which were rapidly quelled by the *maître-chef*.

Quietly in a corner, the pastry chef worked away. Above all he was an artist who made delicately moulded petit-fours, éclairs and meringues in fantastic convoluted shapes. Judith learned a lot from him, and from the chef who made sauces; those light, frothy, delicately flavoured concoctions which graced the main entrée dish: fish, meat or game. But the chef she liked to watch most, whose art she admired, was the *sous-chef* Marcel, next in line to the *maître-chef*, who worked with such speed and dexterity in creating the most exquisite dishes that were the specialities of the house.

Marcel Laborde was a tall, ascetic young man with the face of a poet. His cheeks were cavernous and his eyes large and dreamy. He was a serious man who very seldom smiled. He never laughed but, just occasionally, his lips would part and one would know that, at least, he was amused.

Judith had first met Marcel on the ski slopes. He was a keen and experienced skier and, although she was a beginner, they had become acquainted in a ski hut when they were marooned with others during a blizzard.

After that they scarcely met again until she returned to the kitchens as an apprentice chef as part of her course and, for a time, she came under the guidance of Marcel. She realized that from every point of view he was an artist, and not only in the kitchen. He painted, he played the flute and he always took his holidays in Venice or one of the great art capitals of the world.

All this she found out very slowly because Marcel was a solitary; a man of few words. He was an exacting master and expected much from his pupil but, after a time, he invited her to a concert the Suisse-Romande orchestra were giving in Geneva.

From then on she learned more about him. For instance, that he was quite wealthy; that he had his own apartment in a block a few metres from the hotel. That he drove a pre-war Mercedes and that he loved wearing good clothes.

From time to time Judith had to return to England on business connected with the development of Aylestone, and he was always interested to hear what she had to say when she got back.

In the years she'd been in Switzerland Judith had little time for fun or for socializing. She'd made very few close friends of either sex because people tended to move around a lot. Many of the men and women who worked in the hotel were married and had their own lives. Also she was somehow rather apart, belonging nowhere. She found it difficult to make friends among the staff, and she knew this was probably because she was a foreigner and also because they had little in common.

But life in the hotel was a task of total dedication that she realized would be the pattern of her life henceforward if she gave it over to helping to make Aylestone one of the great hotels in the world. In its way it was a calling, a vocation, but she welcomed it.

At first it had been very difficult, bewildering and, even, frightening. Judith Prynne had nearly given up; packed it all in. But it was she who had finally persuaded her parents to accept Drake's offer and turn Aylestone into the most splendid stately home hotel certainly in England and perhaps, even, in Europe. She could hardly return with her tail between her legs and say now that she'd discovered how hard it all was, she'd changed her mind.

For a long time Greville and Angela Prynne had vacillated. Angela considered it might possibly be the entrée into the good life; a life, at last, of leisure and ease, free from worry. Gran didn't want to leave her wing. But Greville had dreams of returning to India where he imagined that, on some sun-covered slope, there would be a place for him.

Moira maintained her attitude of splendid indifference with the carefree attitude of the younger sibling, who thought that whatever happened she would be cosseted and provided for as she always had been. She rather shared her mother's hopes that Bond Street would be more accessible from a *pied-à-terre*; but it was Gran who, having claimed that she had somehow been through to her late husband, cast her vote: the Admiral, she said, was definitely of the opinion that Aylestone should be restored provided the family remain at home in the wing.

Looking back on it now, that had been just the beginning, the easy part. The negotiations with Drake had been tough. He was more than a match for the easy-going old-fashioned Prynne family solicitor, Mr Williams, whose experience of the property market was rudimentary. In the end other solicitors were retained whose own skills and deviousness matched those of Mr Drake, and a hard bargain was driven.

Drake would pay for the restoration of Aylestone and its equipment and refurbishment as a hotel. He would provide working capital; in his estimation, even by present rates, several million pounds. In return, he would want sixty per cent of the profits and an equal say in the running of the hotel.

A new company was to be formed with Greville as chairman and himself as executive director and all the family on the board, who were allotted a certain number of shares.

By the time it was all tied up Douglas had left Cambridge and announced his engagement to Rosalind as soon as he joined the Drake Organization as a management trainee, and Judith was on her way to the Hotel Daniel in Switzerland.

She had spent the first six months perfecting her languages, French and German, by day, and working in the hotel at night. She began as a chambermaid and became familiar with all the requirements of reasonable and unreasonable guests who were used to luxury; not only to clean linen every day but fresh flowers, turned-down sheets and a chocolate on the pillow at night. She had her allotted set of rooms and every morning she would push her trolley, laden with clean linen sheets, fresh fluffy white towels embossed with the monogram of the hotel, tiny bars of soap, cosmetic aids and fragrances for both men and women and, of course, the chocolates, made by a well-known confectioner.

In the afternoon she studied her languages, and in the evening she was back in the hotel preparing the rooms for the night. There was no time at all for play.

The first thing Judith learnt was a quality that did not come easily to the Prynnes: a certain invisibility, the art of appearing when one was required and disappearing when one was not. She learned tolerance – one was perpetually at the beck and call of other people – and she learned that the standards of other people, even the very rich, were not always as impeccable as one's own. Some of them were dirty, however polished they appeared on the surface; some were slovenly, had bad manners and were altogether her inferiors, except that their money enabled them to be served and she had to serve them. She learned a lot about people's natures and their generosity or lack of it; but above all she learned how to be humble. To be humble without being obsequious. And that, most definitely, was an attribute that did not come easily to a Prynne.

From the bedrooms she descended to the kitchens, to the sculleries where she washed up all day long, or fetched and carried for the chefs who either ignored her or issued harsh orders that had to be instantly obeyed. There was a distinct hierarchy in the kitchen. Every individual chef was a master, a king in his own sphere whether he made sauces, pastry, cakes, hors d'œuvres or the grand entrées.

Finally, her German and French perfected, Judith donned normal clothes and ascended to the office where the bookings were made and the complaints were investigated: the control room from which the hotel was run. Only uniformed men or women were employed at the desk in the reception hall where they welcomed guests, issued keys and answered the innumerable questions that poured in every minute of the day.

Now, in her third year, Judith was learning how to cook and, at home, a sumptuous hotel was rising metaphorically from the ashes of the Prynne ancient family home.

Marcel finished putting his glaze on the *carré d'agneau*, one of the many variations of a dish he was expert in. Judith watched him as he surveyed his work, like an experienced surgeon, or a master craftsman, before he was satisfied. Even then he made little adjustments until it was taken away, totally absorbed in the tiny refinements that made each finished dish a work of art.

'*Parfait*,' he pronounced after a moment, stepping back and taking up his cloth to wipe his hands. He turned to see Judith staring at him.

'Sorry, I am boasting.'

'But it *is* perfect,' Judith replied in her, by now, almost perfect French. Then she said *sotto voce*, looking round, 'I think you are a much better chef than Roland.' But she recoiled as he shook his head and put his finger to his lips.

Gustave Roland was the *maître-chef*, the prima donna of the kitchen, a man given to terrible outbursts of temper. He was considered spiteful, vindictive and jealous. It was no secret that he was very jealous of Laborde and did all he could to demean him. Some said he would like to have got rid of him altogether.

'I'd actually like to talk to you about something later on,' Judith said as Marcel moved on to another dish. 'Could we meet for a drink after work?'

Marcel, seemingly unperturbed by the invitation, consulted his schedule on the wall and shook his head.

'It is not possible today,' he said. 'I will be here until midnight as we have a gastronomic dinner, and all the chefs involved go afterwards into the dining room to hear compliments about their work. Well,' brief smile, 'we *hope* there will be compliments. What about tomorrow? Ah no. Tomorrow there is also a big occasion.'

'What about the morning?' Judith suggested. 'Coffee in one of the bars? I'm not on duty until noon.'

'That is a good idea,' Marcel said. 'But a better one is why don't you come to my apartment? It is not too far from here and we can talk privately, that is if you wish for us to be private?'

It occurred to Judith that the implication was that he was too well known in the tiny Alpine town to be seen drinking coffee with her. It might start people gossiping. He wrote his address on the pad in front of his desk and gave it to her in a manner that seemed to signify that the interview was at an end. Sometimes she found him quite daunting.

Fregères was a small Swiss resort about an hour's drive from Geneva. It was surrounded by high, snow-covered mountains and deep forests, and the Hotel Daniel was on the lower slopes of the nearest mountain. It was the only hotel of any size, though there were many smaller ones and the usual number of guest-houses. On the periphery of the village were new blocks containing apartments, many of which had been built in anticipation of the resumption of the much-needed tourist trade after the war.

Switzerland had not suffered as had the rest of Europe in the war; but its economy was largely based on tourism, and there had been very few tourists between 1939 and 1945. However, like its neighbours France and Germany, Switzerland was resilient and a great building programme was in full swing, catering for the masses whom, it was hoped, would resume one of the great pre-war pastimes.

Judith knew the location of Marcel's apartment, though she had never visited him there. She knew nothing about his private life except that he was unmarried. That much she knew from the little time they'd had for conversation in the course of the concert he'd taken her to. Mostly they had discussed their tastes in music, and she told him something about herself and the development of Aylestone and the family's plans for the future.

As she left the hotel through a side entrance, Judith bumped into Madame Daniel who had a basket in her hand and looked for all the world like an ordinary housewife going shopping. Then she saw that there was a rug inside the basket and, underneath it, something moved.

'Good morning, Madame Daniel,' Judith said respectfully, standing back for the older woman to pass.

'Good morning, Mademoiselle Prynne.' Madame gave her customary beaming smile. It was difficult to guess Madame's age. Maybe she was in the middle fifties, maybe the early sixties. Her son Marc, who also worked in the hotel, was thirty, so it was unlikely she was much younger.

The Daniel family were greatly respected by the staff of the hotel. They were true professionals, masters of a craft that had been in the family for nearly a century. Very little was known about the private life of the family but it was suggested that Madame Daniel was a cousin and so had the life of a hotelier in her blood as well.

'My little cat is sick,' Madame said, pointing to the basket as Judith closed the door after her.

'Oh, I hope not too badly sick.'

'Something wrong with his stomach.' Madame made a grimace and rubbed her own well-rounded belly. 'Maybe he caught a mouse and it disagreed with him.'

Judith was rather startled at the admission that a hotel as august as the Daniel might have mice. 'I mean outside in the woods,' Madame corrected herself hastily as the significance of Judith's expression dawned on her.

'Of course,' Judith replied.

For a while they walked along the main street of the little town, Madame acknowledging people to the right and left with a smile, a wave of her free hand. Naturally she knew everyone.

'I hear you're soon to leave us, mademoiselle?' Madame said in a rare pause between greeting acquaintances.

'Alas yes, madame. I have been here nearly three years.'

'And I hope you have learned a lot from us.'

'It has been a wonderful experience, madame. I don't think there is anything about running a hotel that I do not know.'

Madame appeared to consider this statement.

'Maybe you should have gone to one or two more. There are ways and ways of running a hotel, even if we at the Daniel think ours is the best.'

'I intend to do that, madame. I want to travel round Europe and America after our own hotel has opened. Because, of course, it is being run by my father and brother.'

'And what do *they* know of hotel management?' Madame Daniel enquired, knitting her eyebrows together severely.

'My father was a professional soldier. He is a very good manager of men. My brother has taken courses in law and accountancy and then there is the backing of the large Drake Organization behind us.'

'Quite,' Madame said, looking out for traffic before she crossed the road to the large white building where the vet had his quarters. From the basket came the plaintive miaowing of the sick cat.

'And where are you off to, mademoiselle?' Madame Daniel enquired.

'I thought I'd have a walk before I go on duty at twelve.' Judith had expected the question and so her answer was ready.

'Good day to you, then,' Madame said, smiling at her and at another acquaintance just behind her. 'Take care.'

It was February and there had been a fresh fall of snow. Judith set off for the edge of the town taking care not to slip on the slush, or get bogged down in the drifts that lay by the side of the narrow roads. She raised her head and sniffed the air, and the cold made her eyes tingle. That lovely smell of freshly fallen snow, combined with the keen mountain air, was something unique to this landscape and she knew she would miss it, although Aylestone was in the country too and the air there was very fine, but not comparable to Switzerland.

It took her about ten minutes to walk to Marcel's apartment block and a few minutes more to find it on the fourth floor. It was in a modern building with a new elevator and, as she stepped out of it, the door opened and Marcel appeared in front of her smiling.

'So, you found me,' he said, extending his hand in greeting.

'It wasn't very difficult! This is the most modern building in the town. I was accompanied half the way by Madame Daniel.'

'Oh?' Marcel stopped in front of his door, his eyes instantly alert.

'Don't worry, I didn't tell her where I was going. She was going to the vet with her cat.'

'I see.' Carefully Marcel closed the door behind him and Judith entered a large sitting room with, at the end, a magnificent, huge picture window. This looked right on to the mountain and the ski lift that rose above the town carrying its human cargo to the finest *pistes* at the top of the slopes.

'What a lovely view,' Judith exclaimed.

'It is very fine,' Marcel agreed. From the kitchen came the smell of freshly ground coffee. He folded his arms and stood beside her. 'It's funny how one never tires of looking at the mountains. Of course all day long I see very little; but I love it here.'

'Did you ever live in the hotel?' She turned to him with a look of interest on her face. 'In fact I know very little about you.'

'Oh no. I didn't train at the Daniel; and it was not my first job in Switzerland.'

'Were you here before the war?'

'No. I was only thirteen when the war began. I was in Rouen, which is my home town. But already when I was sixteen I began to learn the work that I wanted to do in the small restaurant kept by my father. It was he who sent me to Switzerland. I tell you I had enough of living in hotels. When I became *sous-chef* at the Daniel I determined to live out.'

'And when will you become head chef?'

'Ah when?' Marcel looked at her enigmatically. 'I think Monsieur Roland has many years left at the Daniel. I will have to look elsewhere for the post, when the time comes. Here, let me get you some coffee.'

Marcel disappeared into the kitchen and emerged in a moment with a tray on which there were two cups of *café filtre*, a jug of cream, a bowl of sugar and, beside them, a plate of *langues du chat*.

Judith sat down in a comfortable, tweed-covered chair from which she could still see the mountain and the gentle motion of the ski lift. Beside her the boiling water slowly dripped through the fresh coffee grounds into the cup.

'Tell me,' Judith said, after she had inspected the progress of the coffee. 'Why did you look startled when I said that I didn't tell Madame Daniel where I was going?'

'Did I?' Marcel's expression was now inscrutable. 'Well of course what we do is our own affair. Why should she know our business?'

'Quite.' Judith removed the top of the *filtre*, saw that it was empty and put two lumps of sugar into her black coffee and put the cup to her lips.

'Mmm, it's good,' she said, after sipping it appreciatively. 'I just wondered if *you* might have guessed the nature of my business?'

Now it was Marcel's turn to look startled. He wore corduroy trousers and a brown check shirt and Judith realized that he had curly brown hair which she hardly ever saw. He looked like two different people in uniform and out of it.

'The nature of your business? I don't really understand you.'

'I thought you might, as I've just come back from England.'

'No, you are being mysterious.'

'I want to offer you a job. We need a chef at our hotel. Naturally we only want the best.'

'You mean you want me to work in England?'

'Yes, at Aylestone. We want to employ the best people in the world and you *are* one of the best.'

Marcel lowered his head and Judith thought he blushed.

'That is most kind of you, Judith. But I am very happy at the Daniel.'

'With Mr Roland?'

'Well, he is a cross I have to bear.' Marcel gave a slight

53

shrug of his shoulders. 'It is worth it because of the esteem in which the hotel is held.'

'But wouldn't you prefer to be your own boss?'

Marcel raised his head and gazed at her.

'You mean I would be *maître-chef*?'

'Of course. I wouldn't think of employing anyone over you. You would be able to set the tone and style of the cuisine for Aylestone. You would be completely in charge of the kitchens and, if you came early enough, you could select your own staff.'

'But I am under contract to Monsieur Daniel.'

'Oh!' Judith gnawed the side of her fingernail. 'I didn't think of that. How much longer has your contract got to run?'

'A year.'

'We shall have to get the Drake Organization's lawyers to try and break it. That's *if* you want the job.' Judith groped in her handbag and produced a brochure which she had folded in half and handed to him.

'This is our first brochure. You will see what sort of place it is and it tells you a little about it and us. We are opening in September and we would very much like you to be there. Maybe the Daniels would not be difficult about releasing you?'

Marcel grunted.

'That I doubt. Also,' he gazed towards the window, 'I'm not sure I want the job, Judith, although it will be a big chance.'

'It will be a *very* big chance,' she said with emphasis. 'You could be one of the great chefs of the world, much sooner than you would otherwise. Because I am sure you will one day, whatever happens. Only now it will be sooner rather than later.'

'Mmm . . .' Marcel turned the pages of the sumptuously produced brochure. 'I'm not sure. I don't know if I want to work in England, though it looks a beautiful place, sure, magnificent. And this is your family home?'

'Was,' Judith grimaced. 'The inside has practically been gutted; but the outside is as it was. We have left it largely because it *is* so beautiful; but a lot has had to be changed inside, lifts put in, etc. We are already behind the schedule so there is no time to lose. Of course you must come over and see it before you decide; but I do hope you'll say "yes"!'

Judith was coming towards the end of her time at the hotel and the days passed very quickly. She didn't go with Marcel when he flew over on one of his weekends off to inspect Aylestone, but when he came back he told her at once that he would accept her offer. He would try and break his contract.

It was a few nights after that, as she was coming off duty, that the telephone rang in the reception where she was working and Mr Daniel's secretary asked her to come upstairs and see him.

Judith thought he wanted to bid her goodbye and smiled as she went into his office; but when she saw his face the smile disappeared.

If it was difficult to guess the age of Madame Daniel, everyone knew that Monsieur was over sixty because he had celebrated his sixtieth birthday with some style a few years before. He was rather a plump man, a true hotelier born to the business and one who enjoyed his food but, particularly, his wine. His greying hair was neatly parted at the side of his head and he always wore morning dress during the day and a black tie and jacket in the evening.

Now he had just changed into evening wear and in his hand there was a large cigar. But, as Judith entered, he sat back in his chair, did not rise – he was customarily the most courteous of men – and did not invite her to sit down.

Instead he came to the point at once, tapping the ash off his cigar on the side of the large glass ashtray.

'I have asked you to come and see me, Mademoiselle Prynne,' he said in a clipped, staccato voice expressive of displeasure, 'because I wanted to tell you personally how disgusted I am that you, of all people, should repay the hospitality you have had in this hotel in such a shoddy manner.'

'I don't know what you mean . . .' Judith began, when her eyes fell to a letter on M. Daniel's desk with the name of the Drake Organization at the top of it. 'Oh. I see.'

'Oh indeed, mademoiselle?' M. Daniel thumped the letter. 'Stealing my top chef. Was it a nice thing to do?'

'I hoped Monsieur Laborde would break the news to you personally. He said he was going to. It is simply that he feels he will never get to the top here, and he is an ambitious man.'

'Nevertheless he has a year of his contract to run and we shall be sure that he sticks to it. As for you, mademoiselle, you may pack your bags and leave us as soon as you can, *and* there will be no diploma, no letter of recommendation from us *ever* – you can be quite sure of that.'

'Monsieur Daniel!' Judith burst out. 'How *can* you say that? You know I have been an excellent pupil. I have served my articles here diligently and you have always praised me. You cannot deny me what is my due.'

'On the contrary I can and I do, mademoiselle,' M. Daniel said, standing up to his full five feet four inches, some three inches shorter than Judith. 'I feel that to attempt to steal my best chef is an act beneath contempt and, believe me, it is something I shall never forget. For you my lack of recommendation will prove a grave disadvantage at the beginning of your career in the hotel business, whether your family owns the hotel or not.'

'I think you're very unreasonable, Monsieur Daniel.' Judith's eyes were beginning to smart. 'How *can* you say that Monsieur Laborde is your best chef when you have a genius like Monsieur Roland? Monsieur Laborde is *sous-chef*, or have you forgotten that?'

'On the contrary, I have not forgotten.' M. Daniel's impeccable control was beginning to desert him. He advanced round the desk and thrust a finger straight at her. '*You* know that Laborde's talent is superior to that of Monsieur Roland. *Everyone* knows it. It is he who gives the accolade to this hotel. I have been thinking of ways to get rid of Roland and promote Laborde. I was to offer him the post of head chef and now . . .' he turned and banged the letter with his hand. 'This!'

'Then I think we shouldn't *dream* of stealing Monsieur Laborde from you,' Judith said with dignity, 'if that is really the case. There are, after all, other chefs in the world. Please keep Monsieur Laborde and see what happens when you try and demote Monsieur Roland or get rid of him. I think you will have a storm on your hands that might surprise even you. Good-day and goodbye to you, Monsieur Daniel. I shall be leaving the hotel within the hour.' She turned towards the door and then suddenly she stopped, as if in an afterthought, and faced him again.

'Having said that I would, nevertheless, like to thank you for what you have done for me at the Daniel. You may choose not to give me a certificate or a reference, but you have given me the very best training in the finest Swiss tradition, and I assure you I am grateful for it and always shall be. You and Madame will always be welcome guests at Aylestone. Please say goodbye for me to Madame Daniel, and to your family.'

And with that she bowed gracefully and swept out of the door; and, within the hour, in accordance with her promise, she was gone.

Gustave Roland was physically an immense man, vastly overweight, with a full beard, a heavy moustache and thick sideboards beneath his tall chef's hat. His appearance was fearsome and he had a temperament to match. He was the undisputed master of the kitchens of the Hotel Daniel and had been for many years. Underlings of every degree of capability had come and gone, some after a very short time.

But, in his way, Roland was a culinary genius and thus he was tolerated not only by the hotel management, to whom he was consistently rude, but by everyone who worked for or near him. It was he who had given the hotel its gastronomic reputation, its two stars in the Michelin Guide. It was because of the reputation of M. Roland that Marcel Laborde had applied for the job of *sous-chef* in the first place.

But the pupil had, in fact, begun to surpass the master. Roland had been at his job a long time and he had grown lazy, less exact and meticulous in his work. It was rumoured that the hotel might be about to lose a star unless the genius of chef Roland were reactivated. But, instead of trying harder, Roland had grown even more quarrelsome and the heat in the kitchen had often more to do with him than the temperature of its ovens.

But Roland had pets; he liked the ladies and, despite his grotesque appearance, for some reason they appeared to like him. He had a little network of female spies scattered throughout the hotel who brought to him daily reports of what was happening in its various parts, and thus he was not slow to learn of the scene between Mademoiselle Prynne (a lady whose style he had instinctively admired, an admiration that had not been reciprocal) prior to her abrupt departure. She had left the hotel without saying goodbye to any of the staff with whom she'd worked for nearly three years, and the reason was soon common knowledge.

If Roland detested anyone it was his deputy, whose work he consistently tried to belittle and undermine. He was intolerant of everyone whose skill threatened to rival his own. But no one had threatened to do so more than Marcel Laborde. Roland had even been known to try and ruin some delicate dish by the simple expedient of adding too much salt or seasoning when Laborde's back was turned, and he was constantly claiming credit for dishes which were not his and strutting about the dining room afterwards to receive the congratulations of the diners.

But now it was whispered, and with authority, that he was about to be supplanted and, when the news reached his ears, his rage was terrible to behold. There was a clash of knives in the kitchens as he prepared to carve the roasts for the restaurant, and those around him felt that that was not the only blood likely to be spilt on a day which was, luckily, M. Laborde's day off.

M. Roland stood there sharpening his knives, eyes glinting wickedly around, and then he attacked the sanguinary cadaver as though it were a live human being.

Luncheon that day was a disaster. The reports of confusion in the kitchen led to confusion in the dining room. Petrified waiters mixed up their orders and the wine waiter upset a bottle of 1929 Haut-Brion over the lap of a distinguished guest. The unease was palpable. One guest choked on her food and had to be escorted to the ladies' room and several of the men had too much to drink and the effects showed.

M. Daniel stayed in his room, aware of what was happening but not knowing what to do about it. For once in his life he remained inactive, immobile, staring at the map of Switzerland on the wall and wondering what action he could take to avert the fact that the reputation of his hotel was slowly beginning to crumble in the dining room downstairs.

At precisely three o'clock the door of his office was violently thrown open and M. Roland appeared, his face puce, every bristle of his massive beard quivering as though it had been electrified.

59

'What is this I hear?' he shouted. 'That *I* am to be *replaced*? I, Roland, who have received more honours and accolades than any other chef in Switzerland. That I am to be put out to pasture when a man who is not fit to wipe my shoes is to replace me? Is that what I hear?'

'No, no,' M. Daniel replied cravenly, shrinking into the protective cover of his winged leather chair. 'No, it is not that at all. You are completely mistaken, Gustave.'

M. Daniel levered himself up in his chair and gently began to mop at the perspiration that had gathered on his brow.

The chef, who by this time had advanced half-way across the room, stopped abruptly. Then he too pulled out his handkerchief from the pocket of his apron, removed his chef's hat and performed a similar operation on his own brow.

'I heard I was to be replaced by Laborde,' he said in a querulous tone.

'You should not believe such stories.' M. Daniel got smartly out of his chair and approached the chef with the caution of a heifer who finds itself alone in a field with a bull. 'Such a thing is out of the question.' Then he wagged a finger at M. Roland, whose eyes had assumed a cunning gleam. 'I have been asked to relieve Laborde. Naturally I am not pleased. He is an excellent chef . . .'

Roland shrugged his massive shoulders dismissively.

'I'm sure even *you* admit that, Gustave. Besides I know you don't like him. But replace you? Never!'

'I heard Mademoiselle Prynne was behind this request and this is why she so precipitously left the hotel.'

'That *is* true.' M. Daniel crossed one hand piously over the other and leaned against his desk for support. 'Naturally I was annoyed. Maybe I said some things I didn't mean. After all, we in this hotel had given Mademoiselle every facility and how am I rewarded? She tries to steal one of my best members of staff. But not *the* best member.

She would not dare to do that. She would not dare even to attempt to steal from me the great Monsieur Roland, Chef d'Honneur, holder of so many prestigious awards . . .'

'I would let him go,' Roland said off-handedly. 'He is not half as good as you think he is, or as he thinks himself. I have to cover up for him a lot, I can tell you. More than you realize, Monsieur Daniel.' Roland appeared preoccupied by a study of his nails. 'Let Mademoiselle Prynne find out what sort of chef he really is. As a matter of fact, monsieur,' he said with an unctuous smile on his face, 'a cousin of mine is beginning to perform extremely well at the Auberge des Neiges in Montreux. With a little more tutoring from me he would make an excellent deputy. I don't know if you would consider . . .' He raised his eyes and studied those of his employer, realizing, at that moment, that at last he had him completely under his control. How fortunate it was that Madame Daniel, who had a little more spirit and was not so afraid of him, was spending a few days in Lausanne visiting her niece.

It was, after all, always the women who made the problems, never the men.

Chapter 4

Aylestone opened in the autumn of 1956 complete with its head chef M. Laborde who came, full of accolades, from Switzerland, including a glowing testimonial from M. Jules Daniel, owner of the Hotel Daniel, who had reluctantly agreed to release him. It seemed an auspicious start.

At the same time there also arrived a testimonial about the competence of Mademoiselle Judith Prynne to engage in every aspect of the business of hotel management. She had not only completed an exacting course in all aspects of the work, but had mastered the French and German languages so that she could converse freely in both.

But Judith felt little triumph about her victory. There had been so much to do, so many problems to overcome. However well trained one was, there was nothing like experience, and that none of them really had. They had the best builders, decorators, designers and consultants; but there were still numerous little anomalies, irregularities and inconsistencies which were incompatible with the running of a first-class hotel. There were lights that did not go on, and taps that either would not turn on or off; there were clashes between wallpaper and curtaining, and a bed that collapsed, luckily before it had its first occupant.

There was the nature of the opening to decide upon and the kind of celebration it should be. But it was a particularly good time to open because at last Britain, with the rest of Europe, was beginning to cast aside the shadows and the aftermath of war ten years after it had officially ended. The Conservatives had established themselves firmly in power and rationing had finally come to an end.

And yet, and yet . . . there was trouble in Egypt. Colonel

Nasser nationalized the Suez Canal and rumblings of discontent cast a gloom among the Allies.

Eventually it was decided to hold a house party of invited guests, with Greville and Angela Prynne host and hostess rather as if they were entertaining family friends. It was a particularly good time of the year for the opening of the hotel, with the leaves on the trees in the park surrounding the house turning to the browns, russets and golds of autumn, and the great log fire in the hall, where everyone was first welcomed to the hotel, lending verisimilitude to the impression of a family home.

For it was intended to present the image of a family home, but the stately home of a great family, as the Prynnes had once been.

Those in charge of the Drake Organization did nothing by halves, especially as George Drake was now related to the family by marriage. Two years before the opening, after he had spent a year abroad, Douglas married Rosalind. Thus George Drake, a man of vast wealth but humble origins, had taken a more than personal interest in the transformation of the derelict house into a hotel of renown. He had put a talented team of designers in charge of the refurbishment, Tom and Tessa Kennedy, who were of the new breed who would transform the theory and practice of design in the post-war world. The Kennedys travelled around Europe in search of inspiration, and finally decided on a decorative scheme that would incorporate simplicity of style with opulence.

Everything had to be the best: the best woods, the best fabrics woven by the most skilled craftsmen, the best Scandinavian cabinetmakers for fitted furniture in bedrooms, and the finest antiques from the sale and auction rooms of Europe for the lounges and the historic dining hall. The presence of the minstrels' gallery made this essentially Jacobean, a style that is easy to copy, but there was nothing in the least phoney about it. Although it was difficult to find original Jacobean furniture, they did: from old halls, where families scarcely knew the value of what they possessed; and from antique boutiques in Paris, Venice and Rome, where the prices were grossly inflated. The specially woven curtains and upholstery incorporated elements and ideas from the seventeenth century that would have deceived an expert, and from the centre hung a wrought iron candelabra which carried real·candles which were changed every day.

The hall that greeted guests presented an image of warmth and welcome. They walked through it to the reception which was functional and unostentatious and manned by one or two functionaries in morning dress. Luggage was carried by footmen who wore aprons over their plain waistcoats and black trousers during the day; at night they wore red or blue tailcoats with brass buttons.

The initial guest list was drawn up with care. It was intended to invite people who were influential without being tainted by any hint of vulgarity.

The Prynnes in their time had accumulated a good number of acquaintances: people of title; the odd politician who was now a minister in the government; captains of industry and, of course, a scattering of service personnel who had achieved positions of great seniority.

All the Prynnes, men and women, had been to the best schools, had stayed with the best people during holidays, and kept in touch with them afterwards. There were numerous Prynne relations among the landed gentry, or who were something in the City, and one or two who were close to the throne.

They had no trouble in filling the place for a party, but a lot in keeping would-be invitees away. For days after the opening was announced Angela or Greville were called personally to the phone by someone who'd remember some close connection with the family, some favour done in years past.

But to no avail. In charge of publicity was Maurice Asher, who had been at school with Douglas and now had his own public relations firm. He had designed everything, from the expensively produced brochures to the press handouts, and the treasured invitations to view that were sent out only to the top papers and magazines.

The gardens, which had been redesigned and laid out by experts from authentic eighteenth-century drawings of Aylestone and its surroundings, were patrolled by guards with fierce dogs, and the large wrought iron gates by the lodge were manned by a uniformed security guard who had only to press a button to summon aid. It was most impressive.

Naturally there was no vulgar sign outside to denote that the venerable home of the Prynnes had been changed into a hotel; just the word AYLESTONE engraved in the stone on either side of the gates, and a tantalizing glimpse through the trees of the huge sandstone mansion at the end of the long, long drive.

On the day of the official opening the guests began to assemble for tea, as was customary in country houses. As their cars drew up at the main door the doors were opened by well-trained footmen, who removed the luggage before the cars were driven round the back. Here there were garages that had been constructed out of the old stables which had been moved further away from the house.

The family waited in the hall to greet the guests, Angela in a day dress of green watered silk with a softly ruched bodice and a pleated skirt by Victor Stiebel. She wore a tiny hat of the same material with an upswept brim and a long plume which slanted over her forehead. Angela had not known such finery – nor had she the chance to try it – since well before the war, and the days spent in the best London couture houses in preparation not only for the opening but her role as hostess were among the most exciting in her recent life. Greville wore a Harris tweed suit which struck the right note for an English country gentleman of property, and Doug a lounge suit which seemed correct for an up-and-coming entrepreneur.

Rosalind was not a natural beauty, but money could make up for a lot of what she lacked; and her black belted suit by Dior with a pearl-grey blouse was beautifully tailored to a figure accentuated by very high heels. Hatless, her upswept hairstyle gave her added inches. In the background two beautifully behaved, impeccably bred red setters lolled by the fire, and an equally domesticated blue Burmese cat perched nonchalantly on the back of one of the chairs, its blue eyes gazing arrogantly at the assembled company.

Behind the scenes, a clipboard and stopwatch in his hand, Maurice Asher kept an eye on preparations minute-by-minute and the Kennedys ran to and fro answering the frantic summonses of everyone, from chef to chambermaid, about last-minute hitches and alterations.

From her office on the first floor Judith controlled the staff, the comings and goings of all the functionaries. On the wall lists of schedules and maps with pins indicated the whereabouts of the various members of staff, whose duties were carefully plotted.

For the grand opening dinner Judith did not appear out front at all, but stayed in the kitchens to help Marcel who, understandably, was undergoing an attack of first-night nerves. This was despite the fact that his talented nephew, Raoul, had come from Marseilles as *sous-chef*, and that all the staff had been personally engaged and tested by him and were experts in their specialities.

Mignons of Scotch salmon poached and served in a hollandaise sauce were accompanied by champagne, a Krug 1937, which had been the last great year before the war. Jacques Peret, a knowledgeable *sommelier*, had been engaged from France, and it had been his pleasant task to purchase the wines from the cellars of numerous vintners, some still struggling to get back on their feet in the aftermath of war, from all the great wine-producing countries of Europe. The cellars below the house were maintained at a temperature of 12° Centigrade and each wine for the opening weekend had been selected by Jacques several weeks previously. The reds had also been personally decanted by him and served at the exact temperature at which they should be drunk.

The clear consommé after the salmon was served with a pale fino sherry imported directly from Jerez in the old casks in which it had been aged, and the burgundies which accompanied the Boeuf rôti à la Bordelaise were '34 Richebourg and a '27 Echezeaux from the great vineyards of Romanée-Conti.

Each table had eight people, one of whom was a member of the family. Judith's place on the first night was taken by Moira, who had thoroughly enjoyed the years of transforming the family home as, having proved herself quite useless at any task she was given, she had consequently been paid to stay away. She had spent some time in Paris, Madrid, Vienna and Rome, from which she returned in time for the grand opening with a young man she introduced to her disapproving parents as her fiancé. He was a personable young American of Italian origin, a painter who lived in Rome. His name was Richard Valenti and, as his manners seemed impeccable and his disposition helpful and polite, he was successful in dispelling the doubts, as well as some of the flutters that affected almost every member of the family at that splendid opening dinner.

In the minstrels' gallery a group of talented musicians played medieval instruments and thus introduced for the first time to some members of the British public the delights of authentic music of the Renaissance.

Angela had changed from her day dress by Stiebel to an evening dress by Mattli of black satin with bare shoulders;

an embroidered bodice hugged her figure and a long, gathered skirt embroidered with thousands of tiny sequins reached to her feet. Gone, long gone, were the days of cardigans and skirts, the perpetual cigarette in the nicotine-stained fingers and the harassed expression on her prematurely ageing, careworn face.

Hours at the top London beauty salons had produced wonders. A clever face-lift had removed the wrinkles, and the tiny little tell-tale tucks and folds were artfully concealed by her hairline. Softly feminine curls led to an upswept chignon which in turn yielded to a large black velvet bow.

All around her women in beautiful gowns conversed with men in tails and starched fronts, and the red- and blue-coated waiters moved skilfully in and out among the diners supervised by the watchful eye of another Frenchman, René Poytevine, the *maître-d'hôtel*. The blue coats were for the young *commis* waiters, the red for those in charge of stations which comprised several tables. There were to be no snags, no awkward moments to interrupt the evening, except that after the sweet – tiny swans made of fluffy meringue, their hollowed-out backs filled with strawberries – Greville stood up to propose the health of the Queen and to announce that everyone could smoke.

Deftly again the highly trained waiters removed plates, refilled glasses and, for the umpteenth time, brushed almost invisible crumbs from the tables with silver-backed brushes into minute silver pans.

'Coffee, I think, in the drawing room,' Angela said, glancing at her neighbour, whose cigar was being lit by a waiter hovering at his elbow.

'Excellent idea.' Matthew Jenner leaned back and glanced round at his wife who sat opposite Greville at the next table.

'A superb dinner, Angela. You can't possibly keep up this standard.'

'Oh can't we? But we must.' Angela greedily lit the cigarette for which she had yearned all evening. 'So much money has been spent on this place that it will take years to get it back.'

'We shall come again,' Sir Matthew said. 'I hear you're offering fishing and riding . . .'

'And golf,' Angela added. 'Haven't you got a very low handicap, Matt?'

'It's eight,' Sir Matthew said with a note of pride. 'That is the first thing on my agenda tomorrow morning.' He leaned over and lowered his voice so that his neighbour, the wife of a member of the House of Lords who hoped to be the next Lord Chancellor, would be unable to hear.

'Who is that very good-looking young man next to Moira?'

'Well, she *calls* him her fiancé,' Angela said in an aggrieved voice. 'We know absolutely nothing about him. He's an American, of all things. We *did* so hope for a title. Moira had the entrée to all the best places, but what can you do? You can't control them, can you? Not like you could before the war.'

'There's always Judith,' Matthew laughed.

'Oh Judith will never marry a *peer*!' her mother cried. 'We'll be lucky if she marries the chef.'

'Are you serious?' Matthew looked surprised. '*Your* chef?'

'She brought him over from Switzerland, after a lot of fuss. She says he's a genius.'

'He is.' Sir Matthew nodded his head enthusiastically. 'The perfection of this dinner is something I cannot recall since before the war. I hope we are to meet this paragon.'

'He's awfully shy.' Angela glanced at Greville and looked at her watch. 'But I think he will put in an appearance after dinner tomorrow night.'

'Well that will be very nice. Judith *and* the chef . . .'

'Oh don't, *please*.' Angela shuddered, putting a hand on his arm. 'I was only pretending . . .

'Yes, but great chefs are great people . . .'

'I can't think what Greville's mother would say. Put it straight out of your mind,' and, smiling, Angela rose as Greville gave a sign, saying *sotto voce*: 'Shall we lead the way, Matt?'

Lady Prynne, meanwhile, had been sitting at the same table as Doug so that he could keep an eye on her. It was many, many years since Gran had dined in such style and, for once, she had been parted from her toque and wore a tiara that was borrowed for the occasion from a famous jeweller in Regent Street, as all the Prynne silver and jewellery had long been sold in an attempt to pay the bills.

Gran gave way to a tiara, but she insisted on wearing the dress she had worn for the Coronation dinner of King George VI and Queen Elizabeth, as she and her husband, as a senior Admiral, had seats in the Abbey. It was a very beautiful gown of purple silk, richly embroidered over her well-corseted bust. Across her shoulders was a mink stole which she had carefully removed from the mothballs in which it had lain for the last nineteen years, and she was led from the dining room by Doug bowing most graciously right and left to the company assembled around her. They moved from the dining room to the drawing room where already the staff was assembled with coffee and liqueurs waiting to be poured the instant someone took a seat.

It was a genial atmosphere. There was plenty of laughter, a show of high spirits as cigarettes and cigars were lit, and the aroma of coffee and vintage brandy filled the air.

Matthew Jenner's wife Margaret had joined her husband and, as Greville came up, she kissed him warmly on the cheek.

'It's a triumph, dear. You deserve to be very successful.'

'Not me, Margaret,' Greville said, returning her embrace with a chuckle. 'I have done nothing.' He turned and pointed behind Margaret's shoulder. 'There is the man who has done everything. Paid the lot. God knows it has cost him a fortune.'

'But it is your home still, isn't it, Greville?' Margaret looked momentarily dismayed.

'In a way.' Greville pulled a face. 'We can live here but we no longer own it outright. It is owned by a company of which that chap, Drake, is chairman, and all the family has a portion of the shares. I expect he has the right to throw us out if he can muster enough people.' Ruefully Greville shook his head. '*I've* no head for business. Never had.' He gave one of his charming, deprecating smiles as Douglas made his way through the throng and whispered in his ear.

'Lord Morris would like a game of billiards, Father. Are you game?'

'I believe I'm set up to play bridge with Arthur Fearnley and Admiral Mustoe and, er, Lady Keith, I believe. You'd better get someone else for billiards.'

'But Lord Morris . . .'

'All right, I'll come and see him myself and explain.' And murmuring an apology Greville trotted off in the direction of the peer with whom he was at school and in the Army.

Margaret Jenner, head on one side, smiled at Douglas.

'You remember me, don't you, Douglas?'

'Of course, Lady Jenner.' Douglas took her hand. 'Have you met my wife?'

'I was introduced to her before dinner. What a charming girl she is. But I want to see Judith too. When I last saw her she was still at school.'

'Not tonight, I'm afraid. She's in charge of the whole show. She's nursing our chef through his first-night nerves.'

'And doing it very well. Dinner was superb.'

'Judith does everything well,' Doug said, looking round

for his wife. 'She seems to have found her vocation. I didn't really know she had it in her.'

'Aren't people full of surprises?' Margaret Jenner waved at someone across the room. 'And now I must go and have a word with your mother and ask her how she's managed to shed twenty years.'

'Ask her the name of the beauty salon,' Douglas whispered in her ear, 'but don't ask the price!'

Margaret Jenner patted his cheek and laughed as she slipped away.

George Drake was standing in front of the fire in a manner that was distinctly proprietorial. He had a large cigar in one hand and a balloon of the finest cognac in the other. His face was a trifle flushed, but he was quite sober. He was a man who would never drink to excess or allow anything to befuddle his brain, which he kept alert to all possibilities. He enjoyed fine wines and good food, but everything in moderation.

He liked Douglas well enough and he knew Judith was a hard worker. Angela and Greville . . . well . . . he screwed up his eyes. They were here for the ride. Anyone who had left money and property in India after Partition could only be taken for a fool.

Moira he knew less well. She was a younger, prettier edition of her mother and, as he watched the gathering of distinguished guests circulating in the drawing room he beckoned to Rosalind, who came over to him and took his hand.

'Enjoying it, Daddy?'

'Are you, darling?'

'Very much. It's a big success.'

'Then I'm glad. Who is Moira Prynne's young man?'

'Isn't he handsome? Would you like to meet him? I'll go and get Moira,' Rosalind said darting away from her father's side, but she did not have far to go.

Moira and Richard had entered the room and after a few words with them, Rosalind pointed to her father who went over to them with an outstretched hand.

'Daddy, this is Richard . . . I'm sorry I don't know your name,' she finished apologetically.

'Valenti, sir. How do you do?' and the young man stepped nimbly forward and took George Drake's hand. 'We did briefly meet when I arrived but obviously you don't remember.'

'Forgive me,' Drake said apologetically. 'So much to do, so many people to see. Did you say Valenti?'

'Yes, sir.'

'But I understood you were a painter?'

'I am, Mr Drake.'

'But you're American?'

'That's right.' Richard maintained his easy, unaffected manner but he tapped his toe rather impatiently on the floor as if the inquisition bothered him.

'Isn't Valenti a very well-known name in America?'

'It could be.' Richard sounded evasive and Moira, looking curiously at him, touched his arm.

'Obviously he's being modest.' Drake smiled at Moira. 'If his father is *the* Valenti I'm thinking of he is a very important and powerful businessman. Leo Valenti I think.'

'That's my father,' Richard said lowering his voice.

'Is he *very* famous?' Moira looked bemused.

'I've never met him,' Drake said, 'but I've done business with him. He's a very smart man.'

'Oh *that* couldn't be Richard's father,' Moira said tucking her arm through Richard's. 'He is the proverbial penniless artist. He lives in a garret in Trastevere . . .'

'But how *fascinating*,' Angela butted in, having joined the group just in time to hear Drake's announcement. 'And there we all were thinking that Moira . . .'

'Are you playing bridge, darling?' Greville interrupted

73

her. 'There's a table next door waiting for you to make up the four.'

'Greville ... such a coincidence.' Impulsively Angela seized his hand. 'George knows Richard's father. Isn't it a small world?'

'I don't actually *know* him,' George began, but Angela swept on.

'He's an important businessman,' she volunteered. 'Not that *that* means a thing of course.' She sounded a little drunk.

'It means absolutely nothing,' Greville said firmly. 'But we have duties to fulfil, darling.'

And, bowing, he skilfully drew her out of the group.

'Isn't that a piece of *luck*,' Angela said, fumbling with her earring as she gazed at herself in the mirror. The door to Greville's dressing room was open as he moved back and forth until he stopped by the door in the act of untying his bow.

'What's that?'

'Richard being wealthy. We thought he was a pauper. So did she.'

'*She* appears rather upset by the whole thing.'

'She's such a silly girl! She would. By marrying a pauper she'd make things just that little bit harder for us. I'm afraid our daughter is very spoilt and would rather have enjoyed that.'

'Oh I don't think so, dear.' Greville emerged in his dressing gown and sat on the chair by Angela's dressing table.

Though a fortune had been spent on the house as a whole, the wing where the family lived remained relatively untouched. However, the antiquated system of central heating, which hadn't functioned properly for the last thirty years or more, had been replaced by a modern system which now heated the entire house from a central boiler in the basement. Thus the fireplaces were ornamental, though Gran insisted on having her fire lit every evening, especially as the nights were drawing in. In her experience fires were reliable; one never knew what could go wrong with a central heating system, and often did.

George Drake, though generous in fitting up the hotel, didn't think much time or money should be spent on the family living quarters. Because of this insistence on keeping them, much needed revenue was being lost to the hotel. Thus the living quarters remained little changed.

Greville leaned back in his chair and put his hands behind his head.

'I think you're being rather unkind to Moira. Personally I'm delighted if it's true.'

'But don't you think he'd *say*? That's what I can't understand.' Angela, by now undressed, began to take off her make-up. 'I mean,' she turned towards her spouse, hands mechanically revolving around her face, 'wouldn't you say *you* were wealthy if you were?'

Greville considered the matter. 'No,' he said at last, 'I don't really think I would. I'd rather respect the chap for not mentioning it.'

'Unless,' Angela paused and, eyes wide, she looked at her reflection in the mirror, 'unless he'd something to hide.'

'Don't be ridiculous, darling. I think you've had too much to drink.' Greville gave a yawn, stood up and patted her on the back. 'Don't worry about Moira. She has her head screwed on. A wealthy man might be cautious about gold-diggers. Not boasting about money is a rather attractive feature, I think. Well, it's been a very successful evening if you ask me. Good-night dear.' And off he went to bed.

Downstairs in the kitchens everything was quiet. It was almost dark except for the light in the *maître-chef*'s room where Marcel was going over his menus for the following day, despite the pleas of Judith, who sat back in her chair, every bit as exhausted as he was.

'If you go on like this, Marcel, you'll kill yourself. I didn't mean that to happen when I offered you the job.' She glanced at the clock on the wall with the large second-hand relentlessly circulating on the dial. 'It's two now and you say you have to get up at six. That's less than four hours' sleep!'

'I have to,' Marcel said without looking up, rapidly covering the page with his small, neat handwriting.

'But Raoul or René can do the breakfasts.' René was the second *sous-chef*, a young man who'd trained at Claridges.

Marcel looked up with an exaggerated sigh.

'Judith, please, don't argue with me. I am in charge here, and I want everything to be perfect, everything down to the last detail. Fresh rolls have to be baked for breakfast ... there is luncheon to prepare and the huge dinner tonight.'

Judith put her head in her hands. It was too much. They had all taken on too much. With such a large staff, with so many people in charge of individual departments, she had never dreamed there would be so much work to do, so many details to see to. If Aylestone, by any chance, remained full it would be almost impossible to cope, or so it seemed now.

'You're very tired yourself,' Marcel said kindly. 'Why don't *you* get some rest? I thought you were to attend the dinner tonight? Rather, last night.'

'It was impossible,' Judith said. 'I thought Mother and Father would be of more help. As it is they're behaving as though they were guests! I suppose we should have expected it, but George Drake is quite cross about it already.'

'But he has behaved like a guest too.' Marcel closed his ledgers and sat back, running a hand over his pale face.

'Yes, but he's got a right. He's put in all the money. Mother and Father have put in nothing and they are being quite well paid. Mother even has a dress allowance. I think they should be doing more.'

'Did anyone *seriously* ever think they would?' Marcel gazed at her without smiling. 'Your parents are the most delightful people, but as soon as I met them I knew they would not carry any of the burden of running the hotel. Your brother, now, and sister-in-law . . .' Marcel frowned and, standing up, removed his apron.

'Don't you like them?' Judith looked concerned.

'I like your brother very much. But your sister-in-law . . . well I'm not so sure. The daughter of Mr Drake . . .'

'She's awfully competent. But I don't know that she wants to get involved in the hotel. She's in love and she wants a nice house and a family.'

'Isn't that what every woman wants?' Marcel closely watched the expression on Judith's face.

'Not every woman,' Judith said, and with an enigmatic smile began to go round the kitchen, switching off the lights.

Chapter 5

Everyone agreed that the opening of Aylestone as a hotel was a great success and the invited guests went away well pleased to spread the news. It travelled but it didn't travel far or fast enough. It was a very expensive place in which to stay and the perfection of the menu, the excellence and variety and, sometimes, rarity of the ingredients made eating there prohibitively expensive except for the very rich.

Even the very rich had not yet grown accustomed to spending a lot of money in the aftermath of war. Moreover there was an increasing tendency to go abroad for holidays on the part of a people which had been confined – except for those who had fought overseas – for over five years. The package tour trade had not yet become as popular as it was to be, but it was growing. The aeroplane was expanding the world of travel to places people would never have thought of visiting for a holiday in pre-war days.

But perhaps it was the effect of the Suez war that affected the hotel business most. The years of peace had so far always been overshadowed by the threat of Russian aggression and the atomic bomb. Now, with the invasion of Suez by the British and French troops in the month after Aylestone opened, many people thought that the world was on the brink of another war. That Armageddon had finally arrived. They were not inclined to go and spend enormous sums of money at an expensive hotel so near London. In a way it had been an unpropitious time for it to open.

The hotel was never completely empty. There were always several couples, mainly American tourists, curious enough to see what living in a stately home was like, and the restaurant was often booked out, especially at week-ends. News of its superb cuisine had spread like wildfire, and half the people who ate there were gastronomic experts from various papers and journals who then went away and gave it the kind of write-up which encouraged even more. The experts were always anonymous; but they became easy to spot. They looked at each offering critically, and sniffed each wine suspiciously. But the work, the artistry of Marcel Laborde, was considered a triumph and his reputation spread.

The upkeep of the hotel was astronomical. The over-heads were colossal because there was such a large staff, often not fully employed. The reputation of the hotel was based on quality, on service, so no one could be laid off in case a disappointed visitor became critical and the criticism spread.

Doug grew more nervous and fidgety and spent a lot of his time in his office going over the figures, wondering how costs could be cut without the service being impaired. Judith remained calm, treating every day as a fresh experi-ence in which something could be learned, and Marcel was absorbed in his work, the invention and testing of new dishes. He shopped personally in Covent Garden twice a week and food was sent down fresh; the finest cuts of meat from Smithfield; fish carefully packed in ice from Billingsgate.

But by the end of November they were still not making money and George Drake was known to be displeased.

'We can't possibly break even, never mind make a *profit* in two months,' Judith exploded one day after the senior staff had had a dressing-down from George.

'I didn't expect to break even for a year,' George replied testily. 'But I didn't expect that money would drain away as it has.' He held up a sheaf of papers and shook them at her. 'This enterprise has already cost me millions of pounds. Millions and . . .' he looked around at the assembled company: Judith, her brother, Maurice Asher, 'where are your parents today, may I ask, Judith?'

'Mother's in town. I think Father's playing golf.'

'Does he *ever* do anything else?'

'With one of the guests,' Judith replied coldly, 'who needed a partner.'

'Still, I think your father considers that we have done up this place to please him – as a personal gift to the Prynnes. Does your mother *ever* do anything? For example, if she could supervise the housework we could dispense with a housekeeper.'

'You could hardly expect Mother to do that!' Judith protested, 'She hasn't had the training.'

'Oh, hasn't she?' Drake sneered.

'No, she hasn't. She is a very good hostess when there are guests. That's all you ever asked her to be. She'd be hopeless at domestic detail. They lived abroad, don't forget. If you like I can take on that; but I still think it's too soon.'

'Much too soon to start firing people,' Maurice Asher said nervously, as if aware that his name might be first on the list. 'Once you do it gets the place a bad reputation.'

'In my view you were too extravagant.' Judith gazed at Drake calmly. 'You needn't have spent as much money as you did doing the place up. I believe the consulting fee of the Kennedys alone was a hundred thousand pounds.'

'I suppose *you* could have done that too?' Drake commented caustically.

'Yes, I suppose I could,' Judith replied. 'I think you set the tone. You were fired with terrific ambitions and expected to make a fortune at once. The hotel business isn't like that.'

'No it isn't,' Doug said, supporting Judith. 'I've been all over the world studying it.'

'Then *you* should know how to run it better,' Drake snapped at him. 'That trip alone cost us a small fortune.'

Rosalind, who was there by invitation, sat with her back to the room where the meeting was taking place, looking out of the window. The trees were almost bare of leaves and it was possible to see the river lazily wending its course to the sea below. She recalled sitting in the same place the year before with all bedlam going on around them and how happy and excited they'd been then. How very different was the tone of the meeting now. Slowly she turned to face her father, arms akimbo.

'I think you're being a bit unreasonable, Daddy. Of course it will look bad if we start sacking people. If you ask me we should advertise a Christmas party. You know, so many days all in.'

'It's a bit late for *that*,' Doug said dubiously.

'No it isn't. Get an advert in *The Times* and the *Telegraph*. Maurice can ring up some of his friends in the Street.'

'It will have to be costed carefully.' There was excitement in Judith's voice. 'Frankly I think it's a splendid idea. Marcel will be thrilled.'

'And kindly tell Marcel to stop ordering caviare from Russia,' George said testily. 'He can get the Danish variety, like anyone else.'

'Oh he would *never* do that, I'm afraid,' Judith replied loftily. 'Marcel will never drop his standards for anyone, even you.'

To some extent the idea for a Christmas party worked. Judith herself rang up some of the people who had been invited to the opening, and among those who agreed to come were the Jenners and Sir Harry and Lady Montcalm with their son and daughter-in-law. Maria Sillitoe, the actress, said she'd come with her new boyfriend, but just for Christmas Day and night.

Judith was very careful to keep George Drake's doubts from the temperamental Marcel, who set to planning the menus with gusto. But it would be no ordinary Christmas fare. There would be a lot of inventions, a mixture of the traditional with the new.

One casualty, inevitably, and as he'd feared, was Maurice Asher, who was told directly by Drake that his services were being dispensed with. Drake felt the PR man was too capricious. None of the other senior staff knew until it was over, but Judith was furious, saying that George's unilateral decision would harm the hotel. She tried to call Drake but he refused to take her calls or return them. Finally she wrote him a note, but by that time it was too late.

By Christmas the routine of the hotel had settled down. The housekeeper was kept on, but the situation would be reviewed in the New Year. Judith and Douglas were a good team, dividing the administration between them; to their irritation Rosalind also took it into her head to try and play a part though she had no official position. Rosalind was eager to do the things Judith had said she would: she and Doug had a small but beautiful house about a mile from the hotel, and she was pregnant with their first child.

But Rosalind was ambitious too; and she was restless at being cast in the domestic role when so much was going on a mile up the road. She'd arrive just before lunch in her little Morris Minor and the way she talked to staff and asked to see reports seemed to indicate that she considered herself her father's deputy.

Judith began to resent it.

'I was afraid she would be a bit of a pain,' Judith said to her mother, who was making up in the mirror before dinner on Christmas Eve, having welcomed the guests for tea rather as she had at the opening party in the autumn. She wore a new creation, part of an ensemble made by Hardy Amies for the occasion.

'She's not a girl I'm over-fond of myself, frankly.' Her mother, peering at herself with her large blue eyes, smeared lipstick at the corner of her mouth with her little finger. Then she fluttered her heavily mascara'd lashes and pronounced herself satisfied. 'I suppose Doug married her because she was Drake's daughter.'

'I think he married her because he loved her.'

'Oh, Doug could have done much better than *that*!' Angela said with a malicious smile. 'Such a plain little thing. She does her best . . . but you can't make a silk purse out of a sow's ear. Can you?'

'Mother!' Judith stepped back from her perch near the dressing table. 'That is a horrible thing to say. We can't help how we look, and Ros *is* smart! I don't think she's plain at all.'

'Oh dear, Judith,' her mother sighed. 'That's your trouble. You always want to see the best in people.'

'Is it a fault?'

'It's not a fault, darling, but it's foolish. If you go to such lengths to deceive yourself you might make mistakes elsewhere. If you're in business you can't afford to be like that.'

'How do you know?' Judith began to smile.

'I *know*,' her mother said, tapping her head with a wise smile. 'I've been around a long time. Believe you me . . .'

She halted as Judith came over to her and put her arms round her:

'Oh, Mother.' Judith hugged her and then drew back, still smiling.

'Yes, what is it darling?' Angela looked surprised.

'Don't ever change, that's all.' Then she kissed her on the cheek.

'Why Judith, you haven't been so affectionate for ages.' Angela, in turn, patted her daughter's cheek. 'You've grown up rather well yourself, darling. I wish we could find *you* a nice man.'

'When have I got the time for romance, Mother, I ask you?' Judith, releasing her mother, stopped to peer at herself in the mirror and ran a comb through her hair.

'Aren't you coming to dinner, dear?'

'No, there's too much to do in the kitchen. René has had the 'flu and Marcel is in a bit of a state.'

'When is Marcel *not* in a state?' her father asked, entering the bedroom from his dressing room and smelling a fresh hot-house rose he had just pinned to the lapel of his dinner jacket.

'Not very often, actually. As you don't go down to the kitchen much I don't think you can really know what goes on there, Daddy.'

'I *hear* things,' her father said with a knowing smile.

'I bet you do. I think you gossip too much with the servants, Dad, getting them to do little favours for you. Don't think *I* don't know what goes on.'

'I've no idea what you mean.' Her father studied the flower in his buttonhole, then preened himself in the mirror, above her mother's head.

'You treat the family wing, Dad, as though it were part of the hotel.'

'Well, isn't it?'

'No. It isn't. Whenever I see one of the footmen carrying a tray across the hall he's on his way here. You have your meals served up here, and they're perpetually fetching you drinks.'

'Don't forget, my dear daughter,' Greville said with an edge to his voice, 'that I sold my birthright to that mendacious Jew.'

'George is not Jewish,' Judith said in astonishment at her father's outburst. 'Besides, after the concentration camps, I wonder you could make a remark like that'

'Oh don't be dramatic, Judith.' Angela got up and clasped her hands around her neat waist. 'The Jews will never change.'

'But George Drake is not Jewish!' Judith stamped her foot in exasperation on the floor.

'Well if he isn't, then he's learned a lot of their tricks. I've never known such a mean-minded man. Your father and I are extremely sorry we ever got involved with him. Given second sight . . .'

'Given second sight, Mother, you would be living in some poky little house on the edge of the town wondering where the next cheque was coming from. You've a lot to thank George Drake for, even if he were Jewish, you and Dad, and please don't forget it.'

Judith turned abruptly on her heels and went to the door without another word, while her mother and father exchanged glances. When she'd gone Greville said:

'Time for a quickie, dear?'

'I think so.' Angela smiled and sat down to do her nails as Greville produced the gin bottle from a corner cupboard together with a bottle of tonic and two glasses. 'Judith is much too intense for this business. Frankly, I don't think it will last, Grev, do you?'

'What's that, dear?' Greville concentrated on pouring two stiff measures of gin.

'This hotel thing. I always thought it was a lark.'

'Well it is rather serious.' Greville handed his wife her drink and sat opposite her, carefully sipping his own. '*If* it goes, we go.'

'Oh, but you can't say *that*!'

'I do say that. Drake will sell this place lock, stock and barrel over our heads, and we shan't have much to show for it.'

'You're not serious, Greville?' His wife looked at him in dismay.

'Oh but I am. We got a poor financial arrangement, there's no doubt about that, because we had no choice.'

'But I thought you were a director of this outfit?'

'I am. We all have shares, as well. But the family only

owns forty-five per cent. Drake and his family own fifty-five. They can outvote us and outsell us any day.'

'But that's *monstrous*! It should never have been allowed.'

'At the time it seemed fair. We had a derelict house and some land and nothing else. We weren't in much of a position to argue.'

'But I always thought the house remained ours?'

'Oh no, darling.' Greville finished his drink in one gulp. 'The house no longer belongs to us but to the company and the company is part of the Drake Organization. They could buy us out and that would be it. Mind you, we'd have a tidy bit of money, but it's not the same thing is it?'

'Not at all,' Angela said, her eyes narrowing. 'I might have known that Jew would get it all his own way.'

Downstairs in the hall, Gran was sitting on an upright chair looking very regal. She had on the gown she'd worn for the opening and a rather ancient feathered hat that looked like a discarded bird's nest on her head. Both hands clasped the head of her cane and, as she sat, her head turned from side to side as if she were looking for someone or something. Finally one of the guests who was passing stopped and asked politely if he could be of help.

'That's most kind of you,' Gran said. 'Have you seen the Admiral?'

'I beg your pardon?' The guest bent his head politely. He was on the staff of the Swedish Embassy and had seen the announcement of the Christmas party in *The Times*.

'My husband, Admiral Sir Jasper Prynne. You must know him.' Gran looked patronizingly at the Swede. Her half-hooded eyes gleamed with a knowing intelligence, and her highly rouged cheeks and strong, thin nose bore a resemblance to some predatory bird. The Swede was impressed.

'I do not know the Admiral, madame, but I shall certainly go in search of him.'

'Thank you, most good of you,' Gran said. 'You could ask one of the footmen. Or,' she put out a hand, 'there's my granddaughter Moira. She will know.'

Moira, dressed in a short evening dress of green velvet, came towards her grandmother, a smile on her face as she glanced at the diplomat.

'What is it, Gran?'

'Your grandfather, darling. Have you seen him? I haven't seen him since morning.'

'Let's go and look for him,' Moira said smiling fixedly at the Swede who bowed low and continued on his way through the hall. Then Moira tucked her hand through her grandmother's arm and said quietly but severely:

'Now, Gran, you must *not* do that in front of guests. You know that Grandpa has been dead since before the war.'

'Oh, Moira, what a cruel thing to say,' Gran said querulously. 'I saw him this morning.'

'You forget, Gran,' Moira said tapping her hand. 'Your mind wanders. How much whisky have you had?'

'I only had a drop in the bar,' Gran said, feeling a little hurt. 'Then I came and sat here to wait for your grandfather to take me in to dinner.'

'Well Richard will take you in to dinner instead. You like Richard, don't you Gran?'

'Who's Richard?'

'He's my fiancé, Gran.'

'I didn't know you were engaged,' Gran said looking at her with interest. 'No one *ever* seems to tell me anything. When are you getting married?'

'In the summer.'

'Oh that will be lovely,' Gran said cheering up. 'I shall enjoy that. Will it be a large wedding in St Margaret's?'

'Hardly, Gran,' Moira replied, as Richard Valenti

appeared in the corridor dressed for dinner. Evening dress suited him with his dark, Italian looks and curly black hair.

'There you are,' he said putting an arm easily round Moira's waist. 'Are you ready for dinner?'

'The gong hasn't sounded. I think there's champagne in the drawing room first.'

'Oh how lovely,' Gran said enthusiastically. 'I *do* love a party.'

One on each side of Lady Prynne, they walked towards the drawing room, where quite a concourse had already assembled. Cars had been arriving in the drive all evening and the restaurant was booked out over Christmas. It was, indeed, very like the opening party all over again, and the hotel had never been as full since. Judith circulated among the guests while her mother, who should have been doing this, was sitting at the bar holding court and drinking. George Drake was in a far corner talking to one of the guests and then, through the crowd, Judith saw Matthew Jenner and went over to greet him:

'Matthew, how nice to see you.'

'And you, Judith,' Matthew said, kissing her cheek. He looked around, his eyes smiling. 'How are things? Going well?'

'Pretty well.'

'Full up?'

'Not quite. Full up in the restaurant.'

'I'm surprised the hotel isn't full.'

'We left it a bit late to advertise.'

'Still, surely, its reputation . . .'

'It's early days yet, Matt,' Judith said. 'Please excuse me. I've seen someone I have to give a message to.'

Matthew stood back as she hurried past him but his smile was replaced by a frown. He saw George Drake in one corner deep in conversation, and Greville and Angela at the bar gaily entertaining a group of people he didn't know. Suddenly Drake looked up and caught his eye and, ending his conversation, came over to Jenner with hand outstretched.

'How nice to see you, Matthew.'

'And you!' They shook hands. 'What splendid company you have here. Maria Sillitoe is the great star of the West End at the moment.'

'So they say.' George appeared unimpressed.

'Not too happy, George?' Matthew enquired. 'I thought Judith hurried away rather quickly when I asked her how things were going.'

'The hotel isn't full.' George pulled a face.

'It *looks* very full.'

'That's because people are here to dine. You'd think it would be full at Christmas.'

'But have you given it a chance, George? It's only been open three months.'

'Four. We opened at the beginning of September.'

'Even four months isn't a lot.'

'I like to see quick profits.'

'Then you shouldn't have gone into the hotel business.'

'We spent so much on publicity. I mean, we may not have opened until September, but there were articles about the place, the blasted historical Prynnes, all year. And look at them!' Drake gestured towards the bar. 'You honestly would think it was their family home!'

'Well it is.' Matthew, who liked the Prynne family better than George Drake, looked amused.

'It is *not*. We had to go down to the foundations to restore it. The structure was rotten with woodworm. When I came on the scene it was a ruin. In fact it *may* have been better to have pulled it down and started all over again.'

'Surely it had a preservation order . . .'

'Oh there are ways to get round that. Pull it down first, then ask permission. That's what I always do. It works too. That, and a few cases of whisky in the right quarter.'

Matthew smiled without amusement, but said nothing.

89

There was little love lost between the two men who, besides being business rivals, came from different backgrounds. Drake considered himself more successful than Jenner though perhaps he envied his membership of the baronetage, his links with a famous public school. Jenner despised Drake, but envied his success, his acknowledged acumen.

'If it doesn't work I'm not holding on to it. I've too much invested in it.' Drake stubbed out his cigar in an ashtray of heavy, leaded crystal.

'I'm sorry to hear you say that.' Matthew looked concerned. 'The Prynnes would be devastated.'

'Then they should work harder to do something about it. The parents are parasites. I think they think I restored it as a home for *them*. Angela spends all her time in London at Harrods or Harvey Nichols or at some beauty salon or other. Greville is always on the golf course. I think he thinks I laid it for his private enjoyment.'

'Judith . . .'

'Judith works hard. She has to. She is responsible for a lot of it and she knows what is at stake. She knows *exactly* what is at stake.'

'Laborde is a genius.'

'I have no complaints about the chef; but do you know we have about three members of staff to see to the needs of every guest? It's absurd. You can imagine how many hang around doing nothing when we're not full. Yet I'm told that if we sack people the news will be bad publicity.'

'True.' Matthew suddenly smiled towards the door where Lady Prynne was being led in by Richard and Moira. 'Excuse me,' Matthew said, and went over to greet them.

'Lady Prynne! How good to see you.'

'Oh, Matthew.' Gran's eyes looked troubled. 'Have you seen the Admiral? No one seems to know where he is and I fear he may be lost.'

Matthew looked round, apparently concerned.

'No, he is nowhere to be seen, Lady Prynne. But I'm sure you have no need for alarm!'

'I saw him this morning. Not since . . .' Gran wandered off looking vague.

'Do go after your grandmother,' Matthew urged Moira. 'I don't think Mr Drake would be too pleased if she started asking the Admiral's whereabouts of the guests.'

Moira went after her grandmother, catching her arm just as she was in the act of approaching a prominent member of Parliament.

'It's really very sad,' Richard said looking after her.

'Oh she's perfectly all right,' Matthew assured him. 'She's a little eccentric, but not mad. Not mad at all.'

'But if she thinks her husband is still alive . . . Moira said he died in *1938*.'

'Maybe she does see him, who knows?' Matthew smiled at the young man next to him. 'I hear the wedding date is fixed.'

'In the summer. We hope my father can come over for it.'

'Will it be here?'

'Perhaps. Neither Moira nor I want a lot of fuss and, as we are of different religions, we thought a registry office wedding, followed by a reception here.'

'What a good idea. Let's hope the place is still here.'

'Oh?' Richard looked at him sharply. 'Is there any reason it shouldn't be?'

'I've just been talking to Drake. I'm not sure how much the family knows, or you know. Maybe I shouldn't have said anything.'

'I can't believe he'd let it go after just a few months. It would be scandalous.'

'He's a very tough businessman. I wondered, quite honestly, why he ever got into it. It's not really his style. Now, a popular restaurant with a quick turnover . . . but a hotel like this. It takes a long time to get a return on investment.'

'Business bores me, I'm afraid,' Richard said, yawning.

'You're a painter?'

'Yes.'

'Successful?'

'No. But then Van Gogh wasn't very successful in his lifetime.'

'I hope you don't share his fate.' Matthew laughed and, as his wife came over, he held out his hand.

'Have you met Moira's fiancé, dear? Richard Valenti. He's an artist.'

'I know.' Margaret Jenner shook Richard's hand. 'You may not remember but we had a talk at the opening party. I told you I couldn't understand Picasso and you were telling me . . .'

But just then the gong sounded and everyone turned towards the door as though they were hungry.

'Feeding time at the zoo,' Matthew said, steering his wife towards the door.

Richard Valenti felt uneasy in the Prynne family home that wasn't a home. It was hard to relax even for a moment, and he suspected Moira's parents didn't really like or approve of him. They were the kind of people who were so used to hiding their true feelings that one never knew what they thought. Whenever he appeared he was greeted by that bland smile of great charm which was neither sincere nor insincere. It was detached, objective, uninvolved. There had been a little of that in Moira, too, on his first sight of her at a private view in Rome of some paintings of a mutual friend. He couldn't take his eyes off such an elegant, beautiful girl, who wandered around the room in a white suit, pausing quite unselfconsciously before each painting as if totally unaware that the eyes of most people in the room were upon her.

Who was she?

And that was how Moira Prynne came into his life.

It had been at a difficult time in her life and, like all the Prynnes, she was evasive, even secretive. She was reluctant to discuss family business with him.

The relationship had been slow to develop. For a time she left Rome and went to Paris, but soon she was back again and he knew he was in love with her.

At dinner he found himself sitting next to Judith, his future sister-in-law. He didn't know whether by accident or design. Judith and Moira were dissimilar both in temperament and appearance. There was an air of fragility about Moira that made a man want to protect her, while Judith was strong; clearly someone who could look after herself.

The dining room was lit solely by candles for Christmas Eve. It was beautifully, tastefully, unostentatiously decorated with holly, mistletoe and other seasonal emblems. A huge fire curled round the logs at one end of the room. In the minstrels' gallery the Renaissance ensemble played medieval Christmas music.

Judith wore black. It was a good colour for her because of her auburn hair, her grey-green eyes. She was someone with natural colouring who needed little make-up besides a splash of orange lipstick. Opposite her, her sister was her very antithesis: blonde, fragile, feminine. Even her voice was pitched half an octave higher.

'You've done an awfully good job,' Richard said, breaking into his bread roll. 'It must have been a lot of work for you.'

'Not just me,' Judith smiled at him. 'It has been a lot of work for all the staff, but particularly Marcel, the chef. He is a perfectionist.'

'That's obvious.' Richard sank his knife into the quenelle of sea trout with lobster sauce. 'When I was here last I thought the food superb.'

'I'm afraid we hardly knew you then.'

'It makes no difference.' Richard smiled at her.

He was an attractive man, Judith thought to herself. His accent was that of a Bostonian rather than a New Yorker and his manners were impeccable.

'Did it surprise you when Moira told you the story about our home?' she ventured at last.

'You mean being turned into a hotel?'

'Yes.'

'Do you mean did it surprise me or shock me?'

'Both.'

'Well, of course, it didn't shock me. Moira never concealed the fact that the family hadn't sufficient means to carry on as they had in the old days. Few people have. She never pretended you were rich. When I first met her she was unhappy about what was happening; but now I think she is used to it. I think she may even like it. You can see that your parents are enjoying themselves.'

'Oh enormously; but they're very naughty. They don't do any work.'

'That's why they're enjoying themselves. I'm going to play golf with your father tomorrow. I hear he has a handicap of ten. Moira and I also intend to go riding tomorrow. It is really like a very nice home ... from home.'

'But how long will it last?' Judith lowered her voice and he leaned closer to her.

'Last? Every time I'm here the place is full.'

'You have been here twice and both times there were parties. Most of the time it is empty.'

'But it's very early days,' Richard said. 'Unfortunately I know nothing about the economics of hotels.'

'It is pretty much like the economics of any other business. It either works or it doesn't.'

'This will surely work, in time.' Richard continued to gaze at her. 'But you don't think so?'

'I shouldn't be talking like this.' Judith critically watched the waiter as he removed her plate and another one appeared who deftly brushed off the crumbs with the silver-backed brush. 'But as you're almost family . . .'

'Please go on.'

'Mother and Father don't like George Drake. He's the backer.' She pointed towards a table at the end of the room, to a man with his back to them. 'He is the one with the money. He is getting impatient. He expected it to be an instant success. I don't think he'll have a lot of patience if it isn't. You've no idea how much he's done. Everything had to be right.'

'Ah, it is. It is magnificent. But I would have thought a year, two years . . . at least. I'll ask my father.'

'Is he in the hotel business?'

'No, but he is a businessman. He comes to Rome quite often.'

'Matthew Jenner seemed very impressed by your father.' Richard acknowledged the compliment.

'He is an impressive man.'

'Didn't he want you to go into the business?'

Richard shrugged.

'He couldn't stop me wanting to paint. He didn't try. I'm the only child, so it was a blow to him.'

'And your mother?'

'My mother is dead.' Richard paused and frowned. 'She had a heart condition.'

'I'm sorry.'

'It was five years ago.' Richard shrugged. 'I decided to make my new life in Rome. Now I have Moira . . .'

'Excuse me, Miss Prynne.' The *maître d'hôtel*, who had been hovering near Judith for a few minutes, now bent urgently over her shoulder. 'I wonder if I could have a few words?'

'Now?'

'At once if possible, madame. There is trouble in the kitchen.'

'Excuse me,' Judith said to Richard, standing up and dropping her napkin on the chair. Quickly she followed the *maître d'hôtel* out of the dining room. 'Tonight of all nights.'

'It has been brewing for some time, madame.'

'But chef . . .'

'It is chef who is involved, and I'm afraid it also involves your sister-in-law.'

'Mrs Prynne . . .'

By this time they had gone through the green baize door to the kitchens, from which already there were sounds of a commotion. Judith pushed back the swing doors and saw Rosalind, with Douglas behind her, confronting Marcel who stood on the other side of the central serving table on which stood several large turkeys waiting to be carved.

Marcel, however, was not carving them. He stood with his arms crossed and glanced up as Judith came through the door. Suddenly the babble of noise died down and Doug and Rosalind slowly turned.

'Judith,' Doug said. 'You're not on duty.'

'Nevertheless . . . is there anything I can do?'

'No thank you,' Rosalind said pertly. 'We don't interfere when you're on duty. I thought you were having a well-deserved night off.'

'*We?*' Judith said with emphasis. 'I thought Doug was the manager here, not you.'

'Don't be rude to Ros,' Doug said, but he looked uncomfortable.

'On the contrary, I'm stating a truth, Doug. She has no official position here; no place in this kitchen. Something here is wrong enough for Henri to demand my presence.' She turned to the *maître d'hôtel* but he had returned to the dining room.

'It is as well you are here, Judith,' Marcel said, uncrossing his arms. 'Because I cannot fulfil my task here in the kitchens any longer.' He began to unfasten the strings of his apron. 'It is as well that I complete my duties and return to France.'

'What on earth are you talking about?' Angrily Judith crossed the room.

'You should ask your brother *and* sister-in-law.'

'What does he mean?' Judith turned to Doug who looked distressed.

'He means . . .' Doug began.

'I mean that I can no longer work in this hotel. I have not the freedom you promised me.'

'But you have every freedom.'

'No I have not.' Marcel shook his head in a gesture that Judith knew only too well. 'Everything I suggest is changed. Orders are given to my staff that countermand mine. I have had enough.' Marcel succeeded in removing his apron and threw it on a chair. 'I am no longer the *maître-chef* at Aylestone.'

'Thank goodness for that,' Rosalind said with a smile and turned to her husband.

'Just *what* do you mean?' Judith said to her, hand on hip.

'I mean, Judith,' Rosalind said sweetly, 'that Monsieur Laborde has no idea of the kind of food we like or expect in England. He has no idea how to deal with staff. Ask him,' Rosalind pointed a hand at Raoul, who had remained in the background. 'Ask him what *he* thinks.'

'I may ask him in my own time, but not now.' Judith's voice began to rise. 'Who has engineered this confrontation? Do you realize that it is Christmas Eve and we have sixty guests upstairs waiting for their dinner? This is absolutely preposterous. What brought it about?'

Rosalind and Marcel simultaneously pointed across the room at each other.

'Doug, I *implore* you . . .' Judith turned in desperation to her brother.

'There is a conflict, Judith, between Marcel and Rosalind. She is, you know, a trained cordon bleu chef . . .'

'No I didn't know.'

'Well she is.'

'I thought she studied history at Cambridge?'

'She did but after that she did a course.'

'A *course*,' Marcel sighed dramatically, 'lasting a few weeks. While I have spent my entire life in the kitchen.'

'But I didn't know Rosalind had any *authority* in the kitchen,' Judith continued speaking to her brother. 'As far as I know she has no authority at *all* in this hotel.'

'May I remind you it is owned by *my* father,' Rosalind said.

'Part owned,' Judith corrected her. 'But he certainly didn't give you authority over the *maître-chef*.'

'Doug asked me to keep an eye on the kitchens.'

'Did you, Doug? Without consulting me?' Judith looked at him with concern.

'May I remind you, Judith, I am the manager.'

'And I . . .' Judith paused. 'Well I may not have an exact title, but I understood I was clearly involved in running this hotel as well.'

'You're the housekeeper,' Rosalind said coolly. 'Or you will be soon.'

'Indeed? We'll see about that!'

'My father intends to make a lot of changes after Christmas.' Rosalind, pregnant and by now breathing heavily, leaned against the table. 'This hotel is ludicrously overstaffed. No one in charge has had enough experience. We can't attract people without more appeal. British people like British food. Father thinks the menu is too fiddly.'

'What's wrong with roast turkey?' Judith pointed to the table. 'It's terribly British.'

'But *quenelles*! Whoever knows what they are or how to eat them?'

'Well no one seemed to have any difficulty that I saw. And they're extremely difficult to make. They were beautiful, incidentally, Marcel.'

Marcel, whose face was the colour of his white coat, scarcely acknowledged her. Suddenly seeing the look in his eyes, the despair on his face, Judith felt desperate.

'Look, please let's call a truce, just for Christmas. I don't think even your father wants to disappoint our guests, Rosalind. Later we can deal with the whole thing.'

'I am still going,' Marcel said, re-crossing his arms.

'Please, Marcel,' Judith put a hand on his arm, 'for me.'

'I am not taking orders from *her*.'

'Just for me, for tonight. For Christmas.'

Marcel hung his head for a moment as if deep in contemplation, then he uncrossed his arms and reached for his apron. With a swift gesture he beckoned to Raoul and gave him rapid instructions in French.

'Just for tonight,' Marcel said, turning his back rudely on Rosalind, his eyes on Judith. 'Just for Christmas, and you.'

Despite everything the dinner was a success, though the sorbet course seemed to take rather a long time, and then the waiters hurried in with the magnificent turkeys paraded on their silver dishes before the assembled guests.

Judith slid into her seat beside Richard, her face hot, little tendrils of her hair clamped to her brow.

'Something wrong?' Richard murmured.

'You can say that again.' Judith looked at him, gave a lopsided smile and shakily brought her glass to her lips.

George Drake prided himself on keeping fit. He did not smoke, drank very little and ate sparingly. Consequently he was one of the few people able to rise early the following morning and take out a horse to exercise it in the fields.

He was an expert horseman and bred horses at Newmarket. But that morning he was deeply engaged in thought and took little notice of his surroundings.

After his ride he returned the horse to the stable, where it was rubbed down by the groom. Then he walked up to the hotel and was about to go up to his room when a figure dressed in a red dressing gown wandered through the hall and looked at him with the trusting eyes of a child.

'Mr Drake?'

'Yes, Lady Prynne?'

'Have you seen the Admiral?'

'No, I'm afraid I have not.'

'Oh, but I'm sure he said . . .' Gran, her face puckered with bewilderment, slowly looked round.

'May I escort you back to your room, Lady Prynne?'

'That is very kind of you, Mr Drake, but the Admiral will be here soon. We are to take breakfast together.'

'Lady Prynne.' Drake seized her hand and tucked it through his arm. 'Please come with me.' Then he led her out of the hall, in case early guests should be about, and ushered her into a small writing room next to the drawing room. There he let go of her arm and bade her sit down. Gran looked confused, almost tearful, a little frightened.

'The Admiral won't know where I am,' she said fretfully, wringing her hands. Drake sat opposite her and leaned forward, hands folded in front of him. He sighed deeply.

'Lady Prynne. Your husband, the Admiral, is dead. He is not here and he is not likely to be. He is dead. He died, I believe, shortly before the war. Now, Lady Prynne, you must get that into your head, if you are to continue to stay here. Admiral Prynne is dead. He is no more; no longer with us. It is no use going round asking for him, and it will be very bad for the reputation of this hotel if our guests should be sent on a wild-goose chase looking for someone who is no longer alive. I'm afraid that if you cannot believe that your husband is dead, Lady Prynne, I shall have to ask you to leave and live elsewhere. I am having enough difficulties getting this hotel going without having our guests frightened away by non-existent ghosts.' Breathing heavily, Drake stood up and offered his hand. 'Now, Lady Prynne, may I take you to your room and restore you to your family?'

Politely he bent towards her but was greeted by the sightless, bewildered stare of a frightened child.

Chapter 6

By lunchtime on the day following Boxing Day most of the guests had departed except for a few who were staying on for New Year. They included an American investment banker and his wife, Mr and Mrs Dwight C. Smallbone, and a prominent English golfer who wanted to practise on the excellent Aylestone course.

From her office window Judith could see the drive and, during the morning, as the cars left, she watched them one by one until, at the gates, they turned into the road and set off in the direction of London. Then she would wander back to her desk and stare almost sightlessly at the papers in front of her. None of them seemed to make any sense and, restlessly, she arranged and rearranged them. Lists, lists and more lists . . .

But it was over. It had been successful, at least for the guests; and disaster, in the kitchens or anywhere else, had been avoided.

But an atmosphere of uneasy calm hung over the house because this afternoon there would be confrontation. A meeting had been called in her parents' sitting room in the wing, out of earshot of the guests. It was difficult to be calm in the circumstances and, just then, she longed for the comforting help of a friend; someone who could understand, who would be objective. Fleetingly she thought of Matthew Jenner; but he had been one of the first to leave in the morning after complimenting her and her staff at the success of the occasion. He had pressed her hand and asked her to call him if she ever needed anything.

She had promised she would, warmly shook his hand and kissed his wife on the cheek.

Then there was Richard; she found him sympathetic. He had warmth, empathy; but he was not yet family. Besides, why draw him into family affairs? As it was, he and Moira had gone up to London to see a show and dine with friends.

Judith had a sandwich and coffee in her room. The time seemed to drag. Reluctantly, at last, she got up and slowly made her way to the west wing of the house where the family lived.

As she opened the door into the family sitting room a cameo picture presented itself that she knew would linger in her mind for ever. Her father stood by the mantelpiece filling his pipe, his stick, as usual, hooked over one arm. At his feet was one of their dogs, obedient as always. Greville wore his customary tweeds, a check shirt with a knotted woollen tie. He was what he had always been: the English gentleman, perfect in deportment and manners. At home by his fireside surrounded by his family. And if it was no longer his home or his fireside, he gave no impression of being anything but at ease and, as Judith came in, he smiled at her.

Next to him, also looking utterly relaxed, was her mother. She wore a woollen suit over a plain Pringle jersey, a row of pearls round her neck. One beautifully manicured hand rested elegantly on her knee, and the scarlet-tipped nails of the other played with the coat of the second dog sitting at her feet. On her father's left was Doug, smoking a cigarette. He wore cords and a polo-necked jersey, but he looked ill at ease and kept on flicking the ash from his cigarette into the fire behind him. Alongside him on the sofa sat Rosalind, her black hair bound by a red band which perfectly matched the cherry-red dress with a high neck and buttons down to the waist. The belt was black and her high-heeled patent leather shoes were also black. She looked pale and, though also perfectly composed, had shadows under her eyes as though from lack of sleep. She kept on looking at her father, who was standing by the window, his hands behind his back, gazing out towards the river flowing below. He too wore tweeds, plus fours with yellow socks and well-polished shoes. His iron grey hair was brushed straight back from his forehead and his rather puffy red face and freshly shaved cheeks had a bluish tinge.

Gran was absent, either because she had not been invited or had preferred for obvious reasons to stay in her room.

As Judith softly closed the door behind her, Angela smiled at her elder daughter and, patting the dog, said, 'I think we can begin.' Greville loudly cleared his throat and, after a lot of play with his pipe, which appeared to have gone cold, took it out of his mouth and left it in his hand and addressed his wife.

'I think you've got something to say, Angela. Maybe you should begin.'

'Very well.' Angela stopped patting the dog and, joining her hands on her lap, looked straight at George Drake, who had turned towards her.

'I think I might as well be frank and come out with what is the matter, George. We asked to see you because of an incident that happened two days ago concerning Greville's mother.'

'A lady of some eighty-two years,' Greville said, pointing the stem of his pipe at Drake.

'I am quite well aware of how old your mother is.' George's brows knotted together in the middle of his forehead.

'My mother is not an *old* woman, that is the point.' Greville glared at George as though he were addressing some recalcitrant subaltern on the parade ground. 'Eighty-two is not, as far as my mother is concerned, *old* and she is not senile. Yet you seem to think she is.'

'She . . .' Drake tried to interrupt but Angela swiftly interrupted him.

'My husband and I strongly object to the way you spoke to his mother when you met her in the hall on Chrismas morning. As far as we can ascertain she was offending no one; she was simply wandering round in her own house, as she sometimes does, in search of her husband. She is doing no harm to anyone.'

'None at all,' Greville said. 'Perfectly natural thing to do.'

'But her husband is *dead*,' George said.

'Yes, logically, she knows that perfectly well. There is no need to spell it out.'

'None at all,' Angela affirmed indignantly. 'She is quite aware of what she is doing. At times, however, occasionally she wanders off, in her mind you know, and then she wanders back again. Lots of people do it.'

'*Not* in a first-class hotel,' Drake said, with an edge to his voice. 'I cannot have old ladies off their rockers wandering about in any hotel of mine asking guests if they have seen someone who has been dead for donkey's years.'

'But *they* don't know that.' Greville tried to look reasonable. 'Mother just says: "Have you seen the Admiral?" and they say "no". *They* don't know he's dead.'

'But what if they find out?'

'Why should they, and what harm would it do? My mother is merely a little eccentric. She is forgetful; she is not mad and she is not dangerous.'

'She was terribly hurt by what you said,' Angela added reproachfully. 'She has not come out of her room since.'

'Thank goodness for that.' Drake got his handkerchief out of his pocket and carefully mopped his brow.

'Mother said that *you* said that if she did come out again you'd have her put away. She said you were quite brutal.' Greville jabbed his pipe at Drake again.

'Brutal,' Angela echoed in ringing tones. 'She assured us that *you* were no gentleman.'

'I was not brutal.' Drake stamped his foot on the

threadbare carpet that had not undergone restoration and refurbishment with the rest of the hotel. It had been taken out of the old drawing room and cut down to size for the family's use. 'I was merely telling your mother that her husband is *dead* and she shouldn't behave as though he were alive. She mustn't wander about asking for him. She was in her dressing gown in the front hall! *Anyone* could have seen her.'

'Mother knew that no one would be up at that time on Christmas morning.'

'Why was she doing it then?'

'She was looking for her husband,' Angela said, as if making an obvious point to a child of doubtful intelligence. 'Can't you see that?'

'But her husband . . . Oh, I give up!' Drake threw his hands in the air and completed a circular motion as if, metaphorically, he were clutching at straws. 'I give up. This whole place is beyond me. It has got to stop.'

'What exactly has got to stop?' Greville enquired sternly.

'Everything. For a start, the family treating it as though it were merely a comfortable country home.'

'But it *is* a comfortable country home,' Angela said in some surprise. 'Very comfortable.'

'But it is *not* a country home.' Drake shook his head vigorously. 'It is a hotel. That is what you don't seem to realize. It is being run *not* for the well-being of the Prynne family, who have made themselves very comfortable indeed, but to make a profit. It is not for you, it is for your guests, and there are not enough of them. Do you realize that? Do you realize that every day we remain open is costing me thousands of pounds?' Frantically he began to stab the air again in front of him with a stretched finger. 'And I can't see it getting any better while a mad old woman is allowed to wander around the place in her red flannel dressing gown and you, Mrs Prynne, spend your time propping up the bar and entertaining male customers.

Meanwhile your husband spends all *his* day walking round the golf course. It is hopeless, out of the question, it must stop. Look, I feel I must tell you . . .' but suddenly he seemed to change his mind and his voice faltered.

There was silence, a pregnant pause. Angela's air of haughtiness vanished and her crumpled face looked as though it were about to collapse in tears. The colour mounted on Greville's cheeks while he furiously plucked at the bowl of his cold pipe.

'There's a lot more we have to discuss.' Judith waited for a moment as if inviting George to continue, but he remained silent. 'That was not the only incident this Christmas, as you know full well, George.' She went on, 'It was trivial compared to the fact that our chef has threatened to leave.'

'Leave? Marcel?' Drake's expression was thunderstruck. 'Why has he threatened to leave?'

'Because your daughter has made it her business to interfere in the kitchen. Did you authorize her?'

'Well I . . .'

'Did you?' Judith continued to gaze at him.

'She *is* a cordon bleu cook.'

'She only has a certificate.'

'She wanted something to do.'

'Then you should have asked us, or did Doug know?' Judith transferred her gaze to her brother who had risen and now had one arm on the mantelpiece, his eyes studying the floor; but he said nothing.

'As far as I know, Doug has no objection. Rosalind thinks the food is too fancy. I think she is right. I suggested . . .'

'But you had no right to suggest.'

'You don't run the hotel, Judith.'

'Neither do you.'

'Yes, who does run it?' Angela looked about her with interest. 'It's never really been made clear.'

'Theoretically you and Greville are supposed to run it. In practice Doug is the manager.'

'And Judith? What does Judith do?' Rosalind looked at her sister-in-law with ill-concealed dislike.

'Well Judith is trained . . . she spent three years. . .'

'But she has no actual *position*, has she?' Rosalind insisted.

'Well it was understood that she would help Doug.' Greville looked vague. 'She was never given an official position as such. We would all muck in.'

'But Judith mucks in *everywhere*. She makes it her business to be here, there and everywhere, just as though she were the boss. You'd think *she* ran it. Does she ever ask Doug? She appointed the chef, the *sommelier*, the *maître d'hôtel*, all from France or Switzerland.'

'Doug agreed,' Judith said quickly. 'I never did anything without consulting him.'

'It's true,' Doug intervened at last. 'I was very busy. At the time we never thought of defining Judith's role. We were all family.'

'Exactly.' Rosalind gave him a sweet smile. 'I have as much right to interfere as she has. After all, I am the manager's wife. I am family, too.'

'She is his sister. Oh dear, oh dear,' Angela said with a worried look. 'It's all a mess, isn't it?'

'It is all a mess,' Judith agreed. 'It *is* a mess and it's no wonder. We were really amateur beginners. We thought we knew everything and we didn't because none of us had had practical experience. Well, now we know better. We can all learn from our mistakes. I propose that, with the New Year, we should forget the past and begin again. I will talk to Marcel and . . .'

'In that case I think you will all be relieved to hear that I have an important contribution to make,' Drake said firmly. 'I was going to save it to tell you later, but it had better come out now. I have decided to appoint a general manager over you all. He will assume absolute control of the hotel, reporting directly to me, from 1 February. His name is John Redmain. I like him and I'm sure you'll like him too, and he'll soon lick this place into shape.'

It was hard for the Prynnes to admit it, but there was a good deal of wisdom behind George Drake's decision to appoint an independent manager. For the weeks following the announcement they did all in their power to resist it, and discord at Aylestone continued. Several members of staff left, including Marcel's nephew from France, who said he was on the verge of a nervous breakdown.

The housekeeper left and was not reappointed, and this very onerous task was given to Judith, who felt she had been downgraded already and was now reduced to the drudgery of domestic service. It was her job to count the sheets and the towels for the maids in the morning, the new bars of soap and bathroom accessories, as well as detergents, washing powders and lavatory paper.

On the other hand there was seldom the need to change even half the beds every day. Despite the success of the Christmas party, the number of clients who visited the hotel in January remained few. But then, it was pointed out, January was a poor month for the trade. Some hotels closed down altogether in January, some for the rest of winter.

It was too late now, but maybe the grand opening should have been in the spring.

Although his arrival was deeply resented, and little was done to make him welcome, John Redmain was an admirable choice. He was about forty-five and had been in the hotel business all his adult life. He had a wife and two school-aged children and had bought a house five miles away from the hotel. He made it quite plain he wanted to keep his private and business life completely separate. He arrived at the hotel at eight-thirty each morning and left at about six when Doug and Judith took it in turns to assume responsibility until John Redmain came on duty again.

The new manager was a large, genial man who wore thick-lensed spectacles and his life seemed to have been governed by the exercise of tact. He soon defined the position, the very complex and unsatisfactory position, at Aylestone. He could see that the presence of the Prynnes on the premises, plus their lack of experience and their failure to communicate either with one another or, particularly, George Drake, was the main cause of the problem.

He agreed that Marcel Laborde was an accomplished chef, who in no circumstances should be allowed to leave; but the kitchen needed rationalizing and everywhere there were too many staff.

The hotel trade was seasonal and to expect to be full all year round was ridiculous. He sacked at least half of the full-time personnel and began to engage staff from the locality on an occasional basis, who could be easily laid off.

Judith didn't like this. The service at Aylestone had been superb, the waiters well trained and experienced. Unemployed men from the district could not begin to match up to them and there were few to be had. They were thus forced to hire women and Judith had a prejudice against women serving in first-class restaurants. She thought it immediately gave the place a 'homely' feel as they went about calling everyone 'dearie', and pausing too long to chat. This was nice in itself but undesirable in a place with the pretensions of Aylestone.

Judith knew that the tone of the place would go down and it would become an ordinary country house hotel like any other. Not enough time had been given to maintain, let alone build up, its ambition to achieve unrivalled excellence.

John Redmain got on least well with Judith, but with the other members of the family he was more fortunate.

He played golf with Greville, whose approval he immediately won not only on account of his handicap but because he had been awarded the MC in the war. He enjoyed a drink at the bar with Angela, and was kindness itself to Gran, with whom he spent a lot of time helping her look for the Admiral. As a family man with ageing parents himself, he quite understood the problem. He won round Doug by his tact and professionalism, his lack of side. Doug knew that a couple of years spent travelling and staying as a guest in the best hotels was no substitute for working experience, years and years of grind in the sculleries, the kitchens, as hall porter, in the reception, behind the bar and doing the accounts. Judith had this sort of experience, but she was too impatient to put it into practice. She had wanted to begin right at the top and stay there.

By the spring Aylestone had been reorganized, and its fortunes revived. A PR firm had been hired and the brochure revamped. Marcel had as his deputy chef a good plain English cook, and roast beef and roast lamb became *de rigueur* rather than dishes which originated in France: curious cuts that the English were unused to and exotic sauces which were too rich for their simple palates.

Families began to arrive and special terms were introduced for children. A playground for them was added to the park and a nanny engaged. The elegant Rolls and Bentleys were replaced by family cars, station wagons full of dogs and small children. Local businessmen or commercial travellers took to popping in for a drink and the Rotary Club asked to have a weekly meeting in the billiard-room.

It was all very different from the original concept of a stately house hotel of international renown.

One day that summer Judith was in the linen room when the door opened and Marcel came in.

'Do I disturb you?' he asked, closing the door gently behind him.

111

'Not at all.' Judith looked up and smiled. 'I've just finished counting the sheets.' She ran a hand through her hair. 'It is really getting hard work. I shall have to engage a new housekeeper.'

'Do you like it?' Marcel sat down on one of the laundry baskets and crossed his arms. Judith thought he looked tired. But then she had had really very little time to observe him. They were both too busy.

'Like what?'

'Like this?'

'My duties you mean?' Judith looked at him in surprise. 'Not much.'

'It's not what we wanted, is it, Judith? Not what you or your family intended?'

'No.' Judith slumped beside him on the wicker basket. 'It's not at all what we intended.' Her voice had a note of defeat.

'Not the grand hotel we had in mind,' Marcel went on. '*You* had in mind. The standards are falling all the time. No one now ever orders my beautifully prepared dishes, my new inventions, my culinary masterpieces. I waste my time going to Covent Garden. It has become a very ordinary hotel; a run-of-the-mill family hotel, and that is not what we wanted when we planned in Switzerland.'

'Not at all.'

'So I have made up my mind to leave, Judith. I wanted you to know first. My contract was for a year and it expires next month. I am going to tell Mr Redmain today that I shall not be renewing it.'

'Oh, Marcel.' Judith grasped his arm. 'Oh *please* don't go. Why you . . . the whole thing was based round *you*.'

'It was a dream, Judith,' Marcel said sadly. 'It lasted a very short time. We got the wrong kind of backer. We should have had someone with a *lot* of money and a *lot* of patience. But I believe Mr Drake isn't very satisfied, either. He is a very hard man to please.'

'For what he spent on it he is not getting enough back. We have had to lower the prices to get the people in. He didn't expect that. Like us he wanted a grand hotel. But twenty-four bedrooms with private bathrooms are not enough. I believe that some of the bathrooms are going to be converted into bedrooms and there will be a bathroom at the end of the corridor.'

Marcel shuddered.

'At the Hotel Daniel we certainly didn't have *that*.'

'Somehow the English can't manage it – I mean to have a really grand hotel, and attract a crowd as well.'

'The Daniel only attracted the best.' Marcel had a note of reproof in his voice. 'It never attempted to attract *tout le monde*.'

'But it attracted a lot of wealthy people who wanted to ski. In England we don't have that kind of facility. What can people do here except play tennis or golf, or ride?'

'It's quite different.' Marcel nodded. 'I see that now. But still it is not for me.'

'What will you do?' Judith asked gently. 'Go home?'

'I'm reluctant to go home. I thought I might maybe try and start a restaurant of my own. In London perhaps . . . do you like that idea, Judith?'

'It's a *marvellous* idea,' Judith said enthusiastically, clasping her hands together. 'I can just see you being a great success. I shall miss you, though. I shall miss you very much.'

'Then why don't you come with me and help me?' His voice was so very low that she had to lean towards him to catch what he said.

'Are you serious?'

'I know you're not happy here.'

'But it is my home.'

'It's no longer your home. You are like a fish out of water.'

'I respect John Redmain.'

113

'I respect John Redmain and I like him; but he is not the kind of man I really want to work for. His standards are not those of excellence. He is a good manager for an average family hotel.'

'My parents . . . I don't know what they'll say.'

'They won't be surprised. Anyone can see you aren't happy.'

'Does it show so much?' Judith put a hand to her face.

'Very much. You have lost your bloom; you have lost a lot of weight too. I am concerned about you, Judith, because,' Marcel leaned over to her, 'I suppose you know that I feel for you more than a . . . mere friend?'

Judith felt the blood rush to her face as his hand, beside hers on the basket, closed over hers.

'Marcel, I had no idea . . .'

'That's because I don't wear my heart on my sleeve; also we do not have a lot of time to spend together. But a day I do not see you is like a day without sunshine. I know how you feel, I know what you think. It is a sudden declaration, but you have become someone very important in my life . . . and I wonder, Judith, if I am in yours?'

'Yes you are, of course. Only . . . I never thought seriously about it. I never thought about it at all.'

'Then you don't love me, Judith?'

Marcel, who had the mobile features of a mime artist, looked immeasurably sad.

'Of *course* I love you,' Judith burst out. 'But not. . . not . . .'

'Not . . . sexually?'

'I don't know, to be honest.' She put her hands once again to her face in an attempt to hide her feelings, which were totally confused. When she did look at him she saw that his eyes were concentrated on her, and she was aware of a beauty, a yearning in them that she had never seen before. She realized that, although she had always liked Marcel, it was the first time that she was aware of any

114

feeling other than friendship, companionship. In him she was now beginning to see things she had not seen before. Was it, therefore, the beginning of love?

'You'll have to give me time,' she said, at last.

'You can have all the time you want; but I really need someone to help me. I have no idea where to start or how, how to organize myself. All I can do is cook. The rest you will have to do.'

'And the money,' Judith said slowly. 'Have you thought of the money?'

Marcel threw his expressive hands in the air.

'You will have to arrange that too. I have a little money, but not wealth of that kind. You know London; you will know the best place to look for premises. You will know where to get finance. You see how I need you, Judith.'

'I'm beginning to,' Judith said with a shy smile.

But was it love; or did she only think it was?

Chapter 7

Greville Prynne was practising his swing on the carpet when Judith came up to talk to them the following afternoon. Angela was having a cup of tea after her afternoon rest, and Gran was sitting in the sunshine by the window reading a book, or pretending to read. Maybe she was dozing too.

Angela noticed something about Judith's step as soon as she came into the room and she looked up, her hand on the handle of the teapot. Her fluffy blonde hair, caught by the sunlight, seemed to shimmer like a halo around her head, but her face looked careworn despite the sparkle of her bright blue eyes. Angela Prynne was one of those women whose youth had been transformed by their appearance and, as they grew old, they found it hard to accept that those years had gone. They wanted, and tried, to be perpetually young.

'What a lovely surprise, darling,' Angela said. 'You hardly ever pay us a social call these days. Tea?'

'Yes please, Mummy.'

Greville swung the golf club right over his shoulder, just missing the shade of one of the lamps, and Angela frowned.

'Greville, if you break the screen of the television set we shall never get another.'

'They're going to have colour anyway,' Greville said, putting his club in the corner. 'So they say. This one will soon be obsolete. What brings you here, Judith? Not enough to do?' Her father laughed heartily, a little cruelly, at the thought.

'I've come to tell you that I'm leaving,' Judith said, having decided in advance to dispense with preliminaries.

116

There was a noise from the window seat as Gran started and her book fell off her lap.

'Leaving?' Angela said in such a loud voice that Judith put a finger to her lips.

'I wanted to tell you first. John doesn't know.'

'But you can't *leave*,' Gran wailed. 'What on earth will we do without you?'

'You'll survive, Gran. I think you're all right here, at least for a while.'

'Why do you say something like that?' Greville looked sharply at her.

'Well nothing's ever permanent, is it? Or it doesn't seem to be. A year ago we thought we had an extremely smart hotel and . . . well.'

'It *has* gone down,' Angela said with a grimace of distaste. 'I never thought to see *quite* such common people. One wonders where on earth they get the money from. People like that never used to be able to afford to stay in hotels before the war.'

'Darling, you can't just *leave* us,' Greville addressed his daughter, gulping his scalding tea and wincing. 'We could never survive here without you. They don't need us but they need *you*. Without you we'll be kicked out.'

'I don't think so, Dad. John likes playing golf with you, that's a plus in your favour. He also seems awfully fond of Gran.'

'But it's not a question of *liking* or being *fond*,' Angela said severely. 'You know as well as we do that George Drake would love to see the back of us. If you go he'll find some excuse to kick us out.'

'He can't. It's written in the agreement that you will continue to inhabit the wing.'

'I know he wants to develop it,' Greville said solemnly. 'He still isn't making enough money on this place in proportion to what he paid for it. He wants to make it even bigger.'

'Well he can't. The lawyers will see to that.'

'He'll find a way round it. There's sure to be an "out" if he looks hard enough.'

'Daddy, I can't just stay here because of that,' Judith said. 'You know that our dream of what Aylestone ought to be has gone sour. We're now short of staff. Frankly it's not what I wanted and I'm unhappy. Also I do have my own life, and I'm leaving for another purpose.' She paused and gave a little gulp. 'I'm to be married.'

'Married?' Greville growled. 'Who to?'

'Marcel. He asked me to marry him yesterday. I hadn't thought about it before but I did overnight, and now I think it's a good idea.'

'Good idea!' Angela said with a brittle laugh. 'There's more to marriage than that, dear. Anyway I always thought he was . . .' she raised her eyebrows, leaving the word unsaid.

'Well he isn't.'

'They usually are.'

'Well if you mean what I think you mean, he's not. He wouldn't want to marry me if he were.'

'Oh, you don't *know*, then.'

'Please, Mother,' Judith said, raising her voice. 'I find this conversation distasteful. Surely I can marry who I like?'

'Of course you can, darling, only usually one has a hint that one's offspring is interested in a person, like Moira and Richard. But you and Marcel. . . the idea simply never crossed our minds.'

'It didn't cross my mind, either,' Judith said slowly, 'to be quite honest. I think the two things came together. When Marcel told me he was leaving and asked me to go with him, it seemed right. I felt that I couldn't do without him. That's the test, isn't it? Then you know how involved you really are.'

* * *

George Drake was not sorry to see the back of Judith Prynne as well as his temperamental chef. It was true that he would dearly have liked to break his connection with the rest of the family; but it wasn't easy. He might own fifty-five per cent of the business, but their forty-five per cent was useful and powerful. If his fifty-five per cent was ever split, or the subject of a takeover, the Prynnes would be in a very strong position.

It was also the Prynne family home and they enjoyed both it and their new lifestyle. It reminded them of the grand days of the Raj; of servants and sundowners on the slopes of the Khasi hills and all the aspects of colonial life they had particularly enjoyed, and grown used to.

Angela lazed away the day to her total satisfaction. She rose late, bathed and dressed leisurely, and sometimes played bridge in the afternoon before changing for dinner.

Greville rode, played golf and did very little until it was time to don his dinner-jacket and pretend to be in charge after John Redmain had gone home.

As for Gran, these days she seldom emerged from the family quarters for fear of bumping into George Drake, for whom she had conceived, not unreasonably, a dislike. He threatened to shatter her illusions, disturb her secrets, break into her dreams that the Admiral had just popped out for something and that that dear, old-fashioned way of life still existed.

But for Douglas Prynne the situation was less satisfactory; it was anomalous, humiliating, and the result was a deteriorating situation between himself and his father-in-law, and mutual rancour between himself and his wife.

It is quite easy to fall out of love if the emotion was never particularly strong in the first place, and after three years of marriage Rosalind Prynne's feelings about her husband were equivocal. It was difficult to shake off that heady feeling of first love, of being sexually attracted to an attractive man. But the reality was less perfect, less reassuring. Now, in the critical light of a stale marriage, she saw Doug as a man with no particular talents, one who was easily swayed. In her father's hands he was putty; and in comparison with Judith he was weak. Now that Judith had walked out on Aylestone, Doug had realized his dependence on her, and he didn't know which way to turn.

John Redmain was not a strong manager but he knew the trade; he knew what he was doing and how to run a hotel. He knew all the logistics of staffing and ordering and managing, and the much-travelled Doug only found out too late how little he knew.

He was made under-manager, directly subject to the orders of John Redmain, and his position was inferior, a sharp reduction in status, much as he tried to make the best of it.

Doug and Ros, as the family called her, lived in a detached house on the other side of Little Hatchem, a village about five miles from Aylestone. It was a modern, stone-built house; an elegant residence by most standards, but Ros was used to better and she had quickly become discontented. They had a son, Philip, born the year after their marriage, and another baby was now on the way.

Ros felt her role was not simply to be wife and mother, a support to a man she had begun to despise. At Cambridge she had been ambitious for a career, a life of her own. Now, by her thoughtless marriage undertaken too young, she felt she had thrown her chances away.

She had tried to interest herself in the affairs of the hotel, but had been told not to interfere. However capable she was, however willing, she was seen in a purely domestic role which she resented. The changes at Aylestone had embittered her even more because of the diminishing status of Doug, whom she felt too subservient to her father.

One morning a few months after Judith and Marcel had left Aylestone, Ros was, as usual, sitting disconsolately across from Doug nibbling at her breakfast while he, as usual, was reading *The Times*. Occasionally a hand would appear round the paper and pick up the toast he was eating or the cup from which he was drinking. Between them was three-year-old Philip, who kept up a constant patter of chat that neither of his parents took the slightest notice of.

Every now and then Ros would reach out and tap him briskly on the wrist or snatch something away from his mouth but, on the whole, these routine breakfast mornings hardly ever varied in their unmitigated awfulness.

Ros objected to Doug reading the paper. He protested that he was not good in the mornings and that, anyway, this was the only time he had in the course of his busy day to read the news. She, on the other hand, had the whole day in front of her. Ros would sit and sigh, alternately reprimanding Philip or trying to provoke a response to her complaints or comments, largely rhetorical, from Doug.

Philip was a bright, alert little boy, sandy-haired like the Prynnes. He had warm brown eyes and freckles and nothing seemed to diminish his high spirits, not even the friction in the house or the frequent rows between his parents. He was content to eat his breakfast, as messily as possible, and try to interpret the signs between his parents while maintaining a continual monologue, almost under his breath.

Suddenly a wrist shot out from the paper and Ros knew Doug was going to look at the time and say: 'Good God, I'm going to be late.'

'Good God! I'm going to be late,' Doug said on cue, and threw the unfinished paper on the floor beside him – another habit that irritated Rosalind – while gulping the last drops of coffee in his cup.

'Won't it be nice when you don't say *that*,' Rosalind said.

'Say what, dear?'

'What you just said.'

'What did I just say?'

'Oh heavens, Doug, you say it *every day*. "Good God! I'm going to be late."'

'Well if I say it every day,' Doug said, with an attempt at a smile, 'you should be used to it now.'

He finished his toast and, scraping his chair back, got up and planted a kiss on Philip's head, ruffling his hair as he did so, while Philip giggled and tried to catch his father's hand.

'Oh God,' Ros said pushing back her chair, 'if you only *knew* how I hate this routine.' She threw her napkin on the table to coincide with the word 'hate'. Doug, who was half-way out of the room, paused and looked at her.

'Could we talk about it tonight?'

'You're always too tired at night.'

'I haven't time now, darling, really.'

'You're going to go off to have an absolutely marvellous day, aren't you, Doug?'

'Hardly . . .'

'Full of things to do, interesting people to see; a few drinks at the bar, a good lunch . . .'

Doug marched with heavy steps back to his chair and sat down again, looking anxiously at Philip. Philip, however, was contentedly drooling his boiled egg down his chin and rubbing his hands in it.

'Ros, please. Tell me what it is you want.'

'I want to be part of the hotel, too,' Ros replied. 'I thought that was obvious. I've asked you and asked you ever since Judith left; but you always manage to deflect my question or ignore me.'

'Ros, it is *nothing* to do with me. I'm no longer in charge.'

'You're well in with Redmain. Besides, my father . . .'

'Your father has left John *completely* in charge. Besides, darling, you're having a baby in a few months.'

'But after that . . . You've no real idea how bored and fed up I am. You've never replaced Judith . . .'

'We've reorganized the whole structure. We have a new housekeeper, a very capable woman called Doris Malcolm. We have rationalized the staff. Honestly, Ros, I don't know what you could do.'

'*If* I'd realized my life was going to be like this . . .'

'Like what?' Doug looked at his watch again.

'Marriage to you . . . like this!'

Doug once more nervously glanced at Philip, but raised voices between his parents were everyday occurrences and Philip Prynne must have thought that this was the way everyone behaved, other families the world over. In a few minutes his daily nanny would arrive and take him out to the nearby park. He always looked forward to that.

'Do you think it's *really* good for Philip to hear this day after day?' Doug said.

'It isn't day after day. Do you realize I spend about twenty out of every twenty-four hours in this damned house doing nothing? I have a first-class brain, Doug, a Cambridge degree . . .'

'I *know* you have, Ros.' Doug leaned over and attempted to take her hand, but she abruptly drew it away from him.

'I'm sure my father never meant my life should be one of unrelieved domesticity and boredom.'

'Then talk to your father.'

'About what?'

'About a job. Maybe he can take you into his organization. After all he gave me a job before Aylestone. He could make one for you.'

'And I'd go up to town every day?' Rosalind's face expressed astonishment.

'Why not?'

'What about the new baby?'

Doug heaved his shoulders in an exaggerated sigh.

'Darling, you really *ought* to have thought that one out. You wanted a second child.'

'Aylestone is so *near*.'

'There simply isn't a place, Ros.'

'I'll ask my father to make a place.'

Doug was beginning to perspire with frustration. He was already late for the morning meeting of senior hotel personnel presided over by John Redmain in the general manager's office.

'Right then, ask him. See if he'll go over John's head. I doubt it. Redmain is a man of very set views. He is quite capable of standing up to your father's bullying tactics in a way, I must say, I never learned.'

'Bullying tactics . . . I like that.'

'Yes, bullying. Your father is a tyrant, Ros, who gets everything he wants by his barnstorming manner. He promised me the job of running the hotel, *my* family home and a business in which *my* family continued to have a prominent share. What has he done? Demoted me! He completely reneged on his promises.'

'You were incapable of standing up to him. That's your fault.'

'What could I do? He was my father-in-law. He might have sacked me.'

'I'd have thought better of you if you had.'

'Oh really?'

'Yes, really.'

'You would really have liked me to go round looking for a job?'

'I think I'd have respected you more if you had, Doug. It was very humiliating, the way Father treated you.'

'*Now* you tell me!'

'What kind of man would let himself be demoted? Only someone with no sense of self-respect.'

Doug's face began slowly to turn puce and even Philip

seemed mesmerized by it, and leaned forward keenly to inspect it.

'Daddy very red,' he said pointing it out to his mother.

'Daddy very cross,' Doug said, clutching his son's hand. 'What kind of man, you ask, Rosalind? I'll tell you what kind of man: a very unhappy and frustrated man. One who has seen his family divided, his ambitions thwarted, his hopes blighted. And a man who is now very sorry indeed that he ever became involved with someone as ruthless, selfish and unprincipled as your father.'

Doug got up again, quickly kissed Philip and hurried to the door while – her own face, by contrast, very pale – Ros sat back in her chair and slowly began to massage her stomach.

After a few moments of looking at her anxiously, Philip, who was an affectionate, loving little boy, even a perceptive one for his age, got down from his seat and clambered up on her knee. Rosalind put her arms round him and hugged him, burying her face in his hair.

Despite its proximity to the Mother of Parliaments and the home of the Monarch, Victoria Station had emerged relatively unscathed from the war. The great tower of the Roman Catholic Cathedral of Westminster had survived undamaged, although the inside of the cathedral itself, begun at the turn of the century, was far from completed.

From the station streets radiated out on all sides to the centre of the metropolis; north towards Hyde Park Corner, south towards the river. It was in one of these smaller streets, a mews behind Victoria Street, that Judith discovered just the kind of building she and Marcel were looking for. It had once been a grocery shop with residential premises overhead.

The shop was in an area which had survived a stick of German incendiary bombs, and many of the houses, once smart private residences before the war, were run down and boarded up. In time the bright post-war entrepreneurial builders would start to restore them or, in some cases, raze them to the ground, blocks at a time, and build tall, ephemeral office buildings or blocks of flats, Atomic Age architecture, in their place.

The street which Judith alighted on was in a maze of streets criss-crossing Victoria Street and Horseferry Road, which led past Westminster Hospital to the river. It was not far from the Army and Navy Stores, that grand emporium of better days in the twenties and thirties, and due for redevelopment itself.

The premises were ideal because planning permission already existed for commercial use and there was a flat where they, as busy people – Marcel doing the cooking and Judith the running and managing – could live over the shop.

The site was ideal, the situation was ideal; but Marcel and Judith lacked a very important commodity. Neither of them had access to the substantial amount of money that would be necessary to buy the lease of the premises and do them up in the style they had in mind for the sort of restaurant they wished to run.

Judith had found a room near Victoria, just behind the station, and Marcel had rented a small flat in Kensington. He then went back to Switzerland to dispose of his flat in Fregères and try to raise some capital.

But it was not enough, and it all took time, much too much time, during which Judith did temporary work as a waitress at Lyons Corner House on the corner of Oxford Street and Tottenham Court Road. It was not quite the sort of life she had intended and she often wondered whether they had made a mistake. It was a strange time: a strange part of their lives and, above all, a very strange romance.

They had decided to postpone their marriage until the

formalities of the purchase were complete. Their honey-moon would be a holiday before the formal opening of the restaurant.

From time to time Angela came up and circumstances now forced her to stay with Judith. She had the bed while Judith put up a camp bed for herself. Angela moaned about Aylestone and how the place was, in her eyes, going even further downhill; but Judith now never went there and she no longer thought of it in any sense as 'home'.

In effect Judith felt rather homeless, stateless, a drifter. It was a very difficult time of her life, and one on which she was to look back with a considerable amount of pain in later years.

One night when Angela had returned from the theatre after a day spent at the beauty parlour, her hairdresser's and several establishments selling clothes and furs in Bond Street, she said:

'Matthew Jenner was asking after you.' She was taking off her make-up, carefully spreading the cream over her face, as if some magic could expunge, once and for all, those dreadful, ageing wrinkles. She turned to look at her daughter who had already bedded down after a tiring, fruitless day and was trying to sleep. 'Judith! Did you hear what I said?'

'Yes, Mother.' Judith raised her head from the pillow and squinted into the light.

'I always think he rather fancies you, you know.'

'What do you mean, *fancies* me?'

'Likes you, *you* know what I mean. He always asks after you and was dreadfully upset when he found you had left.'

'I can't think why.'

'Well he's an attractive man and you're an attractive woman, well, *quite* attractive. I always think you could make more of yourself.'

'Thank you, Mother,' Judith said, with an ironic smile.

'While we're on the subject of men,' Angela continued thoughtfully, 'why don't you and Marcel live together?'

'Why should we?'

'I think it's very strange. But then I always did think it an odd relationship.'

'Thank you again, Mother. *May* I now go to sleep?'

Her mother, clad in her dressing gown, got up and, swiftly crossing the room, perched on Judith's bed.

'Seriously, darling, I think you could get quite a lot out of Matthew if you played your cards right. He as much as said so.'

'What *do* you mean?' Judith sat upright on her bed and wrapped her arms round her knees.

'You know . . . it's obvious he's not in love with his wife. They have no children. He is a *most* attractive man, I always think. If I were younger . . .'

'I'm surprised at you, Mother,' Judith said. 'What are you getting at?'

'Matt could help you an awful lot. He is a millionaire several times over. He's a very old friend of the family. He told me that if you needed help you had only to ask . . .'

'What do you mean if *I* needed help?'

'I told him about the difficulty you were having getting things off the ground, working at Lyons and all that. I said Marcel is away most of the time trying to find cash. He said you should give him a ring . . .'

'I wouldn't dream of such a thing. He's a bit too old for me.' Judith angrily fluffed up her pillows and, laying her head on the pillow, tried to get to sleep again.

'It's just a thought . . . no strings attached, of course.'

From the window of Jenner Securities in one of the new towers that were being constructed in the bombed-out City of London, it was possible to see as far as Hampstead Heath on one side and Crystal Palace on the other side of the river. Below them lay the dome of St Paul's, once the tallest building in the City. Many things were being done now that would ruin the London of Christopher Wren; but it would be a long time before anyone tried to stop the booming, ugly post-war buildings.

Shading her eyes, Judith admired the view, aware of the bulky figure standing behind her.

'Lovely,' she said. 'Really lovely. Hideous to look at though, this building, I mean.'

Matthew Jenner shrugged his shoulders. 'Can't have everything. Glass and prestressed concrete are the products of the post-war world. They make things possible that were not thought of before. We need more offices and, as ground is expensive, we must build high. Can't be helped. It is an ephemeral age, don't you think? One not meant to last?'

'I hope you're wrong.' Judith crossed the room and sat down on the other side of his large desk, whose only ornaments were a leather blotter and a crystal writing set.

He sat down, too, and lit a cigarette. 'I'm very glad you rang me, Judith. I know times are hard for you, you don't need to tell me.'

'It's difficult to raise capital without collateral. Mother suggested it,' Judith said with an air of defiance. 'She thought you might be quite interested in getting into catering.'

'We *are* in catering.' Sir Matthew pulled a file from the drawer to his right. 'We are going into foodstuffs, distribution, all that kind of thing. We might buy a chain of hotels from the Gartree Group if we can get them at the right price. They've gone down since the war. You know,' he leaned forward fiddling with his cigarette, 'the war did funny things. People like you lost money and people like Drake made a lot. We're somewhere in between, but doing quite nicely now.' He paused and gazed at her. 'You're not too fond of Drake, are you?'

'Not too keen. He's inconsistent and I very much regret

that we ever got involved with him – as a family, that is. It was all because in that heady time Ros and Doug were in love. We all should have thought much more about it, but I was as much to blame as anyone.'

'I think he might be beginning to regret it too.' Matthew frowned.

'Oh?' Judith looked at him with interest.

'He's too diversified. He's basically a man who should stick to steel and its subsidiaries. He's a machine man.'

'But he can't do that now that it's nationalized.'

'No, but plenty of things are made of steel: motor parts, machine tools and so on. I think it was the vanity of owning Aylestone, of being associated with the Prynnes, that appealed to him. My goodness, that place has gone down.' Matthew grimaced. 'We shan't stay there in a hurry again. Now to the point of our meeting.' Matthew leaned eagerly across the desk. 'I gather you need capital for your restaurant?'

'More, much more, than we thought. More than the banks will lend us. We can just about manage to buy the lease and do the place up. Marcel has sold his flat in Switzerland and raised some family money. But one needs more than that to start a business . . .'

'Quite . . . and to get a reputation.'

'We really want to be as Aylestone was meant to be, with no slipping of standards: excellent food, good service, exquisite wines.'

'London badly needs a restaurant like that!' Matthew appeared to share her enthusiasm. 'A lot are springing up, but I think you and Marcel are just the right people to run it. I have a lot of faith in you both, Judith.' He drew a piece of paper towards him. 'You in particular. Now, tell me, how much do you need?'

Judith looked at him, trying to find words that would not be offensive yet which would leave him in no doubt as to her, and Marcel's, position.

'No strings?' she asked.

'None at all, of course not. At least,' for a moment an odd expression came into his eyes, 'my company would, of course, want an interest, depending on how much you need; but as you can afford the lease and repairs you won't need a great amount. We'd have to draw up the details but, say, a quarter? What do you think?'

'I'd have to think about it, and discuss it with Marcel.' Judith looked dubiously at him. 'But I suppose you can't get money for nothing?'

'Not these days,' Matthew said pleasantly. 'But of course we wouldn't interfere. Oh, by the way, what's it to be called?'

'*Prynne's,*' Judith said with a smile. 'Simply, *Prynne's.*'

PART TWO
Dreams of India
1961–1966

Chapter 8

The young Valentis occupied a large apartment in a modern block behind the Via Condetti, the most fashionable part of Rome. They had, after all, married in Italy in the summer after the family home opened as a hotel and had not been back since. For a year they had travelled; first to the States, to meet Richard's father and then, through South America, to Australia where they took a ship to Singapore. They toured the Far and Near East before arriving in Rome sixteen months after they were married.

It was a good way to get to know each other, though, for them, there were none of the hardships of travel: no need for cheap trips or bargain holidays. Richard Valenti was a wealthy young man and everything was done stylishly and in comfort. Still the proximity, the enforced closeness, was quite a good way to begin a marriage and by the time they settled in Rome, where Richard resumed his career as an artist, they understood each other quite well.

Moira was not a profound girl; she had none of the depths of her sister and she was content to drift. She loved clothes, fast cars and the company of the smart set and Richard seemed the perfect partner. He was attractive, clever and wealthy; she had not realized quite how wealthy when she married him. His family money enabled them to roam freely and independently around the world, pausing where they wished for Richard to sketch or paint. He was now assembling an exhibition to be held at the end of the year in his studio in the Trastevere district.

One morning, about a year after they had settled in Rome, Moira was sitting at the Café Greco in the Corso waiting to have lunch with her husband. They seldom met for lunch because Richard rose late and he liked to spend the day at his studio, while Moira invariably had a date with friends among the social, fashionable set of which she was a prominent member. However Richard wanted her to look at a gallery which he thought might be a possibility for his exhibition.

Moira sat smoking and drinking a Campari-soda, glancing frequently to the street outside where people hurried along in the cold wind. Next to her a man was reading the London *Times* and, as he turned the page, she saw, in large capital letters, the words:

GLITTERING OPENING OF A NEW RESTAURANT:
'PRYNNE'S' COMES TO TOWN.

Moira felt so excited that she leaned over and said:
'Would you mind if I had a glance at your paper? I have seen an item about someone I know.'

The man looked from behind his paper and smiled.

'*Prego, signora*,' he said politely, handing her the paper. 'Please have it. I am about to leave.'

And he stood up and began jangling the change in his pocket.

'Please,' Moira said, feeling suddenly awkward. 'I can easily buy one.'

'It is my pleasure,' the stranger said gravely and, bowing, took up his briefcase and walked towards the cash desk.

Moira quickly hunted through the folded paper and found the item she sought:

On a grey day in February a little colour came to London with the opening of a fashionable new restaurant a stone's throw from the Houses of Parliament and sure to be popular with members. Indeed at its opening the whole of London seemed to be there, though how they squeezed in it was hard to know. The owner is Marcel Laborde, who was *maître-chef* at Aylestone, the celebrated hotel on the Thames which he also helped to launch.

Now, backed by Sir Matthew Jenner, he has acquired new premises in Victoria which have been refurbished to an exacting standard. Before coming to England, Marcel Laborde worked in France and at the Hotel Daniel in Switzerland.

The restaurant is named after the family of his wife, and co-owner, Judith, who was one of the Prynnes of Aylestone, a family with established roots in the England of the Conquest.

Her husband admits that his wife, with her strong personality, has been the driving force behind the restaurant which she now intends to manage while her husband works in the kitchen.

On the night of the opening . . .

'Hello, darling, sorry I'm late.' Richard bent and kissed Moira on the cheek, beckoning to the waiter as he sat down. 'Beer, please.'

'*Prego, signore.*' The waiter looked at Moira's glass but she shook her head, and showed the paper to her husband:

'Look, there's a report on the opening of the restaurant in *The Times*. Isn't that exciting? I wish we'd been there. It was quite a "do". By all accounts it's a success. Listen to this.'

She then went on to read the account of the reception and the dinner that was served after it. Richard licked his lips:

'Makes me feel hungry. I think Marcel will have a big success on his hands there.'

'With Judith behind him he will. *The Times* is right.'

'You think Judith is the stronger personality?'

'Oh, Marcel is strong, too, in his way. He is very stubborn; but he is only interested in cooking and Judith has the organizational drive and flair.'

'I think my father would like Judith.' Richard's eyes focused on the menu which was brought to them.

'Oh? Why do you say that?' Moira looked enquiringly at him.

'He likes strong women. If they are beautiful, too, it helps.'

137

'But Judith is happily married.' Moira looked rather shocked.

'*Cara*, I didn't say he would want to marry her or even have an affair with her. I merely said I thought he would *like* her. Don't you?'

Moira looked at the plate of antipasto which had been set before her. She had found Valenti senior rather terrifying. Richard, who was tall, slim and elegant, didn't resemble him at all. Valenti senior was of medium height but powerfully built. He had a large head which seemed out of proportion to the rest of his body; but in no sense did it make him seem deformed. On the other hand he was not strictly handsome; but his eyes, deeply sunk in his face, were mesmeric. He was like his name: leonine; one of the most formidable people she had ever met. No wonder her dreamy, artistic husband had wanted to distance himself from such an awesome and demanding parent.

Moira began to pick daintily at her *hors d'œuvre*, which was accompanied by mineral water. Richard was eating spaghetti and, with it, half a flagon of chianti. He had a healthy appetite but his wife was still figure-conscious, even in advanced pregnancy.

'It wouldn't surprise me one day if Judith needed your father,' Moira said suddenly.

'How do you mean?' Now Richard looked surprised and, putting down his fork, fingered the stem of his wineglass.

'You never know, but if Matt Jenner ever let her down she would need money, and your father obviously has pots.'

'But Father isn't interested in restaurants.'

'I think Judith has more ambition than that. I wouldn't be surprised if one day she tried to buy back Aylestone and run it the way they wanted to in the first place. I think the restaurant is just the first rung of the ladder.'

* * *

138

One morning, not long before her baby was due, Rosalind woke up early, aware of a sensation of wetness around her. She jabbed her elbow into Doug's rib and said:

'Get up. Hurry! I think the waters have broken,' and, as Doug started out of bed, Ros threw back the sheets and nearly fainted when she found herself lying in a pool of sticky, bright blood.

What happened after that was something she found hard to recall. Doug told her, after it was all over, that he had called the doctor, called an ambulance, and she was rushed off to hospital. However it was too late to save the baby and, she was told, she was lucky to have escaped with her life.

Rosalind felt that this was another one of those unjust, and undeserved, pieces of misfortune which seemed to have dogged her in recent years. Accordingly she sank rapidly into a depression which the doctors assured her and her husband was quite normal. She would lie in bed all day and look at the ceiling or, after she was moved home, gaze out of the window and make unreasonable and continual demands on the harassed nurse engaged to look after her. She became capricious and would sometimes refuse to see people, who might have travelled quite a long way to bring her some present or words of comfort. One school friend who came down from the north of England was sent back without so much as a glimpse of her erstwhile friend.

But when George Drake was announced there was no question of his not being admitted to see his daughter, who even made an effort to pretty herself up and greet her father from the bed with a bright, affectionate smile. He looked anxiously at her as he stooped to kiss her, laying a huge bunch of flowers beside her on the bed.

'I'm terribly sorry, darling.'

'Thanks, Daddy ... and thanks for the flowers. They *are* beautiful.'

George glanced round. 'It seems like a flower shop already. I should have brought something else.'

'Really, Daddy, these flowers are the nicest.' Rosalind patted the place beside her on the bed. 'You're *just* the tonic I needed.'

'I hear you haven't been well, darling.' George anxiously stroked her brow. 'Down in the dumps?'

'Horrible to lose a baby so near time, Daddy,' Rosalind said, a mite tearfully. 'I thought the waters had broken and there I was . . . soaked in blood.'

George shut his eyes and pressed his daughter's hand.

'There was some sort of rupture inside. Rare, but it happens.'

'You can always try again darling . . . in time,' George said with a forced kind of cheerfulness.

'Oh I don't want another baby, Daddy. I've quite made up my mind about that. I don't think I could *bear* to go through it all again. It *is* frightening, you know. Supposing I'd been alone in the house; that Doug hadn't been here?' Rosalind put a hand to her mouth. 'It doesn't bear thinking about, does it?'

'Doesn't really,' Drake said and put his hand on her lap. 'And don't; just you hurry up and get well.'

'Oh Daddy,' Rosalind clasped his hand with a sigh. 'It is *so* good to have you here. I wish . . .'

'What, darling?' George frowned.

'Well, maybe Doug wasn't *quite* the right husband for me. He's changed.'

George looked disturbed and carefully got off the bed. Then he went over to the window, hands in his pockets, and stared out.

'How has he changed, pet?'

'He's not what I thought. He's not a *doer*, is he, Daddy? He's a *leaner*.'

'He's not like Judith, that's for sure,' Drake said.

'Oh Judith! I don't mean pushy like her.'

'Seriously,' George turned to face his daughter. 'He might have done better to *be* pushy. To know what he wants and go out and get it, as she did. I couldn't understand him letting himself be pushed aside so easily for John Redmain.'

'He's a bit afraid of you, Daddy.' Rosalind looked sulkily at her father.

'He's too much of a gentleman,' George said decisively, 'but that's no bad thing in a husband, dear, and he's very fond of Philip. He dotes on him. What is it *you* really want?'

'I'd like a job frankly, Daddy, when I'm better, and I feel better already seeing you.'

'What sort of job?' George again began to look puzzled.

'Well I'd like to work at Aylestone, but Doug is against it. I discussed it with him when I was first pregnant. He was dead against, wouldn't even listen.' Rosalind slyly, carefully inspected her long, pretty hands. 'Couldn't you *make* him give me a job, Daddy?'

'Doug has no power. John Redmain's in charge, Ros. I have no influence with him at *all*.'

'But you must have. You're his boss.' Rosalind looked astonished.

'Yes, but he does have a free hand. He insisted on it. Besides, it wouldn't be right for me to force him to employ my daughter.'

'Then can you employ me, Daddy?' Ros pleaded, hands outstretched.

'In what way, darling?' George, looking confused, sat down on her bed again.

'Anything. Your personal assistant. I'd do anything.'

'You can't type, dear.'

'I can learn.'

'You have no experience. Believe me it's not as simple as you think. Besides . . .' Drake paused and sharply drew in his breath. 'Things really *aren't* going all that well. I lost a

141

packet on the Aylestone project. I didn't really know what I was doing. I wouldn't mind pulling out if another offer came my way. The banks have lost faith in my judgement and aren't too keen to lend me money. It's not the time to take on new staff, old girl.'

'But couldn't I *help*?'

'I'm afraid there's nothing you can do, pet.' George affectionately patted her arm. 'And do keep this to yourself; don't tell Doug. If this sort of thing gets around it's bad for business.'

'But what can I *do*?' Rosalind wailed. Suddenly years of boredom, frustration and routine seemed to stretch endlessly before her.

'Well, you could take up shorthand and typing as you suggested,' George said brightly.

'I'm a Cambridge graduate, Daddy.'

'I know; but you let that go, didn't you, dear? You threw that, and the chances that came with it, all away when you married Douglas Prynne. You plumped for marriage and motherhood, dear. Can't have everything. I'm afraid that it's too late to do anything about that now.'

After her father left Rosalind began to weep. She wept so hard and so long that the doctor was eventually called and prescribed a sedative. He told her husband she'd take a long time to get over her illness.

But Ros was not weeping because she was sick or depressed. She was weeping for those lost chances, for the waste of a life.

Sir Matthew Jenner, Bt., was an ambitious man. He was also a devious one. He looked an amiable man, full of jovial *bonhomie*, but by nature he was a predator and seldom did anything from which he would not benefit.

Unlike George Drake, who was his rival, he had served in the war and had thus missed the chance of profiting from it. In fact he very nearly lost his life. While he was overseas the business, Jenner Securities, founded by his father, and for which he had been made a baronet, was poorly run and when Matthew joined it in 1945 it lacked either funds or clear direction.

Jenner had been thirty when the war ended and he had taken over control of the business using his war record – which was, indeed, distinguished – his old school tie, his father's name and title, to make the business grow as rapidly as he could.

Based on foodstuffs, it had had a poor war. Rationing and controls did little for businesses which relied on food for profits and Matthew realized the need to diversify if he was to expand. Food was not completely derationed until 1954, nine years after the end of hostilities.

But Matthew was energetic, diligent and not overscrupulous. He had married a wife who had money of her own and he used it to further the business. He had a flat in Mayfair and a house in the country. He was well satisfied with what he had achieved, but not satisfied enough. He was anxious to expand even further and the ambitions of Judith Prynne appealed to him. He had an instinct that, if he followed her star, he would rise too in the world of smart restaurants and good hotels, a trail already blazed for him by Judith.

Sir Matthew was a socialite. He liked to be seen at fashionable parties, the opera and first nights. He was usually, but not invariably, accompanied by his wife Margaret, who had little taste for society. She was country born and bred, though 'county' rather than a daughter of the soil. She loved horses and dogs and messing about in wellies. The Jenners had little in common and this disparity widened as they grew older and their marriage longer.

Sir Matthew was an old family friend of Greville and Angela Prynne. He greatly approved of their elder daughter who was the kind of attractive, clever, ambitious woman who appealed to him. He was pleased to do all he could to help someone he'd known for years; but he felt, he knew, there was profit in it for him too.

Matthew Jenner now sat at his large desk reading the *Financial Times* when an item of news caught his eye:

'Sharp fall in Drake shares; gloomy profit forecast.'

The article then went on to describe the troubles of the Drake empire due to poor half-year results and a lack-lustre performance.

In general, the troubles that have afflicted George Drake may be laid at the door of over-expansion in unwise investments. In particular his venture into the realm of luxury hotels has been disastrous, and one may well ask oneself what made a normally astute businessman sink millions into a profitless venture like the refurbishment of the ancient home of the Prynne family which, as a hotel and however it is run, has consistently failed to make a profit. Perhaps this could be ascribed to carelessness, or lack of foresight. Expertise in one area of business does not necessarily lead to success in another. A self-made man who started his working life on the shop floor, George Drake has made his millions from steel and, after nationalization, products based on steel. This is an area in which he is an expert, whereas of the hotel and catering industry he knows nothing.

There then followed an analysis of the Drake share performance which Matthew digested carefully. As he came to the end of the article he sat back in his chair with a smile, the paper still in his hand.

After a while he pressed the intercom button to his outside office and said softly on the phone to his secretary:

'Get me George Drake on the phone, would you?'

In the early morning Judith would lie and listen to the sounds of the city wakening up. For most of her life she had lived in the country; she considered herself of the countryside. For nearly three years she had lived in Switzerland. Yet there was nothing to compare with the sounds of a great city the size of London waking up in the morning.

First there was the noise of the dustcart making its rounds; the whine and grind of machinery. Then came the sound of milk bottles clanking along in the milk float. The soft cooing of pigeons beneath the rafters, or on the ledges of the windows, continued onwards from dawn and, finally, as if to remind one that one was in the heart of the metropolis, came the sonorous tones of Big Ben sounding the hour.

Seven o'clock. Time to get up.

It was a horrible moment and one which she never became used to, even though she had had to rise early most of her life; at boarding school and, especially, during her time at the Hotel Daniel, when she often had to get up before six.

Inevitably, she and Marcel went to bed late. Sometimes it was not until two. It was very hard to have to get up at seven. But then, they had chosen a singularly hard life.

A hard life but a rewarding one, and today it was her turn to shop at Covent Garden and procure the best of the day's produce brought in both from the country and abroad.

Marcel was a heavy sleeper. Just as well that he was not woken by the sound of the dust lorry, the milk floats or the chimes of Big Ben. But he had an exhausting day. They were open for lunch as well as dinner six days a week. Sunday was his only day of rest and then he often didn't get up until evening, but stayed in bed all day sleeping or reading the papers. That was also the day they made love.

Judith gazed at her sleeping spouse, his tousled hair, the curve of his mouth, his stubbly cheeks and felt, once again, the shock that she often did feel on seeing him there at all. Sometimes it was like looking at a stranger; as though he were someone she didn't know and would never know any better. She had never really known him well before, despite their professional compatibility, but it was marriage that had made her realize what a complicated, unfathomable,

145

unrevealing man he was; a man full of secrets, locked in his own private world to which only he had the key. A man of contrasts.

Yet he was also a kind and thoughtful man; a gentleman in every sense of the word: polite, considerate, thoughtful, cautious. When he touched her it was with respect rather than passion. When he made love to her it was in a tentative way, as if he hoped she wouldn't mind. In physical matters he was distinctly unsure of himself.

Neither of them had had a lover before their marriage. For both of them it was a difficult time; difficult, and hard to endure because, as a woman, Judith realized that she had hitherto repressed the passionate side of her nature. She had expected that he, as the male, would know everything. Instead she found someone who was as uncertain as she; who was cautious, fumbling, a little clumsy, constantly apologetic. For many months they did not make love successfully at all.

Nevertheless love and understanding did grow, Judith thought, slipping out from beside him and covering him up. It was not passionate, headstrong, novelettish love; but tenderness and respect. She imagined that there were better lovers than Marcel, men more sure of themselves, and she imagined that she, herself, would perhaps never be quite satisfied by him. Yet he was a friend, a companion. Soon now, he would be a father.

They were pleased when she became pregnant. They had wished for a family. Marcel said that all chefs were family men, so that they had someone to whom to teach their art. They did nothing to prevent conception, but it did not happen for some time.

Judith was a strong girl and she had a good pregnancy. She was able to carry out her duties either in the restaurant or behind the scenes, or shopping and bargaining at the market. In a month or two she would give it up and after that her baby would be born.

Later that morning she was greeted at the market by the men whose produce she selected at the booths in the big arcade by the side of the opera house. There were avocados and oranges from Israel; melons, asparagus, artichokes from France; oranges, melons, grapefruit from Spain; grapes from Belgium and South Africa; strawberries flown in from the United States; pears, mangoes, pineapple and paw paw . . . some of these she had never seen before. They had not been seen on the market since before the war.

Then there were the mundane vegetables which had all to be of the finest quality: potatoes; various kinds of greens; cabbages, sprouts, broccoli, lettuce, tomatoes . . . and, as she wandered around with her pencil poised over her pad, she was followed by a Covent Garden porter who collected her purchases and put them in boxes on his barrow. Then at the end he took them to the white van parked in Bow Street with the PRYNNE'S sign written along it in blue. PRYNNE'S with the family crest just over the loop of the Y.

Judith was always called Miss Prynne.

'Morning, Miss Prynne,' the marketeers said touching their caps, producing stubs of pencil from behind their ears to note down her orders. From the cafés in the market came the enticing smell of frying: bacon and egg, fried bread, sausages, chips . . . sometimes it made the mouth water and, in the early days of her pregnancy, it had sometimes made her nauseous; but still she came. The pubs in Covent Garden, open very early in the morning, were full not only with market personnel, merchants and porters, but with revellers in evening dress who had been up all night, lurching drunkenly from one party to another and finally to a last bottle of champagne or something to eat in a Covent Garden pub. Some people never knew when it was time to go home.

By ten o'clock the shopping was over. Henry, the

restaurant's handyman, had remained at the wheel in case he was moved on by the police, and Judith watched as the porter stowed the cartons, cases, sacks and boxes safely into the back of the van. Then she gave him a few notes, for which he thanked her, climbed in beside Henry and, gingerly, they started to navigate their way through the traffic that was already slowly strangling the centre of London, until they got to the Strand. Then past the Savoy, through Trafalgar Square, up Parliament Street, past the Houses of Parliament and Westminster Abbey and into the narrow maze of streets that was home.

Judith loved her mornings in the market, the smells, sights and sounds of a city within a city: a city dedicated to fruit, flowers and vegetables. She loved it when it was cold and the blue sky seemed like a canopy beneath which the porters wore mufflers to keep the cold from their pink faces and the merchants rubbed their chapped hands together, stamping their feet briskly on the cobbled stones.

But in summer it had a special charm. Then there was a proliferation of gorgeous flowers scenting the air, the plenitude of colours delighting the eye, dazzling the senses. There was an air of jollity and well-being and the men quaffed large pints of ale in the open, their chests bared to the sun.

When it was cold Judith sometimes stopped for tea and hot buttered toast in one of the cafés; but today she decided to wait until she got home.

For by now 32 Emmott Mews was home. It was also their place of work, where they were painstakingly creating a reputation for excellence. They were now booked out every day, sometimes for weeks in advance. Eminent people came to dine at night, and prominent businessmen and politicians brought their clients, constituents, and influential acquaintances there for lunch.

By the time Judith got back everything in the kitchen was moving like a well-oiled machine towards the first event of the day, which was lunch. The vegetables were peeled, the starters and *hors d'oeuvres* were being prepared under the experienced eye of René the *sous-chef*, who had joined them after his contract had expired at Aylestone.

The *commis*-waiters would arrive shortly after ten and start to lay the tables with freshly starched cloths, gleaming, highly polished silver and stiff white napkins.

Marcel usually appeared at about ten, too, when everything was under way. The main dishes for the day were his responsibility, the *plat du jour*, a blend of culinary wizardry and artistic imagination. Dishes were often ordered in advance together with the wines, and in the cellars the highly experienced *sommelier* was already preparing the fine champagnes, burgundies and clarets that would be served with the main meals.

Marcel was already down when Judith got back. He was going over the menus with René and called to her as she came in.

'We have a very special guest for lunch today, Judith. Someone related to you.'

'Not my parents again, I hope,' Judith said with a wry smile. Naturally they neither offered, nor were expected to pay for what they ate.

'No, your sister's father-in-law.'

'Leo Valenti?' Judith said with interest. 'How do you know?'

'Moira phoned a short time after you left. He is flying in from Rome about now and wants to meet a friend here. I said that only by juggling the tables can I fit him in; but, of course, we must.'

'Of course,' Judith murmured, sitting down on a chair by the table. 'I simply *must* have something to eat.'

'Are you all right, *chérie*?' Marcel looked at her solicitously.

'Perfectly all right. Just hungry.'

'You should eat before you go.'

'I should, but I don't.' She stood up and touched him briefly on the arm. 'I can see you're terribly busy down here, dear. Maybe someone could bring up my tea and toast?'

'I'll send Antoine,' René said authoritatively. 'And you *should* rest more, Judith. You look tired.'

Judith felt tired and walked rather wearily up the back stairs to the private quarters. She was tired, but she refused to give in. When she had the baby she would rest for a month or two, but no more.

Upstairs she found a lot to do. She did all the accounts, all the ordering that could be done, replacements of crockery and so on, by phone and took many of the bookings, though the phone was switched through to the restaurant when the *maître d'hôtel*, Charles Ivens, arrived. He was a discreet, experienced man, half French, old enough to be left in charge yet young enough to accept orders when necessary. He did not resent Judith's overall control.

Her tea and toast were brought up by the young *commis*-waiter and laid on a table beside her while she telephoned Smithfield with a routine enquiry. Marcel or René usually bought the meat, fish or game personally once or twice a week, and these were kept in the cold larders or the huge outside fridge which was big enough to walk into.

Judith finished her breakfast and made some more calls until Charles called up to say he had arrived. She was just about to switch the restaurant line to the restaurant when the domestic phone rang and, after asking the caller to hold on while she completed her task, she sat back and put the phone to her ear, thinking it might probably be Moira about her father-in-law.

'Judith?'

'Yes, Mother.'

'How are you, darling?'

'Fine.'

'Not working too hard?'

'No, Mother.'

'Judith, the most *extraordinary* thing has happened.'

'What's that?'

'Matthew offered for Aylestone! He wants to buy it from Drake. Isn't that wonderful? It must be the *most* marvellous news for us.'

Judith did not come down into the restaurant until two. Even were Moira's father-in-law not here she would always check that the sitting was going well, standing behind the desk where Charles did the bills and took the bookings, looking over the reservations.

She knew who he was as soon as she entered the dark dining room lit, even at lunchtime, by lamps. At a couple of tables naked flames burned where some dish, bœuf Stroganoff or crêpes, was being prepared in front of the clients. The smell of good food mingled with an air of *bonhomie*, of pleasing satiety, the quintessence of a good restaurant.

From the back he did look, as Moira had told her, rather like a large toad. He was thick-set and, in profile, his face was a curious shape dominated by a very large nose. As he turned she saw that he had a long upper lip, eyebrows that almost met in the centre of his face, and very deep-set black eyes. His hair was thick, black but slightly greying and brushed back from his forehead. He wore a well-cut dark blue suit, an American-style shirt buttoned at the collar and a pale-coloured tie.

He glanced quickly at her as she entered the room and their eyes seemed to lock. He wasn't supposed to know who she was, and she didn't actually know who he was; but they knew. Some instinct made them aware of each other from the very beginning, as if it had been predestined that they should meet. He was, as she knew he would be, fascinating.

151

At the same time Charles, dressed in his black jacket, striped trousers, white shirt and black tie, murmured:

'Mr Valenti's over there, Madame.'

'I thought it must be.' Judith went over to the corner table and put out her hand.

'How do you do! I'm Moira's sister.'

Leo Valenti rose to his feet, a considerable presence, but shorter than she was, his knowing eyes prescient.

'You're not at all like your sister, Judith.'

'I'm not meant to be.' She didn't know whether or not the remark were complimentary or critical.

Valenti put his head on one side, gazing at her, and then he seemed suddenly to remember his manners. 'Do forgive me, Judith, this is Mr Harold Schweppes of the Baron Bank.'

'How do you do?' Judith, aware that her senses were reeling from the impact of her meeting with Valenti, but trying to attribute it to her pregnancy, murmured politely: 'Do, please, sit down.'

'Won't you join us?' Valenti pointed to his chair, but immediately a waiter appeared with a chair which he held out for Judith, who sat down and joined her hands on the table.

'I hope you enjoyed your meal?'

'Excellent,' Valenti said with relish. 'I'm so grateful you could fit us in. My friend here says it is almost impossible to get a table at short notice. *I* said I had a contact.'

Judith smiled: 'How are Moira and Richard?'

'Fine, fine.' Momentarily Valenti's thick brows knitted together. 'I can never understand my son, of course, but then I am not an artist. Are you interested in art, Judith?'

'Very much. Why can't you understand him?'

'I was always ambitious. I wanted to make money. I can't understand anyone who doesn't. Can you?'

As he played with a spoon on the table she saw that his hands were well kept and very white, as though he spent a lot of time on them. The overwhelming impression he conveyed was of restless energy, a man who moved a lot, who could hardly ever be still. As he sat down again he seemed to crouch and it was this, with his receding brow and jutting nose, that made him resemble a painting of a slightly sinister medieval pontiff. She could see very little of Richard in the father. Although his clothes were American, and his accent intercontinental, his looks were Italian. He was an Italian, born in Italy to Italian parents; but his demeanour, his presence, seemed to defy boundaries. He was a true cosmopolitan with the air and manners of a diplomat.

'I can understand people who don't want to make money quite well.' Judith shook her head, after dealing with one of the waiters who enquired if she wanted anything. 'Most of my family don't. My husband is also interested only in his art, which is in the kitchen.'

'Then you are the one behind all this?' Valenti looked around as she nodded.

'I'm impressed,' he said.

'Thank you. It was Marcel's idea, of course, that we had a restaurant. But we weren't married then.'

'And when is your baby due?'

'Very soon; but it doesn't keep me from working.' She got to her feet and held out her hand. 'I'll ask Marcel to come up and see you before you go.' She held out her hand. 'I'm so pleased to have met you, Mr Valenti.'

'Leo, *please*,' he said, rising and taking her hand. 'For my part I hope we meet again very soon. I'm sure we shall.' Then he bent his head and kissed the back of the hand he held tightly in his.

Not long after her first meeting with Leo Valenti, Judith gave birth to a son whom she and Marcel called Michael. He was a strong, vigorous, full-term baby and his father prophesied he would be a great chef, though on what evidence it was hard to say.

Judith recovered quickly from her confinement, engaged a nanny to look after Michael and was soon at work not only supervising the affairs of the restaurant, but in discussions with Matthew Jenner on behalf of the family over the future of Aylestone.

Michael was about six weeks old when the family, with the exception of Marcel and Moira, foregathered in the drawing room of the family quarters to hear what Matthew had to say.

After his opening statement he looked around the company and smiled. He was a man obviously at ease with himself and the world, and he had an arm flung casually over the back of his chair, his legs outstretched before him.

The family sat round him. Gran, bright and alert, had taken everything in, though asking no questions.

Judith particularly had questioned him carefully. They didn't, Judith had explained, want to step from the frying pan into the fire. But in reality the Prynnes had little option but to agree. Drake controlled the majority of shares; but, even then, the family in opposition, with its forty-five per cent, could be very difficult indeed.

Marcel hadn't wanted to be included in the family gathering that met with Matthew Jenner to consider his offer. His work was still his hobby, his art, his life, and anything outside it a distraction.

'I take it you all approve then?' Matthew drew in his legs and prepared to get up.

'Of course we approve, don't we, Judith?' Greville looked at his daughter, who had emerged as the business brains of the family.

'Well, for one thing we don't have much option,' Judith said carefully. 'George controls fifty-five per cent. But what sways me and makes me want to give it my whole-hearted approval and say that the family is solidly behind him is that Matthew wants Aylestone to revert to what we originally intended: a first-class hotel. I would add that, as a partner and a backer, he has been very good to deal with. *Prynne's* owes him a lot.'

'Thank you, Judith.' Matthew smiled at her. 'That's it then. Oh!' he appeared to be on the verge of rising when he changed his mind and sat down again. 'There is one other thing you may not be happy about . . .'

Judith looked at him apprehensively.

'You might not like this very much,' Matthew went on, 'and perhaps I should have mentioned it before.'

Judith sat forward in her chair clutching the arms. Matthew finally got up and began to wander around the room, avoiding the eyes of those gathered round him. 'I really feel that if the hotel is to be what we want it to be – and remember I'm buying a loss-making business, as Aylestone has never made a profit – I will need this wing.'

He stopped abruptly as if he didn't know what else to say.

'This wing?' Gran looked around for enlightenment. 'What does he mean?'

'I mean, dear Lady Prynne,' Matthew made an elaborate bow, 'that I have very reluctantly to ask you to give up living here.'

'Oh, that's impossible,' Gran said, with her angelic smile. 'Besides, the Admiral wouldn't like it.'

'I am quite aware of that,' Matthew said gravely. 'But, nevertheless, I have to insist on it if this deal is to go through.'

'But it's in the agreement.' Angela spoke at last, as if coming to her senses after a deep shock.

'I know, and that means I must have your consent. I'm sure I shall.'

'Not mine,' Angela said, crossing her arms and sitting back in her chair.

'Nor mine,' Gran said firmly, 'and *nor* will Jasper.'

'Quite so.'

Matthew went to the window and his fingers drummed on the pane. Rain spattered over the lawn, the flower beds, dripped from the branches of the trees. He turned and appeared to gaze at a spot on the far side of the room. 'Then I must tell you that, if you don't agree, I can't possibly go ahead.'

'Well that's it then.' Greville looked very annoyed. 'It's all off. Drake will have to keep it. We can't possibly lose the family home *completely*. Been here since the Conqueror.'

'Drake won't keep it, I can assure you,' Matthew said. 'If he doesn't sell to me he will sell to another group, and they will want the same thing. No hotelier will tolerate an entire wing being given up to the family.'

'But where will they go?' Doug, who felt he had most to gain from the sale and wanted to keep in with Jenner, now seemed the most upset.

'Anywhere they choose. I will buy them a house in exchange for the wing.'

'But . . .' Greville stuck his pipe in his coat pocket. 'What about me?'

'How do you mean?' Matthew's voice began to sound weary.

'Aren't I going to run round in my monkey suit?'

'I'm afraid not,' Matthew said firmly. 'I do not include you and Angela in my plans for the hotel, though thank you for what you've done.'

'Then what will I do?'

'Aren't you retired?' Jenner looked surprised. 'I would think continue to do what you have always done, play golf.'

Greville began to splutter. 'I . . .'

'My dear Greville,' Jenner said patiently. 'You and I know that in the years since this has been a hotel you have had a very good time, whatever you say. The Prynnes have continued to indulge themselves in a lifestyle they could never otherwise have afforded. I'm not saying this has to stop; but it will not continue here on this spot. You may come and play golf here any time you like, or use any of the facilities. You continue to be a shareholder, together with the rest of your family; but you will not have anything to do with the management,' he said with a note of finality.

'What about Doug?' Ros demanded at last as if finding her voice.

'If we are to succeed, and it is in all our interests that we succeed, this hotel will be professionally managed and run. Good as Redmain is, a generous settlement will have to be made and, unfortunately, he must go.' He turned to Judith, now slumped in her chair, trying to meet her eye. 'I have an idea of which I think you all might approve. Judith has made a startling success of *Prynne's*. I have been very impressed by the way she has managed it . . .'

'Marcel was involved too,' Judith interjected.

'Of course,' Matthew nodded, 'but *you* have managed it; you set it up, you arranged the finance. I think if you and Marcel could be persuaded to take over Aylestone and succeed as well with it as you have succeeded with your restaurant, we shall all be very happy indeed. Happy, and much, much better off.'

Chapter 9

Aylestone reopened in the spring of 1962 under new management. It was extensively refurbished and redecorated and the family, reluctantly prised out of their precious wing, were rehoused in an old stone house surrounded by lawns about five miles down river. Despite its charm, the place found little favour with them, but there was nothing that they could do.

This time the publicity was discreet, controlled, the emphasis being on its renowned restaurant under the personal supervision of *maître-chef* Laborde of *Prynne's* in London. Judith made the columns of many papers on account of her connection with the hotel and her success as a restaurateur. She was gossip-worthy. She began to be the sort of person who was talked about, written about, interviewed and deferred to.

She was that modern phenomenon: a businesswoman who had charm, looks, a successful marriage and a baby. She was photogenic, well connected and she dressed at couture houses.

But this time, at least, Aylestone quickly became a success. Matthew's hunch had been right. It was soon making money, and was almost constantly full of wealthy Americans and Middle Eastern potentates.

Judith stuck firmly to the dictum of César Ritz, which was that a grand hotel should be for the entertainment of the wealthy in discretion and luxury. No lists were ever issued as to who was staying there, and if someone wanted anonymity there, they got it. The staff at Aylestone were as discreet as those employed by the Royal Family; maybe even more so. Tell-tale memoirs were strictly prohibited by contract.

Everything a guest wanted was to hand and they were charged accordingly. Aylestone became one of the most expensive hotels in Europe and even in the depths of winter would-be guests were turned away. It was rather like being a member of an exclusive club with entry restricted only to the well-connected or the very rich.

Naturally Judith found that her lifestyle changed too. She enjoyed wearing smart couture clothes and bought herself an expensive car; but otherwise she had few luxuries and little private life. She and Marcel were forcibly separated by the fact that he remained in London, where his main love was the restaurant, and Judith, perforce, remaining in charge of Aylestone, lived in the small flat reserved for her on the top of the old family wing.

But she saw little of that either. Like the famous Ritz she seldom thought of anything other than her work, although there was a part of each day she liked to spend with her son. Two years after the new Aylestone was opened Judith somehow managed to have another baby, a girl, who was given the name Pauline. She then felt her family was complete.

By any token, however, the family life of the Labordes was a strange one. Husband and wife very seldom met and when they did it was mostly to discuss business. A young chef had been brought over from France to be in charge of the Aylestone kitchens, though under the supervision of Marcel. He had been found in a restaurant in Provence when Marcel and Judith had taken a brief holiday the year before Pauline was born, and his talents were remarkable. His name was André Hebert.

Yet almost immediately discord grew up between the talented, temperamental Hebert, who became a law unto himself, and Marcel, who, in his opinion, as well as that of others, considered himself without equal in England, certainly, and probably most of France as well. The chefs admired each other but their rivalry was immense. Marcel would come over weekly to discuss the menus with André, so that shopping at Billingsgate, Covent Garden and Smithfield could be done for both establishments at the same time, only to find that they were changed once his back was turned. Much of the expensive raw materials went to waste while André perfected his brilliant, imaginative dishes which eschewed most of the best-known methods: *darne de saumon au beurre de cassis* or his *veau à la Montchâteau*.

Judith, increasingly aware of this rivalry, had her own problems: a new baby who needed a lot of attention, which Judith wished to give, plus a hotel whose reputation soared, and, lastly, a family who hardly gave her a moment's peace.

For the Prynnes – mother, father, Gran and the spirit of Sir Jasper – had disliked being bundled out of the ancestral home, for whatever reason. In Gran's opinion the Admiral didn't like it at all and constantly complained about it, through her. Angela and Greville found their lifestyles had suddenly changed. They were no longer persons of consequence or importance and increasingly their dreams turned to India . . . If only . . .

If only they had *stayed*.

At first her parents had continued to motor over to the hotel as though it were a home from home; but this had to be stopped. Eminent businessmen, or men of affairs, objected to having to include Greville in their game just because he had once owned the place. Angela became more reckless at the bar, where people bought her drinks, and, on one terrible evening that Judith could not recall without a shudder, fell off her stool.

Gran had to be forbidden visits to her old home unless she was under heavy escort. Never for a moment was she allowed to wander off alone in search of her errant husband.

The family – Doug included, though he remained as general manager – felt in time that they had been fobbed off, and their attitude towards Judith and her husband changed. There were constant personal complaints, a barrage of telephone calls, and a stream of never-ending reproaches.

'How *could* you . . .'

'If only we'd known. If only we were back in India.'

One night, after a tiresome evening with her family which contained a full recitation of their miseries, Judith's patience snapped.

'I wish you'd go back to India, Mother! If you like I'll gladly pay the fare.'

Gran, who had been nodding by the fire, raised her head, and Angela, always the most volatile member of the family, burst into tears and threw herself against Grev, who removed his pipe from one part of his mouth to the other and patted her back.

'Rotten thing to say, Judith,' he murmured between clenched teeth.

'I don't see why, Dad. All *I* ever hear is how good India was. You are so dissatisfied with life here that I would indeed gladly pay the fare for you to go there on a visit. I didn't mean permanently.'

'On a visit?' Angela's tears dried miraculously and she looked up at her husband. 'What do you think, dear?'

'Oh, a *visit*?' Greville finally removed his pipe from his mouth. 'Who would look after Mother?'

'Oh I don't expect anyone to think of me . . . or Jasper,' Gran wailed. 'No one thought of us when they ejected us from our home. I expect we'll be put in an old people's refuge and forgotten.'

'Don't be silly, Gran.' Judith looked at her watch. 'Of course you'll be taken care of. I'll see to that.'

'I suppose it's all right if you've got the *money*,' Angela said with a look, 'to do these things.'

'What things, Mother?'

'Pay for us to go to India, pay for Gran to be looked after. I don't think you realize, Judith, how narrow and self-centred you've become.'

'Angela, please.' Greville put a hand on his wife's arm but she shook it away.

'I want to continue, Greville, now that we've started.'

'*You've* started.'

'That this conversation has started.' Angela threw herself into a chair. 'Why am *I* the only one to say what we all feel? You complain to me that Judith has become self-centred and arrogant; why don't you tell *her*? You're her father.'

Greville mumbled something and thrust his pipe into his mouth again, as Angela, with a peevish look, addressed her daughter.

'It's not only that we're concerned about you, Judith – your attitude to us; but your attitude to Doug and Ros. You have never given your brother credit for his abilities. You make all the decisions about the hotel without consulting him.'

'I have to make the main decisions. Matt put me in charge. But I do refer to Doug and leave the day-to-day running to him. You surprise me, Mother. I thought we got on quite well. As for Ros,' Judith bit her lip, 'it's true we don't get on too well, but neither has she experience in running a hotel. I know she wants a job, but I can't give her one. I can only employ professionals.'

'You're very hard, Judith.'

'I'm sorry you think that, Mother.' Judith got up and straightened the skirt of her stylish two-piece. 'I don't mean to be.'

'But you are. The truth is, Judith, that all your family, with the exception of me, have become afraid of you. They

162

daren't speak their minds. And if they're afraid of you, you can imagine what everyone else must think of you, too.'

Marcel lay awake, aware of Judith tossing beside him. Once or twice he heard Pauline cry out from her bed in the next room, and quietly he got out of bed to look at her. Michael was a heavy sleeper and seldom woke at nights. Yet, for all her tossing and turning, Judith never woke and Marcel realized that her restlessness was caused by nightmares.

Judith had come back in a very agitated state after a visit to her parents; yet she wouldn't tell him why or what had happened.

She was not the sort of person who was very easily disturbed; years and years of coping with crises had taught her to take one thing at a time, put one step after another.

She had taken two aspirins before she went to sleep; but when he asked her to talk to him she wouldn't. Or rather she said she couldn't.

This inability to communicate was an aspect of their relationship which had grown more marked since the birth of Pauline. They had never been soul-mates, there had always been a reserve in their relationship; but now they seemed to have little to discuss at all other than the children and work. Marcel knew that Judith was preoccupied and that there was a lot to worry about; he longed for her to share her burdens with him, but she didn't. And it was the same with him; when he was worried he wanted to worry alone.

After he had settled the child, instead of getting into bed Marcel went over to the chair by the window and sat in it, drawing the curtains slightly so that he would see the dawn slowly rising over the trees.

It was spring, a beautiful time of the year, and the park around Aylestone looked at its best with the river glimpsed on clear mornings between the trees. But today was a dusky, dewy dawn and the sun seemed very slow to rise, if it would be visible at all.

After a while he was aware that the restless movements in the bed had ceased. Judith lay still. He knew that she was awake and, after a while, he rose and went over to the bed, gazing down at her.

'Are you all right?' she said, turning to glance at the clock with its illuminated dial.

'Are you?' He sat on the bed and put a hand on her brow, tenderly, gently, as though she were a child.

'Why, what's the matter?' She caught his hand and looked at him and he realized how beautiful she was; how beautiful, and how vulnerable.

'You were tossing about in the bed, *ma chérie*, crying out in your sleep.'

'I wasn't aware of it. I took a sleeping pill.'

'Ah, I thought it was for a headache.'

'That too.' She still had her hand on his.

'Judith, can't you tell me what's worrying you? Can't you confide in me? You know that I love you. I want to help you. I feel that since Pauline was born there has been a gulf between us.'

Judith removed her hand from his and brushed the hair away from her hot, sticky brow.

'Marcel, I think we've taken on too much,' she said suddenly, in a strained, untypical voice. 'Tonight for the first time in my life I began to be afraid.'

'But of what, my darling?'

Soothingly again he began to stroke her and her taut body seemed to relax at his touch.

'Everything. Your constant quarrels with André; the struggle we have to keep up the standards here; and now tonight . . . my parents told me I was remote and arrogant and that everyone was afraid of me.'

'But that's not true,' Marcel protested.

164

'Why should they say it, then?'

'Maybe they are jealous. Who, for instance, is supposed to be afraid of you?'

'Mother said my family are afraid of me. That I don't treat Doug or Ros well – particularly Doug – and that everyone, meaning I suppose the staff and, maybe, you, feel the same. One suddenly begins to wonder if one has ever really looked at oneself. What sort of person have I become?'

She had not protested at his gestures of intimacy, letting his free hand slip inside her nightdress and cup her breast.

'You're trying to buy me off,' she said with a slight, provocative smile.

'Just to soothe you, my darling,' Marcel said, bending to kiss her. 'After we have made love we can talk a little more seriously, perhaps?'

It was true in a way, the power of love. Judith lay beside Marcel drowsy and, momentarily, released from her torments.

Marcel was a tender, caring lover. In their lovemaking they experienced neither the heights nor depths but a gentle release, a satiety of body and mind.

'Maybe we should do this more often?' Marcel murmured. 'Sometimes I feel we've got out of the habit.'

Yet it had never really been a habit, a focal point of their life together. She looked at him and smiled, but said nothing. It would be cruel to tell him, now, that, more often than not, after their lovemaking she felt not sated but dissatisfied.

'Can't you tell me what's wrong?' he asked her.

She lay on her stomach, her face on her hands, and frowned:

'The fact is, Marcel, that a lot of things are going wrong. It's nothing specific.'

'The hotel is running beautifully.'

'But what am I to do about my parents? I have offered them a holiday in India. They can go back permanently if they like. But, if they do, what shall I do about Gran? I can't put her in a home and I certainly can't have her here asking all the guests if they've seen Grandpa!'

'It really *is* most extraordinary, that habit of your grandmother's,' he said with a chuckle. 'Do you think she really believes it?'

'That he's there?' Judith paused to think. 'Maybe it's become such a habit she really thinks he is, or maybe it's a kind of reassurance. Or maybe it's a way of escape. Tonight she included him in the conversation as well, and she knows that we know he's not here.'

'Has she always been like that since he died?'

'It seemed to begin after the war, when Mother and Father came back. I can't explain it; maybe a psychiatrist could. Now I think it has become a habit, or maybe a way of drawing attention to herself.'

'We could certainly have her living here, at the hotel, maybe with a nurse.'

'But it would mean giving up one of the main rooms. Matthew wouldn't like it. He wanted her out.'

'Matthew now does as you tell him. He relies on you.'

'But he keeps a very firm financial hold. He would lose a lot of money if he gave up a room to Gran. We couldn't do it, I'm afraid.'

'She could live with Doug.'

'That's a thought; but what would Ros say? You know things between me and Ros have never been easy. We've never really liked each other much and I know that she resents, maybe more than Doug, my position here. Mother says she would like to do something in the hotel.'

'Why can't she?'

'I couldn't stand it. *That* would lead to conflict. Anyway, she honestly has no experience. And I don't think Doug and she should work together. It's not a good idea. Sometimes I think we need someone like another John Redmain . . .'

'And what would you do?'

'You know,' Judith turned over, hands behind her head, thoughts of sleep now abandoned. 'I would like to open another *Prynne's*, a little more ambitious. I thought of a small hotel, maybe on the Scottish borders?'

'Are you serious?'

'Quite serious.'

'And you'd leave here?'

'I don't know. I mean we're really working body and soul for Matt. There are too many problems pleasing other people that we don't have on our own. We own *Prynne's* and we could own the other hotel. If you ask me it would be some sort of solution.

'In many ways I think it's time we moved on.'

Marcel usually came over to Aylestone at the weekend, as *Prynne's* was closed on Sunday. This was the day he would have liked to rest; but it couldn't always be. It was also the day on which he saw his children, and he was a devoted father. He and Judith might dream of the day they would have a home away from both hotel and restaurant. But neither had the time even to look for one. Every day of the week, including Sunday, was taken up with some activity or the other.

It was rare that husband and wife had the chance to talk as they had during the small hours of the morning, and Marcel felt in a happier state of mind when he went down to the kitchens later on to review the past week and discuss menus for the coming one.

Marcel did not particularly enjoy his weekly meeting with Hebert, a man with whom he differed by temperament and origin. Hebert was from Marseilles, whereas Laborde was a northerner from Rouen. Marcel was careful, thoughtful, meditative, whereas Hebert did everything by instinct and shunned the methods of his compatriot. Hebert also liked to drink, whereas Marcel never touched a drop while he was at work.

Yet one had to admit that Hebert was an inspired chef, and Marcel was sometimes reminded of the rivalry between himself and M. Roland at the Hotel Daniel.

Marcel left Judith in her room and, dressed in a blazer and grey flannels, went down to the kitchen humming a tune under his breath as he did. There were times when he wondered whether he and his wife would have many more years together, they led such separate lives; but on days like today, after the rapport they had once again established in the course of their lovemaking, he felt more optimistic. When his meeting with Hebert was over he intended to take his children for a drive and then, in the evening, they would dine at some restaurant along the Thames Valley where they were unknown, just to make comparisons.

It was eleven in the morning when Marcel got to the kitchen where the familiar bustle before Sunday lunch was in progress. The *sous-chef* was at work on one of the benches and from the ovens already came the enticing smell of roasting meat: the traditional English lunch was well under way. The pastry chef was busy at his table with his delightful confections, and various minions scuttled in and out between the gleaming steel pans and cauldrons, the ovens and scrubbed wooden benches. But of André Hebert there was no sign.

Marcel wandered through the kitchens, stopping to inspect this dish or that, lifting the lid of a pot simmering on the stove to sniff the contents. He paused for a word with the pastry chef, who was making the mixture for the Yorkshire pudding even though he was a fellow country-man of Marcel's.

'I hear your Yorkshire pudding is excellent,' Marcel said with a chuckle. 'Well done, François.'

'Thank you Monsieur Laborde,' the chef smiled with

pleasure. 'Don't forget I learned how to make it at Claridges.'

'Then you were fortunate. I never learned how to make it.' Marcel looked at him. 'Is Monsieur Hebert here?'

François went on with his mixing, his tall chef's hat sliding to one side, the expression on his face noncommittal.

'I think you should ask Mr Hartman where he is. I really don't know.'

'Has he not been here this morning?' Marcel looked surprised.

'You really should speak to Mr Hartman, Monsieur,' the chef said diplomatically. 'It is not for me to comment.'

Feeling both surprised and a little ill at ease, Marcel went over to the *sous-chef* who was now discussing something with the *sommelier*, James. Both smiled as he approached and, in true Gallic fashion, shook hands. Then for a moment or two he discussed the wine with the wine waiter, the merits of the particular vineyards, shippers and vintages of the wines selected for the day. Finally James smiled and withdrew towards his cellar.

'Where is André?' Marcel enquired of the *sous-chef*.

'I have not seen him today, Monsieur Laborde.' John Hartman was carefully folding a thin strip of pastry over a saddle of lamb which he had allowed to cool.

'What do you mean you have not seen him today? It is not his day off, is it?'

'Not that I am aware, sir.'

'Is he ill?'

'I am not aware of that either, Monsieur Laborde.'

'Really, John, you must be straight with me,' Marcel said irritably. 'It is already eleven and he should be in the kitchen on a day like today when the hotel is full. I was not aware he would not be here. I understood Thursday to be his day off. He knows quite well we have an appointment on a Sunday.'

'I can't help you.'

The chef shook his head and Marcel's feeling of irritation began to turn to rage.

'When he does come down will you tell him I was here and that I am annoyed. If I do not see him, kindly ask him to telephone me. I shall be out for the rest of the day after lunch with my family.'

'Very well, sir.'

'Is everything in hand for lunch?'

'Yes, sir, and for dinner. Everything is prepared and perfectly under control.'

Marcel nodded and continued his weekly inspection of the kitchens, nodding and smiling to the workers there. But he felt instinctively that the atmosphere was not as it had been. There was some restraint, a lack of warmth, a cautiousness which rather disturbed him.

He was thinking about this as he went slowly upstairs and through the entrance lobby where Judith, dressed in an attractive lightweight grey spring suit with a red blouse, was inspecting the arrivals register. Momentarily Marcel paused, just out of sight, admiring what he saw: his elegant wife framed against the beautiful background of large bowls of artistically arranged spring flowers reflected in the shiny surfaces of mellowed, polished wood. Behind her stood the formally attired head receptionist and, behind him, hung the brass key rings of the various rooms glinting in the sun which streamed through the open door at the far end. Marcel gave a sigh and, resuming his walk, saw Judith look up, her face breaking into a smile as she saw him.

'Guess who's here, Marcel?'

'I have no idea, my dear.' He put a hand lightly on her arm to show her he had not forgotten the intimacy of the early morning.

'Leo Valenti arrived late last night.'

'Have you see him?'

'I only saw his name in the arrivals register.' She glanced at the head receptionist and closed the book.

'Is he alone?'

'Apparently.'

'Odd he didn't let you know he was coming.' Marcel frowned.

'Maybe he wants to surprise us in order to see what we are really like.'

Judith affectionately linked her arm through his. 'Are we ready? The children are eager to be off while the sun lasts.'

'Aren't we lunching here, darling?'

'I thought we'd picnic seeing it's such a fine day.'

'Excellent idea.' Marcel nodded and looked at the head receptionist.

'Have you any idea where Monsieur Hebert is, Arthur?'

'Isn't he downstairs?' The receptionist looked mystified.

'No.'

'Funny, now that you mention it I saw him go off to the golf course,' Judith said suddenly. 'It didn't register at the time. I was preoccupied with the list of arrivals and Valenti's name.'

Marcel gazed at her. 'You saw him go *where*?'

'He was carrying his clubs and dressed in plus fours. I imagined it was his day off, and that you would know about it. Well, that's what it looked like.'

'I know nothing about it. We always have a meeting on Sunday morning.'

'I never gave it a thought,' Judith said frowning. 'Perhaps he has forgotten.'

'Perhaps. Arthur,' Marcel said with an air of authority in his voice. 'Would you be kind enough to send one of the staff to fetch Monsieur Hebert from the golf course and remind him of our appointment? I shall wait for him in our flat. Perhaps,' Marcel turned to Judith, 'we should have a snack here, after all.'

'Is that wise, dear?' she said gently. 'To take him away from his game?'

'Yes it is wise, *and* necessary,' Marcel said shortly. 'He had an appointment with me, besides which,' Marcel glanced at his watch, 'he is supposed to be overseeing Sunday lunch, a very important occasion. Or perhaps, as it is so late, I should do it myself?'

'But what about John?' Judith, sensing a row, looked and sounded dismayed.

'John Hartman is perfectly capable; but he is *not* the chef.'

'He is in charge when André has *his* day off . . .'

'But that is not today and André is in charge. Yes I will go and take his place until he returns from his golf. *Golf!*'

And, with a sharp exclamation, Marcel went swiftly along the corridor and disappeared through the door that led to the kitchen.

Judith remained looking after him with a worried frown. The receptionist stood with the telephone still in his hands, his eyes on her face.

'What shall I do, Miss Prynne? Shall I send for Monsieur Hebert?'

'You'd better, Arthur. Or I don't know what will happen. As for our day out,' she looked sadly towards the sunshine flooding through the door, *'I think that's off.'*

The conversation had taken place very quietly, out of sound and sight of the guests, some of whom were making a late appearance. Many were dressed for walking and others were going towards the bar with papers under their arms. One or two were obviously going riding or were off to the golf course.

It was a happy, restful, relaxed atmosphere and Judith stood for a moment or two looking around her.

'Please telephone the nursery, Arthur, and tell Nanny that, for the moment, we shall not be taking the children for a drive.'

'Yes, madam,' the receptionist replied, reaching for the internal telephone.

Judith opened the arrivals register once more to check on Valenti's room number and then, when Arthur had conveyed her message, she dialled Valenti herself. After a few seconds he answered in his deep, gravelly voice.

'Valenti.'

'Leo. It's Judith Prynne.'

'Judith! How are *you*?'

'Very well, and you?'

'I'm fine.'

'I hope I didn't disturb you; but I wanted to welcome you to Aylestone.'

'And I want to tell you how very pleased I am to be here. How pleased, and how impressed.'

'You should have let us know you were coming. Marcel and I can't always keep an eye on arrivals.'

'I didn't wish to trouble you. Tell me, Judith, it's a lovely day. Do you have time for a drink before lunch?'

'That would be nice.'

'Shall I see you in the bar in . . . say, half an hour?'

'Perfect. Until then.'

'*Au revoir*.'

Judith replaced the phone, aware that something had happened to her. The feeling of calm, repose, of peace, had gone. Instead it was replaced by the churned-up feeling in her stomach of excitement, of anticipation. Immediately she forgot all about the conflict between her husband and the *maître-chef* and went up to her room to make sure that, for Mr Valenti, she looked her very best.

But why?

When she got down he was sitting in the window seat, his legs crossed, arms folded, looking towards the garden. He wore well-cut, well-pressed grey slacks and a blue pullover over a white open-necked shirt. He looked very casual but supremely elegant and, as he rose to greet her, she decided that everything he did would be done with grace, elegance and style as though he had been born to it. There was an air of stillness, repose about him which was curiously restful.

This was all the more remarkable when, as far as she knew, his family had been peasants from the Italian South who earned a living tilling the hard, ungrateful and unyielding soil.

Judith had changed into a light tweed check dress with a round neckline and a single row of pearls. Large buttons went as far as the waistline. She knew that this well-cut couture dress showed off her figure, and that high-heeled black calf shoes enhanced the effect. Her hair was brushed straight back from her brow and she wore tiny pearl clips on her ears.

'My dear Judith, how are you?' Leo looked admiringly at her as he took her hand. Then he gazed into her eyes. 'You must forgive me, but I feel we already know each other very well, although we only met once and that a few years ago.'

'That's a good sign,' Judith said lightly. 'How is my sister?'

'She's very well, but I only saw her for a short time.' Momentarily, she thought his face clouded. 'I was in Italy mainly to look for my son.'

'Looking?'

'He has a habit of going off, sometimes for weeks. Has Moira never mentioned this?'

'No, never.' Judith felt disturbed. 'Where does he go?'

'Oh, to the hills, the sea. As an artist he says he must be free. But, with a wife and two small children, I say he has others to consider.'

'Why would Moira not tell me?'

'Perhaps she didn't want to worry you – and,' Leo said with his charming, reassuring smile, 'Rikki always comes back. This time when he does, however, I shall tell him that I'll cut off his allowance if it happens again. Now . . . to more pleasant things. I have ordered a half-bottle of Veuve Clicquot. I think it is the perfect pre-prandial drink, don't you?'

'Perfect,' Judith said.

'And half a bottle is just enough.'

'Quite . . .'

'As for lunch . . . I hope you will be able to join me. Or is it not the done thing to be seen lunching with *la patronne*?'

'But I am only *la directrice*.'

'You do not own the hotel?' Leo looked surprised as the waiter appeared with the wine in a silver bucket. 'I thought it was your family home?' Valenti put a hand out to feel the bottle, frowned and said: 'A few minutes more, perhaps.' The waiter bowed and turned the small bottle covered with cubes of ice.

'It used to be my family home; but we no longer own it.'

'Then who owns it?'

'An organization called Jenner Securities. Really I'm very surprised you didn't know this.'

'Your sister said I must go and stay at "your hotel". She told me how it belonged to the family.'

'Of course we still have a large share; but not the majority.'

'That is too bad.' Leo clicked his tongue sympathetically, once again touching the champagne.

'I'm sorry it's not cold enough for you,' she said. 'It is kept in a very cold cellar.'

'Then perhaps it *is* cold enough.' Leo smiled at the waiter who seemed to appear out of nowhere, like the perfectly trained servant he was. 'Perhaps I'm too fussy.'

'You can never be fussy enough here, Leo. We aim for perfection. If you find the least thing not to your liking please let me know. However today the lunch should be all right as Marcel has taken charge of the kitchen.'

'Really. He is down there?' Valenti looked delighted. 'He *is* a very busy man.'

'He doesn't usually on a Sunday, but . . .' Judith paused as the hall porter who, from the corner of her eye, she had seen coming towards them, paused by her side.

'Yes, James?'

'Could I have a word with you, in private, Miss Prynne?'

'Of course.' Judith rose, excusing herself to Valenti, and went a few paces towards the door with James.

'What is it, James?'

'I'm afraid that Mr Hebert says he will finish his game. He refuses to return to the kitchen.'

'Did you tell him my husband expected him?'

'I think that message was quite firmly conveyed to him, madam. But he would not change his mind.'

'Very well, James. Thank you.'

'Should I tell Monsieur Laborde, madam?'

'Maybe you'd better. He should know exactly what's going on.'

'Thank you, madam.'

The hall porter bowed and went swiftly out of the door while Judith, rather slowly and thoughtfully, went back to her guest.

'Trouble?' Valenti enquired, studying her face.

'Just a small problem. It will be sure to sort itself out by the time we have finished lunch.'

'Good. Then we *are* eating together.'

'Naturally,' Judith said with a smile. 'Is the champagne now chilled to your satisfaction?'

The dining room was full, but the meal was perfectly served without a hitch. Judith only had a light collation and Leo Valenti had a full meal including roast beef.

'Perfect,' he pronounced when he had finished. 'Your

husband is a master chef. Tell me,' he looked at her with a perceptive air, 'has something gone wrong in the kitchen?'

'Does it show?'

'Nothing to do with the food, I assure you; or the service. Both were impeccable. But your sister told me that I should go at the weekend because Marcel had a day off on Sunday. She thought I would enjoy spending time with both of you.'

'Today that was not possible,' Judith murmured. 'But as yet I can't tell you why, simply because I don't know the real reason.'

'I see,' Valenti smiled. 'Every good hotelier I have ever known – and I have known many – has had this gift for discretion, without giving offence. I see you are one of them. Was it always something you wanted to do?'

'No.'

'But you trained in Switzerland, I understand. You see, I know a lot about you.'

She refused to be distracted by the caress in his voice, and replied matter-of-factly:

'Yes, I trained in Switzerland but it was *not* always something I wanted to do. When I was about eighteen it became obvious that we could no longer afford to live here. The family simply hadn't the means. My parents opposed turning it into a hotel. They wanted to sell it; but I rather liked the idea, so did my brother.'

'Douglas I have yet to meet.'

'You will this evening. It is true that Marcel and I usually have Sunday off; but not today. Doug will be here about seven.' Judith looked at her watch. 'I'll introduce you.'

'I shall look forward to that.'

Valenti had a hearty appetite. He finished his lunch with perfectly made, creamy rice pudding.

'Now that,' he said, almost licking his lips, 'I call a good meal. A very good, perfectly cooked English meal. Tell me,' he glanced round the room, 'may I smoke?'

'Of course.'

'Some people don't approve of it these days, especially in America, because of the supposed link with cancer of the lung.'

'In that case perhaps you'd better not,' Judith said with a smile when, to her astonishment, Valenti impulsively clasped her hand.

'Sorry . . .' he said, releasing it immediately, and fumbled in his pockets for a match but the waiter, inevitably hovering, came forward with a light. Valenti took his time about lighting his cigarette and then, exhaling, sat back in his chair.

'I'm sorry. I shouldn't have done that. Seized your hand . . .'

'That's perfectly all right. I feel complimented.'

'Of course you would say that. You're most gracious, just like your sister. Like all your family, I suppose. I am, as you probably know, the son of an Italian peasant. Sometimes I forget my manners. We are an impulsive race . . . but still I must tell you, Judith, I find you most attractive. I hope you're not offended. It is a case of a man admiring a beautiful woman . . .'

Suddenly Judith was aware of a noise that seemed to rise over the heads of the diners, and made everyone look up in surprise. It was a roar that reverberated about the dining room and then it died down again like the aftermath of an avalanche and, in an instant, Judith saw the *maître d'hôtel* Simon Raeburn look up in alarm from his desk and then glance in her direction.

'Excuse me,' Judith drew back her chair. 'I'll join you for coffee in the lounge . . . when you're ready.' She glanced at his cigarette and then, as calmly as she could, and with reassuring glances towards her guests, many of whom she knew, she hurried through the double doors into the kitchen, from which the noise had come.

As she thrust them open she clasped her hands in horror

178

to her face at the sight of the scene confronting her. For, in the centre, engaged like two combatants in a ring, were her husband, dressed in white, and André Hebert, still wearing his golf clothes, his heavy checked sweater and plus fours. Round and round they went, each man violently clutching the arms of the other like wrestlers while the staff, registering various kinds of emotion from shock to unalloyed pleasure, stood in a circle watching.

The faces of both men were red; each muttered imprecations under his breath as round and round they continued to go, neither seeming to have any chance of gaining control over the other.

With a swift intake of breath Judith crossed the room and, grasping Marcel's arm, tugged at him. She signalled to John Hartman, who was standing by one of the stoves with a look of stupefaction on his face, to do the same thing with Hebert.

'Stop it, I say,' Judith cried in a ringing voice. 'Do you know you could hear this in the dining room?'

For a moment neither man took any notice of her and then, as if what she had said had at last percolated into their brains, they stopped, each leaning exhaustedly on the other, sweat pouring from their faces.

Marcel at length released his opponent and Hebert stood back with John Hartman; but both protagonists continued to glare at each other as if it would take very little to start them up again.

'Did you hear what I said?' Judith hissed. 'It was heard in the dining room. Do you want to destroy the reputation this hotel has tried so hard to achieve, at a stroke? This sort of thing I cannot and will not have. Do you understand?' She shook Marcel vigorously by his arm, while his look of anger turned immediately to remorse.

'You heard it in the dining room?' he whispered hoarsely.

'Yes and, for a moment, all the diners stopped eating. I don't think anyone could believe their ears.'

'Then I apologize,' Marcel said humbly, standing with his back to the wall. 'I'm afraid that I completely lost control of myself. It is a thing that has never happened before. Never. But you must know, Judith,' tenderly he touched the side of his face, 'André Hebert struck me first. I'm afraid it was something I could not tolerate.'

'He *struck* you?' Judith repeated, looking at the *maître-chef*, incongruously clad in plus fours, who remained by the side of John Hartman as if turned to stone.

'Across the face.' Gingerly Marcel fingered the spot. 'I'm afraid I cannot tolerate his presence on these premises for a moment longer. I must demand his dismissal.'

'Look,' Judith glanced anxiously at Hartman. 'I think you should come upstairs . . .'

'Out of the question. Luncheon is not yet finished.' Marcel flung out his arms and began vigorously to roll up his sleeves. 'Meanwhile please get that animal out of my sight.'

'Would you come with me, please,' Judith said urgently to Hebert. '*If* you please . . .'

'I'm afraid I am not answerable to you, Miss Prynne.' Hebert now had the air of a man who had regained control of himself. 'I am directly responsible to Sir Matthew and he is not here.'

'You are answerable to my husband,' Judith said, leaning towards him. 'All the kitchen staff are. Now please leave this kitchen at once, as he has requested.'

'I'm afraid I can't.' Mulishly, Hebert crossed his hands in an attitude of rebellion. 'I am answerable only to the Chairman of the Group.'

'You are answerable to *me*, do you hear?' Marcel's voice began to rise again. '*Me. I* am the *directeur de cuisine*. You are answerable to me; but have no fear. That state of affairs will not continue for much longer. From now you are dismissed and you had better go upstairs, pack your bags and leave, or neither I, nor my wife, will be responsible for the consequences.'

'I'm afraid that is out of the question.' Hebert's voice also rose. 'I am not answerable to you or Miss Prynne and neither of you has the power to dismiss me. In fairness to the hotel, which does have a reputation, largely built up by me, I will now leave this kitchen and return to my room. But I shall be back at four and I shall expect you to be out of here, Mr Laborde, from this moment. Because I shall not tolerate *your* interference in the affairs of my kitchen for a moment longer, and when Sir Matthew does hear of this I will tell him quite clearly: either you go, or I go.' And, picking up his golf bag, André Hebert, invested with a curious kind of dignity, made his way solemnly to the door while those around him stood back to allow him to pass. No further word was spoken.

Matthew Jenner, summoned from his country house, stood with his back to the fire in the general manager's private office. He had arrived at eight while dinner was in full swing under the command of André Hebert. Judith, who had spent the afternoon trying to reason with Marcel, was pale but controlled, and she sat in her chair, arms crossed, gazing at the chairman of the group, to whom she had just told the story from beginning to end. Marcel had decided to remain in their quarters, thinking Judith was the best person to deal with the situation.

'Mmm,' Jenner reached in his pocket for his cigarette case. 'Tricky.'

'Did you ever tell André Hebert he was answerable only to you?'

'Of course I didn't.'

'Then he is answerable to Marcel?'

'Yes . . . I suppose so. To you and Marcel.'

181

'What do you mean?' Judith interjected. 'Either he is or he isn't.'

'It has never really been defined, has it?' The chairman looked uncomfortable.

'But Marcel is *directeur de cuisine* of this hotel. That *is* defined.'

'Yes, but we have never said that the *maître-chef* is responsible to him. It's a funny situation, one we never thought would bring trouble.'

'Nevertheless, Matt, one *assumes* that if he is not responsible to Marcel, he is at least responsible to *me* . . .'

'I suppose I'd better have a word with him,' Jenner said after a while. Judith raised her head in astonishment.

'You mean you're going over our heads?'

'But my dear I must, mustn't I? After all, you sent for me.'

'I sent for you to dismiss him. He will only take dismissal from you.'

'Yes, but I can't dismiss him until I've heard his story. It wouldn't be fair.'

'Then you're undermining our authority.' Judith rose and went to the window, swiftly drawing the curtains now that it was getting dark outside. It was silent too, except for the late song of a solitary blackbird. With what nostalgia she recalled this peaceful sound from her childhood . . . last thing at night and first thing in the morning. When at last she turned, Matthew was lighting his cigarette and she thought that, in the light of the flame, she saw a gleam of triumph in his eyes.

'Matthew,' she said, pausing so as to choose her words carefully and deliberately. 'I think you can say that we have a crisis here. It is the first real crisis since Aylestone was reopened. Marcel, as you know, is a man with very strict principles. He will not have his word undermined by someone who is responsible to him, and there is no doubt in my mind, none at all, that that was the situation between

Marcel and André Hebert who was personally engaged by him. It was also Hebert's turn to be on duty today. That is not in question. He flagrantly chose to play golf, thus precipitating this state of affairs.'

'But what has happened between them to cause this?' Matthew blew smoke into the air. 'Why did Hebert deliberately go off to play golf when he knew he had a meeting with Marcel?'

'I don't know. He won't tell me. In fact he refuses to address a word to me.'

'Then something is obviously wrong, isn't it, Judith?'

'Obviously.'

'Very wrong, and I must see what is the cause of it and why. It's only just that I should hear his story.'

'You must support us, Matt. That is just, too. If not you undermine the entire foundation on which our authority is based.'

'I must be fair.' Matthew appeared to hesitate. 'I must be *seen* to behave justly. Look, if you like I will ask Hebert to appear here in front of you. If I command it, he must do it.'

'All right,' Judith said, uttering a sigh. 'I agree. But Marcel . . .'

Matthew interrupted her to shake his head.

'No Marcel,' he said. 'I absolutely insist on that.'

Hebert came very unwillingly to the interview. He kept his employer waiting until dinner had been served and, when he appeared in his chef's uniform, his manner was arrogant. He looked disdainfully across at Judith sitting on a chair in a corner of the room. Her hands were tightly clenched, and she looked very pale.

'I asked Miss Prynne to be here,' Matthew said before Hebert could speak.

'Nevertheless I would rather see you alone, Sir Matthew.'

183

'I'm afraid she must be here,' Matthew replied patiently. 'She is the managing director of the hotel.'

'I'm not having Laborde then.' Hebert pronounced the name contemptuously.

'Miss Prynne has agreed that it will just be you, me and herself. Now, Hebert, I understand you said you will only be answerable to me?'

'That is correct.' Hebert was sweating profusely, whether from nerves or the heat of the kitchen it was impossible to say. 'I have never understood I was answerable to her, and I must tell you Sir Matthew that I will no longer take orders from her husband. That is *final* . . .' Hebert gesticulated wildly in emphasis. 'Quite final.'

'But why is this, André?' Matthew said gently. 'He is a fine chef.'

'I am a fine chef too. I am *maître-chef*. I was *not sous-chef* when I was appointed. You know that I was trained at the Hotel Montcalm in Nice, one of the finest hotels in the south of France. I considered it an insult to be *under* the instructions of Monsieur Laborde, much as I admire his reputation; to *be forced* to discuss my menus with him . . .'

'Nevertheless you did agree,' Judith said quietly. 'And you have done it for a year and a half . . .'

'But no longer,' Hebert interrupted her. 'Not for a second longer do I agree. That is suspended now, at once, for all time . . .'

'Then why did you not *say*, instead of doing it in this rather discourteous fashion?' Matthew demanded.

'I had to make a stand, Sir Matthew. I thought this was the best way to do it. Action, I thought, not words. I will *show* them I no longer mean to continue like this. I will *not* be under the control of Mr Laborde. I am *maître-chef*. That is all.'

'But Marcel is one of the finest chefs in the country.'

'So am *I* one of the finest chefs in the country.' Hebert

184

thrust out his chest. 'I do not need Laborde to tell *me* what to cook or how to cook it. I do not require him to buy for me. I will make my own menus myself, and do my own buying myself. Either that . . . or I go,' and he thrust a menacing finger in the air, waving it melodramatically around his head.

'Supposing I let you go then,' Matthew said. 'Is *that* what you want?'

Hebert shook his head vigorously.

'No sir. It is not what I want. I like it here. I like Aylestone, and I work very hard for it, for you, for my guests who send me many compliments about my marvellous food.' Hebert theatrically put his fingers to his lips and kissed them. 'If *I* go who will you get? Monsieur Laborde? But who will cook for him in London? Even he, that marvellous chef, cannot be in two places at once . . .'

'Please don't be so *rude*,' Judith burst out. 'Your tone of voice is *most* insulting.' Hebert looked at her in some surprise.

'Really, Miss Prynne, I do not intend to be rude. Your husband is an inspired chef. You tell me so, he certainly tells me so constantly; but others say I am as good as he is. I am marvellous too. Everyone tells me. So, is it not logical that each of us, marvellous in our way, should be in our own kitchens, in charge of our own cuisine?'

And with that he paused expectantly, looking boldly from one to the other.

Finally Matthew, who appeared to have heard this tirade with a good deal of instinctive sympathy, looked first at Hebert, to whom he smiled, and then at Judith.

'Do you know, Judith, I really think he has a point,' he said softly.

Chapter 10

There was a tap on the door, and Judith called: 'Come in,' without looking round.

'I just wanted to say goodbye,' a quiet voice said behind her. Judith swung round in her chair and, standing up, put out her hand.

'I'm terribly sorry,' she said. 'I sort of stood you up yesterday.'

'I gathered it was something you couldn't help.' Leo Valenti came into the room with that easy familiarity of a person who feels he is welcome everywhere. He wore a single-breasted blue barathea suit with a white shirt and a dark tie. Everything about him, from his attire to the faint perfume of expensive after-shave, was quiet, tasteful, restrained yet, somehow, with a hint of opulence. 'Some crisis in the kitchen?' he enquired, taking her extended hand.

'I'm afraid so. I was caught up all day, though I should have tried to send you a message.'

'Was Marcel included?'

Judith pointed to a chair. 'Very much so, but I don't want to bore you with the dramas of this hotel.'

'But I'm interested, really.' Leo seemed reluctant to let go of her hand, but did so, sitting in the chair indicated by Judith. 'I also dabble in the hotel business. I am keen to extend my involvement.'

'Really?'

'Oh yes, not in this country, perhaps, but certainly in Europe. I already own a hotel and casino in Palm Beach, and hotels in Amalfi, Palermo and Corsica, plus a chain of fast-food restaurants in Canada.'

'Is that why you wanted to look at us?' Judith put her head on one side.

Leo assumed a curiously enigmatic expression. 'One never knows, does one? Let's say I was interested to see what it was like. And it is good. Excellent. First class. A very high standard.'

'Thank you.' Judith lowered her head. 'I'm afraid, however, yesterday's fracas won't have impressed you.'

Leo leaned forward to reassure her.

'But it happens *everywhere*, my dear, even in the best hotels.'

'I don't think so.' Judith's eyes looked troubled as they met his.

'But I assure you it does.'

'It wouldn't happen in the Ritz.'

'It *does* happen in the Ritz. I was staying there once before the war when their entire staff staged a sit-in.'

'Really?' Judith looked surprised. 'What happened?'

'I think the admirable Monsieur Auzello saved the situation; but it was very unpleasant for the management, I can tell you, and much much more serious than what happened here yesterday.'

'Well, it's good of you to say so.' Judith rose and wandered over to the window.

'You may confide in me, you know,' Valenti went on. 'After all, I am family.'

'It's kind of you . . . well.' At last she had what she had always wanted, a confidant, and, impulsively, Judith turned towards him. 'Marcel and the *maître-chef*, Hebert, do not get on. Yesterday Hebert issued an ultimatum.'

'And what was that?'

'Either he left or Marcel . . .'

Leo nodded sagely, absorbing it all.

'And what did you do?'

'I had to send for Matthew Jenner, as chairman and president of the group which now owns Aylestone.'

'He was here last night?'

'Hebert insisted. He would only talk to him.'

'And what happened? He supported your husband, of course.'

'He didn't, as a matter of fact. He thought the incumbent *maître-chef* more important than the *directeur de cuisine*. There's some sense in this. Marcel only comes here in a consultative capacity and Hebert is very good; but it was the way it was done. It was badly done.'

'There was a confrontation?'

'Exactly. Hebert went off to play golf when he should have been in consultation with Marcel. By this discourtesy he forced the issue . . .'

'And what did your husband do?' Leo's expression was sympathetic, his voice gentle.

'He went back to London last night. He was very angry. He wanted me to go with him, but I couldn't.'

'You run the place yourself?'

'I am the managing director, though my brother is the general manager. One of us always tries to be here. We have a resident manager, but he is relatively junior and last night Matthew Jenner told me he thought Doug should move in. Doug wouldn't like that.'

'But what will *you* do?'

'Well,' Judith shrugged, 'funnily enough, Marcel and I talked only this weekend of severing our connection with Aylestone. We own a restaurant and we would like to own a hotel. This may decide it.'

'Where would you like to own the hotel?' Leo enquired idly.

'I'm keen on Scotland. I have actually seen one I rather like.' She stopped as she saw Leo shaking his head, his arms folded against his chest.

'What is it?' Judith asked.

'Scotland is too far . . . what about here?'

'Aylestone? But we couldn't possibly afford it. Do you know how much it's worth?'

'I can guess.'

'It's out of the question.'

Now Leo rose and joined her beside the window. For a moment he stood there brooding, gazing towards the river.

'It may not be,' he said at last, turning round. 'You never know, it may not be.'

'Besides, Matthew wouldn't sell.' Judith vigorously shook her head. 'He's very proud of it. Also it is profitable.'

'But does he own it or his company?'

'His company.'

'And that is Jenner Securities?'

'Yes.'

'I see.' Leo produced a notebook and briefly wrote something in it.

'What's that for?' Judith tried to peep over his shoulder.

Leo snapped his notebook shut and said, with a teasing note in his voice, 'Just writing a little note to myself.' He shook down his shirt cuffs and glanced at his watch.

'Now, my dear, I must go. But let me tell you this.' He placed both hands on her shoulders and looked into her eyes. 'You are a very smart lady, Judith Prynne. I like you and I believe in you and, if you ever find yourself short of capital for any project, anything you have in mind, anything at all, will you let me know?'

Judith stared at him, mesmerized like a rabbit by those dark, compelling eyes, but she could not find the words to answer.

'I mean it,' Leo said, softly tightening his grip on her shoulders. 'Think about it. And now, goodbye.'

And before she could recover her speech he was gone.

All during the spring and summer of that year Judith concentrated on trying to establish Aylestone's reputation

189

as one of the most luxurious hotels in the country. She put out of her mind the struggle for power between Marcel and André Hebert because that had already been lost. There was no point in pursuing it. André had achieved a *fait accompli*. The result was that Marcel refused ever to set foot in the hotel again.

It was not a particularly happy time for Judith, who came to realize that there was more to running a successful hotel than a knowledge of how one thought things ought to be. Three years in Switzerland, restaurant experience and common sense were not enough. She wondered if one could discover all one needed to know in a lifetime.

The trouble was that she was surrounded by true professionals. Most of the important staff had been in the business for a very long time, and this was one of the reasons why Hebert, an artist in his own right, had refused to be subject to Marcel. Yet if Hebert had handled the matter badly so had they, and it was something she learned from.

In fact most of the staff could teach her things she didn't know. The *maître d'hôtel* had trained at the Savoy as a young *commis* waiter, had slowly climbed the ladder from station waiter to *chef de rang*, then head waiter and, finally, *maître d'hôtel* in charge of the dining room. He had served in many large and famous hotels including the Savoy, the Carlton in Cannes and the Gritti in Venice. The head receptionist had begun his career at the Ritz in Paris and had worked at the Ritz in London, Brown's and the Connaught. All of the station waiters had been at their work a number of years, and the *sommelier* had learned his craft at many of the best hotels in Burgundy, Bordeaux and Champagne.

Even the bill clerk was trilingual and had made up the accounts for some of the greatest names at some of the best hotels in Europe, and the housekeeper had learned her business in Switzerland and had worked in America, the West Indies and the Grand Hotel, Manchester.

It was, in fact, in these rather practical, mundane areas that Judith experienced a lot of trouble that summer. One morning Madge, the bill clerk, came to her with an account for £2,500 in her hands due from a guest who was on the point of leaving.

Judith had been telephoning some orders from the office behind the reception and, as she put the phone down, Madge came up to her and presented an account made out in the name of Samuel G. Brown of New York, a well-known financier who had brought a male companion for a few days' golf.

'Yes, Madge?' Judith cast her eye expertly over the bill. 'Is there something wrong with this?'

'Mr Brown asks that it be sent to his company. In New York.' There was an edge to Madge's voice.

'Do they have an arrangement with us?'

'No, Miss Prynne.'

'Then tell him that, most regretfully, we cannot oblige.'

'I have already told him, Miss Prynne, and he got quite angry.'

Judith sighed. 'I see. Where is he now?'

'He's in the hall, madam. All his bags are packed and he's in rather a temper.'

Judith squared her shoulders, opened the wood-panelled door into the hall where Mr Brown and his guest were waiting, not attempting to conceal their impatience and surrounded by an expensive collection of leather suitcases and two golf bags complete with umbrella. Brown wore an overcoat and his hat rested on the pile of luggage. His companion was gazing at the paintings on the wall with the air of a connoisseur. Both looked up as Judith, a gracious smile on her face, came towards them.

'Mr Brown,' she said, putting out her hand. 'So you are leaving us?'

'Oh, Miss Prynne.' Disarmed, Brown too smiled as he shook hands. 'We have had a wonderful time. Unfortunately there is some little altercation with your accounts clerk. The girl doesn't seem to know her business.'

'Oh yes she does, and she *is* acting on quite specific instructions, Mr Brown.' Judith assumed a tone that was at once placating yet authoritative. 'We cannot accept that bills are paid by a company unless there is a prior arrangement. In your case there appears not to be.'

'But you know my company, Miss Prynne,' Mr Brown blustered. 'It's internationally famous.'

'But, unfortunately, without an arrangement with us. If you would care to have this seen to we shall, of course, be most happy to make arrangements for you in future.'

'In that case I'm afraid there will be no future, Miss Prynne,' Brown snapped back, signalling to his guest.

'I am very sorry about that, Mr Brown, and I do hope that you will change your mind but, in the meantime, and on this occasion, I'm afraid I must insist on payment before you leave.'

'And if I don't?' Brown said, drawing himself up and gazing at her haughtily.

'Oh, but I'm sure you will, Mr Brown.' Judith pointed to a table with an eloquent gesture. 'It is management policy. Would you care to sit down and make out your cheque?'

Mr Brown's guest, looking by now most embarrassed, finished his close examination of the pictures and strolled over to his friend.

'Can I take care of that for you, Sam?'

'Of course not,' Brown said furiously.

'Please do let me, if it is an embarrassment,' the guest insisted.

'I assure you it is no embarrassment. Just a matter of principle.'

'Better pay up, Sam,' the friend said with a laconic air.

'I, personally, would sure be disappointed not to be able to play here again.'

'Well . . .' Brown looked indecisively from his friend to Judith, to the table, and back again.

'Best pay up.' The guest steered his friend in the direction of the table.

'Well . . .' Sam said, but he had already reached into his breast pocket for his cheque book.

'Whew!' Judith murmured when she reached the safe haven of her room again. This was the sort of thing one learned from experience. But, like all hotels, they had had several bad accounts and several dishonoured cheques. One couldn't take chances.

She went into her small kitchen to reactivate the coffee percolator when there was a tap on the door and the assistant manager, Neil Beaumont, put his head round.

'May I have a word, Miss Prynne?'

'Of course,' Judith said brightly, but her heart sank. There was something in his tone that presaged another crisis. 'Would you like coffee, Neil?'

'No thank you, Miss Prynne.'

Judith poured her coffee and came into the room stirring it. She liked Neil, but he was a new member of staff and relatively inexperienced. This was his first senior appointment in management. She felt they had taken a gamble in appointing him because he lacked the authority of an older man, although the staff seemed to like and respect him. What, for instance, would Neil have done the night Marcel and André had had their fight in the kitchen?

As resident manager, however, he was in charge when she or Doug were absent from the hotel; and she often wondered if his thirty-year-old shoulders were strong enough for the responsibility.

'Now, Neil.' Judith sat down and pointed to a chair, but Neil remained standing, a letter in his hand.

'I thought you ought to see this, Miss Prynne,' he said, holding it out to her. 'I have tried with Mrs Malcolm; but she can be a very obstinate lady. I knew something like this would happen one day.'

'Oh dear, what is it now?' Frowning, Judith took the letter which was headed by the crest of a distinguished, titled family, her eyes skimming over it quickly.

Dear Sir Matthew,

As you know I have stayed in your excellent hotel, Aylestone, a number of times and on each occasion my wife and I have enjoyed ourselves better than the time before.

However, there is one point I felt I should raise with you, because it might determine our attitude towards staying at Aylestone in future. It might also be affecting other guests.

The point is that we always feel that on the morning of our departure there is a rush to get us out. One day we came up from breakfast and our beds were already stripped and the chambermaids hard at work. As we pay until noon we expect to be allowed the comfort of our room until that time.

However on the last occasion we were there we were trying to enjoy a cup of coffee when the maid knocked on our door and said she had instructions to do the room as it was wanted by another guest. I pointed out that it was only eleven and that we had another hour at our disposal. With that she seemed content, apologized and withdrew.

Hardly any time had elapsed before another lady appeared who said she was the housekeeper and it was she who had instructed the maid to do our room. She said the hotel was short-staffed and would we please allow her the facilities to do it at that instant? I refused, whereupon this lady became quite unpleasant. She said it was wanted for an 'important' guest and her manner was brusque. I mentioned that I knew you personally, but it didn't seem to help at all.

I wonder . . .

The letter then went on to more personal matters and Judith, with a sigh, put it on her lap.

'Lord Avery. Rather a pompous individual, but not someone we would wish to annoy. He *is* right, though . . .'

'But not reasonable,' Neil said.

'Reasonable or not, he has paid a lot of money for a room he was not due to vacate for another hour. And anyway we are not short of staff.'

'I think you had better have a word yourself with Mrs Malcolm,' Neil said. 'I told her the same thing and *she* told me to mind my own business. I do find her rather hard to deal with, Miss Prynne. She's not at all co-operative with me. I feel she resents me.'

'On the other hand she *is* excellent at her job,' Judith murmured. 'She is extremely competent and I should hate to lose her.'

'Sir Matthew sent this round by hand. He asked me to deal with it at once. I think he's written to Lord Avery to apologize.'

'Blast Lord Avery,' Judith said putting her fingers to her temples and massaging them. 'OK, Neil, I'll deal with this.'

'Thank you, Miss Prynne.'

As Neil prepared to depart Judith said:

'Anything else, Neil?'

'No, Miss Prynne, not at the moment.'

'Are you happy with us?'

'Yes, very much so. I mean, usually I can get on with all members of staff, but Mrs Malcolm . . .'

'I'll talk to her later on.' Judith pulled towards her a pile of letters and papers that had to be dealt with.

But, after the door had closed, she put her head back against the chair and closed her eyes.

Sometimes it was all a bit much . . . and for what? To have someone like Matthew Jenner, perfectly within his rights, go over her head? She knew then that she would not go on for much longer like this; that, one day, she wanted to be the overall boss. And suddenly she thought of Leo Valenti and her mind lingered on him for some time.

* * *

195

After an hour or so Judith had finished dictating replies to letters, enquiries and various items to her secretary who also worked for Doug and Neil. Stella Foakes was a young married woman who lived locally, and was ideal for the job, which she enjoyed. She was always a fresh, pleasing presence and Judith liked her and working with her.

'There you are, Stella, that's the lot for the day.'

'Thank you, Miss Prynne.' Stella got up, carefully straightening her skirt as she did. She was a neat, fastidious dresser and sometimes helped out in the reception if one of the staff were away or ill.

'Now I must go and see Mrs Malcolm,' Judith murmured, gazing at her watch.

'Will you be going up to London later today, Miss Prynne?'

'Probably this evening. Is there something I can get you?'

'No it wasn't that.' Stella gazed at her well-kept, highly polished shoes. 'I wondered if Mr Prynne would be in charge, that's all.'

'I expect so. I mean, he's due here at five. Why do you ask?'

'It's just that Mr Prynne has a whole lot of letters to sign from yesterday.'

'But didn't he come here last night?'

'I don't think so, Miss Prynne.'

Judith frowned. The previous evening she had gone over to see the family and it had been very late when she had got back.

'I'll have a word with him, Stella. Maybe he forgot.'

'I don't think he was here, Miss Prynne. His room looked as though he hadn't been in it.'

'You mean Neil was in charge by himself?'

'It looks like that, Miss Prynne.'

'Well, Doug should have mentioned it to me. Oh dear.'

Judith put her hand to her throbbing temples again. 'Sometimes I feel there is too much for me to do.'

'I think there is, Miss Prynne. It's not for me to say but, personally, I don't think you have the support you need. You have been looking very tired.'

'Gosh, does it show?' Judith leapt to her feet and went to examine her face in the mirror.

'In my opinion, Miss Prynne – and it's probably not my place to say it – but neither Mr Prynne nor Mr Beaumont are in your class. They can't deal with things the way you deal with them. They haven't the skills or the experience. A lot goes on here that you know nothing about.'

'No, it *isn't* your place to say it, Stella,' Judith said gently, anxious not to lose a good secretary. 'But thank you, nevertheless, for thinking of me. I'll take your point.'

She crossed the room and opened the door to let the young woman out, then she followed her until she came to the winding staircase at the intersection that had previously been the wall between the family wing and the hotel. To her right was the linen room that served the whole hotel.

It was a large, sunny room overlooking the back of the hotel, and stacked on shelves, row upon row, were the linen sheets, towels, pillowcases, soaps and other essentials for the comfort of guests. In the centre were some large wicker boxes which had just returned from the laundry, and at a table in the corner, her back turned to the door, was the capable Mrs Malcolm wearing a white coat.

Judith paused and caught her breath, aware that her hands were tightly clenched. Of all the staff she least liked Doris Malcolm, though she appreciated her qualities. She had not been responsible for appointing her. This had been done by Doug when she and Marcel had been in France on holiday. At the sound of the door gently closing Mrs Malcolm merely turned her head, but continued checking the lists of laundry just returned in the baskets.

'Good morning, Mrs Malcolm,' Judith said pleasantly.

'Morning, Miss Prynne. Excuse me if I don't stop. I am very busy.'

'I would, however, like to talk to you,' Judith said, standing by the side of the table and looking at the grim, set face staring at the rows of lists.

Doris Malcolm was a woman of thirty-five, about whom little of her personal life was known, except that there was no Mr Malcolm. Whether he was dead or divorced no one knew. Doris didn't live in. She was meticulous, punctilious and did her job well. There was usually no need to ask questions. In appearance she had a rather faded prettiness: pale blonde hair caught by a clip to one side, blue eyes, and a face whose pallor seemed to testify to the many hours she spent inside counting and arranging linen. She had a thin, purposeful mouth that seldom smiled. On occasions this could make her look very severe.

'If it's about Lord Avery, I'm afraid I haven't the time,' Doris said without looking up again. 'I'm far too busy for trivial complaints.'

'Yes, it *is* about Lord Avery,' Judith said firmly. '*And* others.'

'Others?' Doris's head jerked up. 'I was not aware of others.'

'I understand there *have* been others.'

'Who told you?' Doris enquired sharply.

'I am not prepared to say; but I do know there have been complaints from guests required to leave their rooms before noon.'

'We can't run a hotel if people won't leave their rooms,' Doris said sullenly, and Judith mentally noted the 'we'.

'Nevertheless, I'm afraid that if guests insist on staying until noon they are entitled to.'

'Some of the girls have their lunch at noon. There is a lot to do.'

'Mrs Malcolm.' Judith bent her head so that the house-keeper was forced to look at her. 'In that case you must

198

arrange a rota. Not every guest in every room wants to stay there until noon. It is also quite untrue to say we are short-staffed. We most certainly are not. This is a luxury, first-class hotel. Our guests pay a lot of money for their comfort, which must be seen to. We must not offend them, if we can help it.'

'I'm glad you say *if* we can help it,' Mrs Malcolm said with spirit.

'I'm afraid I don't quite know what you mean, Mrs Malcolm.' Judith crossed her hands in front of her and prepared for a fight. 'Are *you* trying to tell me something?'

'Yes, I am.' Mrs Malcolm whipped off the pair of large horn-rimmed spectacles she was wearing and Judith was amazed by the rage in her eyes. 'I notice you don't mention your *husband* or your *brother*, or any of your family when it comes to offending people in this hotel.'

'I don't know what you mean,' Judith said stiffly.

'Oh don't you indeed? Not that terrible row the day your husband had a fight . . . *or* your brother who flirts with the women guests? Your father seems to feel it is the duty of guests to play golf with *him*. He gets offended if they don't, and what about your mother who gets drunk at the bar? Remember the night she fell off the bar stool?'

'That's enough,' Judith snapped sharply.

'*I* don't think it's enough, Miss Prynne.' Mrs Malcolm leaned towards her, pale eyes gleaming. 'A lot goes on here that you don't know, don't care about. If only you opened your eyes . . .'

'I assure you, Mrs Malcolm, I am fully aware of what goes on.' Once again Judith thought of Leo Valenti, remembering his words '. . . even in the best hotels'.

'If you ask me, you're blind, Miss Prynne. You're unfit . . .'

'Mrs Malcolm, I must warn you . . .' Judith raised a warning finger but the housekeeper, clearly beside herself, rudely brushed it aside.

'I'll say what I like.'

'In that case,' Judith said firmly, 'I'm afraid you will have to consider your position here terminated, from this moment. When you have packed and vacated your room, kindly call into the office and get your cards and a month's salary in lieu of notice.'

'I certainly shan't, Miss Prynne,' Mrs Malcolm said, also joining her hands in front of her. 'I have no intention of going, any more than Mr Hebert did. *He* stuck to his guns, didn't he? He won.'

'That was a very different situation. He was indispensable. You, I'm glad to say, are not.'

'I still refuse to go.'

'You'll have to, I'm afraid.'

'I insist on seeing Sir Matthew.'

'Mrs Malcolm.' Judith leaned wearily against one of the wooden racks. 'Please do not presume to put yourself in the same category as Mr Hebert, who is a chef of international standing. Please don't think, either, that, valuable though your work is, you are as important as he is. I may not have agreed with what happened, but I was personally involved. Do you honestly think Sir Matthew has the time to come and see you? If so, I'm afraid you have an exaggerated idea of the office you hold. I frankly could do your job myself, because I've done it before. Even if you were to see Sir Matthew, I'm sure he would support me as the complaint about Lord Avery's treatment has come from him. Now,' Judith leaned forward and deftly removed the lists from under the housekeeper's nose. 'I shall continue checking these while you go upstairs and pack.' She looked up at the clock. 'I think I would like *you* to be out of your room by noon, if you don't mind.'

The peremptory dismissal of Doris Malcolm provoked deep stirrings of discontent, the strength of which surprised Judith, who had not imagined such a cold person would be so popular. Previously she had had occasion to dismiss one or two waiters, a kitchen maid, a porter; but the house-keeper in a hotel was a person of authority, and wielded a lot of power. Because of the lack of information the staff obviously felt keenly that an injustice had been done.

The first to express his unease was Neil Beaumont, who was quickly followed by Simon Raeburn, the *maître d'hôtel*, who had been in the business since he was sixteen. Like all the staff he was very experienced and he obviously felt embarrassed about approaching his employer. Judith was surprised to see him too. She was on her way to the linen room when he knocked on her door. She asked him to come in and sit down.

'I'm afraid it is about Mrs Malcolm, Miss Prynne.'

'You too, Simon?' Judith said, sitting back.

'Someone else has spoken to you?' He looked surprised.

'Neil Beaumont, and I expect more. I didn't realize she was so popular.'

'It is not that, madam,' Raeburn said stiffly, 'it is a question of principle. This hotel is not unionized and that leaves us open to exploitation.'

'I see.' Judith crossed her arms. 'You feel *you* have been exploited?'

'Not I, Miss Prynne, but we feel Mrs Malcolm has. I didn't know her particularly well, in fact I doubt if I exchanged a dozen words with her; but her dismissal, I think, was wrong.'

'I'm sorry.' Judith felt a lump in her throat and recognized the latent fear; fear at the thought she might have made a serious error and set back for years the progress made by Aylestone. She should have called a staff meeting and taken them into her confidence. She had been too peremptory, too authoritative . . . even though she was sure she had not abused her power and was right. Matthew had supported her too. She recalled what Leo had told her about the strike at the Ritz. The Ritz might be able to rise above that kind of thing; but supposing it happened here?

'I'm sorry,' she said again, 'but I don't quite think you know the circumstances. Maybe if you did you would change your mind.'

'I understand the remarks that annoyed you were principally about your family, Miss Prynne?' Simon Raeburn, obviously a man of principle, fixed Judith with a steady eye.

'She was certainly not very nice about my family. But that was not the point. She was extremely rude, personally, to me. She also behaved unsatisfactorily towards our clients, which precipitated the encounter between us in the first place. Altogether I decided she was an unsatisfactory employee, and would therefore have to go.'

'Is there *any* question of her being reinstated if she apologizes?'

'None at all, I'm afraid,' Judith said, 'and I'm on my way to the linen room now. Would you excuse me.' She stood up. 'Thank you for putting your point of view, Simon. It *is* appreciated and I will bear it in mind for the future. But this episode is quite closed. I'm firm about that.'

'Thank you, Miss Prynne.' The *maître d'hôtel* bowed, but the expression on his face remained inscrutable. Judith felt that she had not heard the end of the matter.

And nor had she for, less than an hour later, as she was checking the laundry returns in the linen room, the door was unceremoniously flung open and Douglas stormed in.

'Judith!'

'Doug.' She turned round in surprise. 'You startled me.'

'Judith what is this I hear about Doris Malcolm?'

Doug had been away on leave and had missed the drama which, although it had happened a few days previously, seemed to have assumed a new importance.

'How was your holiday, Doug?' Judith turned back to the table.

'Judith, I demand to know what happened.' She felt Doug's hand come down on her shoulder, and she angrily swung round so that he was forced to drop it. He too looked very angry.

'I'm very surprised you feel so strongly about Mrs Malcolm,' Judith remarked.

'She was an excellent housekeeper.'

'You thought so, did you? Well, others didn't. There were complaints about her to Matthew.'

Doug passed a hand across his forehead. 'I understood she made remarks about the family that you objected to?'

'Well? Wouldn't you? She more or less said Father was a pest and Mother was a drunk. She said *you* flirted with women guests, and she referred to the fight between Marcel and André. All in all she seemed to me to have a personal bias against this family. She was so rude to me I decided I couldn't continue to work with her.'

'Oh!' Doug leaned against the table. 'I didn't hear all that.'

'Who did you hear it from, as a matter of interest?' Judith slowly crossed her arms. 'I thought you only came back last night.'

'I heard it,' Doug bit his lip, 'well, I heard it from her actually. From Doris. She telephoned me at home. She feels very badly treated, victimized. I said I would have a word with you.'

'Did *she* tell you that she accused you of flirting with the women guests?'

'No.' Doug clenched his teeth. 'She didn't mention that; besides, it's utterly untrue.'

'Funny she missed *that* out.' Judith's tone of voice changed. 'Funny, come to that, that she knew. After all she doesn't mix much with the guests or the staff.'

'They know everything. They all talk with one another . . . anyway it's *not* true, and if she did say it I object to it.'

'Then you must take that up with her,' Judith replied silkily.

'I am the manager of this hotel. It would quite out of place to flirt . . . it's nonsense.'

'You *do* use your charm, Doug. I've noticed it too, the famous Prynne charm, particularly with women guests.'

'But that's my job, to be pleasant to guests, not to flirt. I strongly deny that. Anyway, Judith, it's time we had a talk . . . a long talk. I'm not happy about things either and I suspect you know it. I understand there's a strong undercurrent among the staff of dissatisfaction over the way Doris has been treated. There's a move for her reinstatement.'

'She will not be reinstated. I have dismissed her and I shall not take her back.'

'What does Matthew say to this?'

'Matthew supports me. He had complaints about her.'

'I think a reprimand, a warning, would have been enough.'

'It's what I intended, but I can't tell you how insolent and unpleasant she was, Doug. No one could have stood it. She was too provocative.' Judith gazed for a moment at her brother, who stood looking at the floor, a frown on his face. 'Anyway,' she continued as he said nothing, 'I didn't think you knew her well enough to call her "Doris".'

'I knew her quite well.' Judith noticed a defensive note in his voice. 'I call a lot of the staff by their Christian names. It makes them feel at home.'

'You're too informal with them, Doug. That's bad. I think it's because you want people to like you. Nothing wrong with that. But in a hotel like Aylestone you must keep a distance from the staff. If they've been well trained they prefer it. In the Ritz . . .'

'I'm sick of hearing about the Ritz! César Ritz died half

a century ago. Even before the last war attitudes were different. You don't *have* to be formal, remote . . .'

'I'm *not* formal and remote. I would have thought I was a friendly person. But to be intimate with the housekeeper . . .'

'I was *not* intimate! What a word to use.'

'She felt she knew you well enough to ring you at home.'

'She couldn't very well ring me here. Some Nosy Parker would have passed that bit of gossip on to you.'

'Nevertheless, I don't like it. And I don't like your attitude, Doug. It's hardly giving *me* support.'

'And you hardly give *me* support.' Doug's anger was mounting. 'Besides *I* appointed Doris Malcolm and I feel I have let her down. She didn't like you. Hardly any of the staff like you.'

'How *can* you say that?' Judith, feeling enraged, put both her hands on her hips.

'Because it happens to be true. I know that they think you've got too much on your plate and, besides, you've changed. You're too full of yourself. Sometimes I feel I hardly know you myself, Judith.'

'Doug, I'm beginning to think you're jealous.'

'Jealousy doesn't come into it. I care about Aylestone and Aylestone only. You have too many irons in the fire.' Doug pointed a finger at her, his forehead covered with perspiration. 'And I'm telling you what I'm going to do, Judith. I'm going to go personally to Matthew Jenner. I'm going to tell him just how you fired Doris Malcolm and why, and how you've upset the staff. Any more of that sort of behaviour and we'll have a riot on our hands. And after all he's been through Matthew certainly wouldn't want *that*.'

For many weeks after their row Douglas and Judith were scarcely on speaking terms, and their mutual hostility tainted the atmosphere to the extent that it seemed to affect everyone. It quickly became known among the staff at the hotel that brother and sister had fallen out, and there was an instinctive move to support Douglas, who was known to be on their side.

However, many of the staff had, and continued to have, a strong liking for Judith who, in most cases, had appointed them. She was friendly without being over-familiar. She was efficient, fair-minded and extremely capable. The reputation the hotel had acquired was thanks largely to her.

But André Hebert had never liked her, and the kitchen staff were against her. It was a personal, partisan matter which had its roots in Hebert's fight with her husband.

Doug and Judith had to continue to meet, to communicate, because the long-term success of Aylestone depended on it. If there were disagreements the people who must not be aware of them were the customers: that exclusive, pampered breed who paid a great deal for the privilege.

The family were particularly upset and, in many ways, the most affected. They quickly had a distorted, one-sided view of the disagreement from Ros. Greville tried to bring brother and sister together, but without success. He and his wife felt more remote, more isolated from the family home than ever, and their dreams of escape increased.

One morning, a few weeks after the row, Greville was mowing the lawn, pipe stuck firmly in the corner of his mouth. The house was surrounded by a pretty garden and, on that day, it looked at its best. Clumps of bright, brilliant flowers – lupins, sunflowers, hollyhock, sweet william – grew in haphazard profusion against a background of conifers, ash and oak. Along the borders was a thick carpet of nasturtium, polyanthus, geranium, lobelia and variegated petunias: purples, blues, reds, whites and yellows. In and out flew the butterflies, alighting first on one flower, then another, and the harmonious medley of the smells, sights and sounds of summer seemed like a refrain, repeated throughout the land, of an English garden on a summer's day.

The stretches of smooth, well-watered lawn required constant attention and, occasionally, one of the gardeners from Aylestone was sent over to the house to help. But for Greville it was a never-ending task, a warm task, and, after a while, he cut the engine and flopped on to a nearby bench mopping his brow.

On the far lawn Angela and Gran were chatting under a huge chestnut tree. Both wore large picture hats and together they presented a vignette, redolent of those happy, far-off pre-war days.

Seeing Greville sit down, Angela took off her sunglasses and waved them at him. He waved back and, after a minute, Angela said something to Gran and then came over to him and sat down.

'Would you like a lemonade, dear?'

'Love it,' Greville said, mopping his brow again. 'This is getting all too much for me, Angela.'

Angela put a hand on his back and patted him. Then she went into the house, poured lemonade into a glass with ice and took it out to him.

'Thanks,' he said, grasping it and gulping it down.

'It *is* an awfully hot day,' Angela remarked. 'Why don't you come and sit under the tree for a while with Mother and me? She's awfully mis.'

'I'm awfully mis too,' Greville said with feeling. 'I hate this blasted garden.'

'But it's so pretty, dear.' Angela gazed at it forlornly. 'I do, however, know what you mean.'

'Ever think of India?' Greville said wistfully.

'Often. More than ever for some reason lately. I suppose we've been so unhappy, and I'd love to get away.'

'Do you mean it, Ange?' Greville rested a hand on her lap.

'Of course I mean it. I just have to close my eyes to see

207

our bungalow at Tezpur, and the acres of high green tea plants surrounding it that seemed to stretch for ever towards the river. I wonder what it looks like now, Grev?'

'Those certainly were the days,' Greville said, his voice almost breaking with emotion.

'They were lovely, weren't they? Do you remember Azim the dhobi, and Shreelah the ayah?'

'I wonder what happened to them?' Greville mused.

'I think we're still paying their wages.' The nostalgia on Angela's face vanished. 'To think *if* we're still paying their wages ... Grev, we must go back to India! We must at least *see* what the property is like; if the place is still there. Maybe we can do the bungalow up. After all we did buy it for our retirement. It was *such* a pretty place.'

Suddenly, ecstatically, she joined her hands together: 'Oh, those mornings in India, with the mist rising from the river ...'

'The sundowners on the terrace at sunset.' Greville frowned. 'The mosquitoes ...'

'Oh, don't think about those.' Angela waved her hands in front of her as if despatching a swarm of the wretched things. 'Anyway we could have air conditioning now.'

'*If* we could afford it ...'

'Grev, in India we'd be rich! Don't you understand? Look, there we have money. Here we haven't any. We're parasites. Actually,' she stared at him, her lower lip trembling, 'we're not wanted, Grev.'

'Do you mean go back for good?' Greville looked thoughtfully at his wife who, however, continued as though she had never been interrupted:

'That row between Doug and Judith. That decided me. To think of *how* the staff talk about us at the hotel, our home after all ...'

Yes, it had been deeply offensive, wounding, hurtful to be not wanted, thrown aside, rejected, on the slag heap. Laughed at. That was worst of all.

Grev pushed his pipe from one side of his mouth to the other. 'What will we do about Mother? She'd hate India.'

'We couldn't take your mother. Judith would always look after her. She'd never abandon her. Besides, we would never let on we wanted to go back for good.'

'Mother's calling.' Greville gave a loud sigh and opened his eyes that had been half closed, abandoning the dream reluctantly to return to reality once more.

Chapter 11

'*Ciao, cara, ciao – a sta sera!*' Moira put down the telephone, and then immediately picked it up again, searching through her book for another number. She dialled and waited, but there was no reply. She replaced the receiver, started to look through her book, then flung it on the sofa beside her and sat back, arms behind her head, tapping her feet on the carpet. One of her two cats saw the opportunity for a little love and came and jumped on her lap, purring. Moira buried her face in its furry back and listened to that curious, reassuring sound of contentment.

Sometimes she thought that animals were the one consolation she had: animals and children. Yet the children, Alida and Franco, were out with their nanny and the cats couldn't speak. The flat on the edge of the Campo Santa Maria Formosa was deserted except for her and the cats – Galileo and Tikki, brother and sister. They were grey feral cats whom she had taken off the streets of Venice as kittens after they had been deserted by their mother, and facing the uncertain life of strays, even in that city hospitable to the feline species. Moira loved them very much. She felt she had a certain sympathy with cats and they with her.

Rising, she took Galileo to the window, festooned with colourful window boxes, producing a comb from a drawer as she passed, and began to groom him while the sun streamed through the window and Galileo preened himself in the sun.

Moira and Richard, always restless, had moved to Venice just after Franco, the younger child, was born. Richard had grown tired of Rome and Moira had, perforce, to accompany him; but she missed her friends, the smart set who gathered in the Corso to while away the time.

In Venice, however, she soon found another smart set who congregated on the Piazza San Marco, at Harry's Bar, or the bars of the Danieli and the Gritti Palace. Invariably, too, they had titles: contessa, marchesa, principessa and ducessa, even though such honours had been abolished in Italy for over a century. But there was still a lot of wealth in Venice. Many of the palazzos on the Grand Canal and the tributaries off it remained in private hands. There was, in addition, a very strong American contingent of artists and writers, many of whom Richard knew.

But it was still, for her, a lonely life. Moira was not a self-contained person and there were many hours on her own. Richard had a small studio in the Giudecca which he shared with another artist and, from late morning until late at night, she scarcely saw him.

Moira completed her grooming of Galileo and looked round for Tikki, who was nowhere to be seen. Galileo loved these grooming sessions and, immediately Moira started to comb or brush him, hurled himself on his back, a somewhat hazardous procedure when resting on a window ledge. He was a cat with very few brains, which they hadn't known when they gave him his illustrious name; but he had a gentle, loving nature compared to Tikki who was much smarter, but cunning and greedy. She only purred when she wanted food, whereas Galileo purred all the time and loved to be cosseted and cuddled, told that he was loved.

The apartment on the Campo was on the first floor of an old house which had been converted into flats. It was not as large as their flat in Rome had been; but it was much more beautiful, more atmospheric and, with its view over the square towards the market which daily supplied the surrounding populace with fresh produce from the mainland, there was always plenty to see, people to watch, and comings and goings that went on all day.

The back of the house overlooked the canal which ran

past the baroque Church of Santa Maria Formosa to intersect with others that, ultimately, flowed into the lagoon. In summer, in common with most of Venice's idyllic waterways, the canal stank, but then they tried to go away to the mountains or to the open sea.

Moira thought that if they stayed in Venice long enough she would try and persuade Richard to buy one of the spacious, healthier and larger apartments in one of the many modern blocks on the Lido. So far everywhere they had lived was rented, as though to emphasize the transitory nature of their lives.

In the morning there'd been a letter from Judith. Their parents were anxious to go to India and she had offered to pay the fare. It seemed that, at last, it would actually happen and that soon the dream of India would come true.

Moira also had her dreams. She would like to leave Italy altogether and go home. She missed her family because the friends she had, with their superficial manners and extravagant ways, could never take their place.

Moira knew that she had been spoilt and only now, too late, did she realize what a poor preparation it was for life. Her parents had spoiled her and Richard, in the first few years of their marriage, had spoiled her too.

He spoiled her no longer and, instead, had become a distant, erring husband with mysterious ways. It was as though he had undergone a complete change of personality. Yet not for a long time had he gone away without telling her. That period of his life seemed to be past; but it always left her wondering why, and where and what it had been about.

Like many couples, Richard and Moira found they had little in common after several years of marriage. Yet there was still a smattering of love, a glimmer of attraction and, so far, that had been sufficient to keep them together.

Richard considered himself a serious artist and was in certain circles well respected. Yet, for all her efforts, art hardly interested Moira. There was not much that did. She was aware of an emptiness and, now that she needed them, she realized how few resources she had: just herself, the children and the cats for company; no interior life, no real hobbies or interests . . . nothing at all.

After a while Moira put down Galileo, who set up a plaintive wail, and went into her bedroom to look for Judith's letter. The sisters had never been close; but at least Judith was flesh and blood, and if their parents were going to India who knew when they would see them again? The bed was unmade, the sheets thrown back as though someone had left in a hurry. Richard and she hardly spoke in the morning. It was not his 'good' time. In fact Richard had a lot of bad times and Moira began to wonder if he was really ill; if there was something seriously the matter with him.

She found Judith's letter tossed on the table by her side of the bed; a couple of pages had fallen on the floor and, as she bent down to retrieve them, the sunlight gleamed on something under the bed and she lay flat on her stomach and groped for it.

At first she didn't know what it was. She turned it around in her hand and at last, gingerly, put it to her nose. It didn't smell of anything, but with a pang of anguish she realized she was clasping the upper part of a syringe; a tube of glass and metal with the needle missing.

Her hand closed over it but she remained where she was lying on the floor. Then quietly she began to sob. Tikki appeared from some unknown refuge and began to rub herself against Moira in an effort to comfort her.

All in vain.

A camera focusing in on the little group standing in the departure hall at Heathrow would have noticed nothing in particular; the inevitable expressions, forced smiles, a few tears; the usual thing when families met to say goodbye to one another.

Around them other people were doing the same thing, and even the Prynnes would not have stood out among so many. Maybe, however, they looked just a little smarter and more chic than most of the other people bunched closely together; and one or two male eyes might have turned to take in Judith's undeniable elegance, her almost flame-coloured hair, or Moira's neat ankles shown to advantage by her very high-heeled Ferragamo shoes. The little children around them were sweet, that was for sure, and a lot of attention was focused by the family on them because saying goodbye to one another was so difficult. Children became the excuse to avoid a show of true feeling.

'Of course we'll be back,' Angela said, after giving Franco yet another kiss. This was the grandchild she had not seen and, in many ways, he was the one she was saddest to leave. The others might just conceivably remember her, but little Franco, scarcely out of babyhood? Never.

'He *is* a darling,' she continued, raising sad eyes to Moira. 'He'll be quite grown up when I see him again.'

'Oh, Mummy, don't say that,' Moira said, flinging herself in desperation into her mother's arms. 'You said it was just for a holiday.'

'There's a lot to do.' Greville shuffled his feet and looked at the board announcing departures. He felt excited and afraid at the same time, and kept on examining the pages of his passport to be sure that it hadn't expired. But he was in need of this kind of reassurance.

Now that the time had come for departure he wondered if, after all, they were doing the right thing.

Marcel and Doug, anonymous in almost identical grey coats, stood talking, expressions grave, heads close together. Occasionally they shuffled their feet and looked at their watches. They really had very little to say to each other. Ros kept running after Philip who, although he was the eldest, was making a nuisance of himself. He said he wanted to see the planes and Ros tried to tell him that there were no planes to see. Not from here; too far away.

The only member of the family not there was Richard. But his absence was not hard to explain. Moira said he was busy with his paintings, a new exhibition to be held in Venice later in the year. She would never have told anyone, not yet anyway, about what she'd found under the bed just before she left.

Suddenly a number of place names flashed on the board and over the tannoy came an announcement about the Air India flight to Calcutta. Time to board the plane.

'I can't *believe* it,' Moira gasped. 'Oh, Mummy!' She flung her arms round her mother once again, close to tears. 'You *will* come back, won't you?'

'Of course, darling.' Angela pressed her younger daughter to her and the tears suddenly and unexpectedly welled from her eyes and cascaded down her puffy cheeks, covered that morning with too much rouge to hide the pallor of her face.

'I wish now you weren't going,' Moira said. 'I wish you'd *stay . . .*'

'Darling, it's only a little while . . . a few months.'

Greville put a hand on his wife's shoulder, the passports held tightly in his other hand. His face was red, and his bristly moustache stuck out like a brush over pursed lips.

'Time to go, Ange,' he said gently. 'Judith, could you look after your sister?'

'Of course.' Capable Judith, always being asked to take charge. The children scampered around them, the voice on the tannoy spoke again, more urgently, and the din seemed suddenly enormous; unendurable. Judith put her arm protectively round Moira, while Marcel shook Greville's hand.

'Good luck, Greville. Send us some tea.'

'I'll do that,' Greville said jovially, 'providing there is any.'

Moira and Angela still clung to each other despite the pressure of Judith's hand; the children played in and out among them and Doug eventually took Moira's other arm and practically dragged her from their mother.

'Goodbye, Mother,' he said, kissing her on the cheek. 'Sorry . . .' he stepped back and looked into her eyes. 'Sorry you had to go.'

'Now mind you and Judith don't quarrel,' Angela said in an attempt at severity, shaking her finger at him. 'You . . .'

'We won't quarrel, Mummy,' Judith said. 'I promise.' She bent and kissed her mother, aware of that trace of familiar perfume which she had associated with her ever since she had been a little girl: Chanel No 5 and face powder. It permeated her clothes, as well, and the room in which she slept. She hugged her mother very tightly and whispered in her ear.

'Take care, Mummy darling. I do love you . . .'

'I love you *too*, Judith dear . . .' Angela seemed to want to say something, but Greville dragged her away.

The grandchildren, suddenly aware that the hour of departure was on them, threw themselves at their grandparents, and were the last to receive their hugs.

Then, quickly, looking suddenly rather small and frail, the two senior members of the Prynne family joined the queue at the barrier for passport inspection, waved once again and were gone.

Two people in late middle age, suddenly uncertain about their future, going on an adventure into the unknown.

Lady Prynne had decided not to go to the airport with the family. She knew it would be emotional and she couldn't stand too much emotion. She had taken her own farewell

216

of her son and something inside her had told her it would be the last time she would see him.

Maybe in those last days before his departure Greville had confided in his mother and she now knew how unhappy, how really horribly unhappy, they had been.

Gran bore their departure with her customary stoicism. There was a deep vein in the old lady of self-containment because she had lived on her own for a long time and knew that, in this life, one could only really depend on oneself.

She knew her family had not forgotten her and she would not be neglected. A woman in her late forties by the name of Maud Lanchester had been engaged to look after her. She was both a housekeeper and a nurse, and Gran liked her. She liked her a lot more than Angela and, in a way, she felt that, sad though it was to lose Greville, the departure of part of her family to India was not such a bad thing.

Mrs Lanchester was a pleasant, adaptable woman who had travelled a good deal in her life looking after private cases that were often more taxing than Gran. She found Gran a delightful old lady, fully in possession of her senses – not what she had been led to expect – but, then, it was noticeable that Gran hardly ever bothered to look for her late husband unless she had an interested audience.

The weeks after Angela and Greville left passed quietly but harmoniously as Gran liked Mrs Lanchester, whom she called by her Christian name, and enjoyed her company. There was also a daily help and a man to do the garden. Moira and her children stayed on for some time with Gran after the departure of her parents; but after she left either Judith, Doug or Rosalind came frequently to call. Gran never felt neglected, left on her own. Consequently Mrs Lanchester, who found herself in one of the cushiest jobs of her life and one that she hoped would continue for a very long time, grew careless. She enjoyed the proximity of London and Gran never minded if she slipped away for the day; in fact she encouraged her because, although she liked Maud well enough, she found her constant presence a trifle irritating.

One day in the spring, when Greville and Angela had been gone three months, Gran woke up one morning with an idea in her head. It was an idea that grew into a fixation as the day progressed and, that afternoon, she said to Maud:

'When are you going to town again, dear?'

'Do you mean London, Lady Prynne?'

'Of course I mean London,' Gran said rather sharply, tapping her stick on the floor with irritation. 'Where did you think I meant?'

'Is there something you want?' Maud enquired humbly.

Gran thought rather quickly. 'Jacksons in Piccadilly have a tea I am particularly fond of. My daughter-in-law always kept me supplied with it, but sadly . . .'

'Oh, of course I'll get your tea for you, Lady Prynne,' Maud said, jumping at the chance. 'Would it be all right if I went up tomorrow?'

'Perfectly all right with me,' Gran said offhandedly. 'Stay as long as you like . . .' and she waved a hand vaguely about in the air.

'Oh, I should never leave you alone at *night*, Lady Prynne,' Maud said, with her characteristic unctuousness. But Gran didn't mind . . . what she wanted to do could easily be achieved during the day.

The following morning Gran woke as usual and lay in bed listening to the sounds of the house: the Hoover going in the lounge, the tray tinkling outside the door as Maud arrived with her breakfast.

'How are we this morning?' Maud said in her cheerful voice, briskly drawing the curtains back.

Gran always hated that 'we'. There was an air of condescension about it, as though Maud were addressing a child. But she knew it was the way such people behaved.

But Gran was too excited to allow herself to be irritated by Maud on this particular day. Instead she sat up in bed, propped her pillows behind her head and smiled.

'Excellent,' she said, somewhat to Maud's astonishment, because Gran was usually rather taciturn, a little grumpy, in the mornings. 'We're fine. Are you ready for town?'

'I shall be going up on the 9.45 train if that's all right with you, Lady Prynne.'

'Perfectly all right.' Gran pulled her pink bedjacket more comfortably around her shoulders. 'You have a good day and make sure you remember the *tea*.' She frowned as she tilted the teapot towards her cup. 'Jackson's Breakfast Tea, it's called.'

'I shan't forget, Lady Prynne,' Maud said, with a trace of excitement in her voice, 'and be sure *you* have a good day too. Your luncheon is all ready in the kitchen. Then this afternoon, after you have had your nap . . .'

'Oh, I know what to do, I know what to do.' Gran allowed her composure to falter as she waved her hand towards the door. 'Now off you go and get ready.'

And gratefully Maud fled towards the door with never a backward glance.

After she had gone Gran lay back, listening. The Hoover stopped and she heard conversation between the two women. Not long after came the sound of a taxi outside the front door. She held her breath, which she only released when the car started up again and then, her breakfast hardly touched, she put the tray on one side and clambered out of bed with the air and in the manner of a predator.

After Gran had had her bath she dressed with particular care, choosing the dress she had worn for Doug and Rosalind's wedding. It was a very pretty dress made of voile with a pattern of large mauve flowers and a high collar. Around this she draped the strings of the family pearls that were practically her last valuable possession, apart from the pearl and diamond ring that her father had

219

given her on her twenty-first birthday, and the large emerald that had been her engagement present from Jasper. Jasper. How she missed him.

Suddenly her eyes swam with tears, and the image of herself in the mirror misted over as she placed her toque on her head like a crown and pulled the little half-veil over her eyes. When the mist cleared she looked at herself for a minute or two, liking what she saw. She had carefully made up her face, applying powder thickly over those withered, wrinkled cheeks together with a touch of rouge that she knew brought out the colour of her violet-blue eyes. How *Jasper* had loved those eyes . . .

Jasper was constantly on her mind as, carefully, she arranged the veil over her forehead so that it reached just to the top of her nose. Jasper was such a very fine, upright, handsome man; the sort of man a woman was proud to be seen with. With his nautical air and his famous Prynne charm . . .

Her fur was already on her bed and, draping it around her shoulders and grasping her stick, she went firmly into the hall in search of him. The cleaning lady, who was in the act of dusting the banisters, registered surprise when she saw her:

'Are you going *out*, my lady?'

'I am, Agnes dear,' Gran said with a sweet smile. 'Be an angel and call me a cab.'

'But should you be going out, Lady Prynne?' Agnes said with suspicion. 'Mrs Lanchester said nothing to me about it. She left your lunch all ready in the kitchen.'

'Just call me a cab, there's a dear,' Gran said, producing a ten-shilling note from her pocket and pressing it into the astonished charlady's hand. 'And here's half a sovereign for you.'

Oh how *good* it was to see the old place again as the cab swept up the drive. They tried to keep her away, but it was no use. It was her home and she loved it. She loved it more than most because she had lived here the longest.

Angela and Greville, who had scarcely lived there during their married life, obviously could not have loved it at all or they would never have let it go. But people who preferred a bungalow in the middle of a tea plantation in India could hardly be expected to put much value on a stately home.

From the outside it looked just as it always had; the steps going up to the porticoed front door reminded her of the first time she had stepped up them, long before she and Jasper had been engaged. The ivy crept up the walls towards the crenellated roof with its four gables, the rounded windows where she used to have her suite. Behind the house the trees in the wood were yet again bursting into leaf. How many springs had she known? Countless, and today the birds sang so sweetly, as if welcoming her home.

It was her home and it was Jasper's and no one had had any right to take it away from them.

A footman appeared as soon as the cab stopped and he opened the door for her, bowing low as he did. She looked at him but he did not recognize her. This was a bit of luck. She had half expected to be met by someone she knew and ushered straight up to Judith, who doubtless would have marched her straight out again.

Marcia Prynne loved her elder granddaughter, but she was slightly in awe of her. No one had ever thought that Judith, who had not been particularly brainy at school, or shown much of an aptitude for anything except games, would turn into such a successful businesswoman.

'Have you any luggage, madam?' the footman asked after Gran had paid the cabbie and tipped him well.

'I'm lunching here, thank you,' Gran replied loftily, pressing a half-crown into the footman's hand. 'Thank you, my good man.'

221

The footman attempted to take her arm, but Gran gently shook him off and began slowly to climb the few stairs to the porch.

In the lobby one or two people stood casually about. There was the same air of leisure in the place which Gran could never become accustomed to thinking of as a hotel. But, beyond the lobby, the drawing room remained pretty much as it had been, smarter of course, and there was now a corridor that went right to the other side. Beyond it was the lawn, now bathed in the tranquil sunlight of noon.

Gran looked towards it and, feeling a little out of breath, sank thankfully into a chair. The years seemed to roll back as though, once again, she was the châtelaine of this great house, and she could hear the sounds of her children playing on the lawn.

Leaning her head against the back of the chair she closed her eyes. Thank heaven the children were looked after by the excellent Miss Hardy and the nursery nurse Abigail, who had been with her since the birth of Greville. She opened her eyes and a thoughtful look came into them as she leaned forward, cupping her hand behind her ear.

Or was it her *grandchildren* playing on the lawn? Of course that was most likely, as she could hear several voices.

But the main worry was Jasper; he was always disappearing, getting lost, losing his breath and his balance as he wandered through the woods towards the river. It was a great worry and, one day, if he wasn't careful, he would lose his balance completely and fall in.

Suddenly she shot up, face creased with anxiety, heart beating faster, as a man in a grey suit, appearing rather blurred with the sun behind him, came towards her.

'Oh *Jasper*,' she said, clasping his lapels. 'Thank God it's you. I was so worried.'

'May I help you?' the man said in a concerned tone of voice, bending over her. 'Is there something wrong?'

'Oh dear.' Gran quickly drew back from him. 'I *thought* you were my husband . . . have *you* seen the Admiral?'

'The Admiral?' the man said, looking puzzled. Gran could see now that, although he wasn't Jasper, he had a kind face.

'I *do* worry about him,' she said weakly, sinking back into her chair. 'He wanders off, towards the *river* you know. His balance is poor, his eyesight is worse. I always worry about him and that river.'

'Good heavens,' the man exclaimed. 'Has he gone towards the river?'

'I expect so,' Gran sighed. 'He is a seafaring man, you know. He loves the water; but he *will* take risks.'

'How long is it since you saw your husband, madam?' The man glanced anxiously at his watch.

'What time is it now?'

'It's nearly noon.'

'It was about nine o'clock.'

'Oh dear me.' The man beckoned frantically to another guest dressed in golfing clothes who, obviously aware that something was wrong, had stopped to see if he could be of assistance. 'This lady's husband is missing. She thinks he may have fallen in the river. He's been gone *three* hours.'

'I *say*.' The other guest sounded alarmed. 'We'd better alert the management.'

'No time for that,' the first Samaritan said. 'We'd better go down quickly to the river ourselves.'

'Oh *would* you?' Gran sank back, kneading her handkerchief in her hand. 'I'd be so grateful.'

By this time two or three more had gathered and were instructed in rapid authoritative tones by the man in the grey suit, who happened to be the president of a large multinational organization and thus used to giving orders. Then, with one accord, they started to run across the lawn and down through the trees to the river.

Gran watched them go, a look of relief on her face, but

overwhelmed by a feeling of perplexity all the same . . . perplexity and anguish and . . . fear.

Judith, standing at the window of her room, was dictating letters to Stella, who was sitting on a chair, her shorthand pad on her knee. Judith had her back to Stella, a sheaf of letters requiring quick answers in her hand, when she looked down and, to her amazement, saw a stream of people, guests of all ages and sizes, issuing at great speed from the garden door of the hotel and running across the lawn.

'Good heavens,' she cried, lowering the letters in her hand. 'What on earth is going on?'

'What's that, Miss Prynne?' Stella didn't even look up.

'A crowd of guests, running towards the river.'

'Oh, I do hope . . . there hasn't been an accident!' Stella put her shorthand pad on a table and jumped up, crossing the room to stand next to Judith. 'Maybe someone's fallen in the river.'

'I'd better go and see,' Judith said going towards the door.

'Shall I phone down, Miss Prynne?'

'There isn't time. That sort of tragedy is the *last* thing we need.'

Judith hurried out of the room, closely followed by Stella. She decided not to use the lift but took the stairs, two at a time. Below, the lobby and lounge were deserted, an odd contrast to the hectic activity she had observed taking place outside.

Jill, the head receptionist, had her head bent over a ledger on the desk before her.

'Is anything wrong, Jill?'

'Wrong?' Jill enquired, looking up.

'A stream of people were charging across the lawn towards the river.'

'Oh *dear*.' Jill emerged from behind the desk, a look of consternation on her face. 'Maybe I should call . . .'

'Don't call *anybody*,' Judith cried. 'Just you stay here until I get back.' Then she walked quickly through the lobby into the lounge, where the first thing she saw was Gran sitting upright in her chair, dressed to kill, her trusting, childlike eyes, shining brightly, fastened intently upon the open door.

'Gran!' Judith called sharply and saw her grandmother turn round with a guilty start and put her hand to her mouth.

'Oh dear . . . Judith.'

'Gran, has something happened? Have you been here long?'

'Why no. I . . .'

'Gran!' Judith said trying hard to keep the hysteria out of her voice, 'is it something to do with *Grandpa*?'

'Is *what* something to do with him, dear?' Gran said nervously.

'A crowd of people were crossing the lawn helter skelter as though there had been some emergency.'

'Well he is *missing*, Judith,' Gran said plaintively. 'He's been gone now for hours.'

Judith did all she could to repair the harm that had been done to the reputation of the hotel. A paragraph that had appeared in the local paper was taken up by a national tabloid, about the uproar that had occurred in the hotel while the guests scoured the area for the missing husband, who had, unbeknown to them, been dead over twenty years. The initial posse had gathered strength as others had joined it including those playing golf, riding or simply taking a pre-prandial walk in the extensive grounds. It had taken hours to get them all together again and none of them had found it at all amusing. One, who had had his clothes torn in the undergrowth, had even left on the spot, muttering about such people being better locked up.

Questions were asked: why had no staff been on duty to stop this happening? Why had Gran been there at *all* . . . why, why, why? There was no end to it.

To many people it was funny; but it was not funny to those who had been involved, and who had been worried. They expected more for the considerable amount of money they were paying per day for the comforts, services and opportunities for relaxation offered by the hotel. They had expected a better supervision of Gran.

The worst thing, from a professional point of view, was the revelation that Gran was a relation of Judith's, the managing director, or the matter might have been passed over, causing less fuss. The first guest, the man in the grey suit, only got really annoyed when he had been told who Gran actually was.

It had been humiliating, but it had also been sad. No one had been as upset as Gran and, because her granddaughter, who loved her, realized how bewildered, frightened and confused she really was, she didn't have it in her heart to reproach her. The reality was that Gran couldn't help herself. She was gradually sinking into that sad, misty world of senility.

Mrs Lanchester had been summarily dismissed and paid off with a month's wages, as well as two pounds of Jackson's Breakfast Tea, which was never handed over in the confusion. A new nurse was installed whose duties as a keeper were clearly outlined. Gran was never to be left alone.

Then came the summons from Jenner.

Matthew Jenner was a man of great charm; but he had a way of looking that could be particularly unpleasant.

Judith had mostly seen the charming aspect of the man; what lay underneath was a surprise to her.

She had seen it very briefly, fleetingly, when they had discussed one or two things to do with the running of the hotel in the past, and then she had thought: 'There is more to this man Jenner than meets the eye. One should beware.'

But now she realized she had never really known him at all. His charm was not only deceptive; it was probably uncharacteristic of the kind of man he really was.

Sitting in front of his large desk in the City, Judith felt like a schoolgirl. For once she was grateful for the presence of Marcel. It was not often that she'd needed his support.

The invitation from Jenner had come in a formal letter delivered by hand; the date and hour at his office specified. There had been no 'would it be convenient . . .?' Just an order to be there.

'I've *said* I was very sorry,' Judith repeated for about the third time, glancing at Marcel. 'It was a most unfortunate incident, and we deeply regret it.'

'It was particularly unfortunate as Sir Cuthbert Henderson, the chairman of one of the major banks, was there at the time,' Matthew said, riffling through some papers. 'And, even more unfortunate still, was the fact that your grandmother first approached him with *her* pathetic tale.'

'He approached her . . .'

'Well, whatever happened,' Matthew said irritably, 'Sir Cuthbert suffers from high blood-pressure. To be crawling around in the undergrowth looking for someone who is no longer with us . . . He thought it a particularly sick kind of joke, unworthy of a great hotel.' Matthew contemptuously tossed to her a letter on business notepaper listing the complaints of the great man himself.

She took it, read it and replaced it on the table without comment. She had had a few addressed directly to herself and to all she had apologized. Yet the thing that struck her was that there was not one person who seemed actually to be sorry for an old and bewildered woman whose home the hotel had been for over sixty years. This fact made her more angry than anything, representing as it did the kind of attitude of the selfish, moneyed people they were there to serve.

'Well, what do you want us to do, Matthew?' Judith said, without any repentance in her voice. 'I have done all I can. Gran now has a full-time nurse and will never go to Aylestone again. I . . .'

'I want you to resign, Judith,' Sir Matthew said, sitting back and lighting a cigarette.

'Over *that!*' Marcel exclaimed, jumping from his chair. 'It is *absurd.*'

'How would *you* like a crazy old woman wandering over your exclusive restaurant, Marcel, driving all your clients away?'

'She is *not* a crazy old woman . . .' Judith protested.

'I hope *I* would be more charitable than your clients,' Marcel said contemptuously. 'But Judith already knows how I feel about this incident. It makes me despise those who could see neither humour nor pathos in the situation. How seriously, how absurdly those wealthy people take themselves.'

'But *you're* not the one who is going to lose money,' Matthew said angrily. 'It's not *your* reputation. This bad publicity will take years . . .'

'I don't think it will,' Judith snapped. 'People have short memories. As for me resigning. That *is* ridiculous.'

'Oh no.' Matthew slowly shook his head and his expression changed. 'And not only over this. The staff are discontented, did you know that?' He threw another letter over to her. 'You sacked, in a peremptory and arbitrary manner, our very capable housekeeper Mrs Malcolm.' Glancing at the letter Judith's lips curled contemptuously again.

'André Hebert. It *would* be from him.'

228

'He was the only one who had the courage to write. I spoke to him personally. He was here yesterday. He says the assistant manager, Beaumont, also spoke to you and got short shrift. The staff are restless, discontented; you have lost their respect. There was the incident involving Marcel before that ...' Matthew stopped and grimly looked at Marcel. 'There have been too many little things in the past year that cannot be allowed to pass. What is more, profits are down. The restlessness of the staff has had an effect. I understand you are also at loggerheads with Douglas, who supported the housekeeper against you.'

'Did Doug tell you that?'

'No. It all came out when I saw Hebert. A whole can of worms, I can tell you. Doug was, is, very loyal and the staff like and respect him. I shall probably ask Doug to take your place. He loves Aylestone, is efficient and non-controversial and would make an excellent choice. This business involving your grandmother is the last straw. Before that your father and mother caused a lot of comment because of their interference. Your mother was frequently seen inebriated at the bar; she couldn't hold her drink. Your father pestered guests to play golf with him. They resented it. I know they used to own the place, but not any longer; yet they behaved as though they did. You never seemed to attempt to control them. I knew all this, of course, when I bought the hotel. That was one of the reasons Drake was glad to sell. He said he couldn't tolerate the family. You Prynnes seem to think ordinary standards of behaviour don't apply to you. Now yet again it is the family ...'

'In my opinion you're being very unreasonable,' Marcel said stiffly, 'and unfair to Judith. She has done everything ...'

'Certain things she should have prevented.' Matthew heaved his shoulders and gave an exaggerated sigh. 'I hope that she has learned a lesson and, if ever she runs a hotel again, as I know she would like to, she will keep her private and professional life completely separate. That is my advice. Above all one must be professional. Now, Judith,' as he gazed at her the kind, avuncular look she remembered from the past returned to his face. 'I think this is best for us all. For you, the Group, and, above all, Aylestone. You want to own your hotel. Well, now, I am giving you the chance. Our redundancy settlement will be generous. I will buy the Prynne family's shares. It will leave you with a substantial capital sum. I . . .'

He was stopped by the noise as Judith's chair scraped back on the polished floor as she got to her feet.

'Save your words, Matthew. If you wish me to resign I have no option. I have no wish to fight you. It would do nobody any good, but as for selling a *single* share . . . not on your life. Aylestone is almost half ours. I cannot speak for Doug, but no other member of my family will part with a single share because one day, if I have anything to do with it, we will own our family home again . . . lock, stock and barrel.'

PART THREE
Rules of Engagement
1967–1974

Chapter 12

'They're beautiful children,' Lady Forteliot said admiringly, watching Michael and Pauline as they skipped about on the lawn.

'Thank you.' Judith, despite herself, beamed with maternal pride, keeping an anxious eye on them as they ran too near to the swift-flowing waters of the River Tweed.

'If my son had lived, of course we'd never have dreamed of selling.' Lady Forteliot turned and looked sadly at the tall towers, the gothic spirals and ancient stonework of Forteliot Castle, which had been the family home for almost as long as Aylestone had belonged to the Prynnes.

'Was he killed in the war?' Judith knew the answer as, even after the passage of over twenty years, her hostess's eyes filled with tears.

'He was engaged to be married ... such a lovely young girl, Fiona. We still see her and she hasn't ever married. They were so much in love. He was killed in Italy with the Royal Scots Guards. Such a tragic thing to happen with an only son, isn't it?' Lady Forteliot put her hand on Judith's arm. 'But there, my dear, I mustn't depress you. We were not alone in our grief and misfortune.'

'I'm not depressed.' Judith touched the older woman's hand. 'I'm very sad for you; grateful for my own two. Pray God there will be no war in their lifetime.'

'Oh there must never be another war!' Lady Forteliot turned to Judith, a look of horror on her face. 'It is only we who have suffered so much who know what war really is. To lose one's only child is horror enough; but to lose someone who also represents the end of the line ... that is a double tragedy ...' Lady Forteliot paused and gazed once more at the vast castle with its crenellated battlements which stood majestically on a slight incline behind them.

'We had the same feeling about our home.' Judith guided Lady Forteliot to a bench on the lawn so that she could be nearer to the darting, playing children. 'We were forced to sell it, and now that we have I don't know that we did the best thing. It brought us little happiness.'

Judith had told Lord and Lady Forteliot the story of Aylestone and its last unhappy years the previous day when she'd travelled from Edinburgh to take another look at the property in which she had been interested for months. The problem had been to make sure that the magnificent estate with acres of woodland and grouse shooting, fishing rights to a stretch of the Tweed, was not entailed; that permission would be forthcoming to develop it as a hotel and entertainment complex. Finally the authorities had indicated that there would be no problem. The Border areas were in great need of investment for tourism.

All she needed to do now was to find the money.

Forteliot occupied a commanding position overlooking the Tweed about ten miles from the wool town of Hawick. Reached by a long, winding drive, it was set in deep woodland and offered some of the finest shooting and fishing in the country. Judith had heard it was for sale only after an exhaustive search for property in Scotland; exhaustive and also negative because the places she saw were either unsuitable or in the wrong position. She had never considered a private house, maybe subconsciously because of Aylestone, until she saw a picture of Forteliot and immediately its use as a fabulous stately home hotel sprang to mind. She knew she had to have it.

Forteliot was very large, with over fifty rooms, but it was also remote. It was off the beaten track and would be expensive to run. But, as a centre for huntsmen, anglers or golfers, or others bent on relaxation and sybaritic pleasure, it was unrivalled. To it she would also introduce the best chefs, the best staff, who would all have to be paid well because of its isolation. If she achieved what she intended, Aylestone might seem a mere hostelry in comparison.

She and the children had been invited to stay with the Forteliots until they were joined by Marcel, who had not seen it.

Autumn was the best time to visit the beautiful Border countryside and she had little doubt that Marcel would love it as she did. All the same he had been curiously unwilling to make the visit; reluctant to leave his beloved restaurant, which had now been awarded two stars in the coveted Michelin Guide. Nothing would satisfy Marcel until he had three, and until then he seemed to have little interest in anything other than perfecting the art of his already superb cuisine to bring this about.

Dinner that night with the Forteliots was taken in the baronial splendour of the ancient dining room. They were waited on by the one remaining servant, who was the husband of the cook. The couple who helped to look after the castle lived in a lodge in the grounds and had been with the Forteliots since the early years of their marriage.

'We should so like the lodge to belong to them,' Lady Forteliot whispered when the door had closed. 'Unfortunately it is part of the estate . . .'

'I'm sure something could be arranged,' Judith said. 'For instance we would need a lodge keeper and this might suit someone retired.'

'How kind.' Lady Forteliot spoke almost to herself. 'I liked you as soon as I saw you. Duncan liked you too. Even when we realized what you needed the castle for, we preferred you to some of our other would-be purchasers. Frankly it *is* hard to think of some of them at home in these parts.'

'Oh, you've had sheikhs to see it?' Judith sounded amused.

'We had a black man,' Lord Forteliot thundered. 'Imagine, a black man in Scotland!'

'He was from Nigeria,' Lady Forteliot corrected him gently. 'He was a charming man, highly educated, a chief in his own right ... however,' she smiled, almost regretfully, 'the climate was not to his liking.'

'Thank heaven for that,' Lord Forteliot said. 'My ancestors would have turned in their graves.'

Duncan, tenth Baron Forteliot, was old and he was irritable. He was also possessed by a feeling of despair which had gnawed deeply into him since the untimely death of his son ... his pride, his hope, his heir. The light had definitely gone out for him in 1944 when the Hon. Hamish Forteliot was killed at the battle for Monte Cassino.

Now Lord Forteliot needed skilled care, as Lady Prynne did; but he also needed a warm climate for his arthritis which sometimes kept him to a wheelchair. With the money they got from the sale of the castle the Forteliots had decided to take one last long journey and live out their remaining years in the Bahamas. Duncan Forteliot was seventy-eight and neither he nor his wife imagined they would ever return to Scotland.

After an early dinner the baron went straight to bed, and Judith and Alice Forteliot sat in the drawing room watching the glow in the sky as the sun finally sank out of sight.

'It is a perfect time here,' Alice Forteliot said, wrinkling her aristocratic nose nostalgically. 'I *shall* miss it.'

'I believe the sunsets are good in the Bahamas too ... and the climate is so much warmer. This place must be a devil to heat.'

'Oh it is,' Alice said with a grimace. 'The *very* devil. I don't know if you realize how much you will have to spend on this place, Madame Laborde, though I expect that's something that doesn't worry you.' She gazed with approval at Judith's Pringle jumper, tweed skirt, and two rows of pearls which exuded a quiet aura of breeding and wealth.

'But money does worry me,' Judith insisted. 'If the Prynnes had been wealthy we should never have sold Aylestone ...'

'But then you must have made a lot of money ... not that it's any of my business.' Alice Forteliot lowered her head, as if it were still most unladylike to talk about money.

'To be honest with you, we haven't made a fortune.' Judith knew what was going through her companion's mind. 'The restaurant is highly respected, but we are not by any means wealthy ...'

'Then how ... of course I know simply nothing about money, but how does one get it?' An expression of anxiety clouded the normally placid and serene features of her hostess.

'There's no need to worry,' Judith said, tapping her knee. 'For a project as big as this, one has to have commercial backing. No single individual could possibly afford it.'

'Then *how* exactly does one go about *that*?' Alice had snow-white hair and very light blue eyes that twinkled like a bird's.

'You go to the banks, various financial institutions and, with your record, you hope they will support you.'

'Oh, then, you haven't actually *got* the money?'

The vision of the Bahamas seemed almost visibly to be vanishing from the old lady's eyes.

'*Please* don't worry, Lady Forteliot,' Judith said reassuringly. 'I assure you that if Marcel agrees with me that we want this place we shall have no problem finding the money to buy it. None at all, because of the excellence of our reputation.'

* * *

237

Michael and Pauline scampered excitedly round their mother and father as, deep in conversation, they strolled across the lawn and stood gazing into the depths of the swirling river. To have their parents to themselves for even a few hours was a great treat because for some time they had very largely led separate lives.

When she had left Aylestone, Judith had decided to make a temporary home with her grandmother who, having been made aware of the damage she could do, had never referred to her late husband again, a fact that made the trained psychiatric nurse who looked after her think she was wasting her valuable time. It was as though the Admiral, who had haunted her thoughts for so long, was at last truly laid to rest. But being close to her grandmother was home for Judith and the children, and Marcel joined them when he could get away. There was no sign of Greville or Angela wishing to return from their Indian paradise; the home they had left on the green slopes of the Khasi hills had been still there when they returned, ready to welcome them. The dhobi and ayah by then had married each other and had children; so it was a doubly joyful homecoming. India was not Europe, and very little had changed.

Besides Gran's nurse, Judith had engaged a resident housekeeper and a cook, as well as the daily woman. It was quite a staff for post-war years, but one that Gran was accustomed to from the years before 1939. And, after the trauma of her last days at Aylestone, Judith had found a measure of peace; a simple, small household routine appeared as a therapeutic change.

But Judith was not the sort of woman to be idle for long. She grew restless, started studying the trade papers and, having decided on Scotland as the location for her own hotel, began writing to estate agents and inspecting properties.

It had all taken time because she had no idea what

238

exactly she wanted. She had assumed they would buy a place that was already a hotel; but nothing suitable had come on the market. They had just missed a possible place in the Cairngorms, but Judith was a great believer in fate and she knew that if something was meant it would happen. When she saw Forteliot Castle she knew the moment had come.

It was the summer holidays and she and Marcel had not seen each other for some time. Judith had taken the opportunity of spending some time with Pauline and Michael, travelling with them through Scotland by car and staying at some first-class hotels on the way. But nothing had, or could, compare to what she had in mind.

'It *is* lovely, don't you think?' She slipped her arm through Marcel's as, instinctively, they both turned to gaze at the castle.

But to her surprise his attitude had been unresponsive and he stared ahead, frowning.

'*Don't* you like it, Marcel?'

'Of course I like it,' he paused and shrugged, 'as a home; but not as a hotel.'

'But it would make a *wonderful* hotel.' Judith had been so sure of his approval that she felt as though she had received a thump in the chest.

'Do you really think so, darling?' Marcel dug his hands into the pockets of his well-cut tweed jacket.

'Of course I think so, dear. It has all the advantages of Aylestone and yet . . .' She struggled for the words she felt she needed if she was to have any hope of convincing him.

'It is too remote,' Marcel blurted out, before she could complete her sentence. 'You will never get anyone to come here. They say the railway to Hawick is going to be axed by Dr Beeching, so you will not be able to get here by train. Who is going to visit a place so far away? I agree it is like Aylestone, and very beautiful, more so. But Aylestone is only thirty miles from London. That is a different prospect altogether, and yet look at the trouble you had with that! This place is hopelessly impractical and you must forget it.'

'But I've almost bought it . . . I've offered for it. I was so *sure* you'd approve.' Judith felt dumbfounded.

'You haven't signed anything have you?' Marcel said sharply.

'Of course not, but my word . . .'

'You word is not legally binding.'

'But they know I love it.'

'You can still love it, my dear; but love it from a distance. You are letting sentiment overrule reason. As a hotel . . .' Marcel shook his head and looked impatiently at his watch. 'Judith, we might as well get away, as there is no point in staying here.'

'You mean we're just going to walk away and leave them?'

'Why not?' Marcel looked puzzled.

'Marcel, this is about my *sixth* visit to this place. I am on Christian name terms with the Forteliots.'

'I'm surprised at you for getting so involved,' Marcel said crossly. 'It's most unprofessional of you. I thought you were a better business woman. I should have come up earlier.'

'I thought it was useless if we couldn't get planning permission to turn it into a hotel. It has taken months to get so much as a promise. I was sure your approval would be a formality. Oh, Marcel,' Judith clutched his hand. 'It even reminds me of the Hotel Daniel, surrounded by mountains and trees; and,' she stretched out her hand, 'just *look* at this river, this magnificent river stuffed full of trout. Marcel, have you any idea how anglers would give their eye teeth for unlimited access to such a river? And then over there,' she moved her hand, shielding her eyes against the sun. 'It is almost crying out to be turned into a golf course. Why, it could rival Gleneagles . . .'

'Gleneagles,' Marcel sneered. 'Have you *any* idea how absurd you sound? What is this compared to Gleneagles?'

'It's what it can be! Have you no vision at all?' Judith was beginning to feel angry. 'It is much more beautifully situated than Gleneagles. With imagination and flair it could be made perfect.'

'How many people do you suppose we could sleep here, Judith?'

'I thought twenty or so couples. There are an awful lot of rooms. Maybe two suites as well.'

'And *how* many people to dine?'

'Well, that's not so easy.' She flung her head back and gazed at him. 'It will depend on your cuisine. I think people will come from far and wide, myself. Why, in France good food attracts people, no matter where it is or how far they have to travel to get it.'

'This is not France,' Marcel said in a chilly tone. 'It is Scotland, and Scottish people do not, to my knowledge, have the same gourmet appreciation of fine food.'

'Oh that's silly, and so prejudiced! They have beautiful food.'

'It does not compare to the best of French cuisine.' Marcel's tone sounded final.

'But *you* will do that, darling . . . you will make them come.'

'I will not,' Marcel said and spread his feet firmly apart on the ground. 'I most certainly will not. It was bad enough having to go to Aylestone once a week. Do you think I'm going to come up here every week too?'

'I thought that, to start, you might stay up here and leave René in charge in London. He is ready for it. He will appreciate the responsibility.'

'Do you think *I* want René to take my restaurant over from me? Steal my thunder after all I have done to build it up, to try and get the third star from the Guide? Do you think *I* am mad, just when I am on the verge of that happening, to go through all this,' Marcel gesticulated wildly with his arms, 'and begin again? No thank you. I am not such a young man, after all. I have worked very hard. In addition I have endured many insults, much humiliation, largely thanks to you. I can tell you, Judith,' Marcel turned his back to the sun and looked at his wife, 'I was reluctant to become re-involved with Aylestone. I did not think it a good idea when we started again. I knew that place was bad luck, and I was right. I am quite happy, thank you, in what I am doing. I have no intention of being involved in anything as foolish, as hard, and as time-consuming again.'

Judith had never seen her husband in quite such a state, so resolved. The children, attracted by the raised tones of their parents, stood in front of them, twisting and turning, fingers in their mouths.

The sight of them seemed to disturb Marcel and he stooped to ruffle their hair.

'There, my darlings, we shall go quite soon. Judith,' peremptorily Marcel gazed at his watch again, 'you had better go and explain to your friends what we have decided. Give them our regrets. Blame it all on me; say I am the villain. I don't care what you say. I'll wait for you in the car.'

Then, putting out a hand for each of his children, he walked resolutely back up the drive as they skipped excitedly beside him. Judith watched them until they were nearly out of sight, then she sat down on a nearby bench and joined her hands in front of her in an attitude of resignation, undecided as to what to do. After a while she heard a step behind her and, turning, saw it was Alice Forteliot, her own hands deep in the pockets of her long cardigan. For a moment she stared unsmilingly into Judith's eyes then, softly, she spoke.

'He doesn't like it, does he, dear? I could tell he didn't. How disappointing for you.' As Judith didn't reply Alice sat gingerly on the seat beside her, her shoulders hunched up for warmth. Then to her surprise she felt Judith's hand slip through her arm and, as she looked up, she saw Judith's broad smile.

'*Nothing* is going to change, Alice,' Judith said. 'I half expected Marcel to react the way he did. He likes it as a place, but he thinks it will make a lousy hotel.'

'Oh *dear*!' Alice gazed abjectly at her knees. 'I *so* hoped . . .'

'I didn't finish, my dear.' Judith leaned over until her mouth was a few inches from the old lady's ear. 'I *disagree* with Marcel. I think it will make a wonderful hotel, a spectacular hotel, and I'm going to go through with it no matter what he thinks. I back my judgement, not his. Now, tomorrow I'm going to drive you into Edinburgh and sign the form of intent to purchase. This is going to be my very own hotel; mine and mine alone and, as Forteliot is a very old and famous name, with your permission I shall call it just that: Forteliot Castle, under the management of Judith Prynne.'

They hadn't met since he'd stayed at the hotel during the crisis between Marcel and André Hebert. It was quite a long time ago. Occasionally they talked on the phone and Moira sometimes mentioned him in her letters. When she had time Judith worried about her sister and her obviously unsatisfactory marriage. But Moira was a grown woman, a mother of two, and she would not thank her sister for interfering in her private affairs.

Judith had called Leo Valenti in Los Angeles and he'd told her he was coming to London, and invited her to dine. Would she like to bring Marcel? No? He was polite; dinner for two then. He named an expensive, well-thought-of restaurant in Knightsbridge, and the time of their rendezvous.

She was known in the restaurant as, increasingly, she

was known everywhere in the world of smart hotels, elegant places to eat. For her date she wore a short black dress with a flared skirt and a cutaway collar which enhanced the diamond necklace that Marcel had given her when Pauline was born. Her chestnut hair was simply dressed and her eyes were subtly made up to enhance their colour. Men raised their heads to follow her tall, slim figure as she walked across the floor.

'I see you're known here,' Leo Valenti said, a note of approval in his voice as he waited for her to sit down.

'Pierre Constance, who owns it, is a great friend of Marcel's. Everyone comes at some time or the other to eat at our restaurant, you know. We like to exchange visits.'

Leo listened attentively, his head bent in concentration. When he raised his eyes she could see the extent of his admiration as they were fixed on her. '*Prynne's*, I hear, is considered the best restaurant in London. If you didn't own it I would have suggested eating there. This is the second best.'

'It is one of the good ones. Are we really the best? Or are you just saying it?'

For a moment Leo looked at her across the table, the expression on his face now enigmatic. 'When you know me better, and I hope that you soon will, you will learn that I never say things I don't mean. I mean it: *Prynne's is* the best.' He put an elbow on the table and leaned his head against the palm of his hand, studying her. 'I have told you before that you don't resemble your sister, haven't I?'

'Yes, you have. Moira is very like my mother and her side of the family. I'm a Prynne. Now tell me,' she leaned across the table towards him: 'How *is* Moira?'

Leo flickered his fingers on the tablecloth and his expression became grave.

'Is anything the matter?' Judith prompted him.

'Nothing that a lot of marriages don't go through. Yours too, I expect.'

Judith bit her lip and stared at the table, aware, not for the first time, of the subtlety of Valenti's approach. He was a master in the art of discovery. He got the answers he wanted without having to ask too many questions.

'Well, we all have our ups and downs. But I feel badly about Moira. She has asked me to visit so often; but I never have the time. Marcel doesn't like the heat so, in the summer, when we can get away, we go north.'

'To Scotland?'

'Sometimes,' Judith said. 'Tell me, are you psychic?'

Valenti looked momentarily thrown and, as Pierre arrived with the menus, he took the opportunity to have a chat with him, complimenting him on the decor, new since his last visit, the ambience, but above all the menu, intent on flattery.

'You will get the third star before Marcel,' Leo concluded teasingly.

'I don't think so, monsieur, as we have only got one.'

Leo put a hand to his mouth to stifle a smile. 'I'm so sorry. Then I am sure you will soon get the second.'

'We do not pretend to have the magic of Marcel Laborde, Monsieur Valenti.' Pierre paused for a moment to gaze at the ceiling. 'To us, you must understand, he is like a god. His inspiration is almost certainly divine. There are very few chefs like him in the universe.'

Valenti studied the menu, inviting Judith, who was looking embarrassed, to join him. She suggested a few unusual dishes. 'That is, if you like fish,' she added.

'But of course I like fish. Am I not an Italian?'

Finally Leo gave the order. Then the choice of wines was debated for some time both with Judith and the wine waiter. When that important matter was concluded, to the satisfaction of all parties, he crossed his arms and, leaning them on the table, gazed once more at his companion.

'Now tell me why we're here.'

'Ah!' Judith took a deep breath. She might have known he would come to the point straight away.

'If you prefer we can wait until the coffee.' Quite clearly Leo discerned her sense of unease.

'No, I'd like to begin right away though, if you say "no", it will be difficult.'

'I can't imagine myself denying you anything,' Valenti said in his velvety voice with its transatlantic intonation. 'By the way, forgive me for saying so, but you are even more attractive now than when I last met you.'

'What I want is strictly without strings,' Judith said with a glint in her eyes. 'No conditions of any kind, particularly of the personal sort.'

'How well you understand me,' Valenti said with a smile. 'Please don't keep me in suspense any longer.'

Judith spun out the story of Forteliot so that it lasted for as long as the meal – her plans, ambitions, its potential. When she finally finished, the meal was almost over. Leo gave her his entire concentration, at times appearing spellbound.

She was aware of his interest, not only in what she was saying, but in herself as a person. And, as she talked and he listened, she wondered what was the source of his magnetic attraction for her. His deep-set eyes were altogether strange and compelling; and his strong, impassive features, his long nose, added up to a totality of dynamism: a man of vision. His hands were long, strong and capable, but, above all, when he talked he gave an impression of confidence, vigour, determination and speed.

She told him first about her quest; about finding Forteliot touched by the rays of the setting sun in its tranquil position by the side of the Tweed. She described it almost with love: its antiquity, the beauty of its russet stone, its fairy-tale grandeur, the gables of assorted sizes, the twinkling mullioned windows. She outlined the history of the Forteliots, as old, or older, than the Prynnes.

Towards the end, and more prosaically, she told him about the drawn-out applications for permission to turn it into a hotel and, finally, she told him about Marcel's opposition.

'Totally opposed?' Leo spoke at last, elbows on the table, chin resting on his clenched hands.

'Totally.'

'He wants to have nothing to do with it?'

'He thinks it won't work, frankly. I must tell you that.'

'Why must you?' His voice was teasing.

'Because I'm going to ask you for money. Lots of it. You once said . . .'

'I remember.' He held out his hand. 'Don't think I would forget something like that. It is not often that I offer a beautiful woman money. But I meant what I said. If you needed capital you had only to ask. One funny thing is that, as long ago as that event took place, I felt one day, instinctively, that you would need me. It would happen.'

'But, of course, you want assurance that it's a good proposition financially?'

For a moment he looked surprised.

'But I trust you, Judith,' he replied. 'I trust your judgement completely. It was, after all, you who made Prynne's . . .'

'Oh no, that was Marcel.'

'I have known many good chefs,' Leo shrugged, 'but the real secret is not in the kitchen. It is the organization, the logistics. It is *you* who made Prynne's, not him. What will he do without you?'

'I will never let Marcel down.'

'But why, if he doesn't support you? Why should you support him?'

'Because,' Judith levelled her eyes at him, 'he is a great man, an artist. He is gifted but, as you say, he is not commercial. He was being perfectly honest when he told

247

me Forteliot won't succeed and I respect that. Besides he is my husband.'

'Ah,' Leo made a broad gesture with outstretched hands. 'That, alas, I cannot deny. It is an irrefutable fact. So . . .'

'You see, I'll admit I'm ambitious,' Judith went on. 'I would like to open more stately home hotels, but one at a time. Get this one right and then move on.'

'Wonderful!' Leo exclaimed, signalling for the bill. 'And you want me to be your partner?'

'Oh no.' Judith's expression was dismayed.

'No?' Leo looked up surprised, perhaps a little annoyed, at her tone of voice.

'Please don't be offended,' she said, 'but I want to own this place myself. I have had Drake and Matthew Jenner, Marcel. I want this to be mine, and mine alone.'

'But my dear Judith, it will be. I assure you of that.' Leo leaned back and knocked his clenched fists sharply on the table. 'You will be in complete control; but I would not be a good businessman if I believed in you so much that I lent you the money you needed – a substantial sum, I understand – without retaining for myself an . . . interest, shall we say?' He looked at her keenly. 'I believe the situation with Jenner was that he had control and the members of your family owned forty-five per cent?'

'Yes.' Judith avoided his eyes.

'Well, in this case you alone will have complete control and I will retain thirty per cent.'

'Thirty per cent is a lot,' Judith said, biting her lip.

'Then, without me, who will you go to?'

'I don't know.' She too leaned back in her chair and gazed at him. 'I was naïve to think you wouldn't want a share. I thought I could pay you back on "generous terms".'

'You will pay me back, my dear, by making a good job of our enterprise.' He bent towards her, but he did not attempt to touch her hand. 'But we must understand the rules of engagement. We must be quite, quite clear about these. Don't you see it is essential that I have a substantial share if I am to protect not only my interests but you? I want you to be free to be creative. In return you will have what money you need, the best advice, and independence too. You are always to be your own woman but – but,' he held up a finger, smiling beguilingly at her, 'I will always be there at the end of the telephone, a mere aeroplane ride away, when you need me. And, whenever you do need me, I shall come.'

Chapter 13

Douglas Prynne looked with satisfaction at the crowd lunching in the dining room, most of them businessmen lured to Aylestone by the prospect of a good meal and an afternoon's golf, or the opportunity to impress a client from abroad by the hotel's cuisine and facilities. There was the usual sprinkling of residents, but not many, and this was a worry which, momentarily, took the smile off Doug's face.

There were people who said that since Judith had left Aylestone the tone of the place had gone down; but Doug refused to believe this. Appointed general manager, he had taken to the task with enthusiasm, moving into her top floor suite and making the success of the hotel his goal, to try and compensate for the dispiriting side of his life: his marriage. But, even more important, the feeling of inferiority which working alongside his dynamic sister had always given him had gone. He was in a job that he could do well, a business he knew inside out, and a place in which he had lived most of his life.

After Judith left the staff rallied round Doug. She had not, on the whole, been popular. Of course she had her admirers, her flatterers, but André Hebert cordially hated her and Neil Beaumont resented her; they both influenced many of those under them. Judith had been, in the opinion of the detractors, too strong, too tough, too unrelenting. She seemed to think that, to run a good hotel, you had to make it a full-time occupation.

André Hebert, who was a man fond of the golf course, knew better. He started to take more time off and leave the work to his deputy, a cousin of his from France called

Alphonse Hebert. Neil Beaumont was courting and wanted more time off to see his girlfriend; so, in subtle ways, now that the iron discipline imposed by Judith had gone, most of the staff felt able to let their hair down a bit and relax. In other words, sloppiness set in and such an attitude was the death-knell of efficiency and good service.

Doug was about to leave the dining room when he became slowly aware of an altercation taking place in the far corner. Eyebrows were raised, voices lowered. Swiftly the *maître d'hôtel*, who was new since Judith's day, left his desk and went over to investigate the source of the disturbance. Doug remained where he was, in the shadow of the desk by the door. The waiter who had been serving at the table, a *commis* in a long white apron, was, in turn, explaining something to the station waiter to whom he was responsible. At the intervention of the *maître d'hôtel*, both men began talking at once while, of the four men who had been eating at the table, one stood up and angrily threw down his napkin.

Doug thought that if he joined the party it would resemble an affray, draw even more attention to itself, so he remained where he was, hoping that things would sort themselves out. However this was not to be, and a second man stood up and started waving his hands about. Swiftly Doug crossed the floor and recognized one of the lunchers as Gavin Lyon, the marketing director of a large multinational corporation who frequently brought guests from the head offices of the group nearby for lunch. It was Mr Lyon who had first stood up and thrown his napkin on the table.

'Mr Lyon,' Doug said with a smile and a bow, 'I am sorry that something seems to have disturbed you. Is there anything I can do to help?'

'There certainly is, Mr Prynne,' Lyon said, in a tone lacking the cordiality with which he habitually addressed the general manager. 'I was complaining about the quality of the terrine that we have been eating. One of my guests had the decided impression it was bad . . .'

'Oh, that couldn't possibly be the case,' Doug said. 'All our food is fresh.' He looked at the *maître d'hôtel*, who reluctantly stood back.

'Nevertheless my guest,' Lyon turned and pointed to a man who sat with his back to the room, eyeing the terrine on his plate with an offended expression, 'maintains that it is. Mr Bromberg is an American director of our organization. He is accustomed to eating at most of the great hotels and restaurants of the world. Naturally I wanted him to be pleased.'

'Naturally.' Doug smiled at Mr Bromberg and smartly whisked away the offending dish. 'And if Mr Bromberg finds this venison terrine not to his taste he will immediately be offered something else.' Doug made a deprecatory gesture with his hands. 'Venison can be a matter of taste, I do insist on that, sir. Some like it high, some . . .'

'It is not that it is not to my *taste*,' Mr Bromberg insisted in flat Brooklynese. 'It is definitely *off*.'

'Maybe you like it a little less well hung, sir?' Doug suggested. 'In this establishment, where it is freshly made, I can assure you it could not be *bad*. Only the freshest and best ingredients are used.'

'Do you want I send it to our lab to have it analysed?' Bromberg interrupted the smooth flow of Doug, who blenched.

'That will *not* be necessary, sir. If you and your friends would care to inspect the menu and re-order I can assure you that you will find no fault with any of the dishes offered. And naturally,' Doug said, while the *maître d'hôtel* smoothly placed menus under their noses again, 'there will be no charge for this meal which will be with our compliments. That includes wine, of course, Mr Lyon.' Doug flicked his fingers at the *sommelier* who came running.

'Well . . .' Lyon looked doubtful, but the powerful

Bromberg nodded authoritatively and Lyon sat down while the *commis* refilled their glasses.

Then, as though nothing had happened, Doug bowed once more and putting his hands behind his back strolled through the restaurant smiling, pausing to address a guest, either to welcome him or her, or to ask if everything was in order.

When Doug got back to the desk where the *maître d'hôtel* was inspecting a bill he was greeted by a look of hauteur.

'Well, that went off all right,' Doug said, a little nervously.

'I would be grateful if I might have a word with you after luncheon, Mr Prynne,' said the *maître d'hôtel*, whose name was Spens, and he swept away from the desk in order to present the bill to the client who had called for it.

Doug watched him, feeling mystified, but after a few moments he left the dining room and wandered through the hall into the lounge where some of the lunchers were enjoying their coffee.

As usual everything, everywhere, sparkled and shone. Fresh flowers filled all the vases, which gleamed on polished tables, though it was not yet warm enough for the end doors to be open.

Doug looked round, waved to one or two of the people he knew, then returned to the reception to inspect the register.

'Everything in order, Mr Mallory?'

'Yes, sir.' Mallory, who was also new since Judith's day, turned round from the pigeonholes where the letters and keys were kept, with a practised smile.

'Would you tell Mr Spens that I shall be in the flat if he wants to talk to me?'

'Very well, sir,' Mallory said, turning round again as Doug went over to the lift and rang the bell to take him to the second floor.

Outside the door of the linen room he paused, listened, finally knocked and went in. It was empty. Everything was neat and in its place, but there was no sign of Doris Malcolm, who had been reinstated the moment Judith had left the hotel. Doug looked round again, wondered whether to leave a note, decided against it and continued up to his suite, letting himself in with his key.

There, sprawled in a chair by the window and smoking, was Doris, the smoke trailing like a signal over the top of the paper she was reading.

Doug gulped and she looked up.

'Hello, darling,' Doris said, and tipped the ash from her cigarette nonchalantly into an ashtray by her side.

'Doris . . .' Doug began and then stopped. The housekeeper put down the paper on her lap and looked at him.

'What is it, Doug?'

'Well, is it wise, just to . . . come in, like this . . . I mean, Ros or *any* of the staff . . . besides I didn't even know you had a key.'

'I have the keys to all the rooms, Doug,' Doris said with a note of asperity in her voice and, peremptorily putting the paper down, she got to her feet and straightened her skirt over her hips. 'I am, after all, the housekeeper. However, I'm sorry if I offended you.' Then she marched to the door, pressing past Doug, who lunged after her.

'Doris, I didn't mean . . . that is . . .'

'Then what *did* you mean, Doug?' she enquired, turning round, cheeks pink with anger. 'That I am only to come when invited, is that what you meant? That I am only, after all, merely the bloody housekeeper.'

'Oh Doris, please *don't*,' Doug said, vainly trying to take her by the shoulders. 'You're beginning to sound like Ros.'

'Oh am I?' Doris retorted. 'Good enough for your bed, but not entitled . . .'

'Please, Doris, *stop* it!' Doug threw himself into one of

254

the chairs and gave a loud sigh. 'Please, Doris, not *today*. There has just been an awful scene in the dining room. We could have lost a very important customer.'

'A scene, what sort of scene?'

'I don't think there's been anything like it since André and Marcel had the fight that ultimately led to Judith leaving.'

'What was the fuss about today?' Doris said, changing her tone. Then she sat on the arm of his chair and tenderly began to stroke away the bits of hair that stuck to his forehead.

'One of the clients complained about the food. Said it was *bad*. I must say I thought it smelt high, even for venison. But instead of just whisking his plate away the *commis* started to argue with him. Arguing with a client, I ask you! Then Morgan, the station waiter, intervened and finally John Spens went over. I just watched thinking it best to keep away, hoping it would blow over, but then the argument grew too violent. It was too much.'

'You can't handle this kind of thing, can you, Doug?' There was a note of patronage in Doris's voice. 'Now Judith . . .'

'I must ask you not to keep on referring to Judith either, Doris. As for handling the situation, of course I can. I can handle any situation.'

'That's what you say.'

'Doris, you're not being very *loyal* to me, are you?'

'I'm just trying to help you, dear, to get a grip on things. You can, you know. You just lack confidence.'

Then, all at once, his previous feeling of wellbeing vanished and the old fear, the feeling of failure, overwhelmed Douglas Prynne once again. He got up and gently pushed Doris Malcolm away.

'Spens has said he wants to see me. I've asked him to come here. Do you mind, Doris?'

'Not at all,' Doris said. 'Just ring the bell when you need

me, sir.' And without a backward glance she flounced out of the room.

Doug sighed, resumed his seat and lay back again in his chair, passing his hand over his sweaty face.

He knew it. He was in it too deeply; she had taken advantage of him, as he might have guessed she would. A grope in the linen room, an ecstatic hour in his bedroom, had not been enough. And, of course, he should have known straight away it would not be enough.

Doris Malcolm was a frustrated, predatory woman who was also ambitious. In a way she resembled his wife. He would have done far better to try and get what he wanted from one of the chambermaids, who would probably have been contented with a tip.

But Doris! Doug realized he was perspiring freely and his heart thudded uncomfortably in his chest. There was a menace about Doris, a threat. She did not respect him and she could do him actual harm. Why, if Ros ever found out there would be an awful scandal; and bang would go his job as general manager of a prestigious hotel.

Yet how prestigious, really, was it? There had not been any complaints in the dining room as bad as today's, but complaints there were: about careless service, bills that had been wrongly calculated . . . too many complaints and too often. The reservations were falling away; profits were down and very soon, unless he did something, there would be a confrontation with Jenner. But what could he do? And why, oh why, had he decided to take, of all people, the housekeeper of the hotel – a voracious and demanding woman who valued her self-esteem – to bed?

There was a knock on the door and he croaked: 'Come in.' He started guiltily, hoping that Spens hadn't seen Doris leave the room. Of course he used it as an office, as Judith had. Still . . .

'Come in, come in,' he said again with more geniality

and got to his feet as, still with a stern expression on his face, John Spens entered and stood stiffly before him.

'Do sit down, Mr Spens,' Doug said, pointing to a chair.

'I have come to make a complaint, Mr Prynne. I would rather stand.'

Spens had come to Aylestone very well qualified, with glowing testimonials from hotels on the Continent as well as in England. He was an impressive, standoffish man who seemed to enjoy his authority in the dining room.

'Very well,' Doug said, also remaining on his feet. 'What is your complaint, Mr Spens?'

'I take a strong objection to your interference in the dining room today, Mr Prynne. That is *my* domain and not yours.'

'On the other hand,' Doug said with dignity, '*I* am the general manager. I thought the situation was getting out of control.'

'It was not, sir. I can assure you of that. I was coping with it perfectly adequately when you took it into your head to intervene. You made me look a fool, sir; you undermined my standing and authority in front of my own staff. I must warn you that, if anything remotely like that happens again, I shall immediately tender my resignation.'

Once more Doug passed his hand across his face. There were fresh beads of moisture on his brow and yet the room was cool. He made an effort to speak with dignity and authority too:

'I must tell you, Spens, I didn't think you *were* completely in control. I did leave you for a while, but when I saw that the client was Mr Lyon – a very important and frequent customer – and that another of his guests had joined in I felt I had no option but to intervene. Mr Lyon is a close friend of Sir Matthew. If this gets back to him . . .'

'Which no doubt it will, sir,' Spens said, a mean note entering his voice, 'together with the many other faults in this hotel which are not – and I must emphasize this –

what I was led to expect when I was appointed. Far from it.'

'Could you explain yourself?' Doug said, mopping his brow and finding support by leaning against his desk.

'I could indeed, Mr Prynne,' Spens said, his voice warming to his task. 'I was led to believe, by yourself and others, that this was a first-class establishment, on a par with the best in the world: the Ritz in Paris, the Carlton in Cannes, the Excelsior in Rome. Well,' the *maître d'hôtel*'s countenance was briefly lit by an ironic smile, 'it is my sad duty to inform you, sir, that it is not. I worked for some time in the dining room of the Paris Ritz, and Aylestone doesn't even *begin* to compare with it.'

'I think the Ritz was, maybe, an exaggeration,' Doug said uncomfortably. 'The Carlton is far too big, the Excelsior . . . This is a very different sort of hotel.'

'Oh, it is indeed, Mr Prynne. It will soon be a *completely* different sort of hotel. I believe that it once catered for the mass market. If you ask me it will again, and sooner than you think. It is going down, Mr Prynne, and neither you nor any of the senior staff seem aware of the fact.'

'Could you let me have your evidence?' Doug said frostily, surreptitiously wiping the palms of his hands on his trousers.

'One piece of evidence, sir, is that the venison terrine today, as I believe you were fully aware, was, indeed, in no fit state to be put before a customer.'

'It was a bit high?' Doug suggested uneasily.

'It was *bad*, sir. If the gentleman had not complained after he smelt it we should probably have had a severe case of food poisoning. I was quite horrified when I saw the remainder of the terrine in the kitchens. I tried to complain to the chef but the chef, of course, was not there.'

'What do you mean "of course"?' Doug leaned more heavily against his desk.

'He is always on the golf course, sir, or have you not noticed?'

'I know he likes golf.'

'Too much, sir. He infinitely prefers it to his duties. The duties of a *maître-chef* are in the kitchen, not on the golf course. What would people say about *me* if I were not personally there to supervise the dining room?'

'Hebert *has* a very able deputy.'

'But has he, Mr Prynne?' Spens raised his eyebrows.

'Don't *you* think Alphonse is a good chef?'

'Mundane, sir, if I may say so; mundane and careless. It was he, after all, who served the venison which should have been thrown out days ago. As it is he is more and more in charge of the cuisine and I, among others, have noticed that the bookings in the restaurant are down. People will not pay high prices, or return, for inferior food.'

'You should have told me this before.' Doug shakily lit a cigarette.

'I was about to when today's incident occurred. I have only been here three months, Mr Prynne. Not long, but long enough to see that all is not as it should be. I understand that when Miss Judith Prynne . . .'

'I don't wish to hear any comments about my predecessor, thank you,' Doug said crisply, 'even if she *is* my sister.'

'I was going to say that I only heard good reports of her,' Spens said with an air of glee.

'I am not interested in what you heard.' Doug's tone was offhand. 'I am now in charge; but thank you for your comments, Spens. They will be heeded.'

'Thank *you*, Mr Prynne,' Spens said with an expression that indicated his view that he had won the round.

Doug attacked the recumbent body of Doris as if she were an inanimate object so that, after a while, she cried out:

259

'Hey, what's the matter with you, Doug? Get off.' She vigorously pulled herself upright and his body slid awkwardly off hers. He was breathing so hard she could hear the loud thump of his heartbeat. He lay on his face, his body heaving, one hand clasping her thigh, helpless as something, someone washed up by the sea on to the shore.

'That wasn't very *nice*, Doug, was it?' she said sharply. 'You hurt me.'

'I'm sorry,' Doug muttered weakly, patting her bare flesh. 'It's been an awful day.'

'Well, there's no need to behave like an *animal*.'

'I didn't mean to. I'm sorry. Truly sorry.' He patted her again but his eyes remained closed, his breathing still stertorous.

Doris peevishly pulled the bedclothes up to her chin. She felt offended, abused and, at the same time, rather puzzled. If anything, Doug was a timid lover and he had never thrown himself at her as he had that night, butting into her like a battering ram, no thought for her own pleasure.

However he *was* the general manager; he *was* a Prynne and, having got her tentacles around him, she had no intention of letting go.

Doris Malcolm was no longer young. She had given up hope of finding another mate, and reconciled herself to spending the rest of her life as a housekeeper, inevitably at hotels less prestigious than Aylestone, when Miss Prynne had peremptorily given her the sack.

That following year she spent at a hotel in Bournemouth, the bulk of whose clientele seemed to have come there to die. It was an offbeat, low-paid job and she was about to look elsewhere when, out of the blue, had come the invitation from Douglas Prynne, who was a generous man and thought his sister had treated her unfairly, to rejoin the staff. Now she was his mistress.

She knew quite well that it was not what he had had in

mind. A grope was all he'd intended, but Doris Malcolm was not a woman to trifle with. She was not young, but she was not old. She was forty-three, which was a comfortable age for a woman; slightly too old to have, or want to have, children, yet young enough to enjoy the pleasures of sex, to need the admiration of men. The fact that Douglas was younger than she was, and needed a mother as well as a mistress, were additional factors in her favour.

But roughness, no. She gave him a fresh look of disapproval, but he was asleep.

The next morning the reason for Doug's rage and despair, or some of it, was revealed in the newspaper under the headline:

JUDITH PRYNNE OPENS PRESTIGIOUS NEW HOTEL IN SCOTLAND

and there was a huge picture of her standing in front of her imposing castle, glowing with hope and confidence. Beneath her, in quotes, was the sentence:

'I want it to be one of the world's best.'

Still reading, Doris took the paper through the sitting room to the bedroom where Doug was morosely drinking tea.

'Sorry about last night,' he said again as she got into bed beside him.

'That's all right.' She handed the paper to him with a wry smile. 'I suppose it wasn't only the row in the dining room? I suppose it was this as well?' and she pointed to Judith's picture on the front page.

'Well, it was on the evening news on TV. I don't suppose it helped. Of course I knew the hotel was due to open and I'm pleased for her; but all this publicity is ridiculous!'

'She must have had a good publicist,' Doris said consolingly.

'*Judith* is a good publicist,' Doug replied. 'She's the best. Everything she does she does extremely well.'

'Huh!' Doris muttered.

'No, honestly.' Douglas put a hand on her arm. '*Prynne's* in London has got the third Michelin star. One of a handful of restaurants in England to get such an accolade.'

'Well, that's thanks to Marcel, not *her*.'

'No, it's also thanks to her. She got him going; she drew attention to him. She'll do the same with this hotel. She's got the touch, the gift.'

Doris shrugged disbelievingly. 'Well, she lost the touch here, that's for sure.'

'She had too many things against her.'

'She was arrogant.'

'You rubbed her up the wrong way.'

'I don't know why you're defending her,' Doris said derisively. 'She had no time for you.'

'Well,' Doug said after a thoughtful pause, 'she *is* my sister, and she is good and, do you know,' he put the paper down and looked moodily past Doris out of the window, 'I wouldn't be surprised if, one day, she didn't come back here.' He turned his head and smiled wanly at her. 'You just mark my words.'

From the balcony that surrounded the bungalow that the Prynnes had bought in pre-war days, and which they now called home, Greville Prynne surveyed the lower slopes of the Khasi hills, covered with acres of tall green tea-plants which one day would become a fine Assam tea. It was only ten in the morning but this was the time he liked best, and he lay semi-recumbent in his chair, a gin and tonic by his side, stirring the soft belly of the mongrel who lay contentedly at his feet. At this hour, when the brown hills were still covered with a fine morning mist, and with Angela still slumbering, the air was calm and quiet. Peace.

At this hour he would glance cursorily at the English papers, which were usually a week old, sometimes more, and read any mail that had been brought up by the servants when they went to fetch the provisions for the day. The letters more usually consisted of a collection of pamphlets from the various organizations of which he was still a member, the numerous official clubs and groups to which he still subscribed, as a lingering reminder of England. But occasionally there were bills which had escaped the net at home and, more rarely these days, a personal letter from one of the members of his family.

These Greville always read circumspectly; often he didn't open them for days. There were seldom totally good things his family had to tell him and Greville hated bad news. 'Trouble at t'mill,' he would say in a phoney northern accent to Angela as, eventually and goaded on by her, he reluctantly slid his paperknife through the envelope.

Both Greville and Angela were completely content in the paradise to which their dreams had brought them. The bungalow was ramshackle and run down; it needed doing up inside and out. But after a token lick of paint this ceased to worry them. They were still cocooned by thick mosquito nets at night because they had no air conditioning. They sweated over their drinks on the veranda day after idle day. Most of the money they'd had left seemed to have evaporated, yet the views of the hills from the bungalow were there for ever, and they were free.

A few of the friends they'd made before the war had survived. Some had gone home to post-war austerity Britain and hated it as much as Greville and Angela had. Everyone of course was a lot older now; but what did it matter? What did time matter? The climate was wonderful, living was cheap and so were servants, and the supply of alcohol, on which both were increasingly dependent, adequate if one knew the right sources. The day started with gin and tonics and it ended with them, and there were lots and lots of little snifters in between. The whole day was spent in a pleasant alcoholic haze, and who would want it any different?

Greville stirred the dog again and opened a week-old issue of *The Times*, turning straight to the sports news at the back but, as he flicked over the pages, something caught his eye and he found himself staring at a large picture of his daughter Judith against the background of a beautiful old house. By her side stood Michael and, kneeling in front with her mother's arms clasped loosely around her, was Pauline. She in turn hugged to her chest a black toy poodle, its face lovingly upturned towards her. It was an enchanting study by a well-known photographer.

However it was not just another society photograph, although Judith with her family looked the quintessence of the English leisured upper classes at home. It was a feature about a woman whom the byline proclaimed:

'An entrepreneurial success in a man's world: Judith Prynne opens a hotel with a difference.'

The article, also by a woman writer, began:

Judith Prynne, pictured above with her two children, Michael and Pauline, against the background of her newest acquisition, Forteliot Castle, near Hawick, Scotland. Formerly the home of Lord and Lady Forteliot, Miss Prynne (Mrs Marcel Laborde in private life) has turned it into a luxurious stately home hotel, converted at huge cost and where nothing will be spared to give pleasure to the guests. Already Miss Prynne reports bookings well into next year, with an emphasis on the autumn and winter months thanks to the popularity of the site on the banks of the Tweed, which offers all-year-round sporting facilities: fishing, shooting and a superb golf course modelled on Muirfields.

Miss Prynne first made her name in the fifties when she was behind the transformation of the home of the ancient Prynne family into the internationally famous hotel, Aylestone, in the Thames Valley. Miss Prynne later married the head chef at the hotel and she and her husband, Marcel, opened the equally celebrated *Prynne's* restaurant in London, which is one of the few in England to be awarded three stars in the Michelin Guide.

But this venture is very much her own. Neither her family nor her husband are associated with it. Instead Miss Prynne has a new partner, Leo Valenti, an American business tycoon who also happens to be the father-in-law of Miss Prynne's younger sister, Moira. Valenti, who has homes in Italy and the United States, and whose wealth is reported to be fathomless, is very much a sleeping partner. He insists: 'I have utter confidence in Judith's ability to manage. I have left the whole thing entirely in her hands.'

Miss Prynne says that, once Forteliot Castle is working to her satisfaction, she intends to resume her quest for other properties throughout the length and breadth of the British Isles, and thus become the owner of an internationally famous chain of hotels catering for the very rich.

'Hell's bells,' Greville muttered, putting his glass thirstily to his lips. 'Maybe it's time to go back.'

'What was that, dear?' Angela said, staggering on to the balcony and collapsing into a chair next to Greville as, with hands that trembled, she lit a cigarette, put it to her lips and promptly started to cough.

Greville glanced at her, passing her the paper without further comment.

'My goodness,' Angela said, squinting at it, reaching at the same time in her dressing gown pocket for her spectacles. 'Is it something about Judith?'

'I said maybe we should think about going home,' Greville said.

'Going *home*?' Angela, having skimmed the article, put down the paper and slipped off her spectacles, which hung on a chain around her neck. 'But *we've* no interest in Judith's business.'

'The more's the pity, because she asked us.'

'Yes, but we thought we needed the money. We still have our shares in Aylestone, though goodness knows what they're worth. The last dividend wasn't very good, was it?'

'We should have sold our shares to Judith when she asked us,' Greville said gloomily. 'They were worth a bit then.'

Judith had written to them the previous year offering

265

them shares in her new company, Prynne's (UK) Ltd, if they would sell their Aylestone shares to her. They hadn't even taken the trouble to reply. India made one lazy. It was such an easy, indolent life. There were few calls on the grey matter and certainly nothing that could not be left until the day after tomorrow, or even the day after that.

'It's *Mother* I worry about,' Greville said. 'Who's taking care of her?'

'Judith says she's very well looked after. This new woman is excellent, though she guards her like a gaoler. Your poor mother sometimes thinks she would be better off out of it.' Angela put a finger up to her head. 'Though, I must say, that episode at Aylestone *was* very funny, if you could see the funny side. All those titled and moneyed bigwigs searching the grounds for a ghost! Oh dear, how we laughed,' and Angela began to laugh again in the mournful, rather brittle way of one who was not quite tuned in to reality.

Looking at her, Greville thought that if she was not careful she would end up like his mother. Perhaps they both would.

Morosely, he put his glass to his mouth and drank deeply for solace.

Chapter 14

Moira Valenti stood at the window in one of the turrets of the castle which overlooked the river. Beyond the far bank the thick coniferous forest seemed to stretch into infinity though, in fact, it was bisected with paths, some wide enough to take a motor car. To the right, on the near bank, the rolling turf of the golf course began and, in the distance, it was just possible to see Leo Valenti, attired in plus fours, tartan socks and a Pringle sweater, teeing the ball for a drive. With him was Sir William McLaren, head of a large Scottish engineering works with whom Leo was having talks about some international business deal. But this time he had also come to see his daughter-in-law and grand-children, over from Italy on a prolonged stay. Perhaps, also, he had come to see Judith, too.

For, behind her, Judith, also wearing tweeds and a Pringle twinset, stood with her arms folded gazing in the same direction as her sister. Her thick, burnished hair was brushed back from her forehead and secured by a velvet band of the same dark green as her jumper and cardigan. Below them, on the tennis courts to the far side of the lawn, their children, Michael and Pauline, Alida and Franco, were engaged in an energetic game of tennis. It was a peaceful, pastoral scene and Judith sighed content-edly and put her hand on Moira's shoulder.

'I'm glad you're here.'

'So am I.'

Without turning, Moira tucked her own hand in her sister's and, for a moment, they stood like that, each engaged in her own thoughts.

'Shall you ever marry Leo, do you think?' Moira said

quietly, feeling the tremor through Judith's hand as she started behind her.

'I'm still married to Marcel.'

'Yes,' Moira let go her hand and, turning, faced her sister. 'But it's a marriage in name only, isn't it? Like mine?'

'Is yours really a marriage in name only? I always thought you and Richard were very physically attracted?'

'We were. It doesn't last. Do you know I haven't seen Richard for at least three months?'

'What?' Judith exclaimed.

'At least. Maybe longer. Even Leo is worried about him now.'

'Has he been away as long as that before?'

'Oh yes, but I thought he'd stopped. He seemed happier and more settled after we left Rome; but still a very strange person – remote and withdrawn. Very strange indeed. Someone, ultimately, it was very difficult to know.'

'But didn't you think his disappearances strange?'

'Very. Somehow one had to get used to them. He said he wanted to be on his own. The artistic side of his nature "craved" solitude.'

'Does he ever say where he's been?'

'No.' Moira turned to the window again, perhaps to try and conceal from her sister the desolate expression on her face. 'I don't think it's a woman though. I think it's something else.'

'May I ask what?' Judith whispered.

'I think it's something to do with drugs,' Moira said suddenly. 'I have done for a long time. Richard is a heroin addict . . . he injects himself. Either he goes away on a binge, or he goes looking for drugs or selling them. I really don't know.'

'But aren't you *terrified*? My God, what a revelation! How long have you known?'

'Quite long,' Moira said in a calm, collected way. 'You

can't always tell with drug addicts, you know. They're very crafty, like alcoholics. Richard only really showed signs a year after we married, when we were living in Rome. He was erratic, moody – depressed and then elated. I thought he wasn't well and was glad when we moved to Venice. Then, one morning I found the barrel of a syringe under our bed! It had dropped out of his pocket or something. Then I knew.'

'Did you confront him?'

'Not then, but later, when I'd got over the shock. He tried to pass it off, but I presented him with the evidence. He said very little and a short time afterwards he went off again. About a week later he rang and said he would come home on condition I never mentioned drugs ... Well,' Moira gave a gesture of helplessness, 'you can see it's been a strain.'

'Oh my darling.' Judith put her arms round Moira, who leaned against her for a moment or two.

'Worse things happen at sea.'

'Not many.'

'You and Leo,' Moira's voice changed abruptly. 'You didn't answer my question.'

'Yes I did. I said I was married to Marcel.'

'But there's an attraction between you and Leo. It's very obvious.'

'Is it?'

'Yes, to me anyway. Do you realize,' Moira said with a laugh that reminded Judith of their mother, 'that if you married him you'd be my mother-in-law?'

'The question of marriage between us has never come up,' Judith said guardedly. 'I don't want to hurt Marcel. He's the children's father. He is very, very fond of them and they of him.'

'I know; you needn't say it. I understand. Only ...' Moira paused, 'there *are* things about Leo I think you

269

should realize in case you ever do decide to throw in your lot with him.'

'Such as?' Judith caught her breath.

'Oh, I don't mean other women. I don't think he plays around; but he *is* Italian. He would expect you to be a wife. I wonder if the business side would . . . go to the wall?'

'Oh, I don't think so.' Judith visibly relaxed and began to laugh. 'Our discussions have not been as serious as that. Leo would know that I wouldn't want to lose interest in the business. He *knows* how important it is to me.'

'You've done awfully well in these past two years.' Moira looked round at the soft furnishings of the room. The predominant motif of the hotel was, obviously, the tartan; but it was subtly done and every room was furnished differently. The tartans were not obtrusive; but the air of the stately home continued in its hand-woven materials, its antiques, it sumptuousness. Most of the bedroom walls were panelled. There were real log fires and the Scottish theme influenced the cooking. Guests could order venison, haggis, Arbroath smokies and dishes that were a regional speciality. The head chef was a Scotsman, though he was assisted by a Frenchman who had trained at some of the great restaurants in France so that a cosmopolitan cuisine of an international standard could be offered in the restaurant.

But already Judith, having established Forteliot as a going concern, had her mind on something else: a hotel overlooking Derwent Water in the Lake District. It had not yet an outstanding reputation, the sort of reputation that Judith was carefully building up as her trademark: excellence at all levels, and at a price. That, she intended to establish in Lakeland.

That night she said to Leo:

'I feel very restless here. It is time to move on.'

'I wish you'd come to Los Angeles,' Leo said, gazing at the ceiling.

'But what is there to *do* in Los Angeles?'

'See where I live, see if you would like it too.'

'But you know I would never want to *live* there, Leo. I've told you that.'

'Well, I don't live there either; but it would be our home. Beverly Hills is very beautiful.'

Leo turned sideways, so that he could gaze at her, running his finger from one point between her breasts to her thighs, observing how the flesh of her taut stomach quivered as he did.

Supine, Judith's figure had a hint of voluptuousness that was not so apparent when she was upright.

They had been lovers for six months but, still, there were things about her he didn't know and, maybe, never would.

Leo Valenti had found Judith attractive from the day he first saw her, quite heavy with child, walking into the restaurant at *Prynne's*. He had thought, then, 'One day I will have this woman,' and he had savoured the thought for many years until, one day, during a visit to London, it had come true.

Marcel had been away. They went out to dine, discuss the progress of the business and, in their mutual pleasure and satisfaction with each other, went to bed.

Since then he seldom had her out of his mind. He was bewitched by her, and Judith, for her part, found the passion reciprocal. For the first time in her life she was completely, physically and wholly in love.

It was a love that excluded Marcel and the family. Some lovers find it quite easy to compartmentalize their lives and, to Judith, Leo was separate, special; their relationship was on a plane quite raised above ordinary, humdrum life.

Leo bent his head to kiss the top of the leg, just where it

271

became part of the hip, but she put a hand on his head and stopped him. He said abruptly:

'What is it? What's the matter?'

'I feel I should talk to Marcel.'

'But, darling, I *want* you to talk to Marcel.'

'I don't like deceiving him.'

'I haven't asked you to.'

'But I have. I've decided it's wrong. It's gone too far.'

'You told me it was years since you and Marcel made love.'

'It is; but he's still my husband. I don't feel right doing this. Besides,' she caught his hand as he tried gently to obtrude it between her thighs. 'Moira has noticed there's something between us.'

'Most people with any sense would.'

'Then *that's* not right. I hadn't realized it was so obvious. I've been blind. But my children will notice it too.'

'What did Moira say?' Leo's tone was curious. 'Did she approve or disapprove?'

'She said there were things about you I didn't know.'

'Oh?' Sharply, Leo voluntarily withdrew his hand and Judith felt his whole body tense. 'Oh, in what way?'

'Oh, don't be *frightened*.' Judith gave him a teasing look. 'She didn't say *women* . . . not as far as she knew; but she said there were other things.'

'What things?' Leo seemed to have forgotten about making love and nervously reached for his cigarette case.

'I see I've got you worried, haven't I?' Judith's tone grew even more mocking.

'I don't like games.' Leo abruptly took a cigarette out of his case and put it to his lips, whereupon Judith sat up, pulling the sheet over her body, and looked at him with surprise.

'You really *are* worried about something, aren't you?'

'Not at all,' he said stiffly. 'I just don't like people talking about me behind my back. Do you?'

272

'No, but I expect they do. Moira is your daughter-in-law. She knows you well. Did *you* know, incidentally, that Richard had been away from home for over three months?'

'He often goes away,' his father said casually.

'Moira said you're restless too.'

'That's true enough.' Leo exhaled a stream of smoke, his powerful chest working like a bellows.

'And that you would want *me* to be a proper Italian wife if we married.'

'That's not true.' Leo looked at her in a way that always seemed to make her melt. 'I don't expect you to give up the business. I know you love it, it means a lot to you, and I have things to do too. That doesn't mean we can't be married or, at least, that you can't be divorced and that we can be seen in public, like a couple. That's what I really want.' He stubbed out his cigarette and, leaning over her, gently pushed her down, one hand drawing back the sheet which she had pulled across her body. Then he lay on top of her and she clung to him with that intensity of passion which swept away all pretence, all restraint, as they abandoned themselves to pleasure.

It had never been like this with Marcel. She knew it was a platitude but, in many ways, Leo had made her come alive. She was still Judith Prynne, but not the one that so many people had known for so long. As a woman in love she was a very different kind of person from the old Judith: she was newer, keener, fitter and much, much happier.

And when she was not with Leo she wanted to be with him; and when she was she could never get enough of him. In every way he possessed her; penetrated her being. She thought it a wonder that the whole world didn't know, didn't recognize the new Judith. Or perhaps some did.

But did Marcel? And that, now, was what worried her.

It was that pleasant hour of the day between tea and dinner time – *cinq à sept*, that the French are said to prefer for lovemaking. Ostensibly Leo had the room next to hers, so that, when she retired to her room it was presumed she was alone. Moira had gone on an excursion with the children and Sir William McLaren, the engineering magnate who was yet quite an amusing bachelor of only thirty-six, whom everyone called Billy.

The lovers in the bedroom were suddenly interrupted by the shrill tones of the telephone, and Leo crushed his fist on hers and murmured:

'Leave it.'

'But they *know* I'm here. I can't,' she said, struggling a little, shifting him gently so that she could lift the receiver and put it to her ear.

'Yes?' That was the old Judith speaking, not the new one, whose heart was thudding, whose body was inflamed by desire.

'Your husband is on the telephone, Miss Prynne,' the receptionist said in her prim Scots voice.

'Could you tell him I'll ring him back,' Judith said breathlessly. 'I'm just about to get into the bath,' and she slammed down the phone before the receptionist could reply and left her hand on it, aware of the hammer of her heart in her breast.

'Who was it?' Leo murmured, his head resting on her shoulder.

'It was Marcel.'

There was a brief silence and then he said:

'Well, don't let it make you stop.'

'I can't go on.' She pushed her hands against his chest. 'Don't you *see*? It makes me feel horrible.'

'Really, Judith.' Leo withdrew from her and flopped beside her on the bed. She could feel his loss of ardour, his anger. 'You're behaving just like a child.'

'I'm not. I *feel* guilty, and *you* should be able to understand that.'

'Well, I can't . . . all right.' He gave a huge sigh which shook the bed. 'I'm sorry. You'll have to tell him, that's all, otherwise this is going to ruin our lives together.' Suddenly, with the elasticity and litheness of a young man he jumped off the bed, threw his wrap over his shoulders and stormed his way into the bathroom.

Judith lay still on the bed, legs outstretched as he had left her, listening.

Judith had incorporated many of the lessons she had learned at Aylestone in her careful development of Forteliot Castle as a hotel of great luxury. In the case of Aylestone there had been too many cooks to spoil the broth, almost literally; too many people with vested interests and ideas. To the inexperienced Prynnes, running a hotel had seemed a comparatively straightforward business. Most people, having stayed in many in their lifetime, thought they knew what they wanted.

In the light of hindsight the wonder was to Judith that Aylestone had ever really got off the ground and from what she heard indirectly – mainly through Gran's nurse, who was a mine of information – it still had its difficulties.

Judith's vision of a hotel on the Tweed was a combination of splendour and simplicity. The castle was an ancient one and the scenery magnificent; but that was not enough for the kind of hotel she envisaged. She had planned all the details meticulously in conjunction with an architect and interior decorator who had worked with her over *Prynne's*, and whom she trusted to fulfil her intentions.

She didn't want Forteliot to overdo the Scottish element. Too much tartan and stags' heads on the walls would effectively ruin it. But she wanted each of her new hotels to be a reflection of the area in which they were situated; thus, although tartan and Scottish emblems were incorporated in the overall design motif, the livery of the staff was plain: red, green or blue waistcoats, according to status, and black trousers.

She realized that it was important to find favour in Scotland which, after all, had a substantial tourist industry, so she was careful that most of the employees would be Scottish: these included the head chef, the *maître d'hôtel*, the head receptionist, the housekeeper, the cashier and the head porter. They had all been trained in England and abroad, but they had all also worked in Scotland.

Judith wanted harmony where before there had been discord. The general manager had also to be resident, at least until the hotel got going. Here she chose another Scot, Fraser Lyle, who had managed some notable hotels, mostly in Scotland. Fraser Lyle was divorced, which Judith liked too: there would be no wife and family to take his mind off the business. She provided a handsome suite for him on the second floor and, so far, they had worked together in harmony. The deputy manager was an Englishman, Jeremy Armstrong, and he too was single. He had a room on the top floor next to her suite.

In the grounds many of the old castle outbuildings had been adapted into quarters for the staff, as the nearest town was ten miles away and the local bus service was poor.

Communications were a problem. Most of the guests arriving by train had to be met at Edinburgh or Berwick, and there were two chauffeurs constantly engaged in ferrying guests to and fro in the maximum amount of comfort and convenience.

In its style the hotel was not unlike Aylestone. There was a lounge through which guests passed to the reception so that their first impression was of a luxurious private home. The general manager, who was a keen shot and a countryman at heart, had two dogs, obedient, well-trained spaniels who were frequently to be seen in front of the fire, and a beautiful Burmese cat, Sherezad, made herself comfortable among the many cushions.

But nothing was spared in an effort to cosset and pamper the guests. Each male guest had his own valet and each female guest her own maid. Sometimes, if the hotel was not full, they had their exclusive use, though if this was not possible they were shared, but only with one or two other guests. If guests brought their own staff – and some still did – they were accommodated in a staff house in the grounds with bells to connect them with their employers in the castle. In addition there were loaders, ghillies, beaters and expert anglers to assist guests with their favourite sports. There was a golf pro, caddies, and the stables were staffed by experienced horsemen and women.

All this had cost a great deal of money and finance was primarily Judith's responsibility: the management of money and the forecast of profits.

At the time Judith was there with her children, Moira and her family, and Leo, the hotel had been open nearly two years and, due to the advance publicity and rapturous notices in the press and media, it had hardly had an empty room. The Americans, in particular, liked the facilities offered by Forteliot Castle, and they came in droves and at all seasons of the year. For the forthcoming summer the hotel was booked out and Judith thought that finally she could concentrate on her new enterprise, the Ruskin, which stood on a promontory overlooking Derwent Water, not far from the spot where the famous writer and art critic, after whom the hotel was named, liked to walk.

As she had at Aylestone, Judith preferred to work in her suite. She had a desk overlooking the river in a small room off the bedroom, that had once been a dressing room.

The morning after her talk with Leo she sat at her desk doing her cash flow for the rest of the year, occasionally looking out to the golf course where Leo was having his usual fifteen holes with Billy. Fortunately Leo never sulked. When he had emerged from the bathroom the previous evening bathed and shaved, he was his usual imperturbable self – a little more grave, perhaps, and unsmiling, than was usual with her but, after she too had bathed and dressed, they had dined with Billy and Moira in the best of spirits. Afterwards the men played billiards.

By this morning his equilibrium seemed fully restored and he had gone off after breakfast in his plus fours, tartan socks and yellow sweater, a pipe clasped firmly between his teeth. Earlier they had discussed plans for the day, because this was their last at the hotel for some time. They planned to go to London, spending a few days at Derwent Water en route, and then fly to Los Angeles.

Judith had always managed to put personal problems to one side when she was working; but today it was difficult. She dictated her letters to the amiable secretary she shared with Fraser Lyle, Mildred Mactavish, and then she went again over cash forecasts with Lyle and the cashier, who was also a trained accountant. That done, she stood for some time gazing out of the window to where, in the distance, she could see the figures at play.

Suddenly, below her on the lawn, she saw Moira with the four children and, although she leaned out of the window to wave, Moira could neither see nor hear her. The children had fishing rods in their hands and Moira, who had become an accomplished water-colourist, was carrying her equipment. The five of them took the path along the river bank in the direction of the two golfers, now about a quarter of a mile away.

Billy was an attractive young man, Judith thought, watching the figures of her children, their cousins and aunt recede into the distance. He was unmarried and he was very rich. At dinner the night before his fascination with Moira was obvious, and he had paid her a number of compliments. How nice it would be . . .

There was a rapid series of knocks on the door and calling 'Come in' she turned to see the cashier, Tom Guthrie, with whom she had already had a lengthy conference that morning.

Tom Guthrie had spent most of his life working in hotels

among their ledgers and accounts. It was not a glamorous job, but it was an important one and Judith had scoured the country to find the best.

Tom Guthrie, who lived with his wife in a small cottage on the estate and had two grown-up children, was the sort of person it was difficult to recall. He seemed to have perfected the art of anonymity – a chameleon-like ability to appear to merge with the landscape – which seemed to suit people who deal with money and allied matters. He was of medium height, balding, had a moustache and large round glasses behind which now his eyes blinked rather rapidly.

'Hello, Tom.' Judith went over to hold the door open for him. 'Did you forget something?'

'No . . . I, er.' Tom adjusted his spectacles and Judith was surprised to see a film of perspiration on his forehead and that his cheeks were unusually flushed.

'Aren't you well, Tom? Is there something wrong?' she asked anxiously, indicating a chair. 'Do sit down.'

Tom Guthrie ignored her invitation and continued to hover. In his arms he was clutching the ledgers they'd been inspecting that morning.

'It's just that . . .' Tom's voice went hoarse and he pushed up his spectacles again, keeping a finger fixed firmly for a moment or two on the bridge while he continued to blink at Judith owlishly. 'I wondered if we could have a word in private?' he whispered, glancing behind him at the door.

'Of course, it's private here; but please sit down, Tom. You're making me feel rather nervous.' She retuned to her desk.

'I didn't *mean* to, Miss Prynne.' Tom sat cautiously down, his eyes rooted now to the floor. 'I have debated for a long time whether to talk to you and, if so, what to say. It *is* very difficult . . .'

'You've really got me worried, Tom,' Judith said with

an embarrassed laugh. 'Please try and tell me what's bothering you. This isn't like you at all.'

'It will be very *confidential*, won't it, Miss Prynne?'

'Utterly. Now, what is it?' Judith joined her hands on her lap and gave him an encouraging smile. 'Out with it, Tom.'

'I really don't know how to begin.' Tom sat on the edge of his chair, but his unease had lessened a little. 'It's very embarrassing for *me* to say this and difficult too.' He paused once again and stared at the ledgers on his lap with a frown then, quickly, he opened one and began to go rapidly through it, his finger travelling down the columns of figures he had carefully and meticulously written there. Then he seemed to settle on a set of figures, looked up at Judith and cleared his throat again.

'I'm sorry to have to tell you that there are errors in these books that I can only account for in one way.'

'And what's that, Tom?'

'Mr Lyle has been drawing too much on petty cash, and has not been accounting properly for the money.'

'Oh, Tom . . .' Judith felt her heart jump and she sat forward in her chair. 'What are you saying? That he's been fiddling the books?'

'I'm afraid so, Miss Prynne.' Tom got out his handkerchief and mopped his perspiring brow.

'But are you *sure*?'

'As sure as I can be.'

'Then why didn't you say anything before? This morning, for instance?'

'I felt I couldn't accuse him to his face. I'm sorry, Miss Prynne, but I hadn't the courage. It's an awful thing to have to do and, as you can imagine, I'm not a very brave man. I have known for some time, but it has been very difficult to know what to do. I would prefer to have done nothing, but this is sure to come out in the audit and if I ignored it I would be blamed. Besides, I know you have a high regard for Mr Lyle.'

'Very high. He seems to have done very well and I was quite happy to leave the running of the hotel entirely to him while I concentrate on something else, another development in the Lakes.'

'I shouldn't do that, Miss Prynne.'

'Are you really saying Lyle is not honest?'

'That's the way it looks to me.'

'But might it not look differently to someone else? There are various ways to interpret figures, aren't there?'

'There are, Miss Prynne, and I took the precaution of having a former colleague of mine check the figures, at my expense and in strict confidence of course. I went to see him in Edinburgh last week and he has confirmed my own calculations to the penny.' Tom couldn't resist a smile of pride. 'You see, it is a relatively simple matter to fiddle the petty cash, so a cashier or accountant has to be extra careful in checking these items. All I can say is that Mr Lyle has been drawing extraordinarily large sums and not accounting properly for them.'

'Doesn't he put in vouchers?'

'Yes, but the vouchers are not accurate and invariably not backed up by bills. When I have asked him to explain he makes some excuse, thinking, no doubt, I would not doubt his word.'

'But have you told him of your suspicions?'

'Oh no, I wouldn't dare. It's not my place, is it, Miss Prynne?'

'So did you ask for an explanation?'

'I did not, Miss Prynne, that is, in so many words. I wanted to talk to you because, in my opinion and that of my colleague, there is no explanation beyond theft. Pure theft.'

'Then how did this come about? Why didn't you suspect before?'

281

'I think he started to cheat about six months ago. That's when drawings on the petty cash shot up. I have always kept meticulous accounts but, of course, the general manager does have authority to draw. According to my calculations he has taken seven thousand, five hundred and forty pounds out of the petty cash for which he has given no adequate explanation; no vouchers, nothing. It is a lot of money.' Tom's lips curled. 'He obviously felt he had a fool in charge of the books. Someone who wouldn't dare speak. It was quite blatant. Now, if I may show you . . .'

Tom leaned forward and, for the next ten minutes, by comparing sets of figures on different pages and in different ledgers, he managed to convince Judith that he was right.

For a few moments she sat in her chair thinking, while Tom Guthrie, thankful that his ordeal was over, started to clean his spectacles which had misted over, peering at the lenses with his shortsighted eyes.

'Do you have *any* idea why he should want such sums of money, Tom? He has a very good salary, a car, free accommodation.'

'I have no idea, madam,' Tom said respectfully, replacing his spectacles on his nose. 'I can only suggest there is something you do not know.'

'He came to us with very good references.'

Tom acknowledged this with a bow of his head.

'But for these figures, Miss Prynne, I would have agreed with them.'

'And you've said nothing to anyone?'

'Other than my ex-colleague, and the name was never revealed to him. He is a *most* respectable accountant.'

'Well.' Judith got up and wandered once more to the window. How odd it was that things could change so dramatically from one moment to the next. This time tomorrow she had imagined that she and Leo would be taking a leisurely drive to Derwent Water, where they would pass a few pleasant days before returning to London and embarking on a plane for America.

Now . . . the future was unclear. Also unclear to her was how she should deal with what was the gravest crisis in her career to date: confronting a man with an international reputation with the charge that he was a thief.

She thanked Tom Guthrie for what he had done, assured him that his confidentiality would be respected and showed him to the door, keeping the incriminating ledgers with her. Then she walked again to the window where, on the golf course, she could see Moira sitting at her easel apparently painting the golfers: her father-in-law and Billy McLaren, or, maybe, it was Billy on whom she concentrated? He was tall and athletic-looking with thick curly hair, almost the colour of Judith's, and when he wore his kilt, which he did with a dinner jacket, he looked like the sort of clean-limbed, upright young man most women dream about.

He was very different from the introverted, artistic Richard, not only in looks, but in personality. He was open, honest and straightforward – or could one use these adjectives so easily when one knew what she did about Fraser Lyle, another apparently clean-limbed, good-looking young man with an open, honest face and a worthy record? It seemed incredible.

Her first thought was to wait and discuss it with Leo: but Leo was impetuous and, she would imagine, lacking the kind of tact Judith felt necessary for this kind of situation. She didn't want an explosion that would worry the guests or cause a scene just when the hotel was full and going so well.

There and then she decided to see Fraser Lyle herself and, having made the decision, she rang down to the reception:

'Is Mr Lyle about?'

'I think he is in the dining room, madam, inspecting it before luncheon with Mr Armstrong.'

'Ask him if he'd be good enough to pop up and see me when the inspection is over.'

'Just Mr Lyle, or Mr Armstrong too?'

'Just Mr Lyle,' Judith replied and replaced the receiver.

Then she sat in a chair facing the door and tried to prepare herself. Crises were frequent in hotels and in restaurants and, early in her career, Judith had tried to cultivate a feeling of detachment when confronted with an awkward situation by making her mind dwell on something completely different. After all, she was not the one at fault; why, therefore, should she feel uncomfortable? But this time she did; it was very hard to stop thinking about the problem in what seemed the considerable time that elapsed between her sending for Lyle and his gentle knock at the door.

Fraser Lyle had straight fair hair, blue eyes, a pink, healthy-looking face and an expression of candour. He smiled a lot and had plenty of the charm that was such an essential prerequisite to those whose profession it is to deal with the public. His early career had been in the army, though he had been too young for the war.

He wore his customary morning suit with a black tie and looked every inch the successful hotelier.

'I believe you wanted to see me, Miss Prynne?' he said with his easy smile, as Judith invited him to sit down. He settled himself comfortably in the chair opposite Judith, crossing his legs.

'Is everything all right in the dining room?'

'Fine, as far as I can see.' He looked at her curiously. 'Why? Should it not be?'

'That's not what I wanted to see you about, Fraser.' Judith sighed and consulted a paper she had on her lap. 'It appears there is some discrepancy in the books and I wondered if you could throw any light on it?' She raised her head and looked straight into his eyes only to see that same open, honest expression, now slightly confused.

'In what way can *I* help you, Miss Prynne? We only went over them this morning. There were no problems then.'

'That was the cash flow for the next six months. I am talking now about the past.'

'The past?' He raised his head and looked at the ceiling.

'The immediate past. Approximately seven thousand five hundred pounds of petty cash is unaccounted for in the last six months. It is rather a lot of money, is it not?'

Lyle shrugged.

'Not particularly in running a hotel like this.'

'But most items of any size are paid for by cheque.'

'That is true,' Lyle nodded his agreement.

'In face *very* little should be paid for by cash . . .'

'Well . . .' That disarming expression had been replaced by one of caution. 'There *are* certain things, of course.'

'Such as?'

'Really, Miss Prynne, one has to have *some* money,' Lyle said, with a note of irritation entering his well-modulated voice.

'But do *you* specifically have to have large amounts of cash, Fraser, and, if so, may I ask for what?'

Judith leaned her head on her hand and looked at him with an air of enquiry.

'Am *I* to understand I am being interrogated, Miss Prynne?' The tone now was one of indignation.

'I'm simply asking questions.'

'Put to you by whom, may I ask?'

'They have been put to me, but I am not at liberty to say by whom. However, I have inspected the figures myself and I feel there is no doubt that, at various times during the past six months, you have appropriated for your own personal use the enormous sum of approximately one thousand two hundred and fifty pounds a month. Well, *I* think that's an enormous sum, anyway. It is certainly large enough to question. Or maybe you don't think so in a hotel of this size?'

'And *you* think I have taken it?' Lyle uncrossed his legs and put his feet together, hands on his knees.

'Yes, I'm afraid I do. I have no choice.'

'Have you proof?'

'In these books,' she pointed towards the table.

'It can only be Guthrie. Have you asked *him* if he has need of large sums of cash?'

'Mr Lyle,' Judith, resorting to formality, stood up and crossed her arms. 'I am quite prepared to institute an independent enquiry by a firm of professional chartered accountants here and now. I have only to phone Edinburgh or London and a team of experts will be put on the next train. However, the evidence that I have seen, with my own eyes, seems without any doubt to indicate that an enquiry would be superfluous. But . . . if you prefer.'

She walked deliberately over to the telephone, whereupon Lyle got up.

'Miss Prynne . . .' she turned round and saw that he had put out his hand. 'What do you intend to do?'

'Call the experts . . .'

'No, I mean if, by any chance, you're right.'

'Why, I intend to inform the police. If it's a clear case of theft from a public company I have no option.'

'But it is not *yet* a public company.'

'Nevertheless we are listed on the USM Market and will seek full listing as soon as we can. Our accounts are published . . .'

'Seven thousand is not such a large figure to lose . . .' Lyle's eyes reminded her of someone caught with his hands in the till. Guthrie was right.

'Nevertheless we do not wish to lose it. However one regrets it, it *is* stealing, Mr Lyle, and you should know the consequences.'

'I should continue to deny it. You would have to prosecute me and it would make a nasty scandal for the group which, so far, is held in high esteem.' He emphasized the *so far* and Judith felt a spasm of anger pass through her.

'So far and will in future, Mr Lyle, if we bring thieves to book. Don't think prosecution will reflect on *us*. It will make other employees take more care.'

Lyle drew from his pocket a large white handkerchief with a hand which Judith observed was trembling. He was trying very hard, but with increasing difficulty, to control himself, his own panic at the prospect of the ruin of his career. He blew his nose violently and then tucked the handkerchief in the sleeve of his black coat.

'I will do a deal with you, Miss Prynne, and I think you will find it to your advantage to listen. I do not admit to the charge of which you are accusing me, but neither do I desire an enquiry. Mud sticks, and I might find it difficult to get a post such as this again, whatever the outcome. Of that I have no doubt.

'On the other hand, Miss Prynne,' Lyle's voice assumed an unctuous note, '*you* have a reputation too, have you not, for honesty, reliability,' he paused and smiled at her, 'fidelity, no doubt? You and your husband are a celebrated couple in the business. Everyone thinks well of you . . .'

'Now, just what are you getting at, Lyle?' Judith said abruptly. 'My private life has absolutely *nothing* to do with business.'

'Well, neither do I consider has mine. And, if you were to ask me if I had a weakness – as you obviously have, Miss Prynne, if your attachment to Mr Valenti is anything to go by – I would be honest and tell you that I gamble . . .'

'Ah . . .' Judith let out a deep breath, but he hurried on:

'I find gambling releases me from the tensions of the business. I gamble on anything, mainly horses, but other things too. I like a flutter, as they say, and that is my affair.

Now you, Miss Prynne, like a flutter, too.' Lyle's smile had become arch, and Judith found herself wondering how she could ever have liked or trusted him. In a trice she had seen a man who now seemed to have not one but many faces. 'But not in the gambling room, I think; though maybe you *are* gambling with your reputation, your marriage, who knows?'

'So what are you getting at?' Judith enquired coldly.

'I would not like to spread the word, at whatever cost to me, because I should be ruined anyway, that you were an adulterer. That this was a little love nest away from your husband, *and* in the company of your children *too*. A few of the national tabloids might quite like this information, might they not? They would probably pay more than seven thousand pounds for it, too. Tut, tut, Miss Prynne, what *would* people think?'

Judith turned to the window. In the distance Moira was still at her easel, but the two golfers had moved on out of sight. Behind Moira on the river bank, Michael and Franco were fishing while a watchful ghillie kept his eyes on them and the two girls were lying in the meadow grass, by the side, chatting. It was a scene of such peace that she dreaded what would happen if circumstances disrupted it. Was it worth it? Prosecution, a court case, and then the blackmail, the threats?

Suddenly she turned and faced the man she had trusted, now engaged in a careful inspection of his finger nails.

'Very well, Lyle, you have made your point. As it happens I am going to ask my husband for a divorce, but, as I can see you are a man motivated by spite, I will not allow you to ruin my life, or the lives of those I love. There will be no prosecution provided that you leave here at once, pausing only to pack. You will say you have to leave for family reasons. If details of my private life are ever leaked, at *any time*, to the press I will not hesitate to throw the book at you. Is that understood?

'Perfectly, madam,' Lyle said with a note, now, in his voice of scorn, 'perfectly understood.'

'I also hope that if you do apply for a post at a hotel again you will never come to me for a reference.

'And now, goodbye.'

Judith turned immediately to the window and heard only the soft click of the door as Fraser Lyle left the room.

Chapter 15

Rosalind Prynne was a disappointed woman. She felt that life had been unkind to her, that she deserved better. She had had a rich father, she was an only, beloved child, and she had married the man she, in turn, loved. But nothing had ever gone right for her and she had been cast in a role she had never really wanted: that of wife and mother.

The Douglas Prynnes had the one son, Philip, who was nearly grown up and, apart from him, Rosalind, who had had so much talent, to whom life seemed to have offered so much, felt she had achieved nothing. She had always lived in the shadow of men: her dynamic father, of whom she saw far too little; her husband, who had been lost to her emotionally for many years; and her son, whom she loved passionately, in the way that only the mother of a single child could.

After Judith had left Aylestone, Doug assumed the general management and he had thrown himself into the running of the hotel. He felt it was essential to be on the spot and spent most nights in his flat on the top floor. When he came home at weekends he tended to be morose, uncommunicative and obviously tired. Despite his enthusiasm, Douglas was not the kind of man who thrived on work. He was a worrier and it got him down. Rosalind suspected he had taken on more than he could cope with.

Doug was more introverted than Judith, more scholarly and nervous. Although she was younger than he was he had always felt she overshadowed him – both as a child and then an adult. For Judith he had long nursed a feeling of bitter resentment.

Rosalind was thus doubly disappointed, in herself and in

her spouse. For Doug had never really risen to the great heights that she had hoped for him in those far-off days when she had married such an attractive, apparently gifted, well-connected man. She had imagined him to be someone with the drive and ambition of her father; but he wasn't. Now, well into their married life together, she saw a man no longer very attractive, certainly not gifted; but simply another careworn, complaining member of the human race and, as his wife, she was tired of him.

She felt that life was passing her by. Maybe it had already passed her. She was over forty and, apart from Philip, she decided she had nothing tangible to show for her life.

Some people might consider that to produce a happy healthy child and run a household was enough. It was nothing to be ashamed of anyway, but Ros was not such a person. Years before she had imagined that she would have a career, at least, something to show for the years of boredom and frustration as the wife of a man who would never really make it to the top.

Doug was good at his job, but he lacked the flair that a great hotelier needed; the kind of charisma that someone like Judith clearly had.

Besides, Aylestone was not doing well. It had been eclipsed completely by the success of Judith and her stately home hotels which had opened with such success, due to good planning, attention to detail and the flair which she undoubtedly had. Like George Drake before him, Jenner appeared to have lost interest until Aylestone had become just another country house hotel with nothing very special about it. It was a kind of albatross, continually bringing bad fortune. Gradually, as had happened before, its prices were lowered and, inevitably, its standards dropped. It began to cater almost exclusively for businessmen who came there ostensibly for sales and management conferences, but mainly to enjoy the sybaritic pleasures of life:

food that was plentiful rather than of gourmet quality, and many, many drinking sessions at the bar.

Judith came frequently to see old Lady Prynne, who was now in her nineties, and Doug and Ros from time to time would meet her at their grandmother's home; but the coolness between the brother and sister remained. It was accepted now that Greville and Angela were lost in the lotus-land that was India, and that they would never return home. Angela was reported not to be in good health.

Thus, imprisoned, cocooned by a life that she loathed, Rosalind grew more embittered, more frustrated, until one day an event that she had dreaded happened. However it would transform her life.

Her father had on the whole enjoyed good health, but for many years had suffered from high blood-pressure. Rosalind was working in her garden at about noon one day when the telephone rang and she leaned in through the open window to answer it.

'Could you come quickly, Mrs Prynne?' her father's secretary said without any preliminaries. 'I'm afraid your father is not at all well.'

'Is it very bad?' Rosalind's voice was strangely composed.

'Quite serious,' the secretary said. 'He was taken to the Westminster. Heart, I'm afraid. Should I send a car to meet your train?'

A few hours later, sitting by his side, it was difficult to recognize the man who had been such a powerful force in her life. His secretary, Eileen, with her usual phlegmatic attitude, had underestimated the seriousness of his condition. So many tubes seemed to come from his emaciated body or lead into it that it was difficult to believe their function was to keep him alive. He remained deeply unconscious and, every now and then, a nurse popped her head round the door of the private room and said: 'Everything all right?' and disappeared before Ros had the chance to reply.

Looking at her father clinging to life – it seemed by a very thin thread – Rosalind felt lost and lonely. She hadn't even been able to send a message to Doug. She still considered Philip a child, though he wasn't, and tried to protect him from unpleasant news.

At about six in the evening Rosalind rang the hotel and asked for Doug. Several minutes passed before she was told he could not be found. His car was not in the garage.

Rosalind left a message saying that her father was ill and asking that her husband should contact her as soon as possible.

Disconsolately she replaced the receiver and returned to her solitary vigil by her father's bedside, aware of her loneliness, her need for companionship, feeling the bitterness of isolation eat into her soul.

For a long time Doris Malcolm had wanted to be Mrs Prynne, but Doug had said that his wife would never divorce him. He didn't add that, in the event of her father's death, Rosalind would be a wealthy woman and, at last, all those years of sterile marriage might bear fruit. He knew that if he left her she would get every penny out of him that she could. If she was rich she, and he, could do as they liked.

But if Ros no longer loved him, Doug knew that she needed him, as people who have lived together for many years often do: they cling and adhere like barnacles to rocks that are frequently swamped and buffeted by the sea. When the tide turns to reveal the drenched rocks once more, there are the barnacles, the whelks and sea moss clinging fast to the outer surface they know. Familiarity is a kind of adhesive which people are loath to sunder.

Doug, in his way, needed her more than he needed

Doris, for whom he even felt a certain measure of contempt. He would, in fact, never have dreamed of asking for a divorce in order to marry her.

Doug received the message from Rosalind when he returned from a visit to a local brewery that wanted Aylestone to stock its beer. For a few moments he pondered what he should do and in the end he did nothing. He was tired, hungry, he needed a drink, and a drive through the night to London did not appeal to him.

Still he had a nagging sense of unease, a feeling that he was doing the wrong thing as he went into the dining room and had a late meal in the company of some of the men who were there for a sales conference, tucking into the scampi, the steak and chips, the chicken in a basket.

Doug felt a spasm of disgust pass through him as he watched them scoffing, tankards of ale regularly pressed to their lips between mouthfuls. It was incredible to think that it had once been an ambition to make this a fine hotel. Who were its clientele now? Businessmen on expense accounts; adulterous couples who were seldom seen in the bar or the restaurant. There were no longer horses in the stables, or a decent chef in the kitchen.

Doug had long ago decided that Aylestone was unlucky. It should never have been turned into a hotel. Gran was vindicated after all; she had always said it would never pay. Maybe she had cursed it?

Doug took his time over his meal, exchanging words with the staff setting tables for breakfast; with a couple of sales managers who had been here before on their annual conference. He didn't even know what they sold. Doug thought back to the time when rooms at Aylestone were booked weeks in advance, patronized by a very different class of clientele, and of André Hebert, and staff like him, who had left long ago for fresh pastures where their talents and skills were appreciated.

Doug stubbed out his cigarette and finished his coffee.

Who was to blame? It was hard to know. He knew that people said Judith had flair and he hadn't; but he thought that more than flair was needed to run a good hotel. One needed a good staff, energetic management and the support of one's family. He had not got the support from Ros a man needed, and his own family had deserted him.

When Doug got to his room he found Doris as usual in his bed, flicking over the pages of the evening paper.

'Gosh, I'm tired,' she said throwing it down as Doug came in.

'Me too.' Doug wearily sat down to untie his shoelaces. 'Ros's father is ill,' he said, looking at her as he massaged his tired feet.

'Oh? How do you know?'

'Ros left a message. He's at the Westminster. Heart attack.'

Doris sat up, leaning on her arms.

'Oughtn't you to be there?'

'Why? What's he done for me?'

'Oh, Doug, I think that's *very* shortsighted of you. He's quite wealthy isn't he?'

'She didn't say he was going to *die*. It didn't sound all that urgent. The old boy will live for years if you ask me. He's always looked after himself.'

'Still,' Doris looked doubtful. 'If he leaves her all his money she'd be well off.'

'Well off?' Doug snorted. 'She'd be rich! However,' Doug threw himself on the bed, fully dressed, and put his arms under his head, 'if you think that would make one iota of difference to us, you're wrong.'

There was a ponderous silence and he knew what Doris was thinking.

'You always told me,' she said eventually in sullen tones, 'that if Drake died and left her his money you could have your freedom.'

'*Freedom!*' Doug said angrily loosening his tie. 'Freedom for what?'

'You'd be free, Doug; you could get away from her. You wouldn't owe *her* anything.'

'And does that mean I'd be free too?' Doug said caustically, turning to her. 'Do you realize I haven't a *bean* apart from my salary?'

'That doesn't *matter*, dear. We've got each other, that's what matters.'

Doug silently passed his hand over his face and closed his eyes. What mattered to him was getting away not only from Ros but from Doris too; from the hotel and all the broken dreams it stood for. If he could *ever* get away it would be by himself, and sometimes he thought he'd take a train or a plane and simply disappear. How lovely that would be.

'Get properly into bed,' Doris said, but there was a note of dejection in her voice as if she could read his thoughts and knew that there was no place in them for her.

Doug slowly undressed, preoccupied by his thoughts; then he went into the bathroom to do his teeth and comb his hair. He looked for some time at his reflection in the mirror and there he saw the face of a man of forty-three who had not only lost the idealism of youth, but who had replaced it by despair. It had the drawn, haggard, anxious look of the sales managers he had so often seen at the hotel, whose livelihood depended on the next set of figures.

Well, so it was with him.

When he got back to his room Doris was lying propped up against the pillows watching him.

'You look really done in, Doug.'

'Well I am done in, aren't I?' Doug said irritably, turning back the sheets. 'I'm spent, fed up. I've had it.'

'Just because of Mr Drake!'

'It's *nothing* to do with Drake.'

'Then what *is* it to do with, love?' She tentatively put a hand over his.

'Well, a lot of it has to do with Matthew Jenner. He's tired of Aylestone and if you ask me he wants to sell it. If it *was* sold I'd be out of a job and what then?'

'When did you hear this?'

'I've guessed it for some time. He told me recently that the prospects were uncertain. He's never really developed the hotels business as he meant to. You can't make a lot of money just out of one; you have to have the know-how, the expertise. You can be sure if it goes, I go.'

'But *why*?'

'Because my name is synonymous with failure; that's why.'

He didn't even kiss her on the cheek as he turned his back on her and tried to go to sleep.

Some time in the small hours of the morning a car pulled out from the side of the Westminster Hospital and drove along the Embankment westward in the direction of the Thames Valley. Neither the chauffeur nor the back seat occupant spoke and when, at last, the outline of Aylestone appeared above the trees, dawn was breaking. The birds had started to sing their beautiful, melodious songs that had nothing in them of mourning or death; only the joy of living and being alive.

Rosalind got out of the car as soon as it reached the front of the hotel, not waiting for her father's chauffeur to open the door. With a nod at him she ran up the stairs and was greeted in the hall by the receptionist, who had just come on duty.

She had hardly time to register who the visitor was before Ros was in the lift, which rose quickly to the top floor, depositing her outside the door of Doug's suite. She turned the handle of the door but it was locked. So she knocked sharply and a sleepy voice called out:

'Just a minute.'

When the door was eventually opened, Doug stood in the doorway yawning and scratching his head. When he saw Ros his mouth fell open, and he stood looking at her without speaking until she said:

'Aren't you going to let me come in?' He scratched his head again but didn't move.

'What is it?' he muttered. 'What do you want? I'm half asleep.'

'Do you *mind* if I come in?' Ros said pushing past him, too fast even for Doris who was used to making hasty exits to the bathroom when one of the staff tapped on the door.

Doris hadn't even time to put on her dressing gown, but stood by the side of the bed, her hands clasped in front of her looking, in her crumpled nightgown, like a schoolgirl caught in a misdemeanour.

'Well, *well*,' Ros said, slowly drawing off her gloves and throwing them on to a chair. 'I *thought* something like this was going on; but with the *housekeeper* . . . *Doug!* What *would* your mother say?'

She cast a cruel, savage smile at Doug who had shut the door and stood watching her in rather the same abject way as Doris.

'After all you *are* a Prynne,' Ros continued contemptuously, 'though I often think you've forgotten it. There's nothing *quite* so sad as a family down on its luck: no money, no prospects, no hope. No future now, either, Doug, for you or me; but I don't suppose you mind that because you've got her.' She looked down her nose towards Doris. 'Actually I'm afraid I've forgotten her name.'

'Doris,' Doug said sullenly.

'Doris!' Ros threw back her head and laughed mirthlessly. 'What on *earth* would your *mother* say to a name like Doris?'

'Oh for God's sake,' Doug said savagely, 'I do wish

you'd shut up and come to the point. Why are *you* here at this ungodly hour?'

'I'm here, Doug,' Ros said evenly, as if she relished the moment, 'because, sadly, Father passed away in the night. I don't need to remind you that I'm now a very wealthy woman, and the first thing I intend to do is rid myself of an encumbrance like you.' Slowly she looked from one to the other, shaking her head. 'I hope that you and "Doris" will have a very happy life together. Very happy indeed.'

The view across Derwent Water overlooked the spot once beloved by John Ruskin, from which he could see the broad sweep of the beautiful lake as far as the Jaws of Borrowdale. The view remained pretty much now as it had been then, and the vast house that had been modernized inside, but whose external fabric had been lovingly restored, would not have been out of place in Ruskin's time.

No expense had been spared to turn The Ruskin into a hotel worthy of comparison with Forteliot Castle. Judith had appointed a general manager who had trained in Switzerland and managed grand hotels all over Europe. He was an American called Karl Bormeister, and he had established himself in his new position very quickly and was popular with his employers, guests and the hotel staff.

Leo and Judith stood at the window of her suite looking at the small boats which chugged across the lake. It was spring and the countryside was at its most alluring, a mist rising from the river. The air was full of birdsong and the cries of new-born lambs who frolicked contentedly beside their mothers in the green fields beneath the lowering fells of Lakeland.

'It *is* a very beautiful part of the world,' Leo said with a sigh. 'I did not know just how beautiful.'

'It isn't always like this.' Judith smiled. 'That's why the

fields are so green. Most of the year it is cloudy and raining, and very cold.'

'Do you think we've done the right thing?' Leo looked anxiously at Judith, who put a hand on his arm.

'What exactly do you mean?'

'If the weather is *so* bad? Will the guests still come?'

'This is England's number one tourist spot. Besides, the guests have everything they need; heated indoor swimming pool, squash courts, massage, sauna. No one ever seems to mind playing golf or riding in the rain.'

'You have a very great talent, Judith.' Leo's arm closed around her waist. 'Now why don't you have a little rest?'

'No time to rest.' Judith involuntarily allowed herself to lean against his reassuring bulk. 'Too much to do. The completion of two new hotels . . . *Prynne's* to launch on the Stock Market.'

'When are you going to marry me?' Leo whispered as if he hadn't heard her. 'You know I'm a very lonely man.'

'That's nonsense, darling.' Judith put a hand up and tenderly caressed his cheek. 'I wouldn't see *any* more of you if we were married than I do now.'

'Is it that you don't want to hurt Marcel? Surely *he* must realize . . .'

'I don't want to hurt him and . . .' Gently Judith released herself and moved away. 'Other things. I have grown to like my independence, my freedom . . .'

'You will have all the freedom and independence you wish with me.'

'Why marry, then?'

'Because I want to show you off. A lot of people don't know about our relationship because we can't tell them. You insist on discretion. I want the whole world to know that I am the husband of Judith Prynne, a woman who, single-handedly, has taken the enclosed world of the grand hotel by storm in creating masterpieces in the Scottish and English countrysides . . .'

'With a little help from my friends,' Judith said lightly. 'I would have got nowhere without you.'

'What is money when you have such talent? You would have raised it somehow. I am privileged that it was I whom you asked.'

'That's very nice of you, Leo, and you have always been supportive; but why spoil something that is so good?'

'You mean us?'

'Yes.'

'It *is* good.' His arm drew her to him again. 'But I want something more and, if you do agree to be my wife, I will give you a present I think you will love. It will be the best jewel in your crown: the hotel to end hotels.'

'Oh?' Judith looked intrigued as Leo, withdrawing his arm, left her side and crossed the room. Producing a folder from his briefcase he came back to her and put it in her hand.

'What's this?' she said.

'Open it.' He looked as pleased as a small boy with a puppy and, intrigued, she sat down, opened the folder and began to inspect the contents, the first page of which was a colour photograph of a large house.

'Aylestone,' she gasped. 'Aylestone is for sale?'

'*May* be for sale.'

'But *why*?'

'I understand Jenner is tired of it. It has gone down. Inevitably it would, as we knew your brother had not the right touch.'

'Don't be hard on Doug,' Judith said sadly. 'You *know* I have a conscience about him.'

'There is no need to have a conscience, my dear. He is simply not as clever as you, and he did not have the support from Jenner you had from me.'

'True.' Judith glanced through the brochure and placed it on her knee. 'But I can't be bribed, Leo. It can't be a condition.' She studied him gravely. 'If I were to marry

301

you it would be for other reasons, not because I want Aylestone.'

'But you do want Aylestone?'

'Of course I'd love it; but not over Doug's head. I must find out what is happening.'

'My fear,' Leo said with a deep sigh, sitting in the chair next to her, 'is that you will let your heart rule your head.'

'You know I never do that.'

'Where your family is concerned I think you do. You are so indulgent to Moira ... you are tolerant towards Doug ... you are devoted to your grandmother.'

'Is it a crime to love one's family?'

'No it is not, and I see you're looking at me and, I admit, I am deficient as a father. Maybe it's as well I never had more children.'

'But Richard *is* your only son, Leo, and yet you don't seem to worry about what's happened to him. He's been gone a long time now.'

'Of course I care, and I have tried to find him. I have just not shown my concern and sorrow to you, Judith.'

'I apologize,' Judith bowed her head. It was true there was a lot about Leo she didn't know. Yet there was too much he kept from her, a side of his character she knew nothing about.

'You know that Billy is keen to marry Moira?' Judith went on. 'That's the main reason I want Richard to be traced.' For a few moments Judith studied the lined face of the man opposite her. 'Do you think he has just disappeared, or ...'

'Or what?' Leo's gaze was quite calm and philosophical.

'Someone may have done away with him?'

'You mean *murdered* him?'

'Yes, it wasn't a word I liked to use. But it is strange and it's also very hard on Moira, not to know.'

'I am going to Italy soon,' Leo said with an air of decisiveness, 'and I'll redouble my efforts to find out what has happened to my son but, you know, in my heart of hearts I think that Richard, who always found reality too much for him, has run away.'

'What would he do for money?'

'Who knows? Perhaps he has someone to keep him?'

'Another woman?'

'Or a man.' Leo raised his eyebrows interrogatively. 'Who knows?'

'Oh dear.' Judith gazed towards the lake. 'In that case it would explain a lot. I never thought Richard made Moira particularly happy . . . in that way.'

'As Marcel never made *you* happy in that way?' His expression changed suggestively.

'Yes, but there was nothing wrong with Marcel. He just preferred cooking.'

'Well, maybe Richard preferred painting.' Leo rose and, crossing the room, took hold of her hand and kissed the back of her palm.

'My darling, why worry about others when we have each other? When the sky is blue and the water is beautiful . . . and we have half a day free to do as we like? What a joy!'

What a joy, indeed.

It was late afternoon when Judith woke and listened to his steady breathing. He had one hand flung, palm up, on the sheet and she thought how white and delicate it was; the hand of a gentleman.

The water of the lake was reflected on the high ceiling of the bedroom and its constant movement seemed to dance and play, like shadows. From the open window came the sound of voices as guests gathered on the terrace below them and, from far away, came the hoot of the river steamer as it made its way along the lake, criss-crossing from jetty to jetty.

Judith finally, reluctantly, slid out of bed and put on a

silk robe lying on the chair by the window. Then she picked up the file that she had left lying on the table and, taking it over to the bed, began to go through its contents.

From some source Leo had collected all the material he could about the Jenner organization and its downward course. Some of the material dated from quite a long time ago, and it was obvious either that Leo had carefully followed the progress of the group for some time, or he had done his research well. The photograph of the house had come from a trade magazine and underneath was the legend:

AYLESTONE FOR SALE?

The copy read:

Twenty years ago the ancient Prynne family sold its ancestral home for redevelopment as a hotel. This was first bought by the Drake Organization and the alliance of the two families was cemented when Douglas Prynne married the only daughter of George Drake, Rosalind.

For some time Aylestone prospered as a hotel thanks, largely, to the management of Judith Prynne, the elder daughter, and her husband, master chef Marcel Laborde, who continues to run *Prynne's*, the celebrated 3-star restaurant in London.

After a disagreement Miss Prynne relinquished the management of the hotel which had, by that time, been sold to Matthew Jenner, who had ambitions in the catering field. However, the aims of Jenner Securities were misplaced, and this was to become their only diversification into hotel ownership.

Despite the expert management of Douglas Prynne, who has run the hotel since his sister left it, this venture has not been a particularly successful one.

Of the two, Judith Prynne seems to have more skill, or more luck, because, as well as being part-owner of *Prynne's*, she has opened the very successful Forteliot Castle in Scotland and, recently, The Ruskin on Derwent Water which, by all accounts, is even more sumptuous than Forteliot. Marcel Laborde has been responsible for running the hotel restaurants through his own appointees to the kitchen, but the guiding force behind Judith

Prynne's venture is said to be Leo Valenti, the American entrepreneur.

Mr Valenti is something of a man of mystery. He is seldom photographed, and always refuses to be interviewed. His business interests remain privately owned, and he is not quoted on the New York Stock Exchange. Nevertheless he is said to be a man of immense wealth. However, Miss Prynne has insisted on complete control in everything she does and her own organization Prynne's (UK) Ltd will be seeking a full listing on the stock market later in the year. On the unlisted securities market Prynne's shares have done particularly well in the last eighteen months.

Carefully Judith put the papers back in the folder and curled up on the bed beside Leo, who, she discovered, was now awake and gazing at her quizzically.

'Interested?' he said.

'Very.' She took his hand and squeezed it.

'You will have to get a proper organization, you know, Judith.' Leo's voice became very matter-of-fact.

'How do you mean?'

'You need the machinery to run a company such as yours. You can't manage it on your own with just a secretary and an accountant.'

'I've done quite well so far.'

'Yes, but you can't go on like that. You need offices, a headquarters. That way you will be able to do more work. Don't you see?'

'How do you mean?'

'Buy several hotels at a time.'

'But won't that be impossible?'

'Not if you are well organized. Not if you have me behind you.' His attempt to look modest was unsuccessful, so he went on: 'You can still put the *personal* touch which is such a part of you; but you have a very good design team. They can almost anticipate your wishes. You can buy hotels in Europe and America; but we must find suitable offices, especially with a full stock market listing pending.'

305

'You mean I must set myself up as the boss?' she grinned.

'Undoubtedly,' Leo said. 'You must not only be the boss; but must be *seen* to be the boss.' Then, bending towards her, he took her once again in his arms and hungrily kissed her.

Marcel said:

'Of course I knew it would come to this.' But still he looked sad.

He wore his white jacket and blue trousers; his chef's hat stood on the table in the middle of the room which, after all these years, was still their home.

Officially it was their home but, in practice, Judith was scarcely ever there. The children hardly knew it as home. Sometimes in the school holidays they travelled about or visited various relations.

It had never been a conventionally happy marriage; but the children had remained as unaffected by this as possible. In term time they were at boarding school and were visited by their parents, either together or separately. They accepted that this was the kind of lifestyle their parents led. Their cousins, Alida and Franco, went to the same boys' and girls' schools, so that the small, broken family could, as far as possible, be together.

'We have done our best for the children,' Judith said at last.

'Our best for the children *and* each other.' Marcel's face was drawn.

'You only *really* think of your cooking, Marcel,' Judith said gently.

'And you *really* only think about being a tycoon,' he replied, but his tone was anything but kind.

'That isn't a very nice thing to say.'

'Yet it's true. Valenti is behind all this, I suppose?'

'I just want to be free.'

'But you *are* free. Free to please yourself.'

'Yes, but I don't want to be married to you any more, Marcel. I'm very sorry, but that's all there is to it.'

'Don't tell me, please Judith, that Valenti isn't behind it?'

She still didn't reply, confused and distressed by the venom in his voice, the contempt and despair in his fine grey eyes.

'I *want* us to be friends, Marcel.'

'Tell me, first, that Valenti isn't behind it?'

'I can't tell you *anything*.' She got up and moved restlessly across the room. 'It isn't fair to keep me if I want to be free. I want us to be civilized for our sake, and for that of the children. You have a large stake in the company, and it would be ridiculous for us to quarrel. I want and need your advice and help, but I don't want you as a husband any more, and Marcel,' she paused and gazed at him across the room, 'I don't honestly feel you want me as a wife.'

'That isn't true.'

'You are married to your *cuisine*.'

'That's rubbish. We have *never* had a family life. In France . . .'

'Oh yes in France I'd sit at the table taking the money, counting it out and putting it into my little black bag. Your slippers would be warm when you came in at night, and your coffee and brioche would be on the table waiting for you in the morning.

'Well I am not like that, Marcel, and I never have been. You did not marry a little woman, a good and obedient wife.'

'I married you because I loved you and I *thought* you loved me.'

'I loved you, but . . .' She stopped, aware of the hurt in his eyes.

'But?' His voice sounded like a distant echo.

'It was never a great love, Marcel, was it? It was love but not passion? I missed that.'

'And now you've found passion, is that it?'

Judith went over to a chair, a different one this time, and sat down.

'Yes, in a way. Not only what you think. All right, I love Leo, and I have for some time. I have deceived you, Marcel, and been unfaithful to you. Yet I've hated myself for doing it, and now I hate myself for telling and, inevitably, hurting you. I should have told you before.'

'Why didn't you?'

'Because I didn't . . .' As she looked up he averted his eyes. 'Believe me, Marcel, I wish things could be different because I like you so much.'

'Valenti's bought you.'

'That's *not* true.'

'Body and soul.'

'That *is* a lie. I never went to bed with him because I needed his money.'

'Oh, didn't you?'

'No.'

'Before or after?'

'Please don't be crude.'

'I want to know, before or after.'

'After,' she said at last. 'He had begged me to leave you, but I said I didn't want to. I do love and respect you, Marcel, whatever you say or think about me; but my affair with Leo has tormented me, and now I want you to release me from our marriage.'

'And if I don't?'

'I will get a divorce anyway. I'll wait; but if you do release me in a civilized way, we can be friends.'

'That's what you think,' Marcel said, and getting up abruptly he put his chef's hat squarely on his head as though it were a badge of office that gave him confidence.

'You try and blackmail me, Judith, to do something I

don't think is right. I won't release you until the law compels me to.

'I won't because I think, I know, Valenti is a bad man; a bad man who is also very bad for you and one day, I hope, you will realize this and thank me for saving you from the consequences of your own folly.'

Chapter 16

Upstairs, inside the house, old Lady Prynne lay very quiet and still, oblivious to the sounds of summer outside, of the beauty of the garden or the subdued voices of her granddaughters who, sitting close together on the terrace, were engrossed in conversation.

'Marcel was *bound* to be hurt.' Moira put her hand on Judith's arm in sympathy. 'We haven't made much of our marriages, we two, have we?'

'Not much,' Judith said. 'But yours wasn't your fault.'

'Did you mention drugs to Leo?' Moira glanced at her sideways.

'I didn't dare.'

'Some say Leo is in it too.'

'But that's preposterous, monstrous!' Judith felt a sickening sensation in her stomach.

'Didn't it ever occur to you?'

'Never. Never for a moment.'

'But where did you think *he* got his money?'

'Certainly not like that,' Judith protested. 'He has a huge organization.'

'But it isn't listed. He's very secretive about it.'

'How did you know?'

'Billy told me. He finds Leo very mysterious. Leo is always very reluctant to put anything on paper. All deals are done by a handclasp – gentlemen's agreement, that sort of thing. He's hard to get hold of.'

'That doesn't mean he's a crook!'

'Of course not, but why should his movements be so devious?'

'Some people like to be that way. You can be secretive,

cautious, without doing anything illegal. He has always been very open and generous with me, always.'

'Billy thinks he's rather sinister. I thought I should warn you . . . just in case you *do* marry him.'

'I don't find him in the *least* sinister.'

'Maybe because you don't want to. I know he is a very sexy man. He's a strong man and you need a strong man; but I think his fascination for you has blinded you to his shortcomings.'

'And what are they?'

'He is very ruthless. He drives a very hard bargain.'

'That's not a crime. It's a sign of good business, or so I thought.'

'Billy made enquiries and he felt it was odd that, despite his reputation, so little was known about him.'

'Then why didn't you tell me about your suspicions before?'

'I haven't had the chance.' Moira tried to tuck her hand in Judith's. 'Dear, I hardly *ever* see you. I wouldn't be here with you now if it weren't for the fact that Gran is ill . . . Oh, I wish . . .' Moira leaned back in the deck chair and put her arms behind her head.

'Yes? What do you wish?'

'I wish the clock would go back.'

'To when?'

'To . . . Oh I wish Mum and Dad were here.'

'They'll never come home!'

'You'd think they'd come and see Gran.'

The children had sent wires about Lady Prynne's stroke, but the answer had been a rather long-delayed air letter. Both sent sympathy, but said they were in poor health themselves.

For a while Judith and Moira sat in silence, each wrapped in thoughts of her own while, presided over by the watchful eye of her nurse Miss Hegarty, their grandmother drew nearer to death. There was no chance now for Gran to escape from her bed to go once more on her travels, her perpetual search for the elusive Admiral. Perhaps she would find him quite soon.

Next to her bedside sat Doug, his face in his hands, watching. From the terrace he could hear Moira and Judith talking quietly together.

Doug, the only grandson, had been singularly fond of his grandmother. She seemed to him to be the one enduring link with the past, with the old days when Gran and the family home represented security, safety from oblivion. Now, soon, both would be gone.

Gran was incredibly old; she was nearly a hundred, but her face had that curious plasticity of the very young. Her blue eyes remained open and seemed to twinkle innocently with surprise and astonishment, not in pain or sadness, as though she were already at the threshold of heaven and trying so hard to peep in.

Was he there? Was the Admiral there at last?

The sound of a car drawing up in the drive dragged Doug from his reverie and, murmuring to Miss Hegarty, he crossed to the window to see Ros emerging from the front seat with a large bunch of flowers in her hand. He stood for a long time looking down at her, and as she crossed the terrace she suddenly looked up, saw him and waved; but he did not wave back. He turned round and went to his chair by the side of Gran and said to her, as though she were lucid enough to hear him:

'Ros has come, Gran. She's brought some flowers.'

'How nice,' Miss Hegarty said, as one empowered to act as the voice of Gran. 'Your grandmother *will* be pleased.'

But Gran showed neither pleasure not displeasure; her eyes veering neither to right nor left, but staring straight ahead looking towards the door.

It was as if, any minute now, she was sure it would open and the Admiral, in his brusque way, would come in and give her a kiss.

Downstairs Moira and Judith looked up as Ros rounded the house, flowers in one hand, the other clutching the brim of the large picture hat on her head. She wore a navy blue dress and high-heeled white shoes and looked incredibly smart.

'How *is* she?' Ros said, thrusting the flowers at Judith.

'She will never get better,' Judith said sadly. 'It's just a matter of time.'

'Awful how they let them go on living.' Ros took the seat which Judith drew up for her.

'Well, you can't do anything else,' Judith replied. 'You can't put them mercifully to sleep. It is not as though one were dealing with a cat or a dog.'

'No, I suppose not.' Rosalind appeared unconvinced by the argument. A sick person, instead of being Gran, had become one of an indefinite number: 'them'. 'Is that Doug's car I saw outside?'

'Doug is upstairs with Gran. He was always very fond of her.'

'Well, he showed his fondness in a funny way.' Ros gave a loud sniff. 'He hardly *ever* came to visit her.'

'I understood from Miss Hegarty that he came over quite often.' Judith sounded surprised. 'Perhaps he didn't tell you.'

'Perhaps he didn't. Doug was always very secretive,' Ros mused, and gazed at the two sisters, neither of whom she had ever particularly liked. There had always been an 'us' and 'them' quality about Doug's family, the suspicion that she wasn't quite good enough to marry a Prynne. Nonsense, of course, but that's how she'd felt. And why? After all, she had a degree, she had a wealthy father and she had always been able to hold her own in any company. But still, the sisters made, or she felt they had tried to make, her feel inferior.

Now that would all change.

'Did you know Doug and I were divorcing?' she asked

suddenly, and was gratified to see their immediate reaction of shock. 'Ah, I can see he hasn't told you.' Ros pulled her chair closer to them, appearing to warm to her theme. 'He won't have told you about Doris, the housekeeper at Aylestone, then? Of course not. Secretive Doug wouldn't say a thing.'

'Do you mean Mrs Malcolm, the one I dismissed?' Judith raised an eyebrow.

'That is *exactly* who I mean. Well, she has been Doug's mistress for some time.' Ros's eyes blazed with malice. 'Ah, I can see you don't like *that* too much, Judith.'

'It's nothing to do with me,' Judith assured her. 'I can hardly recall the woman.'

'Can't you?' Ros said. 'I'm surprised. Surely you will remember what a plain, *ordinary* little woman she was. Being a Prynne you must surely be surprised she found favour with your brother.'

'How did you find all this out?' Moira looked at her curiously, thinking it odd that Ros appeared to be enjoying herself so much.

'I caught them at it, my dear. I had rung Doug to tell him my father was dying, and he couldn't be found. It was the night he had his heart attack. Poor Daddy only lived a few hours, as you know. After he died I came straight back to Aylestone to tell Doug and found him in bed with that common little woman.'

'Would it have made it better if it had been someone else?' Judith enquired, an acerbic note in her voice.

'Oh always the mocker, aren't you, Judith?'

'No I'm not,' Judith fixed her eyes firmly on those of her sister-in-law, 'but you seem to find something particularly deplorable about Doris Malcolm.'

'Wouldn't you? You, of all people, a Prynne! What would your mother and father have to say? What would *Gran* say?'

'They had quite a lot to say at the time about Doug

314

marrying *you*.' Moira's acid tongue came quickly to the defence of her brother. 'Though it's such a long time ago we've all forgotten it.'

'Oh I haven't forgotten it!' Ros cried, slightly hysterically. 'Don't think I have. New money, you thought, snobbish lot that you were, without a bean. Don't think *I* didn't know what you *really* thought . . .'

'You couldn't possibly know what we *really* thought,' Judith said, standing up so suddenly that her chair fell over backwards onto the terrace. 'We never actually thought that at all. Moira has let her indignation get the better of her, or maybe her memory is at fault, I don't know. The fact is that it was after the war and those attitudes were over, as far as we were concerned. Maybe not completely with Mummy and Daddy, but *certainly* with Moira and me.'

'I never honestly heard Mummy and Daddy say anything unpleasant about Ros,' Moira said to her sister as though Ros were not there. 'They only wanted Doug to be happy. You're quite right, Judith, Ros's attitude does get my goat. I didn't mean what I said.'

'Anyway this has got nothing to do with why we are here.' Judith perched on the low wall surrounding the terrace, which was half shaded by a drooping willow tree. It was nearly noon on a warm day in high summer.

'I don't see the point now of reproaches and recriminations,' she went on, looking at Ros. 'I'm sorry about you and Doug; but it seems inevitable, whether there was a Doris about or not.'

'How do you mean "inevitable"?' Ros said, looking at her with suspicion.

'Well, I am divorcing Marcel, and Moira is hoping one day to marry Billy McLaren. So . . .' she raised her shoulders in a Gallic gesture of resignation. 'It seems to be all the vogue.'

At that moment Doug came through the door on to the

terrace and his expression seemed to indicate he'd been listening.

'How's Gran?' Judith said, jumping up.

'The same.' Doug ignored Ros and sat in the chair previously vacated by Judith. 'She has a happy expression on her face. Sometimes, you know, I do believe in the afterlife.'

'Good *morning*, Douglas,' Ros said, pointedly addressing him.

'Good morning, Ros.' Douglas turned lack-lustre eyes in her direction. 'I did see you arrive from the bedroom window. I stayed upstairs as long as I could in the hope that you'd go.'

'Charming,' Ros said, looking from one sister to the other as if she regarded them as allies.

'Well I can't honestly see why you've come,' Doug said angrily. 'You never particularly liked Gran, or cared about her.'

'Oh but I know how it feels to grieve unsupported,' Ros said acidly. 'Like *I* was the night Daddy died.'

'Oh for heaven's sake! You didn't tell me he was *dying*. You merely said he was ill. If I'd thought you'd wanted me, of course I'd have come.'

'And left the arms of the voluptuous Mrs Malcolm?'

'I think that's quite enough on that subject,' Judith interposed quickly. 'Besides, if I remember, she was *hardly* voluptuous.'

'She's told you we're divorcing?' Doug asked abruptly.

'Yes. I'm sorry.' Judith leaned over to touch him.

'You're really sorry?' Doug's smile was sceptical.

'Yes I am. Just because I'm in the same boat myself it doesn't mean that I want everyone else there. I think it's rather sad that our parents have remained married for over forty years, but now their three children are all in the process of getting unmarried.'

Ros stood up, selfconsciously straightening the white belt round her dress.

'I think, if I may, I'll just pop up and see your grandmother. I may not see her again. Doug, would you escort me please?'

'Certainly,' Doug said, jumping to his feet, and he led the way from the terrace back into the house while Moira and Judith remained silently watching them.

'A hard nut that one,' Moira said *sotto voce*, when they'd disappeared. 'I would never have believed it, actually. She's certainly changed. One has the impression that all these years Ros has been more unhappy with Doug than we knew. In a way I feel a bit guilty about it.

'We never really knew her very well. I didn't.' Moira leaned forward to light a cigarette and then threw back her head, blowing smoke into the air. 'I do remember though that we, particularly Mummy, thought she was plain. It was not so much who she was, or what she was, or who her father was, but what she looked like.'

'I remember that, too, and Doug was so very handsome as a young man. Now it's the other way about. Her looks have improved and Doug seems worn out. I think Ros feels she's going to be her own woman and make something of her life. Good luck to her.'

'But what about Doug?'

Judith bent her head and studied the ground where a line of ants were, with singular resolution, pursuing their quest from one part of the terrace to another. How huge a vista it must have seemed to them!

'There's something I want to tell you, Moira. It seems that Aylestone might be for sale and, if it is, I might buy it or, rather, Leo might buy it for me.'

'As a home?' Moira's eyes glinted with excitement.

'Oh no. As a hotel; only in the manner we originally intended.'

'Is it likely to happen?'

'Leo has people making enquiries about it now. There was something in the financial press. Jenner Securities hasn't had a good year; in fact in the last few years it's been going down.'

'If you do buy it, what will happen to Doug?' Moira leaned forward, determined to catch her sister's eye.

'I don't know,' Judith said, managing to avert her gaze. 'That's the problem. I . . .'

Suddenly there was a commotion in the hall inside the house, voices raised in argument. Moira and Judith rose with one accord and rapidly crossed the terrace into the drawing room. As they entered Ros was saying:

'You can bet your life that, as it's my money, I shall bloody well do what I like with it.'

'But you know nothing about hotels.'

'Well, nor do you.'

'What do you mean I know nothing? On the contrary, I know everything.'

'Is that so?' Ros dropped her voice until it was scarcely above a whisper. 'If that is really the case you are the most unlucky hotelier I have ever come across, always being thrown out of a job . . . and that's what's going to happen to you now, sweetie. Because if I *do* buy Aylestone – and the accountants are looking into it now – you, Douglas Prynne, will be the first one to go!'

And then there was the sound of rapid footsteps crossing the floor and of the front door being banged shut.

Moira and Judith remained out of sight, looking at each other, in the sudden calm that followed the storm.

Sir Billy McLaren, Bt, in his white suit, panama hat set at a correct angle on his head, looked every bit the man of wealth with aristocratic connections that he was; every bit the Scottish country gentleman with a background of Fettes and the Guards. As he sipped his *cappuccino* on the pavement outside fashionable Florian's in St Mark's Square he had the appearance of someone at ease with himself and the world. In fact the reverse was the case. The pleasant smile on his lips only barely concealed the fear in his heart because, already, he knew that his mission was a dangerous one.

His quest had taken him first to Rome; then to Naples and Sicily and, finally, via Bologna, to Venice. He was on the trail of a missing man; a man who had been missing for almost three years and who, one might have thought, could be presumed dead. But if he was dead how did he die, and why? These were questions which the twelfth baronet of the ancient and noble Scottish house of McLaren felt ought to be answered if he was ever to be free to make Moira Valenti his wife, and the child she was carrying his lawful heir.

Billy was a man happy and sanguine by nature; he was reluctant to face up to difficulties, or unpalatable facts. His life had been an easy progression up the slope of success from birth: he had been loved, protected, cosseted, indulged. He was the most unlikely man to fall in love with a married woman with two children who, in her turn, expected to be protected, cosseted, loved as she had been from birth, almost like Billy.

But, once in love, for Billy there was no going back; only forward and that meant knowing about what had happened to Richard, a man of artistic temperament, unstable and an abuser of drugs. Yet it was not enough for English law to presume his death. One must know.

Billy gazed furtively about him, for his appointment was already late. He looked first towards the Merceria – that fashionable byway which snaked through the narrow streets of Venice as far as the Rialto Bridge. He looked over to the great Byzantine Cathedral of St Mark, but all he saw on all sides were groups of tourists surrounding their guides who, in assorted tongues, explained the glories of that ancient church which held the bones of the second Evangelist who had written the life of Christ.

To Billy's left was an opening through the arcades of shops which circumscribed the square, and it was in this direction that he concentrated his gaze for, he supposed for some reason, that was the way his contact would arrive.

Billy finished his coffee, looked at his watch, sighed and opened the day-old copy of *The Times* he had bought in the hall of his hotel which overlooked the Grand Canal. It was a small but expensive hotel and at first his contact had suggested they should rendezvous there. But Billy was already a frightened man who, in the course of his peregrinations through Italy, had sometimes wondered if he would ever see his beloved again. So many odd things had happened to him – in Rome, in Naples, but particularly in Palermo – that he preferred to make his appointment in Venice out in the open air because someone, he decided, was either trying to frighten him or finish him off.

In Rome he had had a narrow escape from a motor car which had gone out of control in a narrow street, causing him to flatten himself against a wall. In Naples his room had been searched thoroughly enough to leave him in no doubt as to what had happened, though nothing had been stolen. In Palermo he felt as if he were always being watched, and everyone he tried to see failed to keep their appointments with him. At last he had been directed to Venice by a note left in his room. But why, and by whom? He had no idea.

But ever since he had been in Italy he had been convinced that some person, or persons, had known exactly where he was, what he was doing and why. It had been like playing a game which was a mixture of Follow My Leader and Blind Man's Buff.

As the hour drew towards noon and the heat increased, Billy got out his handkerchief, took off his hat and mopped his brow. He was just about to replace it when a voice to his right (not the direction he had anticipated) said in heavily accented English:

'Lord McLaren?'

'Merely Sir William McLaren,' Billy said, extending his hand. 'Not quite the same thing.'

'You must excuse me,' the visitor said, politely shaking his hand, 'but I am not familiar with the English aristocracy.'

'Scottish,' Billy said, thinking, maybe too late, that it was unnecessary to be so pernickety.

'I beg your pardon, sir?' The man wrinkled his brow.

'I am Scottish, from Scotland.'

'Ah. *Scotia*, of course!' At last the man smiled as if he fully understood and, as he sat down, he put a small packet he was carrying very deliberately on the table.

Billy was carefully taking the measure of his visitor who, however, seemed innocuous enough; there were no obvious bulges from his breast pocket or his hips. He was swarthy with a black moustache, but neither of these was sufficient to make him in any way different from millions of his fellow countrymen. Like Billy he wore a cream-coloured suit, but his hat was a brown fedora.

'Will you have a drink?' Billy enquired as the man seated himself comfortably and began to undo the buttons of his jacket.

'Ah, thank you, no.' The visitor spread his hands. 'I do not drink. It is not good in my business. But I would accept a coffee, black coffee, if you please.'

'And what *is* your business?' Billy asked, nervously flicking his fingers for the attention of the waiter.

'Ah!' The man smiled and wagged his finger. 'That you shouldn't ask. But I know you want to see me, and I know what it is you wish to know.'

'And do you know it?' Billy leaned forward, conscious of the sweat trickling down his brow.

'That depends.' The Italian flashed his teeth in a smile of

cosmetic brilliance, which also divulged one or two gold inlays, as the waiter took his order.

'*Café nero, per favore.*'

'*Si, signore.*'

'On *what* does it depend?' Billy said with a quiet air of desperation. 'I have come a very long way and wasted much of my time, yet, despite meeting many people and asking hundreds of questions, I seem to be no nearer than when I first started.'

'You are very anxious, sir, to find out the whereabouts of Mr Ricardo Valenti, are you not?'

Billy was ashamed to admit even to himself the defeat he felt in his heart.

'Then he is alive.'

The Italian once again waved his forefinger back and forth with the precision of a metronome.

'I did *not* say that.'

'But you said his whereabouts?'

The Italian raised his eyes to heaven then looked at the ground.

'Who knows where that is, signore?'

'I think you're playing with me,' Billy burst out angrily. 'I must tell you that I am a busy man, a very busy man, and the quest on which I have been sent has, so far, been a wild-goose chase . . .'

'Ah, "been sent", Monsignore William, that is the question is it not? On whose behalf are you acting? My principals are not clear . . .'

'I am acting solely on behalf of Mrs Moira Valenti, of course! She doesn't know whether she's a widow or a wife. She has not seen her husband for almost three years. He left their flat not far from here, without a word, and all his clothes and effects remained behind as well. These included passport, credit cards and a quantity of money. There has been no word of him since. All this is most unfair on Signora Valenti, and on me, incidentally.'

'You are an interested party?' A sly look came into the Italian's eye as he accepted his coffee from the waiter and immediately began to sip it.

Billy nodded vigorously. 'I want to marry her. We cannot be married if we don't know where her husband is.'

'Can he not be *presumed* to have died, Monsignore William?'

'Not yet, not to satisfy a British court. More time has to elapse. I believe it is at least seven years. Mr Valenti was also in the habit of disappearing without saying where he was going. He was an artist, a man of unpredictable habits. He ...' as he saw the Italian nodding Billy stopped abruptly. 'I feel you know him?'

'Oh yes I know him, or,' the smile returned to the face that could have come out of a group portrait by Masaccio, 'or shall I say I *knew* him.'

'Then he is dead?' Billy, to his shame, felt his heart flicker.

'It is not to say he is dead. If a person says that they "knew" somebody it may mean that they no longer know them. You may not have seen that person for many years, or the friendship may be broken.' An expression of sadness clouded the man's mobile countenance. 'Who can say?'

Billy signalled again for the waiter and asked for his bill. '*Conto, per favore.*'

'*Prego,*' the waiter began to make out items on his pad as the Italian looked at Billy with surprise.

'You are *going*, monsignore?'

'I think I'm wasting my time.'

'Then you will never know the truth.' The Italian shrugged, looking very sad indeed.

'It seems not.' Billy began to count out the change on the table.

'But that is what you came for?'

'I still think you're wasting my time.'

'What a pity.' The fingers of the Italian drummed on the

323

table and his expression grew more morose. 'I, too, have come a long way, Monsignore William, and I *have* the information you require, and the proof. Please do not think that I have not.' He looked meaningfully at the packet on the table in front of him, which Billy now saw was an oblong envelope. 'But I had to be sure of your credentials also, why you wanted to know.' His hand pressed against his heart and he cast his eyes towards heaven. 'Ah, *l'amore.*'

'The proof is in *there*?' Billy asked with increasing irritability.

'For a price.'

'How much?'

The Italian carefully looked round, as Billy had while he was waiting, then, putting his mouth closely to the ear of his neighbour, who was assailed by a strong smell of garlic, he murmured a price that staggered even the rich Scottish baronet.

'But I have not got that sort of money with me!'

'Nevertheless it is what I want. It should not be too much for a man of your means to command, monsignore. You see I am in *very* dangerous waters too. If people knew what I was doing they would probably wish to bury me. It is not in the interests of everyone to say what happened to Signor Valenti.'

'Who for instance?' Billy, despite his air of bravura, nevertheless felt his flesh crawl.

'Ah, alas,' the Italian shook his head sadly. 'It is worth more than my life or, I dare say, yours to tell you that; but it is someone *very* powerful, believe you me.' He put a finger to his lips. 'More I cannot say. It may even be dangerous for me to meet you here. It is such a costly risk for me that I suggested your hotel but,' he paused and smiled sympathetically again at Billy, 'I can understand why you were cautious. The waters of the lagoon, yes? They run very deep, do they not?'

'Come to the point, please,' Billy said, beside himself with exasperation. 'Where is the evidence? I must know what it is.'

'Are you prepared to pay the sum I mentioned?'

'If the evidence is conclusive.'

'And I will have the money in cash?'

'In any currency you like.'

'And when will it be delivered?'

'As soon as I can make arrangements through my bank here, which should not take more than twenty-four hours. But, first, I must be satisfied that what is in the envelope contains sufficient proof and, when I do have the money, may I assume that the purchase will be complete and can I take the proof with me?'

The Italian nodded vigorously then, looking around once more, reached for the envelope and slid open the flap which Billy saw had not been gummed. Quickly he produced a paper and some photographs and these he placed out of sight on his lap as if playing a game of cards, and rapidly inspected them before holding one up which he placed on the table in front of Billy.

Billy bent over to inspect it and immediately shut his eyes with a muttered imprecation. For beneath him was the face of a corpse, a corpse who had been drowned, or who had spent a lot of time in the water.

But, unmistakably, it was the face of Richard Valenti, a man whose features he had carried in his heart for all the long weeks of his quest.

Chapter 17

From his office window Matthew Jenner, hands in his pockets, stared down upon London's traffic as it swirled below him.

Behind him, legs elegantly crossed, hands on her lap, sat Judith Prynne waiting for an answer. Finally Matthew turned to her and, for a few seconds, gazed round the room. Then looking directly at her he said:

'I was awfully sorry to hear about your grandmother. I know how fond of her you were.'

'We all were.' Judith acknowledged his tribute with a wave of her hand. 'Thankfully she died without pain, in her sleep. For a woman of her age it was a good way to go. Still we miss her and mourn her.' Judith looked Jenner directly in the eye. 'She was mentally quite sound to the end.'

'Yes, well, er . . .' Jenner, remembering his confrontation many years ago with the family over Lady Prynne, awkwardly rubbed his nose. 'As for the business that brings you here, Judith, we are not *sure* as yet that Aylestone is for sale.'

'I'm making you a very good offer.'

'I know it's a good offer, but . . .'

'But *what*, Matthew?' Judith looked at him curiously. It was unlike him to be so evasive.

'Well there are other people after it.'

'Drake?'

'Yes.' He breathed a deep sigh of relief and relaxed visibly. 'You knew about it?'

'Yes. I knew that Rosalind wanted to buy it to get even with Doug. But that was very soon after her father's death and, of course, I thought she might have changed her mind.'

'Well she hasn't, and she's swung the entire board behind her. The new MD is a man called Frank Barnard who has been with Drake since his early years. He was close to George. He is very thrusting and aggressive and he wants to keep his job. He has no intention of giving Rosalind the reins and she has no experience; but she is the major stockholder. Technically, I suppose, she could fire him.'

'Have you seen her recently?'

'Not for many years.'

'She's changed.'

'I imagined she had.'

'She's very bitter. She has a thing against the Prynnes because she feels that she has wasted her years on Doug and that he has failed her. I didn't know quite how bitterly she felt about it.'

'She always seemed a very mild person to me.'

'Oh no.' Judith uncrossed her legs. 'She was never *mild*. She was always ambitious, but George didn't want her to work with him and she couldn't find anything else to do. She doesn't think Doug has achieved enough; there is no reflected glory for her as there would be, say, if he were the head of a large organization.'

'Well.' Matthew frowned and stared at the ground. 'It *is* Doug I'm concerned about. He may not have risen to great heights, but he has been a very faithful and loyal employee.' Matthew shook his head and walked back to his desk. 'I don't know quite why we failed to make Aylestone work the way we intended, but we did. I can't altogether blame Doug. But there is a case to be made out for disposing of it. But it did get out before we made any announcement and I think we may auction it.'

'That way you'll have all the multiples rushing in.'

'Yes, but what *we're* primarily interested in is the cash. We haven't had a very good year.'

'So I understand.' Judith recrossed her legs.

'We have too much money tied up and we need to liquefy some of our assets.'

'Ours is a good price,' Judith insisted, 'and we could, maybe, offer more. We're acquiring now, Matthew, and we've plenty of money.'

'I can't think how you do it.' Jenner couldn't conceal the admiration in his eyes.

'We plan a lot; we take a lot of care . . .'

'"We"? You mean you?'

'No I mean "we". I have a first-rate assistant, Martin Newbolt, and Leo . . . Leo, well, Leo is, of course, very supportive.'

Matthew went round his desk and leaned against it facing her.

'Judith, let me ask you about Leo. What exactly *is* his role in Prynne's (UK) Ltd?'

'He puts up most of the money,' Judith replied without flinching. 'But he gets a good return. It's not a charity. Of course Leo has taken a back seat since he heard of Richard's death. That shook him a lot.'

'I read about it.' Matthew nodded sympathetically. 'What a horrible business. To have a photograph of a corpse but no corpse.'

'It *was* horrible for Leo, and also for Moira. Billy returned particularly upset and disturbed by the whole thing. Luckily that bit didn't go into the press.'

'How do you mean?'

'Well I can't tell you everything, Matthew, to be honest. It's confidential; but Billy had the distinct feeling he was being followed all round Italy. That someone, or maybe more than one person, knew about his movements. Of course he didn't get that evidence without a price. He had to pay out a lot of money; but some of that was Leo's money. He wanted very much to find out what had happened to Richard, and Billy was a good emissary.'

'Do you know why he wanted to?'

'Of course!' Judith looked surprised. 'He was Leo's only son.'

'I know, but you'd think Leo would have connections . . .'

'If you're hinting, please don't,' Judith said with some anger. 'I'm tired of insinuations against Leo. As far as I'm concerned he is a completely honourable man.'

'Why didn't he go himself?' Matthew turned towards the window again.

'Billy seemed a better choice. Leo, of course, is known. He couldn't play the cat-and-mouse game poor Billy played.'

'You think there were underground connections? For Richard, I mean,' Matthew said hastily.

A cautious look came into Judith's eyes.

'We guess there were, but we have no proof.'

'The Mafia?'

'I can't say, Matthew, honestly, and if I could I would rather not. I would like to return to the business in hand. Look . . .'

Judith got up and began to pace about the floor and Matthew watched, unable to conceal his admiration of her style, her elegance. If Rosalind had changed, so had Judith Prynne, who had grown into a formidable woman; yet without losing her femininity – or so he thought. She swung round and, seeing the expression on his face, raised her eyebrows enquiringly.

Matthew looked embarrassed. 'I always admired you, you know, Judith. I hope you don't find it offensive, but I always did.'

'I don't find it offensive in the least. I'm flattered.'

'I wish I'd been able to offer you whatever it is that Valenti has. It's not just his money, I know.'

'No, it's certainly not that.'

'It's difficult for a man to see his attraction. Is it power?

329

I'm eager to know, though I suppose you'll tell me to mind my own business.'

After a moment or two's reflection, Judith replied: 'He's strong and he's positive, and that is a very powerful combination – at least to a woman like me.'

'So it's all over with Marcel?'

'Yes. I want a divorce but I have to wait. Marcel won't agree.'

'I didn't think Marcel would make it difficult for you. He's such a generous man. You surprise me.'

'It surprised me too; but he is a Catholic and has old-fashioned views. But after five years I can get a divorce whether he agrees or not, so that's what will happen. We're officially separated.'

'I suppose he thinks, hopes maybe, that, in time, you'll change your mind?'

'He does but I won't.'

'Are you still friends?'

'Not exactly friendly. I was angry about his attitude over the divorce. It's going to happen anyway. But we continue to work together. He is a director of Prynne's (UK) Ltd and the restaurant is half mine. Marcel has control of what goes on in the kitchens of our hotels. So we keep a business relationship, which is a good thing for the children as well as ourselves. Now,' Judith folded her arms and smiled at her old friend. 'I think that is enough personal gossip. We should get down to business.'

'The truth is, Judith,' Matthew said with a deep sigh, 'I'd like to sell to you; but I think I'll take the best offer and, so far, the best offer comes from Drake.'

'We'll top it. Whatever it is we'll top it.'

'Barnard says that too. He is acting on very specific instructions. That's why I think I may auction. I suppose there has to be a limit somewhere.'

'Not to us,' Judith said and her eyes hardened. 'If you auction we shall bid, and we will win.'

* * *

'It's quite beautiful,' Judith exclaimed, looking round admiringly at the soft furnishings, the elegant furniture.

'I thought you'd like it, darling. I had it designed for you, by your favourite team.'

'You've been so secretive, Leo, and when did you find the *time*?'

'I made time.' Leo put his arm casually round her waist and pressed his lips tenderly to her cheek. 'It is because I love you. This is our very own apartment; the rest of the house consists of offices.'

'Did you have difficulty getting permission?' Judith, the practical woman of business, had to know.

'There already was permission. It used to be part office and part residence. The last occupants were the Aristophanes Shipping Group, and the Aristophanes family lived here on the top, as we shall.'

'Their name isn't really Aristophanes!' Judith started to laugh and Leo permitted himself a bleak smile.

'They say it is. Who knows? A lot of us are not what we seem.'

'No, we're not . . .'

Judith regarded him gravely, the joy of the moment gone. Since Richard's death Leo had not been the same. It was natural that a father should be shocked by such tragic news; but Leo's moods had swung violently from exultation to depression. He had gone to Italy, to America, to Argentina in a desperate search for he knew not what. Finally he had gone up to Forteliot Castle and shut himself up in the suite there for the best part of two weeks, isolated, uncommunicative.

And then, suddenly, he had reappeared in London, no wiser about the truth concerning the death of his son but feeling better. Still Judith didn't feel she knew him well; she didn't think she ever would. There was a large part of Leo that was evasive and secretive, and that, too, had been the trouble with Richard. Father and son were too much alike. Sometimes she was actually glad that she couldn't marry Leo because, in some mysterious way, she felt she was being saved from making what might turn out to be a mistake. But these thoughts were banished as soon as they occurred. They made her feel disloyal because, to her, Leo had always been supportive and tender, whatever he was to others, or whatever others said about him.

Now he had bought a house in Chester Square which was to be the headquarters of Prynne's (UK) Ltd. At last they would have an office and a secretariat . . . and a home of their own together.

'I feel we're in business,' she said at last with a smile. 'Thank you, Leo.'

He took her hand and drew her down beside him on the sofa. Then he patted the back of her hand and gazed into her eyes. The death of Richard had aged him and he looked very tired, his face haggard and mottled, his demeanour sometimes that of an old man. He invariably dressed casually, as if he were off on holiday, well-cut flannels and a double-breasted blue blazer over a silk shirt and club tie. The only time he wore a suit was to dine formally with her at a West End restaurant.

'Now, Judith, what is it?' he enquired gently. 'You look very worried. I expected you to be happy about our first home together. Living in rented apartments and hotels is not all that much fun. I *thought* you would be happy. Maybe I should have consulted you. Maybe you didn't want to live, as it were, over the shop, even one as luxurious as this?'

'It's not that at all,' Judith interrupted him. 'I love this house and I love the position. I couldn't have wished for anything nicer.'

'In the mews around the corner we can keep horses and go riding in Rotten Row.'

'You've thought of everything, darling. It's not that at all.'

'Then what *is* it, Judith?' Leo still firmly held her hand and she began gently to stroke the back of his.

'I think we're going to lose Aylestone,' she said at last. 'As you can imagine it's very important to me.'

'But we are not going to lose it,' he insisted in his deep, calm voice. '*I* am going to buy it for you. I promised you that.' His manner was, as usual, very decisive.

'I saw Matthew Jenner yesterday. He is going to auction. So far the highest offer has come from Rosalind.'

'Is this just to get her own back on Douglas?'

'And us, the Prynnes. She once told me that we had made her feel inferior for years.'

'But the Drake Organization does not have endless resources.'

'Neither do we.'

'My darling,' Leo patted her hand again comfortingly, then got to his feet. He went over to a bowl of fresh flowers before turning to her, hands in his pockets, feet slightly apart. 'What you want you are going to have. I promised you that, and I keep my promises. I have never had any difficulty getting money, as much as I need. I have no problems on that score at all.'

'But *where* does it come from, Leo? There's got to be an end somewhere.' But, as she asked the question, she already saw the answer in his eyes. He dropped his lids like shutters and she knew that it was not for her to know. Strange Leo; strange man. Maybe that's why he obsessed her so much.

'I'm sorry,' she murmured.

'I should think so,' he said, gently reproving. 'We agreed long ago never to discuss my money.'

'But that was before we got so involved. Besides I never thought the business would grow so quickly. I feel that, as we shall soon be seeking a Stock Exchange quotation, I must know where our money comes from.'

'Do you suspect me of hiding something, Judith?'

'Of course not!' Suddenly, unexpectedly, she felt afraid. A fear that started low down in her spine and crawled slowly up her back.

'Some people do, you know,' Leo said quite chattily as he walked to the window, producing a cigar from his breast pocket and taking his time about lighting it. '*I* know that. *I* know there is talk about me; but so far,' he spun round and stabbed the cigar in her direction, 'no one has *ever* accused me to my face of anything dishonest . . .'

'Leo.' Judith rose and, crossing the floor towards him, put her arm through his. 'It's just, Leo darling, that you *are* rather secretive. Inevitably it gives rise to talk. You are a global operator, without even a company. This kind of thing makes people suspicious.'

'But why, why?' Leo, looking seriously annoyed, flung his hands in the air. 'Some people like to work that way. I am an entrepreneur, not an organization.'

'But you wanted Prynne's to have a proper organization.'

'That's different.' He smiled at her, beguiling, seductive. 'You can't run a chain of hotels as an individual. But the way I operate is strictly legitimate. I pay my taxes and everything is above board. I like it that way and I intend to keep it that way. Now you must trust me, Judith. Trust me always and completely. Do you understand?'

'I understand,' Judith said but she did not meet his eyes. He continued:

'What money you want for Aylestone you shall have.'

'Maybe, after all, we should be content with what we've got,' Judith murmured.

'What do you mean exactly?' He looked puzzled.

'We already own two very successful hotels, and Martin Newbolt has plans to acquire more. He is looking at a takeover of the Sheridan chain.'

'That is excellent news.' Leo rubbed his hands with the gleeful air of a miser. 'But we will *also* add Aylestone to our list. No one could run it like you, and Rosalind *must* know that. Whatever her motives, she must realize that we are much better equipped to succeed than she is.'

'That will only spur her on,' Judith said dejectedly. 'She is motivated solely by hate.'

At times Frank Barnard found it hard to understand the new majority shareholder and, effectively, his boss. She was a woman who had spent most of her life in obscurity, in the shadow of her father, then her husband; the mother of a grown-up son. Now she had emerged or, apparently, wished to emerge as an entrepreneur in a tough business world of which she knew nothing.

Rosalind Prynne had no experience; but she was a quick learner and Barnard was a little in awe of her. He didn't understand what propelled her or where she got her fire. He couldn't believe that she was solely motivated by dislike of her husband's family.

Rosalind was a woman in her middle years who dressed smartly, drove a fast, fashionable small car and lived at a good address in Mayfair. It had all happened suddenly within a year of her father's death. It seemed thus to her that his anniversary was a fitting occasion both for grief and celebration, because it had enabled her to find independence and carve for herself an entirely different way of life.

Her divorce from Douglas was nearly absolute. There had been no defence for a man caught in adultery. He didn't even try and defend himself, and Ros, in her desire for vengeance, got the most out of someone who had little left to give. She was determined to leave him with as few assets as she could. All he had left to call his own were his few shares in what had once been his family home. It was a melancholy state for a man to find himself in.

The Drake Organization was a public company. Its shares were quoted on the Stock Exchange, and in that company the Drake family did not have a controlling interest. Theoretically the company could be taken over by anyone who secured enough of the shares to gain control and Ros, who knew enough about company law, was afraid that before very long Judith Prynne would realize that it was not beyond her power to gain control of the organization that wanted to buy Aylestone. In a way both women knew it was a war to the death.

However, the Drake shares were strong; the company was now doing well. On the other hand Jenner Securities was very weak and doing badly. It had become too diversified; it had no corporate identity, no mark that set it apart. It dabbled in this and that and its shares had failed to gain momentum, remaining rather miserably at the bottom end of the index.

'If we could gain control of Jenner we would have Aylestone before they had a chance to sell,' Ros remarked to Frank Barnard in the course of their, by now, daily meetings in the boardroom.

'Why on earth would we want the whole group?' Barnard looked at her in astonishment.

'*Then* we would be sure of Aylestone.'

'But Aylestone is all we want; we don't want the other rubbish that has helped to bring him down.'

'Couldn't we sell it off, Frank?'

'But it would take millions to buy out Jenner, Ros. It would stretch our resources.'

'We could borrow from the banks. They would support us, wouldn't they?'

'They might.' Barnard looked dubious. 'But they would ask why we wanted to buy a company which was not nearly as profitable as ours and land ourselves with a lot of products we knew nothing about; a lot of debts and a lot of trouble. They've had labour relations problems too.'

'Isn't there something called asset stripping? Couldn't we sell them off?'

'Rosalind.' Frank Barnard sighed deeply and began to

play with the paper-knife on his desk. 'I *do* appreciate that after many years merely as a wife and mother you feel frustrated, that you have not realized your potential. You are clever, ambitious and anxious to do well, prove yourself your father's heir. But I must point out to you, with all honesty, that you have very little experience of the business world. I must urge you to tread very gently and carefully, or else this organization that your father nurtured with such care will take on more than it can cope with.'

He sat back in his chair clasping his hands in front of him.

'I really find it an intolerable situation where two headstrong women, former sisters-in-law who hate each other, make the acquisition of a hotel a personal issue merely to settle old scores, to the detriment and danger of this group.'

'Thank you very much, Frank,' Ros said with a sweet smile on her face. 'Believe me I appreciate your honesty. Now tell me, do you know any good journalists?'

'*Journalists?*' Frank gasped. 'Don't tell me you want to take over a *newspaper* too?'

'No, I want someone who is good at gossip,' Ros said. 'Trust me.' And with that she made her exit, leaving her bewildered chief executive staring at the closed door.

Philip Lindsay called himself rather grandiloquently a 'special correspondent', but he was a valuable reporter with the *Global Recorder*, an out-of-town newspaper which wielded quite a lot of influence in Fleet Street. He had never heard of Rosalind Drake – who had reverted to her maiden name – or of the Drake Organization. He specialized in parties patronized by debutantes and the *beau monde*, or what there was left of it in the Britain of the seventies. He liked to dredge up things about people that were just short of libellous and print them in his newspaper without attribution. So far he had never had a court case, though he had come near to it, because he always made sure that the information he had came from sources that were truthful and reliable.

It had taken some persuasion to get him to meet Rosalind Drake for lunch; but when a very good restaurant was mentioned in Knightsbridge which was patronized by royalty and the sort of famous people among whom he liked to mingle with his grubby little notebook, he grudgingly promised to free himself from another engagement.

'I suppose you're *awfully* busy, Mr Lindsay,' Rosalind said ingratiatingly over the gin and tonic which preceded their meal.

'To be honest with you I *am* busy, Mrs Drake,' Lindsay said. 'I have also nothing to do with the business world. But you said enough on the phone to intrigue me.'

'And it *will* be confidential, won't it?' Rosalind paused to smile at the head waiter who informed them that her table was ready.

'Mum's the word,' Lindsay promised, intrigued despite himself. He followed her to the back of the room, his knowing magpie-eyes darting about among the tables in an effort to discover if anybody there was lunching with anybody else's wife, or mistress, or boyfriend.

For the first half of the meal Rosalind, who had quite an entertaining line in conversation, chatted about herself, her background, her ambitions but, above all, about her father who had built up single-handedly such a powerful and successful organization . . . which was now threatened.

'I thought you said something about the Mafia,' Lindsay whispered, leaning across the table so that their noses almost touched. '*That* was the bit that intrigued me.'

'You understand it *is* pretty dangerous ground?'

'Yes I do. Sure, sure,' Lindsay said tucking into his sole véronique, washed down with a glass of good Chablis. '*I* don't want my body found in the Thames with a stone tied to it.'

'Well that's exactly what will happen,' Ros said, a note of excitement entering her voice, 'that is, if you aren't careful.'

'In that case it may be too dangerous for me to touch,' Lindsay felt himself changing colour, 'but fire away.'

'You've heard of Judith Prynne, I suppose?'

'Judith . . .' For a moment Lindsay closed his eyes as he consulted the mental address book he carried around with him, stored in the back of his head. 'You mean *the* Miss Judith Prynne . . . the restaurant and the smart hotels.'

'That's the one.'

'There was a piece on her in *Vogue* a month or two ago?'

'Exactly.'

'Don't tell me she's mixed up in the Mafia?'

'She may be,' Ros said mysteriously.

'But how do you know?'

'I was married to her brother. My married name is Prynne.'

'Golly!' Lindsay said, rapidly retrieving his notebook from his pocket and turning over the pages, already filled with shorthand, until he came to a blank. 'Fire away.'

The hotel had once been a stately home overlooking the sea. It had belonged to an art collector who had furnished it with many priceless paintings and pieces of furniture which, after his death, had mostly to be sold to pay the enormous death duties that accrued to his estate.

Before that it had been the home of a family whose ancestors had come over with the Conqueror at the same time as the Prynnes. Perhaps it was this that gave Judith an especial affection for the place as soon as she had been driven to it one gusty March day, when the wind blew in from the sea sending up huge waves which drenched the roads and promenades along the Kentish coast.

She had spent months overseeing the final arrangements: the time when all the new furniture moved in and the newly engaged staff began to appear. She always brought one or two senior personnel from one of her other hotels to help the newcomers to settle in, and sometimes they stayed on.

Some days before the official opening of The Romney, Marcel made his usual appearance to oversee the restaurant for the first few days of business. It was the only time he left his deputy in charge in London. As it was half-term, Michael and Pauline were also there and, for a time, it seemed almost as though they were a family again living in the family flat. The only difference was that Marcel, instead of sharing a room with Judith, had one of the guest rooms on the first floor.

The children were growing up. They would soon be leaving school. Pauline was a beauty who closely resembled her Aunt Moira. Michael looked grave and serious, fulfilling his early promise of being a scholar rather than a chef.

The children loved being with their parents. One of the few times they saw them together. They were well aware of the situation: that a divorce was in the offing and that, when it happened, their mother would marry Leo.

Yet they both liked Leo. He was charming to them, patient and generous; but they preferred their father, and the best thing of all would have been for them to see their parents together again.

On the morning of the opening Judith sat at the table in the private suite with the children, who had just taken a swim in the basement pool. As usual Judith had black coffee and Melba toast while Pauline and Mike had a full English breakfast, cooked for them by Marcel in the small kitchen belonging to the flat.

There was to be a dinner and dance in the evening at the hotel, which was full of the customary distinguished invited guests, and those who had paid a small fortune for the privilege of attending the opening celebrations of a new

'Prynne' hotel. The children were already excited and, as Marcel brought their plates to the table, he said to them:

'Now quieten down. If you're going to be like this all day you'll be exhausted by the evening.'

'Tell us what you're making for the dinner, Dad?' Pauline said with a side-glance at Judith, who was opening the morning mail addressed personally to her. They were mostly letters of congratulation to go with the flowers that had been arriving for days and would, if the past was anything to go by, continue to arrive for the next few weeks.

'What does it feel like to be *famous*, Mum?' Mike smiled across at her as the telegrams began to pile up beside her plate.

'It's true I do feel like an actress sometimes.' Judith grinned back at him. 'But I wouldn't say I was *famous*.'

'Of course you're famous. Everyone at school has heard of you. Even the Head read the article about you in *Vogue*.'

'How do you know?' Judith looked at Michael with astonishment.

'Because he said "Your mother is a smasher! What a lucky fellow you are."'

'And how did you reply?' Marcel enquired as he sat down to join them but also, like Judith, only taking thin toast and black coffee.

'I mumbled something and hurried off,' Michael replied. 'You never know what to say at a time like that.'

'Quite right.' Marcel looked at Judith who returned his glance with a smile that immediately caught the attention of Pauline. Impulsively she clasped her hands together in an attitude of prayer.

'Oh! I do *wish* you two would make it up. I'm sure you love each other, really.'

Marcel immediately grimaced and Judith gazed at the floor.

'Well you do really, don't you? Don't you, Mum?' Michael urged.

She raised her head and met his eyes. 'Daddy and I like and respect each other very much. Love . . . that is something else. Of course we love each other because we have you, and that gives us a bond. We have the restaurant and the hotels . . .'

'But that isn't enough for your mother,' Marcel said. 'There are other things to marriage, as she will tell you . . .'

'Such as?' Pauline's eyes glinted with suspicion and Judith, very conscious of her expression, said:

'I really don't think this is the time or the day to go into it, darling.'

'Is it because Leo has given you so much money?'

'Money has *nothing* to do with it,' Judith said sharply. 'What a horrible thing to say.'

'I'm sorry, Mum.'

'Tenderness, passion . . .' Marcel seemed to be trying to explain something to them. 'But not money. You should know your mother better. She is not interested in money except, of course, as a means to an end. That end is enough capital for expansion of the business.'

'Then *why*?'

'Hush, *ma petite*,' Marcel murmured, leaning towards his daughter. 'Why make this otherwise happy day unpleasant for your mother?'

Abashed, because she was a well-brought-up, well-behaved girl, Pauline picked up her knife and fork while Judith flashed Marcel a grateful glance just as the phone rang.

'I'll get that.' Marcel rose and lifted the receiver to his ear. Then he held it out to Judith. 'It's for you. Martin would like to see you downstairs.'

'Can't he come here?'

'Could you come up?' Marcel spoke into the mouthpiece. 'We're just having breakfast.' He paused, nodded his head and said to Judith:

'It's something that needs your attention in the office. Martin seems to think it's urgent.'

'Tell him I'll come at once.'

Marcel passed on the message and returned to the table addressing his children.

'You see your mother has so many important things to attend to. You mustn't make her unhappy.'

'We don't want her to be unhappy, we just want . . .'

'Ssh,' Marcel said, lowering his voice. '*Tais-toi.*'

He raised his eyes as Judith, excusing herself, disappeared out of the door.

She went quickly along the corridor, savouring with pleasure the clean, elegant lines of the wallpaper, the luxurious pile of the new carpet specially woven for the Group at a factory in Axminster. It was not the intention to have a uniform house style for all the Prynne hotels, but the carpet did give each one a measure of corporate identity. Each stately home hotel, though individually planned and designed, had certain common aspects that existed for the efficiency of the Group, as well as the convenience and comfort of the guests.

There was a deep stairwell which had once been the grand staircase of the family home of the Romney lords, though now two high-speed lifts on either side served the various floors. The house had been built round a courtyard where a sculptured fountain delicately sprayed water into a pool at its base. It was overlooking this tranquil scene that the main offices had been placed, and most of the guests got a sea view which they normally preferred.

When she reached it Judith found the office busy with the bustle of secretaries, PR assistants and the numerous people who were now deemed necessary to launch a Prynne hotel. For a moment she paused at the doorway, unnoticed by those inside, and it briefly crossed her mind that something had been lost from those leisurely, more graceful days, when first Aylestone then Forteliot Castle had been opened for the first time to the public.

Then it was just herself, Marcel, senior staff and the trusted secretary, Rosemary Carter, who now looked after the main office in Chester Square.

Judith sighed deeply and gently closed the outer door after her as Martin Newbolt appeared from the inner office and saw her. As he did everyone else, seeing his expression, stopped talking.

'Good morning, Miss Prynne,' they suddenly cried out in unison, like the carefully rehearsed chorus of a well-conducted girls' school.

'Good morning, everyone,' Judith replied, aware of the awkward pause that had preceded the greeting. 'Hard at it, I see?'

'Sir Michael Wilmott has telephoned to ask if he might bring a guest . . .' one of the girls began, but Martin gave her a forbidding look as he took Judith by the arm and ushered her into the inner office.

'Can't have you bothered with trivia,' he murmured, firmly shutting the door.

'I'm sure she meant well.' Judith took a seat and smiled at him. 'Standing there in the doorway for a moment, Martin, I was just thinking how it was when it all began. Nothing like this.'

'You weren't a public company then, Judith.' Martin, one of the few people who used her Christian name, sat in a chair opposite her; but she thought his face looked worried.

'Is there something wrong, Martin? I mean, more so than usual on opening day?'

'There *is* something rather worrying in one of the papers, Judith. I wanted you to see it before it was taken up anywhere else, though it may well die the death.'

'Something about me?'

'I'm afraid so. Of course we had a press briefing the

344

other day and invited all the journalists who usually deal with this kind of thing. But this paper has a reputation rather like other hard-nosed tabloids: it delights in ferreting out scandal.' Martin gave a deep sigh and held the paper up. 'It looks to *me* as though someone has been getting at "A correspondent".'

Judith took the paper from Martin, produced her spectacles from her bag and put them on her nose.

'"In Depth" by a correspondent,' she read. Then, looking at Martin, 'This seems to be some sort of weekly column.'

'I think so,' he replied.

He sat back, clearly on edge, unable to conceal his anxiety as Judith began to read in her clear, cultured voice:

'This week sees the opening of yet another "Prynne" hotel by the talented Miss Judith Prynne whose family, in the post-war years, has risen from relative impecuniousness to riches.

The Romney, on the coast of Kent, is a splendid new hotel that was formerly the family seat of a line that went back to the Conqueror but which is now extinct with the death in the war of the tenth earl who died without issue. The house, famous for its historical associations together with its unrivalled view of the Channel from the Kentish Weald, fell into disuse until purchased two years ago by the Prynne group and now lovingly restored.

Judith Prynne's success in the last few years has been phenomenal, especially as her own family, which also traces its origins to William the Conqueror, has not been without its troubles. In 1951 it was forced to sell its own historic stately home, Aylestone, to the Drake Organization and for a while it was run by Miss Prynne and her elder brother Douglas. This enterprise was not a success and Miss Prynne left to found, with her husband, the celebrated chef Marcel Laborde, *Prynne's* Restaurant in Pimlico, and two other very successful hotels. However, because of its association for so many centuries with her family, Aylestone probably had pride of place in her affections.

The success of Miss Prynne is in restoring each hotel to the semblance of the stately home it formerly was, and charging accordingly. She is said to take her dictum from César Ritz, the famed hotelier, that everything is secondary to the wishes of the customer. Each hotel is designed individually, though in overall charge are the celebrated team of designers Ian and Tessa Kennedy, and only the most experienced staff are chosen from the thousands, it is said, who apply.

Unhappily, however, Miss Prynne has failed to achieve one ambition. She is said to wish to repurchase the family home Aylestone, which has never achieved the success hoped for it and in recent years, has gone sadly downmarket.

This move, however, is being forestalled by Rosalind Drake, daughter of George Drake of the Drake Organization, which first purchased Aylestone from the family. Mrs Drake, who, since his death, has taken an active part in her father's company, of which she is majority shareholder, is anxious to regain possession of the hotel which is still managed by her former husband Douglas Prynne.

It seems that one may look forward to a takeover battle of dazzling ferocity between Drake's and Prynne's (UK) Ltd for possession of the hotel, and it will be interesting to see the outcome.

An interesting fact is that a perusal of the Prynne annual accounts at Company House fails to reveal where the bulk of the wealth of the company comes from. On paper Prynne's is not wealthy enough to outbid Drake, and yet there never seems any shortage of money for the most extravagant refurbishment.

The *éminence grise* behind Miss Prynne, and perhaps her future husband – for she is said to be estranged from Marcel Laborde – is Leo Valenti, an international entrepreneur, but nevertheless a man whose own origins and the source of whose fortune are shrouded in mystery.

His son Richard Valenti is believed to have died in mysterious circumstances in Italy, a mystery that has never been solved.

'Well!' Judith exclaimed, putting down the paper and whipping off her spectacles. 'What a load of mischief. All innuendo.'

'Nothing actually libellous, I'm afraid,' Martin said with a worried frown. 'I mean he *says* some quite nice things about you and what he says about Leo, well . . .'

'Yes?' Judith looked sharply at him.

'They are true, aren't they? The source of his money *is* a mystery.'

'It is no mystery at all,' Judith said firmly. 'Do you think I wouldn't have satisfied myself that the whole thing was above board?'

'Oh of course, Judith, I'm sure you would.' Martin seemed at pains to reassure her.

'Well you don't seem too sure to me. I'm surprised at you, Martin. Leo does business as a private individual, as anyone is entitled to. He is an entrepreneur and has ample means. That is how he likes to operate. He is the sweetest, most generous and considerate of men and to suggest there is anything sinister ... and bringing in the death of Richard! Why ... I'd just like to get my hands on the person who was responsible for this piece which was clearly meant to slur and wound.'

'And if you did?' Martin seldom saw his boss so worked up, and stared at her with interest.

'If I did ...' Judith joined both hands around her neck and gripped it hard.

Chapter 18

Frank Barnard had joined the Drake Organization as a young graduate after doing his national service in the fifties. He had been very close to the late George Drake and an admirer of his methods, which he took to be based on a philosophy of benevolent autocracy. In other words Drake had been the head, and would brook no rivalry or opposition from his subordinates.

Although George Drake had adored his only daughter, his paternalist views applied to the home as well as his business and he had always refused to give her a job. Her place, he had told her, was beside her husband, helping him and raising her son. George, thus, had very definite views about a woman's role which had never varied throughout his life.

However, when he died he left the controlling share of his organization to his daughter in trust for his grandson, with the wish recorded in his will that she would leave it in the capable hands of: 'my trusted lieutenant Frank William Barnard' to whom he had also left his villa in Spain and twenty thousand pounds.

It was not long, however, before Barnard began to feel the presence of Rosalind within the organization. She was diligent in attending board meetings, asked to see minutes of all the meetings held throughout the group, its plans and its acquisitions.

By the time her father had been dead a year she had her own office and there was very little that went on within the organization that she didn't know about. It was at that time that Barnard heard about her impending divorce and, not long after that, she told him about her ambitions to own Aylestone and relaunch it as the stately home hotel it was once intended to be.

Barnard was aghast. He had explained that, as a group, they knew nothing about hotels, which was why George had long ago divested himself of Aylestone. He thought it was a mistake, an error solely motivated by Rosalind's desire to get her own back on a husband who had deceived her; but he didn't dare say so. He realized that, although he had known her for over twenty years, he really didn't know her well at all or, if he did, she had re-emerged from her long hibernation as someone quite different.

Frank Barnard did not see the piece in the *Global Recorder* about the Prynne family; but he read all the other publicity concerning the opening of the Romney, at which minor royalty had also been present.

One had to hand it to Judith Prynne, he thought admiringly, looking at the sheaf of cuttings his secretary had put on his desk. She had style. There was a close-up of her with the royal personage, with whom she seemed on excellent terms, and an enthusiastic write-up of the fabulous new hotel whose rooms bore a minimum price tag of £100 a night. For this one got a small room, bathroom en suite, but with a back view. For the suites overlooking the sea the price was much higher and the fabulous cuisine, under the overall control of Marcel Laborde, was in the immediate care of a *maître-chef* chosen and also trained by him.

Barnard was still poring over the cuttings when his door was flung open and Rosalind Drake came storming in, clearly with something on her mind.

'Rosalind,' Frank said, jumping to his feet and glancing at the clock which told him it was ten minutes to nine, 'I didn't expect you so early. The meeting isn't until . . .'

'I know quite well when the meeting is, Frank, thank you,' Rosalind snapped. 'Have you seen *this*,' and with an air of triumph, she flung in front of him the *Global Recorder*, which had been delivered to her by hand.

Frank looked at the headline: 'In Depth'.

'Read it,' she commanded, pointing to his chair with an imperious finger. 'Now is the time to strike.'

When he came to the penultimate paragraph he felt his face change colour and, by the time he had finished it, his whole body felt cold.

'What's the matter, Frank?' Rosalind noticed his change of complexion.

'Were you responsible for this?'

'Of course I was,' she replied gleefully. 'The PR man whose name you gave me had this man Lindsay contact me and I invited him to lunch.'

'I would say it was libellous.' Frank's colour had begun to return once the immediate shock had passed, and he sat down rummaging for a cigarette.

'No it is not libellous. I had the lawyers check it. It doesn't even *imply* Leo Valenti is a crook ... which, incidentally, I'm quite sure he is. My ex-husband, Doug, was always convinced he belonged to the Mafia! Of course, we had to be careful not to *say* as much.'

'I should think not.' Frank looked at her uncomprehendingly. 'You went to all this trouble just to get at Judith Prynne? What real harm did she ever do to you?'

'Frank, if you continue to talk to me like that,' Rosalind said equably, 'I shall be making some changes at board level. I have the power, you know, and I shall soon get the rest of the board on my side. I haven't liked at all the stance you've taken on this, and I don't like your tone now. I won't put up with it, you can be sure of that. I've found you, on the whole, most uncooperative.'

Frank stubbed out his cigarette, aware of the sound of a distant, if imaginary, drum beating a farewell tattoo.

'Uncooperative about what, Rosalind?'

'About my plans, my ambitions.' She briskly undid her

coat which revealed a smart Jaeger two-piece underneath. Round her throat was a double choker of pearls and her skilfully made-up face made her look almost handsome. Plain when young, she had now achieved a mature dignity.

'About my plans, my ambitions, Frank. I am not interested in die-casting and cement, fertilizers and chemical compounds. I am interested in the world of fashion, journalism and hotels, and that is the way in which, henceforward, I intend to direct the Drake Organization.'

'Direct?'

'Yes, direct.' Rosalind stood up and, divesting herself of her coat entirely, casually unbuttoned her Jaeger jacket and put a hand on her waist. Then she crossed to the window and looked out over Mayfair. 'Don't worry, you are going to be promoted, Frank.' She turned to him with a smile. 'Let me be the first to congratulate you. I am going to suggest to the board that you are made President of the Group while I assume the humble position of Managing Director.'

'The presidency is a meaningless position,' Frank said after a stunned silence. 'It is a sinecure.'

'Well, you must make of it what you can.'

'But you can't do that, Rosalind.'

'You know I can and I shall.' Rosalind tripped back from the window to perch on the corner of his desk. 'I have an outright majority of shares. The rest of the board is, I believe, impressed by what I have done in the brief time I have been in control, and they were quite determined to vote me in and you out. I said that, in view of your long service with this company, my father's affection for you, I could not dream of such a thing. However, as president, you will have a lot of kudos.'

'Kudos but no power,' Frank said woodenly. 'I am only forty-six. Presidents are usually men of about seventy, contemplating a cushy retirement.'

'Then you have a lot of years of leisure in front of you,'

Rosalind said with her sweetest expression, 'though, I have no doubt, you will be an active and supportive president, and I hope you will remain with us.'

Barnard pushed back his chair from the table and slowly rose, fastening the buttons of his jacket. He towered over the woman who had administered so deftly, and skilfully, this body blow. He began to fear for the future of the Drake Organization with someone so ruthless, yet inexperienced, in control.

'I feel it is my duty to warn you that I think you are being very, very foolish.'

'That is your opinion,' she said.

'I am speaking to you as a friend, as someone who was your father's trusted helper and lieutenant and who has known you since you were a young woman. I am very sorry if, all those years ago, your father misjudged you. I know that, from time to time, you asked him to give you a job and he always refused. It was his way. He was old-fashioned and did not believe in women working. He liked Douglas Prynne and thought he was a good man.'

'He thought he was a weak man. In the end he *knew* Doug was weak.'

'Nevertheless he was honest and trustworthy, and your father thought he made you happy. You have a handsome son who is a credit to you. However, I realize now that, for years, you have felt frustrated, undervalued, neglected perhaps. The post-war years have taught us a lot more about women and their needs. Women's liberation, they are calling it . . .'

'Exactly, and I want to liberate Drake's from stuffy, old-fashioned business practices.'

'But Rosalind, we are good at what we do. We *know* about concrete and casting and fertilizers and chemicals. We know nothing about fashion, newspapers and hotels.'

'But it doesn't stop us acquiring that knowledge, expanding . . .'

'No, but it *should* make us cautious. We should regard Jenner Securities as an example of what not to do. If we expand it must be slowly. Times have not been easy. The rise in the price of oil has made significant changes in our lifestyles, our economy. Inflation has hit us all. I do *not* recommend rapid expansion or diversification at this moment in time . . . or else you might make us subject to a hostile takeover.'

'Oh really?' Rosalind's expression was sceptical.

'Yes, I mean it. The City is rife with rumours, not about us but about predators who are all over the place. We are now a successful company because we are good at what we do. Your father wanted it to stay that way, which was why he wanted me to remain in charge. I sincerely hope you will respect his wishes, based on his experience, and not do anything of which he would not have approved.'

'My father is dead,' Rosalind said slowly. 'It is true that, for over twenty years, I was confined to a home bringing up a child, married to a husband without ambition. I was one of the thousands, probably millions, of unhappy, frustrated women, some of whom take refuge in nervous breakdowns or drink. But I am not like that, Frank. I have done my bit, run a home, raised my son, supported Doug from the results of his own follies. Maybe my father knew what I wanted to do and enabled me to do it when he left me control.

'Well, control I am taking, and I am taking the company with me into the future. We have stood still for too long and, with your help and that of the board, I want us to face that future.'

'Merely to buy Aylestone . . .'

'Merely to buy *Jenner*,' Ros said with a smile, leaning defiantly over his desk. 'Didn't you ever think of that? You mentioned Jenner, a company the same size as ours, less successful, perhaps, but with the same style of lazy, lackadaisical, complacent management. I'm sorry, Frank, but that's how I see it. You're all the same, you middle-aged men with the "old-boy" network and the "old-school" tie. It *knows* about hotels. It may have made a poor job of Aylestone, but it has made a modest profit. Its middle-market hotels are geared to conferences, management weekends and seminars. We can manage those as well as Jenner can, if we take over his group, keep his staff. We can rationalize by regrouping in these premises. We can sell his present site for millions. Aylestone will be restored to its pre-eminence as our flagship, and we shall take a leaf out of Judith's book and plan a series of hotels even bigger, better and more prestigious than hers.

'Once we are successful we might even set our sights on Prynne's.'

Seeing the confusion on Barnard's face, Rosalind, of whom a daemon seemed to have taken hold, threw back her head and laughed, a little hysterically. 'Now, how's *that* for a thought?'

The official announcement of the appointment of the founder's daughter as effective managing director of the Drake Organization surprised the City. It intrigued them as well, yet, inevitably, the price of the shares fell slightly. There was much speculation as to the reason for this change and some comment as to Rosalind's fitness for the task ahead. The presence of women in boardrooms did not inspire confidence in the kind of people, linked by public school and university, whom she had rightly described to Frank Barnard.

If the financial pages of the newspapers were inclined to give the 'thumbs-down' sign, the whiff of scandal, on the other hand, did excite the popular press. So did the fact that Rosalind was the ex-sister-in-law of another powerful woman in the City: Judith Prynne. There was speculation as to the future of Aylestone, the hotel that had never achieved what it had set out to. One paper even unkindly referred to it as 'this huge white elephant brooding over the Thames' and suggested that it might be turned into a geriatric hospital and run by the National Health Service.

Judith read the account of Rosalind's move with some interest as she travelled north to see her nephew Giles, Moira's new baby by Billy. She was also due to inspect Forteliot Castle though, of her three hotels, this one continued to give the least trouble. It was constantly full, constantly admired, praised and written about. It was difficult for anyone to get a room there who didn't give at least six months' notice.

Some said it also helped to have a name listed in the Social Register, or be related to the English peerage. Sometimes, here, money wasn't enough.

Judith thought that the success of Forteliot Castle was due not only to its position, to good management, and to the fact that Scotland was an ideal round-the-year holiday location, but to a certain snobbish appeal. It was the place to be seen at or have stayed at. Its indoor swimming pool, sauna, gymnasium, squash and badminton courts, its unrivalled golf course, were not half as attractive as the chance to boast that there every guest was someone; mere money didn't count.

On the train Judith also perused the latest group accounts which were more than satisfactory, and it was with some pleasure that she found Billy himself waiting to meet her at Edinburgh station, arms held out in welcome, as she alighted from the sleeper.

'Good journey?'

'Fine.' Judith gave Billy her small overnight case. 'Except that I never sleep particularly well in trains; but I had a lot of reading matter. Some of it most interesting.'

'Oh?' Billy led her to the car parked in the forecourt of the station and, as he saw them emerging, the chauffeur jumped out to open the door.

'I thought we might go first to my office,' Billy said, 'if

that's all right with you. You said that you wanted to talk business?'

'Perfect.' Judith nestled back against the leather upholstery of the company Bentley. 'And then we dine tonight with Moira?'

'Well, I thought you'd want to go over before that. If so, the car is at your disposal.'

'How's Giles?'

'Gorgeous.' Billy's face lit up with pleasure. 'I had no idea it was so wonderful to be a father.'

'It does give one a sense of purpose.' Judith smiled back at him. 'I think if it had not been for the children I'd have left England when things started to go wrong.'

'When what went wrong?' Billy looked at her with surprise.

'Between Marcel and me. But he loved the children and they loved him. I couldn't take them abroad with me, and I couldn't leave them. Children are an anchor in one's life.'

'Giles will certainly be an anchor in mine. And I'm very fond of Alida and Franco too. I want them to think of me as their father.'

'I'm sure they do. They knew very little of Richard. They will remember even less.'

'How was he?' Billy, also comfortable against the leather upholstery, looked sideways at his sister-in-law.

'How do you mean? As a man?'

'What was he like to know? Moira never talks about him.'

'He was very nice to know, at least at the beginning. Very charming, but I only knew him in those early days, mainly before they were married. They came to Aylestone when we first opened. He was very handsome and most polite. I didn't know him at all when he started to deteriorate . . .'

'That must have been terrible for Moira.'

'Terrible; and the end was terrible too. Never mind.'

356

Judith earnestly leaned forward, gazing out of the window at the old stone houses lining the streets on their drive to the centre of the city.

The head office of the McLaren Tool Company was on Princes Street, almost opposite the castle which, from its position high above the city, had dominated it so strikingly for centuries.

Judith loved Edinburgh and, for her, the sky almost always seemed to be blue. She and Billy were dropped off on the pavement outside the building where they were welcomed by a uniformed commissionaire, who escorted them across the thickly carpeted entrance hall to the lift.

This took them swiftly to Billy's office where his secretary was waiting to greet him with the morning mail already opened and put into neat piles. Beside this was a list of telephone calls.

'Mr Forbes said it was very urgent, Sir William,' she whispered to him as Judith looked round for a seat.

'I'll telephone him as soon as I can,' Billy said. 'Meanwhile would you get Miss Prynne and myself a coffee, and hold all calls please, Flora?'

'Yes, sir.'

Flora gave Judith a friendly, business-like smile and swiftly left the room.

'What a charming girl.'

'I've had her for years. She's very good. I don't think anyone would notice if I was away for six months.' Billy joined his hands on his desk and gazed across at Judith. She thought once again how lucky her sister was to have captured the heart of this handsome, honest, upright, uncomplicated man. So different from Richard, with his hang-ups and neuroses, his dependence on drugs.

'Now,' Billy addressed her, returning her appraising look, 'I gather something has come up.'

'I need your advice, Billy.' Judith peeled off her gloves and began digging into her briefcase for some papers.

357

Clipped on the top of these were all the cuttings connected with the changes at Drake. She pushed them across to Billy and sat back while he rapidly scanned them. During this time Flora came in with a tray on which there was a jug of coffee, cups and milk, which she smilingly placed in front of Judith.

Judith poured a cup for Billy and put it beside him, careful not to interrupt his reading. To the one for herself, she added sugar and milk, and then she sat back, glad of the peace of the sun-filled room and the sight of the historic castle almost directly opposite the window. After the past few days it was, indeed, very restful.

'Well,' Billy said at last, putting the cuttings back in their clip and replacing them on top of the rest of the papers. 'That was pretty unexpected, wasn't it?'

'I'll say. I knew Rosalind had ambitions, but I didn't think they were as strong as that or that, at her age, she'd get away with it.'

'What do you mean "at her age"?' Billy asked, eyebrows raised.

'She is a mature woman, not to put too fine a point on it, and she has had no business experience. The one and only time she tried to interfere at Aylestone it was catastrophic.'

'In what way?'

'She got the backs up of all the staff, including Marcel. She has always had the conviction that she knows best about everything. However, I didn't realize she was so frustrated in her role of wife and mother. Nor did I realize she hated Doug so much. Maybe it was the affair with the housekeeper that did it.'

'What is their relationship now?'

'Well, not too good, naturally.' Judith carefully inspected her hands. 'He knows that if she buys Aylestone to run it as a hotel he won't be able to stay on.'

'It would be too humiliating to be subordinate to his wife?'

'She simply wouldn't keep him. He'd be out of a job to which he has given his life. Rosalind has a hard streak, you know, Billy. She always did, in a way, but I didn't realize how tough and uncompromising she could be. Of course I hear people say that about me, so I must be careful.'

'I never think of you as hard,' Billy said loyally.

'Well that's nice of you.' She tossed back her head and gave him a smile and he thought how attractive she was as her flame-coloured hair caught the sun and, momentarily, she seemed to be surrounded by an aura of brilliant light. She wore a heather-mixture light tweed suit and a white blouse with a floppy bow. The heather tones suited her, seeming to bring out the intriguing colour of her eyes. It always struck him how odd it was that two sisters should be so dissimilar in looks.

'What are you thinking of?' She looked at him quizzically.

'I was just thinking, to be honest,' Billy said with his disarming smile, 'that you and Moira are not at all alike. Physically at least. Not even temperamentally, really.'

'Moira was the baby, don't forget. Everyone loved and protected her. She was like my mother too, although Mummy could be bossy and temperamental when she chose. I hope one day you and Moira will be able to go out to India to see our parents. They say they're too old to travel, but they would love to see how happy Moira is once again and, of course, to meet their new grandson.'

'If we can we will,' Billy said. 'Now, Judith, can you give me some idea of what exactly it was you wanted to see me about? I don't think it was just to chat about family. Unfortunately I'm a little short of time.'

'Of course,' Judith said, quickly putting down her cup. Billy watched her carefully as she retrieved the papers from him and glanced at one or two of them before looking up:

'I want to buy Aylestone. I think Jenner will give me preference if we can find the money. He doesn't really like Drake or want them to have it.'

'Won't he merely take the highest bid?'

'Oh yes, but ours must be the highest. I've persuaded him not to auction. Just now I don't have the resources for such a purchase. I'm fully stretched.'

'You mean you couldn't buy without my help?' Billy frowned and looked at his desk.

'I don't think so. We could go to the City, but we'd rather not. It takes time and I want to make a pre-emptive bid. Right away if I can. Matt likes us. He's known our family for a long time, and he's loyal to Doug.'

'But what about Leo?' Billy lowered his voice.

Judith looked puzzled. 'Well, of course, Leo's money *is* in the business already,' she explained.

'Well can't he help more?'

'I don't think so. I think he's fully stretched, too. I don't actually know, because he's been away for a few weeks.'

'Where is he?'

'South America, I think.' Judith's frown deepened. 'Why?'

'I just wondered. I thought you were close and that you'd keep in touch.'

'We also have separate lives, Billy.' There was a reproving note in Judith's voice. 'Leo has his business and I have mine. Of course he takes an interest, but I don't consult him on everything.'

'What sort of equity does he have in your business?'

'About twenty-five per cent.'

Billy sat back, sighed and spread his hands palms down on the table.

'Then I'm sorry, Judith, I can't help you. I'd like to, but I can't.'

'Because of Leo?'

Billy nodded, a little shamefacedly.

Judith faltered for a minute, feeling very annoyed. 'Could you please explain?' she said.

Billy got up, appearing uneasy. He walked over to the window with its view of the castle, and stood there for a few moments staring out as if deciding what to do. Then he turned to his sister-in-law, a woman he deeply respected.

'I'd rather not.'

'I see.' Judith bit her lip and bent her head. When she raised it again her eyes looked straight into Billy's. 'Do you actually *know* something about Leo I don't?'

'I'm not sure.' Billy put his hands behind his back and pondered.

'Something criminal?' she ventured.

'No, not really. But I'm uncomfortable having a business connection with Leo. It happened before and it did not work very well. I can't explain why, because he pays bills on the dot, but there's a lack of documentation that worries me.'

'Documentation?'

'Receipts, invoices, that sort of thing. It's hard to keep accounts. He prefers personal contact and word of mouth. Had you been on your own it would have been different. I would have been glad to help.'

'When I needed it, quickly, Leo gave me money. A lot of it.'

'I know.' Billy looked away.

'He's been very good to me. He's never made any demands and he's left me alone.'

'I know all that, Judith. Believe me I would like to help.'

'I wish you *would* tell me, Billy,' she appealed to him. 'It makes me very unhappy to think you distrust someone I love.'

'It makes me unhappy too to speak like this, Judith, especially on your first visit to see Giles; but I didn't ask for the business meeting, you did.'

'I know that. Now I wish I hadn't.'

'So, in a way, do I,' Billy said sadly, knowing that there was now a rift in their relationship, which he deeply regretted.

The grey stone house built on a hill overlooking the Firth of Forth had been the McLaren home for over a century. Billy's father had died in his infancy and he had inherited the baronetcy and the house which, until his majority, was presided over by his mother Bessie. He had a sister who was married to a prosperous Highland farmer.

Judith arrived just after lunch, which she had had in Edinburgh in between some shopping. But her conversation with Billy had disturbed her, and even her joy at seeing Giles could not dispel her sense of unease. Moira noticed it straight away as they sat having tea in the drawing room, within sight of the Forth bridge.

'What's the matter, Judith? You've been looking worried. Is something wrong?'

As Judith didn't reply she said, tentatively:

'Was it to do with your talk with Billy?'

'In a way.'

'You might as well tell me. If you're going to be like this tonight he'll notice anyway.'

Judith put her bag down and gazed at her sister.

'Darling, I thought I'd drive straight to Forteliot after we've had tea. When you hear what I have to say, I think you'll understand.'

And she repeated, almost word for word, her morning's conversation with Billy.

After she'd finished Moira sat for a long time, with one hand out towards the fire, gazing at it.

'Have you any idea *why*?' Judith leaned forward as if to press her for an answer. 'If so, you *must* tell me.'

'I think I have.' Moira turned to her at last.

'Is it something criminal that he knows and won't tell me?'

'I don't know if he *knows*, but he certainly doesn't like Leo very much.' Moira faltered for a moment and a blush stole up her cheeks making her look vulnerable and slightly child-like, perhaps the secret of her enduring fascination for men. 'I don't like him very much either, Judith. It's very hard for me to say this and I'd much rather not have to. You see, you've been so sweet to me and Billy; so supportive.'

'Well *I* like Billy very much,' Judith said with emphasis. 'Nothing will change that. But, about Leo . . .'

'Don't you feel it yourself?' Moira looked closely at her sister. 'Don't you feel there's something wrong?'

'Wrong? In what way?' Suddenly and inexplicably Judith felt once again that stab of fear, the sensation that ran from the base of her back up her spine. Its impact was almost physical and she jerked herself upright, clutching her back.

'Are you all right?' Moira said anxiously. 'I'm sorry if I've frightened you.'

'Frightened isn't the word . . . but, yes, maybe it is. I mean you know Leo almost as well as I do. He *was* Richard's father . . .'

'I didn't so much *dislike* Leo.' Moira seemed to speak with exaggerated care. 'But I did slightly fear him. I still do, and I think Richard did too.'

'Is that why he disappeared? To get away from his father?'

'I don't know; but what connection there was between his disappearance and Leo I don't know either. And that's what bothered Billy and me. Leo seemed basically so unconcerned about Richard's disappearance.'

'But Richard had done it before – often,' Judith said sharply, defensively, though why she should be so keen to defend Leo she didn't know. Moira was her sister and if there was something wrong, she, Judith, *had* to know it.

'But there was a lack of involvement, somehow, between father and son, didn't you find? It was hardly a relationship at all. I think Leo felt disappointed in Richard. He *must* have talked to you about it?'

'He talked to me very little,' Judith said guardedly, realizing she was doing her best to protect the man she loved. 'They were very different. I think he was upset Richard was so lacking in ambition.'

'Ambition!' Moira said with an ironic laugh. 'Richard was *very* ambitious to succeed as a good artist. His involvement with drugs destroyed him and he couldn't see it. He hoped they would make him a better artist but, instead, they killed him ... or someone killed him. Billy ...'

Moira now seemed to find difficulty in continuing and Judith moved anxiously to her side on the sofa and took her hand firmly in hers.

'Don't go on if it upsets you, darling. I didn't want to upset you.'

'Well I'm upset anyway,' Moira said with a distraught look in her eyes. 'Of course I'm upset. We'll never *know* the truth, will we? This business will never finish until we do, until Richard is laid "to rest".'

'You were going to say something about Billy?' Judith encouraged her gently. 'It was just before I came over to you.'

'Well.' Moira kneaded her fist against the palm of her hand. 'Billy felt he was followed all the time he was in Italy looking for Richard. That someone knew all about him, where he was and why.'

'But he had a lot of people to see. A lot of people knew why he was there.'

'Yes; but this other business, this feeling he had, was different. There was something sinister about it and Billy

364

felt afraid. He really did.' She looked at Judith with an air of surprise that someone as strong and sensible as Billy should ever feel fear. 'After the man gave, or rather sold, him the pictures of Richard he warned him to let the matter rest. Billy of course had to inform the police but, after that, he clammed up. He was afraid and he had nightmares. He had . . .' Moira looked tearfully at her sister, who had an arm around her. 'Billy had the feeling Leo knew more than he let on, and so did I. That's why he wants nothing to do with him.'

'But Leo wouldn't do away with his own son . . .' Judith felt so horrified, so frozen, she could scarcely speak.

'I'm not saying he did,' Moira said quickly, 'and nor does Billy. But if Leo *is* in the drugs business – and no one really knows where he gets all his apparently huge wealth – there may be some sort of rivalry, some sort of vendetta. You know, a Mafia thing.'

'You think that *Leo* supplied Richard with drugs?'

'I don't know.'

'Oh I can't believe it.' Judith took her arm away from Moira's waist and got up from the sofa. She began distractedly to pace the carpet, aware of the pounding of her heart, the fear that threatened to engulf her. Moira had sunk her head in her hands and looked as though she were weeping.

'I think you're letting all this speculation run away with you,' Judith said at last, sitting by Moira's side again. She took Moira's hand and shook it. 'It is unfair. I *know* Leo. I know him very well and I love him. I wouldn't love someone like that!'

'You wouldn't know.'

'But I *do* know,' Judith insisted. 'I do know what he's like.'

'I think you see a different Leo to anyone else,' Moira said stubbornly. 'It's because you are in love and it blinds you. I can't understand how you, Judith, of all people, so perceptive and sensitive, married to someone as nice as

Marcel, can fall in love with a man like Leo. There now . . .' Moira sank back and, her face tear-stained, gazed at Judith. 'I've said it.'

'You really dislike him as much as that?' Judith said slowly, unbelievingly, looking at her sister with horror.

'No, it's not dislike; it's fear. There is so much about Leo that we don't know and I'm astonished that you, who are so straight and open, should fall for that. I really am. It's as though he's bewitched you, Judith, mesmerized you. It's as though you're in the grip of some terrible, irrational obsession.

'And it's not like you, Judith darling. It's really not.'

Judith rose once again and walked slowly over to the window. It had started to rain quite hard, battering against the windows which were shaken by the wind, and the bridge in the distance was almost obscured by the haze. She leaned her brow against the cool glass and shut her eyes, feeling her lids burning.

Leo, Leo . . . It was true he was an obsession that clouded her mind and distorted her judgement. So many questions she continually, subconsciously asked herself were never answered because, in a way, she didn't really want to know the truth. Then, remorselessly, a picture of him seemed to etch itself in her brain, his fine eyes – hooded, enigmatic, compelling, slightly mocking – staring at her.

PART FOUR
Dragon's Reach
1974–1980

Chapter 19

Judith was almost asleep, lulled by the gentle motion of the yacht on the still waters of the Caribbean, when the sound of raised voices shook her into wakefulness. She listened for a moment, but the voices died down and became merely a murmur. Then she heard laughter and, shortly after that, the sound of the motor boat starting up on the starboard side to take Leo's guests back to shore.

She lay very still, listening to the staccato sound of the motor as it receded into the distance and then she heard the door next to her stateroom open and knew that Leo would be preparing for bed.

They didn't share a bed except on occasions. It was the same wherever they were, each preferring to sleep alone. Judith had been married too long to think that sharing a bed was ideal unless one's partner had exactly the same lifestyle and kept the same hours. Marcel and she were good in the morning, bad at night, so sharing a bed was compatible. But Leo was very definitely an owl and, though he could get up early when necessary, he hated to go to bed. Perhaps, she thought, now that there were so many unsubstantiated speculations about him, he dreaded oblivion.

Judith had arrived in the Bahamas tired out, and Leo's was the sort of frenetic nature that could keep going all day, but seemed to come especially alive in the evening. His friends would start to arrive at about ten and a card game commenced that would go on until three or four in the morning, sometimes until dawn.

She had come to this holiday with Leo, planned long ago, full of doubts and forebodings inspired by her talk with Moira. But, as usual, the mere sight of him was enough; his very presence calmed her because she knew she was loved and, as the days had passed, she found the bad thoughts were blotted out and she became more relaxed, refreshed and invigorated by the swimming and the sailing, the excursions to the beautiful places around the Grand Bahama Island. In time she found that she needed less sleep, and, although she went to bed at her usual time, saying good-night to Leo and his friends, she often lay awake wondering, thinking . . . when she was on her own she couldn't help it.

It had been an odd kind of holiday; a mixture of excitement, elation yet, withal, tinged with unease. Leo had greeted her rapturously; he had cosseted her, and cared for her, charmed her and loved her and, with him constantly near her, it was easy to pretend there were no shadows, but . . .

His was a curious lifestyle. His yacht was a floating office, complete with the latest in electronic communications so that he could keep abreast of his businesses round the world. It explained a lot of the mysteries that had puzzled Billy and Moira and had haunted her. Of course a man constantly afloat or in the air didn't need a corporation. It was much easier for him to operate the way he did.

He spent several hours of each morning in his office dictating into a machine letters and memoranda which were sent to the mainland to be transcribed. Clearly he had a vast network of activities whose reach and scope Judith as yet knew nothing about. Nor, as far as she could tell, would she ever know. All Leo would discuss with her was what was happening in England: the vexed question of Rosalind Drake and the possession of Aylestone.

Once the morning's business was done the rest of the day was devoted to her and her enjoyment. Lunch was sometimes taken ashore in the seafood restaurants that were dotted along the quays; an inland excursion would follow to view the exotic fauna and flora among the tropical plantations that rose above the tiny villages which clung to the shores of the little islands.

Dinner was often eaten in the company of friends, either on shore or aboard the yacht. Usually it was a fairly formal affair. The men wore white jackets, black ties, the women gorgeous summery evening dresses, and, if they'd eaten on the Island, they usually returned to the yacht for cards, blackjack or *chemin de fer*. This was the time that Judith usually went to bed.

On other evenings, when they dined aboard alone, at a prearranged hour the motor boat would begin to arrive bringing an assortment of people, almost always men, who had come solely for the sake of serious gambling. These were the people that now would be wending their way back to the Island in the misty light of dawn.

Quietly the door opened and Leo whispered:

'Are you awake?'

'How did you guess?' Judith said, raising her head from her pillows.

'I guessed.' He slid into the bed beside her; his body was naked and he put his arms around her. 'I wanted you and I hoped you wanted me.'

'Leo . . .' she began, but she didn't try to resist him as he gently eased her nightgown over her thighs and started to caress her.

'You know I *love* you,' he whispered urgently into her ear. 'I don't want you to go back, but to stay here with me.'

She struggled a little in an effort to reply but he put his hand on her mouth. It wasn't until quite a long time later, when he lay quiet and replete beside her, that she ventured to say:

'How *can* I stay with you here?'

371

'You see I can run my business from my yacht. You can too. I'm serious, Judith.'

'My personal presence at my hotels is vital for their success.'

'For part of the year, at least, you could live here. I need you, darling. I want you with me. You're a necessary part of my life and I don't want you to go.'

'But when we're married . . .' she trailed off, thinking how difficult it was even to visualize that far-off event.

'Yes?' he encouraged her. 'When we're married . . .'

'Then it will be different,' she said at last but, even as she did, she felt she lied.

'It's as if we were married now, so what does it matter?' he went on. 'Do you want me to put some pressure on Marcel? Is that what you want?'

She sensed his eyes on her even in the dim light, and a *frisson* ran through her body that once again had nothing to do with pleasure or desire, but more with fear.

'Pressure? What do you mean, "pressure"?'

'Well, you know what I mean by pressure, my darling.' He put his hand tenderly on one of her breasts. Then suddenly, unexpectedly and rather brutally, he gave her erect nipple a sharp tweak that made her almost scream with pain.

'*Leo!*'

'I'm sorry, darling,' he said contritely, gently massaging her nipple and then kissing it. 'But *that's* what I mean by pressure.'

'You mean . . . you'd hurt Marcel?'

'Not physically, of course not. Just a little pressure . . . threaten him a bit.'

'For what reason?'

'To get him to give you a divorce. What else? I don't see why he should hold it up, or why he should be allowed to.'

'It's the law of our country,' Judith answered weakly.

'But laws are to be broken, *if* they are inconvenient.'

'Is that what's called "putting the squeeze on"?' She tried to adopt a bantering tone, and so well did she succeed that Leo laughed with delight.

'*Exactly*, my dear, although that's more the kind of language that is used in the movies than in real life.'

'Leo, what is it you do?' The question surprised Judith almost as much as it did Leo. It must have lain dormant for so long in her subconscious that it came out unbidden.

'*Do?* Judith, I don't understand you.' Leo raised his head and levered himself up on one arm. 'What made you ask that now?'

'What sort of work can you control from a room full of advanced electronic gadgetry?'

'Judith, you *know* I have world-wide business interests. I have never tried to conceal that from you. Some of what I do is secret because it is to do with the defences of various countries; but most of it is concerned with many and various enterprises I have throughout the world: the Americas, north and south; Europe; the Arab countries and the Far East. My enterprises are truly global.'

'What is the secret part?' she asked, realizing that her heart was starting to beat faster. Vividly she now recalled her talk with Moira only weeks before.

'My dear, if it's secret I can't tell you, can I?' He had a note of bewilderment as well as amusement in his voice.

'Is it to do with drugs?'

'Drugs?' His tone abruptly changed and he looked at her. 'What do you mean, "drugs"?'

'I was thinking of Richard and the way he died.'

'*You* think I have something to do with that?'

'I *have* wondered.'

'You think I would be connected with the death of my own son. My only *son*?' His voice sank to a melancholy whisper. 'How *could* you, Judith . . .'

'No, of course I don't.'

373

'Then just what are you suggesting?'

'I'm not suggesting anything. No,' she was beginning to feel frightened. Apart from the crew they were alone on the yacht, and the crew were all his paid, trusted servants.

But, instead of replying, Leo got abruptly out of bed and reached for the cotton robe that lay on the chair beside him. He put this on and irritably tugged the cord very tight round his waist. The room was full of the morning light and Judith could see he was very angry indeed, his brow furrowed and his lips pursed.

'I'm sorry, Leo, but I had to say it,' she said contritely.

'I'm sorry too, Judith,' Leo replied and left the room.

For a long time she lay there, scarcely daring to move. She realized now something of the fear that had afflicted Billy as he made his way through Italy in search of the truth about Richard, and she was sorry that she'd spoken.

She had said she trusted Leo, but she was showing now, by her words and behaviour, that she didn't. It was as though she were taunting him, regardless of the consequences and, in the process, scaring herself to death.

She got up and went into the bathroom, drawing the hot seawater into the bath as if in an effort to soothe her nerves and calm her fears. Very soon, she decided, she would leave.

And what then?

Two hours later, however, when she appeared on deck for breakfast, it was as though nothing had happened; nothing to explain such an abrupt, unfriendly exit from her room. The table had been laid, as usual, for two, with a pink cloth, starched pink napkins and an attractive central floral arrangement of hibiscus, mimosa and bougainvillaea. Leo looked relaxed in his chair, wearing shorts and a T-shirt and reading some wires that had come in overnight.

He put down his papers as, dressed in white slacks and a green top, she came on deck, putting on her sunglasses to protect her eyes against the strong morning sun. He rose immediately, took her hands between his and kissed her cheek.

'Forgive me,' he said, tenderly placing her in the chair opposite to him. 'You look, as always, ravishing, Judith. I am privileged to be your lover. I can't tell you how sorry I am I upset you.'

'And I'm sorry I upset you.' She still felt nervous, a little frightened and insecure, but she felt that if this fear communicated itself to him her problems would get worse. Surely Leo would never harm her? So the only thing to fear would seem to be fear itself. She smiled bravely as, still with a hand over hers, he said earnestly:

'You obviously have a curious and most inaccurate idea of what I do, my dear, and I wondered how you could possibly think this about me?' His eyes, gazing at her, silently reproached her.

'It's just that you're so mysterious, Leo,' she said at last, meeting his gaze. 'You come and you go; you appear and disappear. You have huge and extensive business interests but no register on Wall Street. People have asked *me* where your money comes from, and this disturbs me because I am unable to answer. One person would not invest in Prynne's because of your connection with it.'

'Oh, indeed?' Leo's eyes narrowed and Judith sensed that this information had shaken him. 'Who was that?'

'I am not at liberty to tell you, you must realize that. It was someone I invited to invest in the company.'

'That annoys me, Judith,' Leo said immediately. 'I have told you to remain independent. There is no need, none at all, to invite others to buy shares. Why go elsewhere when you have me? *That* is not honest. It is underhand.'

'It doesn't give me any pleasure to depend on you entirely, Leo,' Judith said frankly. 'You may consider it independence, but to me it's not.'

'Ah, the modern woman.' Leo shook his head, playfully

but also regretfully, in the way that men manage to undermine the quest for women's true independence.

'But you must understand this point of view.'

'Perhaps it is I who am out of touch, then.' He put his spoon into the paw-paw in a silver bowl in front of him and raised it to his lips.

'Delicious,' he said. 'It must be the most wonderful fruit in the world. Do have some, Judith.'

Judith unfolded her napkin and began to eat and, for some time, there was silence between them. Finally when he finished his fruit he wiped his lips and rested his hands on his lap – a man, apparently, entirely at ease.

'I think you imagine I am some kind of gangster, Judith, engaged in illicit deals. That seems to me to be the basis of your concern. Is that the idea *you* have of me? Or has somebody, or bodies, given you this idea?'

She too put down her spoon, dabbed her lips and looked at him.

'I have, it is true, speculated about your vast wealth. Others have, too.'

'Which is why you, or they, perhaps, suggested drugs? It's obvious I suppose.' He signalled to the steward who was hovering a few feet away and the tall, dark-skinned man stepped forward and removed his dish.

'Tea or coffee, sir?'

'Coffee, please.'

'And for madam?'

'I'll have tea, please,' Judith said with a smile. 'Don't forget I'm English.'

Leo put out a hand and, in one of the frequent and astonishing changes of mood of which he was capable, squeezed her arm.

'My English rose,' he murmured.

'Hardly,' Judith said with a laugh. 'An English rose is someone fragile and fair . . . like Moira.'

'Ah yes, she is an English rose.' For a few moments Leo

sat brooding over the shimmering water, at the boats which hissed like fireflies across the busy bay. 'Is she, I wonder, the source of your concern about me? For concern there surely is, Judith. I sense you constantly looking at me, thinking about me, wondering. It is certainly not just inspired by love. I wish it were. There is a suspicion in your eyes I did not see before. Do you not think I was devastated by the death of Richard? Could you doubt that? How can you say what you say ... that I deal in drugs? Drugs, that undoubtedly killed my son.'

Judith fastened her eyes on the flowers in the centre of the table.

'I'm sorry ... the way you put it makes me sound deeply offensive. I didn't mean to be ... I wondered if some kind of revenge, vendetta ...'

'You think I'm in the Mafia?'

'Of course *I* don't, Leo! I wouldn't be here if I did ...'

'Your language is very strange.' He looked at her, clearly affronted.

'Then I apologize ... again. Leo, I think I'd better leave, today maybe. I'm spoiling this holiday.'

'But I *must* know the source of these rumours!' Leo banged his fist on the table. 'They are ruining my name, and our love ...'

'Richard's death upset everybody.'

'And me! It upset me!' he cried, clearly very distressed. 'Do you consider me a monster?'

'Billy McLaren was convinced that someone knew he was in Italy and was following him ...'

Leo banged the table again, this time his eyes triumphant. 'Ah, I see now where the source of the mischief is. The noble and honest Scotsman?'

'He was very afraid in Italy.'

'If Richard was engaged in something illegal, then he had reason to be afraid. I would be afraid myself.'

'And you honestly don't know?'

'Of *course* I don't know.' Leo's anger was very visible now. 'If I knew I would do something about it. I would try and find my son, try and find his body and give him a decent, Catholic burial.' Leo looked at her for a moment and there was no doubting the anguish, the hint of tears in his eyes.

Silently she reached for his hand and held it as though conveying to him, merely by her touch, her sympathy and strength. Slowly he said: 'When I spoke to you about "secrets", darling, I was talking about certain things that I do for various governments of the world. If you think that was a reference to drugs you are quite wrong. I supply them with electronic equipment, much of it designed in the USA and manufactured in the Far East. Naturally it is of a very secret nature to do with the space programme. Do you think governments would entrust me with this sort of work if they thought I was a drugs dealer? Don't you think that they – the CIA, FBI, Scotland Yard and Interpol – vet me, know everything about me?'

'I suppose they must.'

'They *do*,' Leo said emphatically. 'They *do*. As for the friends who come and see me at night, I know you don't like them and are suspicious of them ... oh yes, don't pretend you're not. They like to gamble. I do too. We play for very high stakes. It is not illegal, you know. It gives excitement to people who are a little jaded, a little tired, bored by life. They're not bandits or drug dealers but mere gamblers and, if you want the truth, if I have a vice, that is probably it. I'm crazy about gambling.' He opened his arms wide and looked appealingly at her. 'There now, I have been honest with you.'

Judith sat for a long time contemplating the sea. It was difficult to imagine that evil could coexist with such beauty and she wanted to believe him; but there was too much unsettled, unsolved, too many things that still worried her.

'Why did you talk about putting "pressure" on Marcel? I didn't like that at all.'

'I want to marry you!'

'Yes, but it was like gangster's talk.'

'It was meant in fun. It was humorous.'

'It didn't sound like it to me, Leo. You also hurt me, physically. My breast is very sore.' And, instinctively, she pressed a hand to it.

He leaned over the table and took her hand, kissing it. 'For that I deserve to be punished. When I can I will kiss it until all the pain has gone. But now, my darling,' impulsively he threw his other hand above his head, 'look at the sea, look at the sky, enjoy yourself! Let's enjoy ourselves now, while we can. Come, I have an idea. Let's take the motor boat and go water-skiing . . .'

'But I'm much too old.'

'Of course you're not! It's fun. It's easy and, if you fall, I am always there to catch you!'

The water-skiing was not, for Judith, very successful though Leo was obviously an expert. But it was fun and when she fell in the water she just swam about until she was rescued by the little boat skimming around the bay.

After skiing they lunched on the island, cold clams with lobster sauce and long soft drinks. Then Leo took her to meet some people who had a house in the hills, John and Iona Smedley. They were nice, ordinary, if obviously wealthy, people who lived on the island and had known Leo for years.

Judith felt that he was trying to establish his credentials as someone who had friends who had known him for years, family roots. At about five they drove back to the quay where the boat was waiting to take them out to the yacht. They had invited the Smedleys to dine with them aboard the yacht at nine.

As the motor boat tore across the bay they sat close

together like lovers, holding hands, and Judith knew that as soon as she got to her room for a siesta and to change before dinner Leo would join her there.

She knew that the more they made love, the deeper would the bond grow, and the harder it would be to break from him. She knew quite well that Leo was as aware of this as she was and that, from now on until the end of the holiday, he would never leave her alone.

They clambered on board helped by the willing, well-trained members of the wholly coloured crew who manned the boat throughout the year. Only the captain was a white man, Don Alvey, from Southampton, England. Sometimes the yacht sailed up to Florida to pick Leo up for the cruise to the West Indies after arriving at Miami in his private plane.

'There is a message for Miss Prynne, sir,' the senior steward said as Judith prepared to enter her cabin on the deck.

Leo took a white envelope from the steward, thanked him for it and handed it to Judith. She stopped in the doorway and slowly slit it open.

'URGENT YOU TELEPHONE SIR MATTHEW JENNER' the message read, and listed several numbers where she would find him.

'Matt wants me to get in touch with him as soon as possible,' Judith said, staring at the words on the paper. 'I wonder what's happened now?'

'After our siesta, perhaps?' Leo said suggestively, but she smiled and shook her head.

'I think it had better be before, if you don't mind.'

'I do mind,' Leo said, not attempting to hide his disappointment. 'And I think you know why.'

'*I* think you're insatiable,' she murmured and she gently pushed him away. 'Do you think I could try and contact Matt now?'

Leo suddenly became very matter-of-fact and looked at his watch.

'You know the time in London. It is . . .'

'Well, he said to call him urgently.' Judith glanced at the paper again. 'I don't think the time there matters much.'

'Clifford will take you to make your call,' Leo said with obvious regret, but politely stepped aside for her to pass him.

Judith followed the head steward, Clifford, the length of the yacht and into a room without windows which was at its heart. Inside was a man, also dressed in the uniform of the yacht, sitting at a console of electronic machinery with headphones to his ears. By his side was a commonplace telephone which he handed to Judith, at the same time offering her a seat beside him.

'I will get Sir Matthew's number for you now, Miss Prynne,' he said, returning to his controls while Judith held the headpiece to her ear.

The first number drew a blank and they were directed to call a second. Judith discovered it was Matthew's office in the City, and she wondered why he was still there in the middle of the night. With considerable foreboding she asked the operator who answered the phone to be put through.

'Judith!' Matthew's voice came over the phone as clearly as if he were in the next room and, with it, the relief he clearly felt on hearing her voice. 'How kind of you to call.'

'It sounded urgent.'

'It is, yes. Judith, there has been a dawn raid on our shares. We are in danger of a takeover and share dealings have been suspended by the Stock Exchange. I don't suppose I need tell you the name of the predator?'

'Drake?' Judith suggested.

'Drake has been buying them secretly as well as overtly. This is why the takeover panel has suspended dealings. I need help, Judith.'

'How can I help, Matt?'

'I desperately need a White Knight, a friend, to rescue us. We can't go on by ourselves, Judith. We're over-extended and under-capitalized.'

'What exactly do you want me to do, Matt?' Judith said urgently into the phone.

'I want *you* to take us over. I want Prynne's to buy Jenner. This way, and I emphasize, only this way can you save Aylestone.'

'But we haven't the money, Matt,' Judith exclaimed. 'I'm heavily into borrowing myself.'

There was a silence for a long time and, finally, Judith said, 'Matt, are you still there?'

'I'm here, Judith.' There was another pause. Then: 'Judith?'

'Yes?'

'What about Leo . . . can't he help?'

After midnight, when the motor boat had taken the Smedleys back to shore, Judith and Leo sat on the deck, their eyes following the lights of the small craft to its moorings on the quayside. It was summoned by radio when it was needed, either to fetch provisions or to ferry passengers to and from the shore.

The lights in the harbour threw an incandescent glow over the small town and, across the bay, among the boats, stationary or moving, myriad lights danced and twinkled, reflected in the still waters of the translucent sea.

Judith wore a white, ankle-length evening dress that had the stark, flattering lines of a Grecian tunic hanging in soft folds from the waist downwards. She wore gold sandals and gold bangles on both arms, which were bare up to the shoulder. Next to her, Leo wore a white dinner-jacket with a black tie. He was smoking a cigar and by his side was a balloon of brandy.

'Nice people,' Judith said, as the lights of the departing boat became tiny points of light in the distance.

'Do I detect an irony in the words "nice"?'

'Not at all.'

'You don't say that about many of my friends.'

'I can't say it about people I hardly know. We've spent some hours with the Smedleys today, and I do think they are charming, attractive people. I hope we see them again.'

'We shall.'

'What does John do?' Judith turned her head to gaze at Leo puffing at his cigar, his profile to her.

'He was a stockbroker on Wall Street. I don't know a lot about him, except that he was wealthy enough to retire quite young and live in the Bahamas.'

'Do they have a family?'

Leo removed the cigar from his mouth and studied the glowing tip.

'I believe they have a son, but I have never met him. I think he's a stockbroker too. Maybe John has a firm . . . I really don't know, darling. Why this interest?'

'I just wondered.'

'Still checking?'

'Don't be silly,' she said, colouring in the dark as he hit a bull's-eye.

'You haven't yet told me what Matt wanted.'

'Oh, it's a long story.' Judith sighed deeply and, stretching her legs, raised her arms high above her head in a yawn. 'I think it can wait until tomorrow.'

'Tell me now, just briefly.'

'It's terribly complicated, Leo. If I start now it could go on for hours. But anyway . . . it may mean me returning home, so I'd rather that we waited until tomorrow and enjoyed what's left of today.'

'In that case I must know,' Leo said, standing up abruptly and tossing his cigar, in one of his sudden changes of mood, into the water. 'You've been very funny and

383

edgy all evening. I think Iona Smedley thought there was something wrong between us.'

'I'm sorry, Leo, I didn't realize. I thought I was behaving perfectly well – certainly *I* felt there was nothing amiss.'

'And then there were all those questions earlier ... You've got me on edge too, Judith.'

'Why, Leo ...'

'I feel that both I and my life are being examined closely under a microscope,' Leo went on heatedly. 'My life, my business affairs, my family, *and* my friends. You've met a lot of people, yet only the Smedleys seem "nice" to you.'

'I think you're reading too much into this.'

'Tell me what Matt wanted.'

'He wanted Prynne's to come as a White Knight to save Jenner Securities.'

'To come as a what?'

'A White Knight – a friendly takeover. He is the subject of a hostile bid from the Drake Organization.'

'Rosalind Drake?'

'She's absolutely determined to get her hands on Aylestone. Matthew told her that he was accepting our offer; that we were exchanging contracts. We were trying to rush the whole thing through. However, with this move, dealings in the shares have been suspended, and all pending negotiations frozen. Of course if Drake takes him over he'll lose his job.'

'And if Prynne's take him over?'

'I think we'd keep him on. It's a very big undertaking. We're pretty small compared to Jenner.'

'But you lose Aylestone if you don't?'

'Perhaps, it doesn't matter now so much.' She rose and wandered to the rail and, leaning far over, looked into the water. A slight, welcome breeze, rising from the sea, fanned her face.

'Don't your family control shares?'

'Our shares never gave us control, just an interest. I'm

not particularly interested in taking over Jenner anyway, even if I could. I more or less told him "no".'

'Why not?'

'What would I do with a company like that?'

'But he's into all kinds of interests.' Leo eagerly leaned forward, looking thoughtful. 'Electronics, components, hotels . . . has he got any more hotels?'

'Several in the medium price range, so that fits in quite well. But I'm really just interested in perfecting what we have. We're doing well, living within our means. Yet I suppose it sounds silly to feel this affection for something that is long past, the family home. It's a bit childish, really, still looking for Mummy.'

'Not at all. I think it's not only understandable in emotional terms, but it's a good investment. The position and situation near to London are marvellous.

'Besides, with Jenner you could be really big, Judith. Doesn't *that* excite you?'

'Well,' she looked curiously at him. 'I can tell it excites you.'

'It certainly does. It would also give me a legitimate interest in the English market, a listing on the Stock Exchange. Something you've always wanted for me.' He looked slyly towards her. 'I would be very interested in increasing my stake in Prynne's and thus providing you with the capital you need. After all, Matthew is a family friend. He's been good to you.'

'Not always. He was horrible, once, to my grandmother.'

'Darling.' Leo strolled over to her, putting his hand round her neck. 'That is a very personal, feminine kind of observation. You must be more business-like, more objective. I know you venerate your grandmother's memory and, believe me, that does you credit. However, you told me that she could also be eccentric and tiresome; and

385

tiresome old ladies have, or should have, no place in first-class hotels – especially if they are related to the management.

'Now, I suggest we telephone Matthew at once. I shall put in process the transference of substantial funds to the Prynne account. By all means leave Jenner in charge, if you personally don't want to assume control. He will always be grateful to you, a useful ally. You would just have a seat on the board.'

'And you?' She looked at him shrewdly.

'I'd be content with a back seat, you know that, Judith; but it could be useful to me, very useful. You see, now that gambling is no longer illegal in Great Britain it would interest me very much to get a stake there. There are huge profits to be made from casinos.'

'*Gambling!*' However hard she tried to avoid it Judith knew the dread, the fear showed in her voice.

'Do you *so* disapprove of gambling, my dear? If so your attitude is very old-fashioned. There is nothing wrong with it, you know. Maybe you have never been to Monte Carlo and seen how an elegant and fashionable clientele entertains itself. If not, you should remedy that situation quickly. It need not be sordid. It only becomes that if it is forbidden, like drinking, drugs and illicit sex . . .'

'Yes I see what you mean.' Judith bit her lip. 'But still, for me it does have an ugly connotation and I wouldn't like to be associated with a chain of casinos.'

'I'm not talking about a *chain*, my dear. Don't leap to conclusions. I am simply, at this moment, offering you the money to help your old friend . . . and admirer, if I'm not wrong. Who can blame him for that?'

And Judith felt his hand tighten on her neck and wondered if it was a gesture of endearment . . . or, perhaps, a threat?

Chapter 20

Marcel looked up from his desk as Michael came in and smiled at him over his pince-nez.

'Good morning, darling.'

'Good morning, Dad.'

'Did you sleep well?'

Michael grunted and leaned across the table to pour himself some orange juice. The family still lived in the flat over the restaurant, though sometimes, at weekends, they went down to the house that Gran had left the family in her will. Michael and Pauline had preferred to remain with their father, and seldom visited their mother in her new home in Chester Square.

'There's a cable from your mother to say she's coming home.'

'Oh?' Michael looked up with interest. 'Is Leo with her?'

'She doesn't say. Why?'

'I hate him.'

'Really, Mikie.' Marcel got up and, crossing over to his son, affectionately ruffled his hair.

'Pauline hates him too.'

'You didn't used to.'

'We do now.'

'But what did he ever do to either of you?'

'Well, he took Mum away. Look what he did to *you*!'

Marcel sat down next to his son, his hand deep in the pocket of his blue chef's trousers. It was eleven in the morning, the hour that he came up to have coffee and do some accounts or ordering, while the under-chefs and the kitchen staff got on with preparations for lunch and dinner.

During the holidays Michael, who was in his last year at school, seldom rose before noon. Pauline was away staying with a friend. Marcel left his hand on the top of his son's tangled auburn hair, the colour of Judith's, whom he closely resembled.

'It's not fair to say that, Mikie. Your mother was in love with Leo for a long time before she left me. It was something she fought against; I know she did. But these things take control, you know . . . well, maybe you will when you're older.'

'I shan't do a thing like that. Besides, you still love Mum, I can tell.'

Marcel took his hand away and gazed sadly at his son.

'I do love her, but in her opinion my love has never been sufficient. She is an emotional, passionate woman and she wants a powerful, passionate man. I was never like that. It was not my style, at all.'

'I think she was very lucky to have you.'

'And I to have her, in the time that I did.'

'Then why don't you let her *go*, Dad, if you feel like that?'

Michael looked really angry, evidence of an inner emotional storm. He finished his orange juice and banged the glass back on the table. The family cat, Tobias, sitting on the window-sill, looked at him with a superior air of amusement tempered with disdain.

'How do you mean, why don't I let her go?'

'Divorce her, so that she can marry Leo. That's what she really wants.'

'Well now . . .' Marcel paused and appeared deep in thought. Michael was used to these long, profound silences from his father. In fact they were not dissimilar in temperament, despite his physical resemblance to his mother.

'I don't think Leo's right for your mother,' Marcel said eventually. 'She may love him and he may love her; but I don't think he's the right man.'

'How do you mean "right"? She's a grown woman.'

'Well *you* don't like him, do you?'

'No, Dad, but that's for a different reason. Children naturally resent someone who breaks up their home. But if Mum doesn't love you, loves someone else . . .'

'I felt I wouldn't be doing your mother a favour by releasing her. Of course she resents it, naturally; but I think that if she marries him, after five years or so, maybe less, she will discover what an awful mistake she has made. She will suffer terribly, but by that time it will be too late. The law allows us to remain married for five years if one partner objects to divorce. I object very strongly, not only because I love your mother, but because I think Leo is wrong for her, a bad man who will harm her. Maybe he will destroy her reputation. Right now, grown-up or not, she is obsessed by him and in no position to make a good decision. I am doing that for her, because I love her and I have a bond with her: that is, you two children.'

'How do you mean, Leo's "bad", Dad? Do you mean he's a criminal?'

'Oh no, I'm not saying *that*,' Marcel said with his customary circumspection and caution. 'I have no *evidence* he is a criminal – but what I do know of him I don't like. Your mother can't see the wood for the trees – she is so physically "in love" with him – and I must do that for her.'

'It takes a brave man to stand up to Mother,' Mikie – as he was known to the family – said, with a note of admiration in his voice.

'You're right, it does. But I have never been afraid of Judith. She might intimidate others, but not me. And, one day, I think, I hope, she might thank me. Would you like me to make you an omelette before I go downstairs again, darling?' Marcel concluded with his usual Gallic *sang-froid* which deceived no one. It was an act, which he was capable of maintaining even when he was deeply moved.

389

On an impulse Michael, who was not emotional either, flung his arms round his father.

'You are a super person, Dad. I can't think why Mum . . .'

'Ssshhh . . .' Marcel said, putting his arms round his son's shoulders and hugging him. 'Like all children from a home where one parent is absent you want us to be together again. Well so do I; but if I felt that she was really in love with someone who was good for her, for you, I wouldn't stand in her way. It's not just that I'm jealous of Leo, which, I suppose I must admit, I am . . . but I do think he's not the man for your mother, and one day I hope she will realize that and, perhaps, thank me.'

Then he got up quickly in order to hide the tears in his eyes, and went to the stove to prepare his son's breakfast.

Judith Prynne arrived home the following day on a flight direct from Miami. She was met at the airport by her chauffeur and driven straight to Chester Square, where the first thing she did, after a bath and change of clothes, was to go down to the office and ask if there was any news.

It was five in the afternoon and the clatter of typewriters stopped immediately as she came into the outer office and a chorus of voices greeted her. Judith was popular among the small staff, whom she treated with affection. But she was also a rigorous taskmaster and expected a lot from them. They arrived early and left late but they were well paid, well looked after and had holidays longer than the average. Her secretary came to the door of her room and stood back as she walked past the girls in the outer office with a smile and wave, into her own room which overlooked the square. It was a large, sunny room, comfortably, even casually, furnished with an oval marble-topped table instead of the usual desk. On this stood a vase of flowers; and letters, papers, cables and telexes had been stacked on it in front of Judith's chair.

'Did you have a good trip, Miss Prynne?'

'Very nice, Alex. Is there any news?'

'There's a lot of news.' Her new secretary, Alexandra Metcalf, who had succeeded Rosemary who was now in charge of the whole secretariat, pointed to the pile of papers on the table. 'I hardly know where to begin.'

'Begin with the bad news.'

'I don't think there's much of that, Miss Prynne.' Alex got out her spectacles in a businesslike fashion, and popped them on her nose. 'A lot of things need decisions. Martin has been inspecting a hotel in Cornwall that, he says, is in a superb position overlooking the sea.'

'Is it already a hotel?'

'Yes. It's called Dragon's Reach.'

'That sounds nice.' Judith put on her own glasses and began to leaf through the papers. 'Yes, I like the sound of Dragon's Reach very much.'

'He says it *is* very run down, but he thinks . . .'

'Ah . . .' Judith pounced on the one piece of paper she had been looking for. 'Did Matthew Jenner telephone again?'

'He wonders if you could have a drink with him this evening?'

'Tell him "yes".' Judith glanced at her watch. 'Do that now for me, will you? Ask him if he could meet me at Claridges at, say, seven o'clock. It's central for us both and after that I have to look in at home . . . I mean see how Marcel and the family are. Would you ring them and ask if I can eat there at about eight-thirty? You could say I might bring Matthew Jenner with me. No, on second thoughts . . . better not. Michael resents my new life enough as it is, and I don't want him to think I always put business before my domestic duties.'

'Very well, Miss Prynne.' Alex got up and went into her own small office next door, where she dialled Matthew's number, smiling at Judith through the glass panel that separated them.

As Judith walked through the doors of Claridges Hotel into the foyer-lounge, Matthew Jenner was already there, and rose to greet her. She had changed into a soft pink woollen two-piece suit by Karl Lagerfeld, and with it she wore a pearl-coloured silk blouse with a round neck and tiny pearl buttons running down its scalloped edges. As usual she was hatless and carried her gloves with her handbag, which had been dyed to the exact colour of her suit.

Matthew kissed her warmly on the cheek, clasping her hand as he helped her to be seated.

'How was the Bahamas?'

'Fantastic.'

'You look marvellous.'

'I feel it.'

'Champagne?'

'That would be nice.'

'Two more glasses of champagne,' Matthew said, signalling to the waiter who hovered by his side. 'I'm afraid I already started, Judith. I got here early to avoid a crowd of journalists who are staking out the office.'

'Is it as bad as that?'

'I've told them that there's a White Knight arriving and they want to know who it is.' Matthew glanced nervously towards the door.

'I hope we can save you, Matthew, but I'm not sure.' Judith put her bag and gloves by her side and crossed her long, elegant legs. 'There *are* strings,' she added *sotto voce*, as the waiter reappeared with two tall flute-shaped glasses on a silver tray.

'Oh?' As Matthew took his glass with an air of apparent nonchalance Judith perceived that, nevertheless, his hand shook. 'I didn't imagine there would not be.'

'You were very good to me, Matt, and I want to be good to you; but Leo is putting up a great deal more money and insists on a fairly heavy whack.'

'That doesn't surprise me. I tried without success to get the money everywhere. Our shares have been so depressed.'

'Leo thinks that he can introduce new outlets for the things he manufactures and,' Judith paused and took a deep breath, 'he wants to set up one or two casinos.'

'*Casinos!*' Matthew looked at her with the same air of indignation with which, two nights before, she had regarded Leo on the yacht anchored off Grand Bahama Island.

'I thought you'd react that way. I did too but, as he pointed out, it is now perfectly legal to gamble in England. He cited the case of Monte Carlo as an example of the kind of thing he wants to do . . . *and*,' Judith stressed the '*and*' and paused again, 'he wants to start at Aylestone.'

'Aylestone!' Matthew's indignation was even stronger.

'He said it's an ideal place. Near London, good position etc.'

'But would *you* like that?'

'Not much, but I see Leo's point. Aylestone has never paid. It has been an albatross round the neck of anyone who has taken it on. Why, I don't know, as we have been so successful elsewhere. Maybe it's a family curse. Leo can see a different type of client being attracted there. Of course we have to get the permission of the Gaming Board.'

'They are very strict. Would they, er, like Leo? He is an American citizen, I mean.'

Judith noticed how quickly Matthew covered his question, so pretended to ignore the insinuation that Leo was untrustworthy.

'As Leo *is* an American citizen,' she replied calmly, 'it would be up to me to apply for the licence. My reputation, I think, is very good. Leo said he had had this in mind for some time. For this, and only this, he will put up the money. And it's a lot of money, Matt, I needn't remind you.'

'I know that,' Matthew said, 'but . . .'

'But . . .?'

'Well, I don't *quite* know how to put it . . .' Matthew wriggled uncomfortably in his chair.

'You don't like Leo? That's it, isn't it?'

'It's not that, Judith.'

'Then what is it? It was you who, after all, suggested asking for his money.' In her voice now there was a distinct note of contempt.

'Yes, but casinos were the last thing I had in mind. The very last thing. Gambling always has unpleasant connotations for me. I don't quite know why.' Matthew rubbed a finger along the edge of his nose. 'Of course, as Leo says, there is Monte Carlo; perfectly respectable casinos in Germany. But somehow . . .' Matthew shook his head and rubbed the space by the side of his nose again.

'You think Leo's a crook, is that it?'

'Oh, I wouldn't suggest it for a moment, my dear.' Jenner leaned over and touched her hand. '*Please* don't think that. But you said you didn't like casinos yourself.'

'However,' Judith said firmly knowing that, yet again, she had been brainwashed by her charismatic lover, 'it's a gambling licence, or Rosalind Drake gets your company. I think you're thinking of Al Capone, Prohibition and all that, Matt. Those days are gone. Gambling is undoubtedly very profitable. In this country it is under strict state control. There is no doubt that we would be able to finance, and rehabilitate, Aylestone with a casino; a splendid, luxurious one. No expense will be spared to attract the best clients, you can be sure of that.'

'Yet, I can tell you're not really enthusiastic.' Matthew signalled to the waiter again and ordered two more glasses of champagne.

'Well.' Judith glanced at her strong, capable hands, at her fingers adorned with some of the expensive jewels Leo had given to her. 'Leo *is* adamant. No casinos, no money. I think he'll get what he wants ... that is, if you want to survive as an independent company under the Prynne umbrella?'

Matthew looked at her for a moment and then he lowered his eyes to try and hide his despair.

'Put like that I don't really have any option, do I?'

'I'm afraid you don't, much,' Judith said with an air of genuine sympathy, and, placing a hand on his arm, pressed it. 'And neither, as a matter of fact, do I.' Suddenly she looked up as she heard a familiar laugh and, through the doors, swept Rosalind Drake with a man Judith didn't know and her twenty-year-old son Philip, who was at Cambridge. Philip was the first to see his aunt and he went rapidly over to her.

'Hello, Aunt Judith.'

'Philip.' Judith got up and kissed him on the cheek. 'You know Matthew Jenner, don't you?'

Philip, who was now a tall, attractive young man with a distinct look of Doug, shook hands.

'Of course. Mother,' he said innocently turning round, 'look who's here ...'

'Please, Philip,' Rosalind hissed sharply at him, completely ignoring Judith. 'Don't make a scene in public.'

'I'm not making a *scene*, Mother,' Philip whispered, looking bewildered as a bright, adolescent flush flooded his cheeks.

'I suspect your mother feels it's not a good moment for a chat,' Judith said quietly in his ear. 'I'm with Matthew Jenner.'

'Oh.' Philip put a hand to his mouth. 'Of course! Sorry, Aunt Judith.'

By this time Rosalind had reached the restaurant door and, ignoring Judith and her son, was asking the head waiter about her table. Several interested eyes in the lounge had observed the scene. The man with Rosalind, whom Judith didn't know, stood back as Philip came up to him. Then he put an arm round his shoulder and shepherded him into the restaurant.

'Blast!' Judith said, watching them. 'I'm afraid that now Rosalind knows quite well who the White Knight will be, Matthew. We'd better make an announcement without delay, casino or no casino.'

'Casino I'm afraid it is,' Jenner said with a sigh, humiliated by the scene he had just witnessed. And he raised his glass to Judith:

'Cheers,' he said.

Most of the diners at *Prynne's* had gone and a few couples remained, quietly conversing across tables with candles, low in their holders, guttering between them. The waiters glided easily in and out among the tables, clearing dishes and putting on fresh clean cloths for lunch the following day. In the kitchen the staff washing up were chattering and the *maître-chef*, who enjoyed a glass of brandy at the end of a day's work, was sitting in a corner with his family, an expression of benign contentment on his face.

Pauline had arrived home from her friends in time for dinner with her mother and brother. The family dinner had been largely taken up with each of the holidaymakers giving an account of their doings. The children listened impassively to Judith's description of the yacht anchored off Grand Bahama Island. Their faces remained like masks, completely unresponsive, whenever Leo's name was mentioned.

Judith knew that her children, who once had seemed to accept him, now didn't like him but, up to now, this had had little influence on her. She had been so much in his thrall that even the opinion of her children made little difference. Of course they wouldn't like the man who would supplant their father. It was perfectly natural. She understood it and mentioned his name as little as possible.

She made her story brief so that Pauline could tell them about her holiday in the rustic simplicity of the Scottish Highlands, and the Bahamas were not mentioned again until after eleven when Marcel joined them. He sat across from her, a small cheroot between his fingers, the habitual balloon of brandy in front of him. There was a wry smile on his pale face. His hair, which was now thin on top, was a little wispy and untidy after he had taken off his tall hat. Looking at him with the affection she still felt for him, Judith realized how different her husband and Leo were. Yet, in some ways, they were the same. They were both ambitious; they both liked nice things; they both relished the comforts that money could bring. They were achievers, but the difference was in their ways of achieving what they wanted. Marcel, a bourgeois from Rouen, believed in the merits of hard work, harnessing his creativity, his genius in the kitchen, not only to provide a living for himself and his family, but to give pleasure to others.

And Leo – what were his origins? He scarcely spoke about them, sketching in a few vague details: a home somewhere near Naples, a small village no one had ever heard of . . . a journey as a boy to America with his parents . . . life in the Bronx . . . an ambition to better himself, to succeed where his father never had. It was the familiar kind of story of success in the New World.

Sitting there with her husband and children, Judith suddenly yearned for this more bourgeois, practical kind of lifestyle, where people worked with their hands rather than did deals with their brains, but also with cunning and, sometimes, without having to work very hard for them. How vividly, now, did she recall the early days before the children were born when she and Marcel had worked round the clock to make the restaurant a success; getting up early, going to bed late, living above the shop. Then the children were born and Marcel was a careful, diligent, loving father who changed their nappies and gave them their night feeds; who looked after her so tenderly and solicitously during her pregnancies and saw that she got plenty of rest. Yes, he had indeed been tender and solicitous; but ... he had never been exciting. There had never been about him the hint of danger that there was about Leo ... and it was that, that excitement, the allure of the unexpected, that more than anything had tempted and, finally, seduced her.

In this glow of nostalgia while the family chatted quietly among themselves she recalled, oh so clearly, so vividly, the first time she'd met Leo sitting in the corner very near their table. How, even at that instant of their first encounter, she was aware of a magnetism that was to prove irresistible. It was Leo who had said: 'If ever you need any capital don't hesitate to come to me.' Even then, she felt, he knew that one day she would; she'd come to him; and he'd take her. It was like a spider, with all the patience in the world, biding his time for the fly. And he had bided a very long time; he'd waited for years as, slowly, with a hint of caution, she'd approached the centre of the web.

'Penny for them?' Marcel's quiet voice broke in on her reverie. 'You are very far away from us, Judith.'

Judith started suddenly and smiled back at him, but said nothing.

'Mummy's still in Bermuda,' Pauline said looking knowingly at her father. 'That, and the good life ...'

'I wasn't, as a matter of fact,' Judith said. 'I was thinking of the early days, when your father and I lived here over the shop and how good they were. In many ways I'm sorry they ever changed.'

'I can remember,' Michael butted in with an air of excitement, 'when I first started at the infants' school round the corner ...'

'And how amazed and delighted we were when the

restaurant began to fill up and we realized we had a success on our hands.' Marcel was also swept along by the tide of memory.

'And when we got our first *star*!' Judith clapped her hands together as though she could recall that precious moment every bit as vividly now as when it had happened.

'Those *were* very happy days.' Marcel put his chin on his hand and tipped the ash from his cheroot into the ashtray. 'I'm sorry they ever ended.'

'Things can never stay the same,' Mikie observed, with the gravity, the wisdom of youth. 'I could never see Mum going on here . . . not as things are now. It's not her at all,' and he gazed at that elegant, aloof, to him, now rather distant creature who was his mother. The mother he best remembered, the one he loved best, was warm, available, and smiling; or was that only a fantasy? The one he had now, and whom he still loved but in a different way, always seemed to have a little frown puckering her brow, lines of worry creasing the corners by her eyes, and down the sides of her mouth. A mother who was preoccupied, who never had the time to do all the things she needed to do, who was surrounded by assistants and secretaries, and was always being summoned to the phone.

'No, we can't return to the past,' Judith said, glancing at her watch as if to confirm her son's view of what she had become. 'I was really wondering how things ever got to the stage they are at now when I am the head of a large corporation, getting bigger if we take over Jenner. Already I own three hotels and am about to purchase another. I'm not sure which was the happier me,' and she seemed, then, to smile rather sadly at her son.

'What's that about Jenner Securities?' Marcel said, the nostalgia rapidly fading from his face.

'I haven't told you yet, Marcel.' Judith said, wishing she'd said nothing. 'There really wasn't time. I thought tomorrow . . . tonight I wanted to be with the family. And it *has* been a lovely evening.'

Suddenly she rose, realizing she was feeling quite extraordinarily tired. She had only arrived that day after a long flight from Miami, and whoever slept well in a plane?

She knew, too, that she had to get away quickly, urgently, from the family because, if she didn't, her weakness and uncertainty would certainly show and the evening might easily end in tears.

She left very swiftly, impatiently, waiting in the cold outside while Mikie went in search of a taxi.

It seemed that she couldn't wait to be gone, to leave all this warmth and nostalgia, the lure of her loved ones, behind.

And a wistful little group stood on the cobblestones in the mews outside, waving her goodbye.

It was well after midnight when Judith got back to Chester Square, letting herself in with the latchkey.

A soft light glowed over the entrance to the lift at the far end of the hall, and on the highly polished table to one side were some messages for her which she leafed through while waiting for the lift to descend.

Her housekeeper was in bed, and the whole house seemed shrouded in an eerie kind of stillness as though it were empty of life.

She ascended in the lift to their suite on the top floor and here there were more lights on low, highly polished tables and a thermos of coffee and a covered plate of sandwiches left for her by her thoughtful staff.

She glanced at the messages: Leo had rung, he would ring again in the morning. Martin Newbolt had set up a meeting with the agent handling the sale of Dragon's Reach.

Dragon's Reach – it was a most attractive name; it had a kind of call, an echo like a good talisman.

Judith gazed round the drawing room, the soft lights reflected on the polished wood, the ormolu clock ticking away on the mantelpiece in front of which was a huge urn of flowers, as no fire ever burnt in the grate now.

It was a beautiful place, furnished meticulously and with care, but it was rather like a hotel. It had the curious, lifeless air of a place where people did not spend a lot of time; where they did not really feel at home.

She put out the lights one by one and went slowly into the large front room with its double bed, its matching wardrobes, its twin basins in the adjoining bathroom: his and hers. This was the room where she and Leo had intended they should live after their marriage: a double bedroom built for two. There would be no separate rooms then. But it would only be one residence out of half a dozen, a *pied-à-terre*, a place where one didn't stay very long.

When she was Mrs Leo Valenti she would accompany her husband everywhere, be seen with him in public constantly, entertain his friends all over the world. There was the villa in Switzerland, the apartments in Paris and Rome, the yacht anchored all the year round off the Grand Bahama Island, the brownstone in New York that she had never seen . . . all these were Leo's homes, his style as an international businessman, a jet-setter.

How long would they spend here together? Long enough to see the family. Scarcely glimpse Mikie and Pauline who, already, were beginning to seem like strangers to her. Even this bedroom, a place for intimacy, had the anonymity, the restrained opulence of a house which, however much one admired and enjoyed its comforts, could never properly be called home.

It could never be like the flat over the restaurant where, all those years before, she and Marcel, starting out on their married life together, with very little money to get by, had seemed so very happy.

Chapter 21

The news that Prynne's (UK) Ltd had made an offer for Jenner Securities, which was welcome to the board of that company, rocked the City. It was unusual, but not unknown, for a small company to buy a much larger one; but what gave this acquisition its spice, its interest to the gossip pages of the daily newspapers, as well as the financial ones, was the fact that two women, formerly sisters-in-law, were at each other's throats. It had all the challenge and piquancy of great melodrama.

Drake immediately put in a counter-bid. Prynne's raised its price. The board of Jenner Securities met to recommend acceptance of the Prynne offer. There was a complicated structure that would ensure that the company remained intact with, at least for a period of five years, Sir Matthew at its head. Drake had given no such guarantees, and there were hints that the parts which constituted Jenner Securities would be carved up and sold off. All Rosalind Drake – that single-minded woman – really wanted to get hold of was Aylestone, which seemed to her the touchstone of her battle with the Prynne family.

There were pictures of the ex-sisters-in-law, pictures of Doug and the unfortunate Doris Malcolm, cited as co-respondent, and whom he had repudiated after his divorce. There was a history of the Prynne family accompanied by a family tree and a coat of arms with the motto: 'onwards'. In the eleventh century it was part of the rallying call to soldiers of the Conqueror.

Oddly enough there was nothing about Leo Valenti and his part in the takeover, for Leo was adept at closing doors after himself and obliterating tracks. Through a very complex series of deals he had channelled a substantial sum of money from America via Bermuda and various offshore islands, so that when it arrived in England it was almost impossible to trace its source. It *appeared* to have come from a reputable English merchant bank, and it never seemed to occur even to the most experienced Fleet Street hacks to ask questions.

Leo only returned to England when the whole deal was complete and had passed Stock Exchange scrutiny. Judith met him at Heathrow and together they drove to London, saying curiously little for lovers who had been so long apart.

'You look tired,' Leo said at last, squeezing her hand, which he had held throughout the drive. 'Or is something wrong?'

'I *am* very tired,' Judith replied. 'You can imagine how hectic all this has been and I'm not sure I'm cut out for it, such big business and high finance.'

'I wish I'd been here to help you; but it wouldn't have been wise.'

'Why not?'

'Trust me,' he replied with his customary enigmatic smile. 'I have been in business, my dear, for a good many years longer than you. The more you want, the less you need let people know. Remember that; it is a good axiom.'

Judith nodded but said nothing.

'And Matthew, how is he?' Leo asked after another long pause.

'Matthew is very well. He's delighted at the outcome and looking forward to thanking you in person.'

'And Aylestone? I trust we can start moving in on that?'

'Moving in?'

'Transforming it, with rooms for a casino according to our plan.'

403

'You still do mean to go ahead with that? Matthew is very much against it.'

'My dear Judith,' once again Leo's anger flared briefly, 'that is the *sole* reason for my interest in bailing Jenner out. I thought I made that quite clear.'

'I still don't see why you couldn't do it in another way.'

'Really.' Brusquely Leo removed his hand. 'You make me lose patience with you. Do you think I'd put up millions of pounds for nothing? This is the only way I can get my investment back. I have better things to do with my money than make acquisitions in companies merely because they are controlled by friends of yours. I can assure you of that. I don't have too high a regard for Matthew's business acumen but, as I told you, this was an ideal way to have a legitimate English company through which to do my business.'

'It's the word "legitimate" I don't much care for,' Judith said, gazing through the window at the dreary outskirts of Hammersmith through which they were being swiftly driven.

'You still seem to think I'm some kind of gangster, don't you?'

'Of course I don't.'

'Say it, you *are* suspicious of me?'

'No I'm not; or I wouldn't associate with you.' She turned her head and gazed at him. 'It's simply that I don't see why you can't do what you do like any other American company which wishes to be involved in the English market.'

'They are all huge corporations. Compared to them, I and you, and Jenner, are shrimps. And I can assure you there are many, many people like me who prefer to operate in this way. We prefer to work swiftly without regulations, restrictions and controls. It is what risk-taking and being an entrepreneur means. You take my word for it, darling, and smile at me, Judith, please. Do you know I was thinking of you all the way over on the plane?' His hand reached for hers and tightened over it again.

Tonight they would lie together in the double bed.

She, Judith Prynne, was still to him a kind of possession: a body over which he had certain rights. He had paid a lot for her, that was certain. Some people might consider she was an extremely expensive, high-class whore. She bought and Leo paid.

She was aware that Leo's gaze was still on her face and she made a big effort for him and smiled.

'Thank you,' he said, smiling back, and leaned over to brush her cheeks with his lips.

A little while later Judith lay naked on the large double bed and Leo sat beside her, also naked, his hand moving gently over her body, caressing it. It was almost dark in the room except for a lamp behind him that seemed to be focused on her like a floodlight. The light also threw his head and torso into sharp relief, like a ghostly emanation silhouetted against the wall.

But Leo was a skilled voluptuary, an accomplished practitioner in the art of amorous dalliance and foreplay. His touch had the deftness, the expertise of long years of experience in pleasing women. He was skilled at arousing her, exposing with ruthless candour not only her needs and desires, but also her vanities: her longing to be admired and loved, to be treasured for what she was.

By the time he took her in his arms the need to couple drew them together with a magnetic force so that they adhered as one person. When they had finished and he lay once more beside her she knew for a few seconds, a few minutes, maybe an hour, that sublime abandon that was the essence, the fulfilment, the accomplishment of love.

Leo seldom slept after making love but lay awake, alert. Sometimes she was curious to know what he thought about. But she would never ask him because, despite the passion of their embraces, there was always a side of Leo that revealed nothing: his private thoughts that occupied that quiet, hidden place in his mind.

How quickly, however, that time of tranquillity passed. Inevitably reality set in; an awareness of place and time; of seconds passing; of actions required and things to be done.

If only one could retain those moments of tenderness for ever.

Half an hour later, after they had showered, Judith sat in front of her dressing-table mirror deftly making up her face as Leo came back into the bedroom from his dressing room, making the final knot in his tie. He wore a plain blue shirt tucked into dark grey trousers and his silk tie, with the name of a famous French designer on the back, was another subtle shade of blue which harmonized with the colour of the shirt. His eyes fastened on her for a moment and he stood behind her so that their gaze could lock. Then his eyes rose above her and he gave the knot he had made in his tie a sharp tug. He began to fasten his cuffs with the gold cufflinks she had given him a long time ago, one of her very first presents, to mark the opening of Forteliot Castle and his contribution to its acquisition.

'What time are we meeting Matt?' he asked.

'He's coming here at eight.'

'And then?'

'I thought we could eat at *Prynne's*. Marcel is keeping us a table just in case.'

'Mmmm.' Leo frowned. 'Is it a good idea to eat there, do you think?'

'Why not?'

'I always think Marcel is cool with me. Mind you, he has every reason to be . . .'

'Marcel is perfectly adjusted to the fact that he and I will divorce, and you and I will marry. His "cool" is part of his nature. He is like that with everyone.'

406

'Then why doesn't he let us marry now? Why doesn't he free you?'

'Soon I will be free.' Judith rose and, turning, kissed him gently on the cheek before walking across the room in her slip to the wardrobe where she had hung two dresses on the outside, not quite certain which one to wear.

'I will soon be free,' she said again, holding up a long black gown by Jean Muir in front of her and deciding whether to wear that or a shorter, yet just as elegant, cocktail dress that Yves Saint-Laurent had made for her at the beginning of the season. 'Which do you think, Leo?'

He gazed at them critically for a moment, telling her to hold out first one then the other, taking his time. Finally he chose the shorter dress, so she slipped it over her head and he came and buttoned her up at the back, after which his lips pressed gently into the nape of her neck.

With such love, harmony, with such togetherness, how could she ever have thought that one day she would leave him and it would end?

Matthew came sharp at eight o'clock. Leo had already gone into the lounge to mix the cocktails, and Judith followed him after she heard the sound of the lift and Matthew's voice as Leo greeted him.

As she entered Matthew came towards her, hands out-stretched. She noticed that the lines of worry which had creased his face during the weeks of the takeover seemed to have disappeared.

'Judith,' he said kissing her on the cheek. 'You look simply beautiful tonight. I love your gown.'

'Saint-Laurent designed it for me!' Judith said with a gay swirl to show its full effect, stopping in front of Leo and accepting the glass he held out to her. The other he gave to Matthew and then he raised his own.

'I propose a toast,' he said, 'to the new merger and the success of the combined strength of Jenner Securities and Prynne's!'

They drank to that and then Matthew lowered his glass.

'I would like to make another toast,' he said. 'To you both who came to my rescue as gallant White Knights when I needed you. I raise my glass to you both and, with my thanks for your help, go my devout good wishes for our joint success in the future.'

'I think we can all say "amen" to that.' Leo drained his glass. 'Is that all right with you, to eat at *Prynne's*, Matthew?'

'It's fine by me.' Matthew accepted a refill from the cocktail shaker. 'It's a good idea because *Prynne's* offers some privacy, and we do have some plans to discuss. I am full of them, I can tell you.'

The evening began agreeably enough. Marcel had ensured that they had a corner table, well out of earshot of their nearest neighbour. He had personally chosen the menu for them and before they arrived the *sommelier* had already decanted the wine. As they arrived Marcel came out to welcome them and escorted them to their table. After wishing them 'bon appetit' he left them to eat, assuring them he would be back after the meal to share a brandy with them.

Marcel's behaviour was so charming, civilized, and Matthew was interested to notice that there seemed to be no visible acrimony between the two men competing for Judith's hand. Or, did they still compete? Had Marcel accepted Leo as the victor, and thrown his towel into the ring?

The three left to their dinner discussed the finer points of the takeover, the disposition of shares, the operation of Jenner Securities as a separate entity from Prynne's; its existence as a viable company and the confirmation of Matthew as managing director, who would have a seat on the new board of the controlling company.

'It all seems perfectly in order,' Leo said by the time

they had almost finished their meal. 'Now all we have to do is apply for a gaming licence.'

Matthew replaced his glass on the table, joined his arms and frowned.

'Oh? You really intend to go ahead with that, do you?'

'Of course,' Leo said. 'That is the whole purpose of my heavy investment in your company.'

'The *whole* purpose? You surprise me. I thought there were many other aspects of the Jenner enterprises that would interest you. Electronics, for instance. I hoped we could talk about my plans in this field tonight.'

'Later,' Leo said with a quick glance at Judith. 'We shall come to that in due course; but first I want to see Aylestone made viable. It is something very close to Judith's heart and, because of that, close to me.'

'I'm sure a gambling joint isn't close to Judith's heart!' Matthew said with a laugh that sounded suspiciously like a sneer. 'If you'd *known* her mother and father!'

'That pleasure was denied me,' Leo said, in a tone so silky and smooth that Judith found it ominous. 'But I know how much her home means to her. It has not been a success; it has not been well thought of. The very name is associated with failure. Now we shall change all that, and very quickly.'

'I think you're most unwise.'

Leo started back from the table and, for a moment, Judith thought he was going to get up and leave. He was always like this when his wishes were countermanded, his motives under suspicion. He could brook no opposition at all.

'Are you telling *me* I'm unwise?' Leo stuck a finger in his own chest.

'Yes, I am.'

'Then you have a bloody nerve, if you'll excuse my language. You are the most incompetent businessman I think I have ever come across . . .'

'Please, Leo . . .' Judith tried to intervene but he held up a hand warning her to be quiet, and continued to address Matthew in a soft, threatening voice. 'I have stood on the sidelines and said nothing because I love Judith, and you are an old friend of hers and she is grateful to you. You once helped her and she wants to help you. Your own incompetence is responsible for your predicament – I have read the balance sheets and I know – and I could have advised Judith to leave you and let you wallow. But no. I decided to be generous, magnanimous, and this is the thanks I get.'

'Believe me, I *am* grateful.'

'You have a funny way of showing gratitude.' Leo beckoned to the waiter, calling for a cigar.

'Prynne's,' Leo went on, 'had used up all its resources when Judith came to me about you. She had nothing like the money required to put in a bid for you. I tied all that up. I put millions of dollars, and other funds, at her command. And *you* have the *nerve* to tell *me* you think I'm unwise?'

'Only on the matter of the casino,' Matthew said in a low voice, looking round as though he didn't want to be overheard. 'Gambling is not yet considered quite respectable in this country. I'm thinking of your image, Prynne's that is, and Aylestone.'

'And I'm thinking of profits,' Leo said harshly, 'and believe me, a well-run casino is the best way to make them fast. Of course gambling is respectable. You have government controls to see to that. Besides,' he leaned towards Matt, tapping the table rapidly in front of him. '*That* was a condition of my help. Judith knew it and you knew it. You can't renege on something that I consider a matter of honour.' Leo paused to select a cigar from a humidor the waiter was offering him. He thanked him and returned to his attack.

'I hoped I could dissuade you.' Matthew paused, in his

turn, to select a cigar. 'I see I can't. Of course I shan't renege, but I will have nothing to do with it. I shall concentrate on other matters. I must tell you that, in my mind, gambling is associated with unsavoury activities. It is something I do not wish to be part of.'

'Then you have no need to be.'

'But Aylestone belongs to Jenner.'

'And *you* belong to *us*.'

There was a profound silence during which Marcel, unseen by Leo and Matthew, had reached their table, and stood behind them listening.

'There is some disagreement?' he said at last, taking the fourth chair at the table which had been drawn up for him. Immediately one of the waiters came up with a bottle of brandy on a tray and several crystal glasses.

'Did you know that Leo intends making Aylestone into a casino?' Matthew asked Marcel peremptorily, as though he were in control.

'Yes.' Marcel began to give instructions to the waiter to pour the brandy.

'Do you approve of it?'

Marcel shrugged his shoulders and shook his head. 'Is it so important?'

'It is indeed!' Matthew replied angrily. 'Very!'

'Matthew associates gambling with crime,' Leo said, as if he found it amusing. 'I think he has got his ideas from old-fashioned movies. In this country gambling is very well regulated, and all the clubs that have got permission from the Gaming Board are closely controlled and supervised. There are no scandals, as far as I know, attached to any of them.'

'What does *Doug* think about the hotel having a casino?' Matthew turned to Judith but, before she could reply, Leo, clearly beginning to lose patience, snapped: 'What Doug thinks is of no importance. He won't be continuing as general manager at Aylestone.'

The renewed silence, even icier than the one before, among the four sitting round the table seemed accentuated by the noise made by the other diners in the restaurant. Finally it was Judith who broke it:

'Oh? Is that so, Leo?'

Leo firmly put his hand over hers and kept it there.

'My darling,' he said, not looking at her, as if he felt himself surrounded by enemies. 'You can't possibly expect Doug to go on running Aylestone with *his* record?'

'What is wrong with it?' Judith tried to take her hand away, but knew she couldn't without a fuss. His hand on hers was a symbol of Leo's determination to impose his will; his total mastery, emotional and physical, over her.

'It is one of complete disaster, as you must know. And that is without even referring to the unsavoury episode with the housekeeper.'

'That's all finished with.'

'Oh, do you think so?' Leo's expression became a scarcely veiled sneer. 'It was responsible for all the trouble we have had with Rosalind or, rather, that *you* and Matthew have had.' Leo fastidiously dusted some speck from the front of his jacket. 'But Mrs Drake has never troubled me for a moment and I don't think she ever will. I would just swat her like a fly if she tried to interfere in any way with any of the concerns with which I was associated.'

'What an unfortunate expression,' Matthew said, turning up his nose. 'I'm afraid this conversation has taken a turn I find rather distasteful.'

'Oh, in what way is that, Matthew?' The sneer had gone and Leo looked like someone who genuinely wanted to know. But no one was deceived.

'The casino, the gambling element which I intensely dislike. The intention peremptorily to dismiss Doug without even Judith knowing. It does appear you are going to take over, Leo, despite your reassurances.'

412

'Not at all, my dear Matthew.' Leo released his tight grip on Judith's hand in order to rekindle the light which had gone out on his cigar. 'I have no intention of that, I assure you; but you do know that Prynne's had not the means to take you over, as *you* requested?'

'Yes I know that,' Matthew admitted, his eyes on the tablecloth.

'I believe you even suggested I might have funds. You, yourself, suggested it. Judith then came to me and I offered her all that she needed.'

'Yes I did and I am grateful, but . . .'

'But . . . not now?'

'I don't know.' Matthew studied the tablecloth. 'There are a lot of things that have arisen which were unforeseen. I thought one of the things we were considering was that Doug's position was safe too. It is the family home which, as far as I am concerned, he has run as well as he was able.'

'But that is only as far as *you* are concerned, Matthew.' Leo, appearing almost avuncular, leaned across the table towards him. 'There was a lot wrong with other aspects of your business which *you* also failed to see in time. Don't think I threw my money in regardless. My financial advisers went very thoroughly into every aspect of Jenner Securities, I can tell you, and they didn't much like what they found. For instance, in most of your endeavours you have a very low yield on capital invested. Your shares were low, your company badly managed and you were just ripe for a takeover. Had it not been for *me* you wouldn't have lasted much longer and you, personally, Sir Matthew Jenner, Baronet, would have been out on your ear. I hope, by now, that I have made that perfectly clear to you?' He paused once again as the waiter, hovering by his side, carefully refilled his glass. He glanced one by one at his companions round the table and continued:

'Don't think for a moment I intend to stay in this country peering over your shoulders. I assure you, as soon

413

as all this has been settled satisfactorily I will be off on my travels. I have every confidence in Judith. But, next year, she and I will be married,' his eyes briefly met Marcel's, 'and she will no longer be resident here full-time either. I want this company run by good people, and I intend to be sure that it is.

'But please don't worry. Something in which so much of my money is invested will be well protected. Now my dear,' he glanced at his watch and at Judith, 'I think it's time we went. We have had a long day and there is much to do tomorrow. Thank you, as always, Marcel, for a wonderful meal.' He stood up and smiled down at Marcel in a way that was decidedly patronizing. Then he turned with the same air to Matthew and patted him on the shoulder. 'Don't be disheartened, my friend. Frankly, I'm grateful we had this talk now. I wouldn't have liked you to have had any illusions that there were not going to be any changes; but don't despair. I have the welfare of a much enlarged concern well in mind, and that will only be for the better. Everything will be taken care of. You can be sure of that.'

Then with another, slightly regal smile he put his arm firmly round Judith and escorted her to the door while Matthew and Marcel remained where they were, as if stupefied.

On the way back to the house Leo and Judith exchanged few words, and when they arrived Judith jumped out of the door before the chauffeur could open it for her, and went straight indoors to the lift.

Leo followed at a more leisurely pace, first giving instructions to the chauffeur about his programme for the next day. The chauffeur saluted, replaced his cap, and drove the car round to the mews behind the house.

By the time Leo reached the drawing room Judith, who preceded him, had already put on the lights and was waiting for him in front of the mantelpiece. Her coat was still on, her eyes smouldering.

As though he had an inkling what to expect, Leo walked over to the box on one of the tables and selected a fresh cigar at leisure, taking his time.

'Can I get you a brandy, darling?' he enquired casually.

'No thank you.'

'I think you need it.'

'I'm quite *sure* I don't. I am very angry, Leo.'

'I can see that.' Leo sat in one of the chairs and stretched his feet before him as he nonchalantly began to light his cigar.

'I have discovered an aspect of you tonight that appals me,' Judith went on in the same tone.

Leo looked up at her as he extinguished his match. 'I'm sorry, but it had to be. There was no point in any of us labouring under false illusions.'

'You treated Matt as though he were some sort of underling.'

'Well, in a way he is.' Leo put down his cigar and gazed up at her. 'I think a man who lets his company get into such a position cannot really be considered an equal partner. Not equal to the likes of you and me, Judith. I have put millions of dollars in to bail him out, and I do not intend for him to go on repeating past mistakes. He has to know who is the master now. I think, maybe, he thought it was you.' Leo paused and smiled. 'Although you are a remarkably good businesswoman, you are not tough enough, my love. You are not sufficiently ruthless. You wouldn't do a hatchet job. You must leave that aspect to me. Every good business has someone who is unpopular. You can blame it all on me but, afterwards, you will see a ship that is more in trim, better run. After all we are in the business to make profits, and I intend to see that they are made. Believe me, when we are married . . .'

'That seems to me now remote,' Judith said, aware that

her heart had started to race. Suddenly she was afraid of Leo again; afraid as she had not been for a very long time. He had lulled her, through his ardour, his protestations of love, into a false sense of security.

'Oh?' Leo looked up sharply.

'I've seen a side of you I find repulsive.'

'But my dear Judith,' he rose and went over to her, trying to take her in his arms. 'This has *nothing* to do with our personal life together.'

'I think it has. You said that when we were married I wouldn't be here all the time.'

'Well, nor you will.' He looked surprised.

'I thought this was to be our home?'

'*One* of our homes! Maybe we'll spend three or four months of the year here, I don't really know. You can't imagine, my dear, that having waited for you all this time, I would consent to leave you behind. If so, your idea and my idea of a wife are very different.'

He tried to kiss her, but she resisted him. She felt threatened and struck at his chest with her fists. Suddenly his expression turned to rage and, pushing her away from him, he moved to the other side of the room.

'Judith, what *is* this?' he thundered. 'After the Bahamas, after our passionate lovemaking this afternoon, what is happening to us?'

'I'm seeing you differently,' she said, sitting down and putting her head in her hands. 'It is a person that I've glimpsed briefly once or twice before, but didn't want to believe existed. Sometimes you frighten me. I don't know what kind of man you are.'

Now, for the first time, Leo looked confused too. He stretched out his hands towards her. 'But I've *always* been like this. Surely you, of all people, knew that? And I do feel that, if business is to create such a barrier between us, then the sooner you give it up the better. You have done a

416

wonderful job, but there is no earthly need for you to go on . . .'

'Just to travel round the world, as *your* wife . . .' She gaped at him, almost speechless.

'Naturally, what could be better? I don't wish to boast, but it's a position that a lot of women would sell their souls for.' He bent over her chair and began stroking her hair. 'Now come to bed, my sweet, and forget about all this. After all, it is there that we really understand each other, isn't it? There is no chance at all of confusion in our lives there.'

Much later that night Judith, still awake, lay by the side of the sleeping man who, she realized too late, was a stranger. He was someone who had for so long obsessed her that she had been unable to see him with any objectivity. How pathetic she must have looked to Marcel and, maybe, her children too.

She realized now that for too long she had been the victim of this singular obsession. She had been illogically and irrationally bewitched, and for many years, by a man whose real personality was hidden from her.

She had allowed him to make her. His money had helped her from the time she had bought her first hotel. She had allowed him to become her lover, a part of her physical existence that was essential to her. She couldn't exist without him: somehow, in the background, he always had to be there. His very absences, even, made him more fascinating. He had made her, without her realizing it, totally dependent on him, transforming her from the hard-working wife of a chef, who bought the food for the restaurant and did the accounts, to a female carbon copy of an international tycoon like Leo. The transformation had been so gradual that it had changed her slowly, without her realizing it.

Yet the night she had eaten with her family after

417

returning from the Bahamas had made her realize what she had become. It was then that she saw herself through their eyes – someone who had forsaken her family for a form of love she didn't really understand. She was no longer Judith Prynne. She was Leo's woman. Maybe he had one in every capital city: how could she know?

Slowly she had trodden across the web to the centre where she was caught fast. Slowly, but deliberately, she had fallen into the attractive, forbidden net that he'd woven with the cunning of a spider.

Chapter 22

Rosalind Drake was a woman who did not take defeat lightly. Yet for so long had she endured her domestic role that she completely lacked the knowledge, the experience, of combating someone as dangerous and as powerful as Leo Valenti. Even though the general public, or even specialists in the City, had remained in ignorance of his interest in the operations of the enlarged Jenner organization, his dominant personality imprinted itself on everything that happened practically from the day that he returned to London to view his domain, impose his views. Yet his control was known only to a few, those who were entrusted to carry out his orders. He didn't stay in England for long and, as soon as he left, his messages began coming over telex, across wires that buzzed and hummed round the world from wherever he happened to be. He missed nothing, his finger on every pulse. In many people such a multiplicity of talents, the ability to contain and know so much, was admirable.

But Rosalind, new to the City and the machinations of the business world, knew nothing about this. She soon realized the extent of her ignorance. Accordingly she was forced more and more to take the advice of the man she had kicked upstairs, made president. She had no alternative other than to rely on his judgement, his wisdom, his experience: Frank Barnard.

But the Prynne–Jenner merger moved too quickly even for one as experienced in the ways of the City as he. For many years gambling had been illegal in England, largely for the very reasons that had made it so suspect in America and other places where it was tolerated. But since the sixties a Gaming Levy Board had kept very strict control over those places to which it issued licences, so that when the respectable Jenner Securities applied for a licence for its newly refurbished stately home hotel on the Thames they were considered ideal. Its link with that vastly successful hotel chain, Prynne's, gave it eminent respectability.

The licence was granted and the new Aylestone was launched as a ritzy, glitzy palace full of black leather and red plush which revolved round its casino. Here people could play blackjack, roulette and chemmy to their hearts' content. They could sleep away their cares in the most comfortable of beds, exorcize their morning blues in the underground pool, in the gym or on the golf course and start again after lunch.

But to play at Aylestone you had to be a member, and to be accepted as a member you had to have a certain amount of money. It became a very exclusive, costly affair indeed.

Rosalind avidly followed the transformation of Aylestone into a high-class gambling joint and frequently discussed the details with her son Philip, who had joined the Drake Organization. He was a competent young man, fresh from university, who one day would undoubtedly be managing director. He was not unlike the young Doug who had first taken control of Aylestone, and he had managed to remain close to both his mother and his father. He was on good terms with his Aunts Judith and Moira, and he got on well with his cousins, particularly Pauline.

But Judith did not want an interest to develop into love. She did not approve of the marriage of first cousins and she had packed Pauline off to America to see the world and complete her education. In her own quiet way she could be just as pragmatic, just as ruthless as Leo Valenti.

Philip had been deeply affected by the alienation between his mother and father. He was a gentle, affectionate man who loved his family and thought family life important. He enjoyed country life and visiting his relations in Scotland, to which his work sometimes took him, as Drake had an interest in the development of oil in the North Sea.

When he travelled to Aberdeen, he invariably stayed on the way with the McLarens in their large stone house overlooking the Firth of Forth. Isolated up there, Moira was always glad to hear news of what was happening to the rest of the family in the south and, particularly, the sister whom she loved but from whom she had felt increasingly isolated. Moira was extremely fond of Philip and found in him one of the few really understanding, sympathetic members of the family in whom she was able to confide.

Philip was having tea one afternoon with his aunt in the course of one of his regular journeys to the North Sea coast when she rested her cup on her lap and said, with a deep sigh:

'I don't suppose you see much of Judith these days, do you, Philip?'

'Not after the row,' Philip said ruefully, accepting a large piece of fruit cake from his aunt. 'Mother felt that she'd had her nose well and truly put out of joint. She hated Aunt Judith after that.'

'They were never close.' Moira moved nearer to the fire and extended her hand to trap its warmth. 'Even from the beginning, when she first met Doug. In their different ways they were both ambitious. And Aylestone, now, is a great success.' She gazed into the depths of the fire. 'Mind you, I don't like thinking of it as a gambling casino. It's not really the kind of activity that I, or Billy – a Scot, you know – approve of.'

'I don't think Aunt Judith would have gone so far without Leo behind her,' Philip said. '*He* was the one who wanted the casino.'

'What a frightening man he is,' Moira said with a perceptible shudder, and Philip looked at her in surprise.

'As frightening as that?'

'I think so. Don't you?'

'I don't really know him. Whenever I meet the family he's not there. I don't think Michael and Pauline care for him much; in fact I know they don't.'

'Judith will marry him, though, I expect.'

'I think the five years are nearly up.' Philip held out his cup for more tea and, as Moira replenished it and returned it to him, he sat back, stirring it thoughtfully.

'Why do you call him "frightening", Aunt Moira? I thought that shudder seemed to go right up your spine.'

'It did,' Moira said, shuddering again. 'It's a long time ago, but when Billy wanted to clear up the mystery of Richard's disappearance he went over to Italy to look for him. He travelled to Rome, Naples, Sicily and finally Venice, which was our last home. Everywhere he went Billy felt he was being followed, that someone knew all about him; where he was, and why he was there.'

'What a horrible feeling,' Philip said, gazing at her with interest.

'It was, and Billy is not a normally nervous man. When he arrived in Venice he was mysteriously contacted, shown the photo of Richard and told it would be his for a large price. It was the evidence we needed if we were to marry.' Moira's voice faltered and she began to rub her arms as though a chill had entered her body. 'Somehow, although we have no proof, we always associated Leo with that. He knew that Billy was going to Italy and why. It upset Billy so much that he came home a frightened man, a changed man. He realized there were forces of evil in the world he hadn't known existed.'

'But surely he didn't think Leo disposed of his own son?'

Moira hesitated for a moment and then said:

'Billy's theory was that Richard's death was a gang killing. He felt – though he never had any proof from that day to this – that Leo was involved, maybe with Richard, certainly opposed to the side that disposed of him. Leo was trying to get information through Billy as to who killed Richard. Billy has remained convinced that Leo is involved with the Mafia ... and hence his enormous fortune. Of course you must never say *anything* about this to a soul – it could be dangerous.' Moira shuddered again and rubbed her arms with both hands.

'Billy and I have been very happy, of course,' she went on after a moment, 'but he is never very at ease in Judith's company. He would prefer not to meet her but, as she's my sister, he can't avoid it. In no circumstances will he agree to meet Leo.'

'Surely Uncle Billy didn't think Aunt Judith was involved,' Philip said, looking aghast.

'Oh no, of course not! It is her association with Leo that embarrasses him. He's quite sure she's innocent and so am I. But she's obsessed by that man. I really believe it's an illness, and she will neither see nor hear anything but good of him. She once asked Billy to invest in Prynne's, but he said he would have nothing to do with anything connected with Valenti. That upset her.'

Moira reached for some logs that lay in a basket by the side of the grate and threw them on the fire.

'Billy thought Valenti was connected with the drugs racket, you know. We all did but, of course, never *dared* to say a *thing*. I mean one doesn't have any proof, does one? Besides, what can you do? What can anyone do?'

'Shouldn't she be told?' Philip said with a worried frown. 'She may be in danger herself.'

'Oh, she knows,' Moira said with a grave, sad face. 'If you ask me, she knows. And as for Leo harming her ... these people always protect their own, so they say. I always think ...'

Suddenly the embers of the fire, fuelled by the fresh application of logs which Moira had thrown on, came to life and flames shot up the chimney with a menacing roar that drowned whatever she was going to say.

From the balcony overlooking the sea brother and sister stood, side by side, watching the fishing boats returning to the harbour with their catch. Behind the boats the gulls flew low as if hoping for some bounty to fall from the nets. Part of Dragon's Reach was still covered with scaffolding as workmen put the finishing touches to the outside fabric of the hotel. Inside, banging continued as new rooms were constructed, bathrooms added, and the general upheaval ensued that preceded the opening of that event in the hoteliers' world: a new Prynne hotel.

'It *is* a heavenly spot,' Doug said, turning enthusiastically to Judith. 'I think the nicest one you've got.'

'Dragon's Reach,' Judith murmured. 'It *has* an air of completion about it, don't you think?'

'In what way?'

'As if it will be the last.'

'The last Prynne hotel?'

'I think so. It's a bit like Mother's and Father's dream of India. They never came back; finally in their old age they found happiness. I feel I could be very happy here at Dragon's Reach.'

'Judith, you're talking as though you and Leo were no longer going to be married.' Doug looked at her searchingly but, for some moments, Judith didn't reply, continuing to gaze across the water towards the bustle and activity in the normally tranquil bay.

'Are you, Judith?' Doug asked, repeating his question.

'Well I'm free to do so now; the divorce has come through; but I'm in no hurry to change my status.'

'Have you and Leo grown apart? Somehow for a long time I've had the feeling you have.'

'Maybe,' she said enigmatically. 'Let's just say there are things about him I know now that I didn't know before.'

'What are they?'

'Suddenly you discover you don't really know someone you've been associated with for years. The crunch came over Aylestone. Oh I know it *is* successful, and perhaps he was right . . . but it was the way he did it. He imposed his will on us all; he got rid of you quite without feeling and, not for the first time, I felt afraid of him. You don't *really* want to be afraid of the man you marry, do you, Doug?'

'You don't,' Doug said sombrely, reaching in his pocket for his cigarette case. 'But it's difficult to get out of now, isn't it? He's irretrievably linked with Prynne's, and Jenner.'

'It will be difficult to disconnect our business interests, for a while at least, but I'm not forced to marry him.' Judith put her arm through his and they continued the walk they had been taking along the terrace stretching the length of the hotel. Beneath this were the lawns and formal gardens which led, eventually, to the sea via a set of steep stone steps cut into the cliffside.

Judith paused by one of the old wooden benches that still remained on the terrace and sat down, her arm through Doug's, taking him with her. In one hand he still held a cigarette between his fingers.

'You've had a rough deal in life, Doug, haven't you?'

'Most of it's my own fault,' Doug admitted ruefully. 'Years ago Rosalind told me I was weak, and I am.'

'You're not. You're very capable. You're not a genius, but few people are. Rosalind was a discontented woman who enjoyed making those around her miserable.'

'Only me – not Philip, or her father.'

'They had qualities of independence you don't have, though I think Philip is rather like you.'

'No, I've let people kick me about. I am weak. I was weak to give in to Doris. She was only interested in me for what she thought I had. When she found it was nothing she packed me in.'

'She wasn't your type. She was a refuge. I've been weak too, about Leo. People think I'm tough, but I'm not. I let him mould me. Whatever his personal faults, Leo has an unerring instinct for business. He is nearly always right. Doug,' Judith squeezed his hand and looked searchingly at his brooding face, 'I'm sorry for what Leo did to you. I know that you loved Aylestone; but I don't think you'd love it any more. Every time I go there I no longer think of it as our home.'

'I'm sure you're right,' Doug said, patting her arm. 'Don't worry about it. I couldn't have managed a gambling joint.'

'But I do worry. You're such a nice fellow and you've had a raw deal. How would you like to manage Dragon's Reach? That's really why I asked you here.'

Doug glanced from the sea towards her.

'Are you serious?'

'Absolutely.'

'Did you talk it over with Leo?'

'No. I don't have to talk everything over with Leo. But I did ask Marcel and he thought it was a good idea. I think this is the sort of leisurely place you'd like, Doug. It will be good for you and you will be good for it. Besides, we're lucky to have you. You're very experienced. You know the hotel business inside out. What's more, I feel we'll establish a home here for the family, rather as Aylestone once was.' She turned her head, looking behind her. 'Maybe that wing which has the sea on both sides; but we'll do it up a lot nicer than Drake ever did for us.'

'He did nothing. It was full of damp. What a bastard that man was.'

'No use looking back, Doug. We must go on, looking forward, and I would love to know that you were the manager here and,' momentarily she looked towards the sea again, 'somehow I feel that Gran would like it too.'

The news soon got round that Doug was back in the family business. It was considered a magnanimous, generous gesture, but some people considered it a little foolish; a weakness on Judith's part. People said that in business the heart should not rule the head, and Doug had failed to make Aylestone pay.

Marcel, however, agreed with Judith. He knew Doug was good if he had someone good over him. When Judith left Aylestone the influence that steadied Doug was no longer there. Now, they were back in harness again, good as a team.

Marcel had the feeling that old times were returning as he inspected the nearly completed hotel and gave it his approval. There was a new vitality about Judith, and he was sure it had to do with the absence of Leo.

'I thought a fish restaurant,' Judith said, looking round the spacious area with sea views that would be the main restaurant. 'You know everywhere we go we specialize in local dishes. Fresh fish from Cornwall; oysters and lobsters. What do you think?'

'I like the idea,' Marcel said cautiously. 'I can't believe that we'll strike lucky again, Judith.'

'Why not?' she looked at him, surprised. 'We have the same principle here as with all the others: planning, good controls, careful execution. Now you think of a wonderful fish chef and he can start planning.'

'I have a wonderful fish chef,' Marcel said.

'Good.' Judith produced the notebook in which she jotted points as she made her way round the nearly completed building. 'What's his name?'

'Marcel Laborde.'

'Yes, Marcel, I know, but who will you put in charge?'

'It's a very nice spot.' Marcel scratched the little bald patch on the crown of his head and smiled.

'You don't mean you're going to retire from *Prynne's*?'

'Why not?'

'You're too young.'

'All right, maybe six months there and six months here. I love the sea.'

'It *is* a very charming place,' Judith agreed. 'I admit I was seduced. Everyone seems very happy here. Doug has settled in immediately. The children adore it. I thought of making it the family home, rather as Aylestone was in the old days.'

'Family?' Marcel said with a trace of bitterness. 'What family?'

Judith's eyes rested solemnly on him. 'Marcel, we're still family – Pauline, Mikie, you and me. Doug is family, Moira and Billy, Alida, Franco and Giles. Philip . . . he's family too.'

'And Ros?' Marcel's eyes narrowed.

'I don't think Ros would ever be happy here.'

'Would she be welcome, though?'

'No.' Judith's expression became defensive. 'Ros has given us a hard run, you know. She's forced me to do things I wouldn't otherwise have done.'

'You could also say that about Leo. Is he family, by the way? *He* has forced you to do things you wouldn't otherwise have done.'

'Such as?'

'Practically everything in your adult life since you met him. Behind all your actions for years I've seen not you but Leo.'

'That's because you're prejudiced, Marcel,' Judith said.

'I admit I'm prejudiced. But the way he has transformed Aylestone into a casino was the last straw. Thank God I refused to have anything to do with the cuisine.'

'Have you seen it? It's very nicely done.'

'I'm not saying it isn't nicely done, but should it have been done? You let him overrule you, Judith, and in your heart you know you're wrong.'

'I don't see how you can tell what goes on in my heart, Marcel. You know, I *want* us to remain friends . . .'

'When are you getting married anyway? Date fixed?'

'Not yet. When it is I'll let you know.'

Judith turned on her heels and left Marcel standing in the middle of the huge, empty room.

Chapter 23

From the top of the grand staircase Judith stood, as she so often did when she was at Aylestone, looking down on to the crowd that thronged the lobby outside the doors leading into the casino. A crowd of sophisticated, elegantly dressed women and men in dinner-jackets smoked, chatted and laughed together like people at some fashionable first night at Covent Garden, or a London theatre.

She herself always wore evening dress, and the slinky folds of her midnight blue gown emphasized her figure which she'd kept well over the years. An older woman had to be careful with make-up and Judith knew just how much eye-shadow or blusher to use, and what colour of lipstick suited her best.

Suddenly her eyes were riveted by the sight of two men who had walked into view. They both had domed, bald heads, smoked long cigarettes and were closely engaged in conversation. One turned his profile in his quest for an ashtray and, instinctively, she stepped behind one of the orange trees that decorated the balcony, cutting off the casino from the rest of the hotel.

There was, she felt, absolutely no doubt about it. Both of the men she was looking at had, at one time or another, visited Leo when she was staying with him on the yacht in the Bahamas.

Well, the sensible practical part of herself reasoned, there was nothing wrong with that. Leo would be sure to tell his friends about his gambling interests in England. All the same she felt that *frisson*, that irrational yet instinctive feeling of fear she had had before, and tightly she gripped the rail of the balcony for support.

'Are you all right?' A voice spoke close to her ear and she turned to find a concerned pair of eyes gazing at her. A strong hand reached out to steady her.

'I think I must have tripped,' Judith said, looking at her feet. 'I'm perfectly all right now, thank you.'

'You look very pale, Miss Prynne. Perhaps you should sit down and allow me to get you a glass of water.'

'I'm absolutely fine,' Judith insisted. 'I'm very sorry . . . you appear to know my name, yet I don't know yours.'

'Webber,' the man said, putting a hand in his inside breast pocket to look for a card. 'Ernest Webber. I was just on my way down to the casino when I saw you falter.'

'Please don't let me interrupt your play, Mr Webber. I'm perfectly all right.'

'You looked as though you'd had a shock. However, I was glad of the chance to be of help. I would also like to tell you what a fine job I think you've made of Aylestone. I've been here a few times over the years, but it's never been as good as this.'

'I don't *think* we've had the pleasure of meeting before, Mr Webber?' Judith looked at him with a puzzled smile. She had a very good memory for faces. 'Yet you obviously knew who I was.'

'Well you're quite famous, Miss Prynne,' Mr Webber said with an air of gallantry. 'I don't think you quite realize how well-known your face is; a prominent and successful businesswoman, rather a rarity even these days.'

'I didn't realize my face was as well-known as that,' Judith replied with a smile. 'May I ask what you do?'

'I'm in Securities, Miss Prynne.' Webber finally produced his card, which gave his name and an address in Threadneedle Street.

'I see,' she said, studying it. 'Do many businessmen gamble?'

'*Every* businessman is a gambler, didn't you know? You, for instance, must have gambled a lot in your career.'

'Yes, I suppose I have. That is, I gambled a lot at first but, later, everything seemed to flow. I was very lucky. How long are you staying, Mr Webber?'

'A few days.'

'And is your wife with you?'

'Alas, I belong to that fortunate, or unfortunate, segment of the population which has never married, Miss Prynne. My life is my work. I travel abroad a lot and so this enables me to have all the freedom I want. I am, however, very attached to my dog who likes nothing better than to come on holiday with me when he can because, of course, he can't when I travel abroad.'

'And is he here with you?'

'Yes, and in your excellent kennels.'

'We used to have two red setters in our family,' Judith said with a nostalgic smile. 'They were chiefly my parents' pets, and when they returned to India the dogs pined for them. It was really sad.'

'And what happened to them?' Mr Webber was obviously a keen animal lover.

'Oh, they remained here. They died natural deaths in the fullness of time, but I don't think they ever forgot my parents.'

'Life *is* sad, isn't it, Miss Prynne?'

'Sometimes, yes, Mr Webber.'

'Well,' the man jangled some coins in his pockets. 'Time to go and lose my money.'

'I hope you make some as well.'

'You never know your luck.' Mr Webber gave a cheery wave and began to descend the staircase and, as he did, he looked back. 'Are you *sure* you've recovered, Miss Prynne?'

'There was nothing wrong with me at all, but thank you for your concern. Good-night and good luck.'

'Thank you.'

Judith stood for some time watching Webber as he

slowly completed his descent and, as he paused at the entrance to the casino, he looked up at her and waved.

She then remembered, with a start, what had caused their unexpected encounter and looked round. But, of the two men with bald heads, there was no sign.

She retraced her steps along the corridor that led to the reception. A few couples sat in the lounge drinking their after-dinner coffee and, from the sound of voices in the restaurant, she knew that it was still full.

In many ways it was the same old Aylestone but, in more important ways, it was not. The people were different: the smart set who drove up from London, had dinner and stayed until four in the morning gambling in the casino before they drove home again. Then there were the serious gamblers who sometimes came from abroad and stayed, perhaps, for a few days; some seemed to stay for weeks.

She paused in the reception, exchanged a few words with the head receptionist, and then drew the guest book towards her, running her finger along the list of names for ones that might be familiar, that might furnish a clue as to the identity of the men she had seen going into the casino. She found Webber. He had given his address in the City; maybe he had a flat there as well, though it seemed unlikely in Threadneedle Street. He had a very firm, clear hand and she paused for a few minutes studying it. There was something about him that had rather interested her.

'Mr Webber has a dog?' she enquired of the receptionist.

'Yes, Miss Prynne, a large red setter. A lovely animal he likes to take for walks. It is, of course, too big for his bedroom, so he keeps it in the kennels.'

'Any idea how long he's staying?'

The receptionist ran his hands rapidly through the card index which contained details of those staying in the hotel and produced a card.

'He came on Thursday, Miss Prynne. He gave no

indication of when he was leaving; but has definitely booked for a week.'

'Thank you,' Judith said and continued on her way, making for the kitchens where one of Marcel's protégés was in charge.

When she stayed in the hotel Judith used the room, if it was vacant, that had once been occupied by Gran. Even though the room was vastly transformed from the familiar den it once was, it still contained a precious, nostalgic link with the past; with her childhood.

Yet, that night, she found it difficult to sleep. She lay for a long time on top of the bed, trying to read; but thoughts kept on obtruding themselves between her eyes and the printed page. Finally she put the book down and the light out, and crept between the sheets.

Of course she *was* tired. She was tired and she was not happy. The talk with Marcel at Dragon's Reach had upset her. She had not been honest with Marcel about Leo, but she wasn't really being honest with herself. It was an aspect of her life that she did her best to blot from her mind; yet soon he would be back, and decision time was near.

How would she feel when she saw him again?

Judith supposed she had some sleep. One often thought one had none, yet time passed. When it was dawn – she was sure she hadn't closed her eyes – she rose to make a cup of tea and, for some time, she sat at the window gazing at the familiar scene which reminded her of those happy days at Aylestone during the war, of school holidays with Gran.

A movement among the trees caught her eye and a large dog rushed out across the lawn in front of its owner who, with brisk strides, emerged from the wood and followed the dog towards the house.

Judith looked at her watch. It was 5 A.M. Had Mr Webber not been able to sleep either; or, had he not yet gone to bed?

She dressed quickly in a skirt and jumper and, daubing a trace of lipstick on her mouth, hurriedly left her room and went quickly along the corridor towards the stairs. She ran lightly down them, past the reception, which was empty – maybe the night receptionist was answering a call – and across the hall into the guests' lounge which was also empty. She went to the far door, towards which she had seen Mr Webber walking from the garden side, and looked out, but there was no sign of him. She opened the door, closed it behind her and stepped onto the terrace which ran the length of the river side of the house. Then she saw the flick of a dog's tail and heard a soft whistle.

Without thinking, she went in the direction of the whistle and realized it came from one of the outhouses that was used as a kitchen store. Just as she reached the door Webber emerged quite casually, stopping to turn and call for his dog and then, when he turned round again, he nearly collided with her.

'Miss Prynne!' he exclaimed. 'You startled me.'

'You startled me too, Mr Webber.' She saw that, far from not having gone to bed, he was freshly shaved, smelt of cologne and wore a yellow polo-necked sweater under his country tweeds. 'What an odd place to find you at *this* hour of the morning.' She pointedly stared at the watch on her wrist.

'You too, Miss Prynne. Or are you in the habit of taking early morning walks?'

'When I can't sleep I sometimes do. But I'm sorry to tell you, Mr Webber, that this part of the hotel is out of bounds to guests and, naturally, their animals. It contains the stores for the hotel.'

'I *do* apologize, Miss Prynne,' Webber said contritely. 'But my dog strayed. Here, boy, to heel,' he admonished as it slunk out of the store and crawled obediently to his side. 'Taggert, sit,' Mr Webber said, pointing commandingly to a spot by his side. 'His name's Taggert,' he explained unnecessarily to Judith. To her he seemed nervous.

'Was the door *open*?' Judith stood looking at the store in astonishment.

'It must have been.' Webber followed her gaze with an innocent air. 'How else could Taggert have got in?'

'Most unusual.' Judith peered closely at the lock. 'I shall have to speak to chef. Now, if you would be kind enough, Mr Webber, to return with your dog to the grounds, I should be grateful. And please don't allow him to stray again, or we shall reluctantly have to reconsider our policy towards allowing guests to bring dogs to this hotel.'

'*Do* forgive me, Miss Prynne,' Webber said, slipping a lead through the dog's collar. 'You can be sure he will be reprimanded, and it will not happen again.'

Later on that week, the incident forgotten, Judith travelled north by car to begin a routine inspection of her hotels.

She began with Forteliot Castle which had been one of her favourites since it had opened. It was here that she could unwind and relax. She could do some fishing, see her sister and brother-in-law and her little nephew if he was home, because he was now at a boarding school.

It was amazing to think that, after Aylestone, the castle was the oldest of her hotels, and the time was fast approaching when it would need refurbishment and redecoration. So, during the day, she wandered through the long corridors, the huge airy rooms, with her secretary making careful notes.

During the day, too, there were telephone calls to make and receive. Invariably a problem cropped up in some part of the Prynne network that needed her attention.

Dragon's Reach was nearing completion, and it was her plan to fly from Edinburgh to Penzance at the end of the week for all those last-minute details that would need her close attention.

Around her now as she stood in the middle of the dining room, outlining her ideas for a new colour scheme, were the general manager of the hotel, Donald More, who had been there since Fraser Lyle had been dismissed; her secretary; the under-manager, Maurice Gowing, and the team of talented designers – the successors to the Kennedys – who were now in overall charge of the group design at all the Prynne hotels.

The sun slanted through the high, stained-glass window of what had once been the hall of the old house, and in front of her Jennifer Ridley, the head of the design team, dressed in jeans and a sweater, hair only casually combed through, was placing on the floor patterns for the new colour scheme that would replace the old one at the hotel.

'You see, Miss Prynne, green *is* a most attractive, most dominating colour and a mixture of . . .'

'Excuse me, madam,' a footman murmured at her elbow. 'You are wanted on the telephone.'

'Alex, would you go and see who it is?' Judith smiled at her secretary who was on her knees, also taking notes.

'It is for you personally, madam,' the footman said. 'I was specifically told to ask for you in person.'

'Who is it, Angus?' Judith enquired, frowning. The name Leo leapt to her mind.

'It is the manager at Aylestone, madam, and he said I must fetch you at once.'

Judith excused herself and hurried after the footman, her mind immediately returning not to the mystery of the American guests but, for some reason, to the open storehouse door. It was an unexplained irregularity that had worried her, subconsciously, for days. She took the call in the manager's office which was empty.

'Yes, Judith Prynne here.'

'I'm sorry to interrupt you, Miss Prynne.' The manager was a man of wide experience called Graham Knight.

'That's all right, Graham, what is it?' Graham's tone was so normal that Judith felt an immediate sense of relief.

'I'm afraid that the police are here, Miss Prynne. The hotel was raided in the early hours of this morning. I'm sorry to tell you that a considerable quantity of the drug cocaine was found in one of the storehouses outside the kitchen.'

As Judith drove up, the drive of the hotel was full of police cars, and a thorough room-to-room search was in progress of the hotel which, until further notice, had been closed. All the guests had been asked to leave after breakfast. Judith had flown from Edinburgh to Heathrow where she was met by her chauffeur, who had taken her to Aylestone. Marcel was on his way and so, apparently, was Doug to lend support.

She was immediately taken to see the officer in charge of the case.

'Of course we realize you personally know nothing about this, Miss Prynne,' a senior policeman explained, after outlining what had happened. 'You are an innocent victim. We know that.'

'Victim?' Judith said quickly. 'How do you mean "victim"?'

'You have been used, Miss Prynne, quite ruthlessly and for a long time.' The man from Scotland Yard produced a notebook from his pocket which he consulted, after laboriously flicking through the pages. Then, when he had found what he wanted, he looked at Judith with a kindly expression.

'I suppose you never doubted Mr Valenti's integrity?'

'Integrity?' Judith heard herself saying. 'Why should I?'

'Quite. I believe you were to be married.'

'There was a probability. But not a certainty.' She felt herself colouring as though already, like Judas, she was guilty of betraying him.

438

'However, it was a relationship which has endured for a number of years?'

'Yes.'

'And you *never* questioned Mr Valenti as to the source of his wealth?'

'Frequently; but his answers were always satisfactory.'

'I'm sure they were.'

'I think my solicitor . . .'

'There will be plenty of time for you to call your solicitor, madam. All we wish to do now is establish a few facts. I assure you, Miss Prynne, it is not our intention to charge you, certainly at this juncture and probably not at all. We have no doubt that Mr Valenti used you, and others, for his own purposes.'

'I suppose you do have proof of what you are suggesting?' Judith spoke as though her voice came from a great distance.

'Well . . .' the detective looked at his colleague and shrugged his shoulders. 'I can't say that we exactly have *proof*. Mr Valenti is much too clever for that; but we are certain that a very intricate web has been woven to bamboozle the authorities here and in the USA, as well as on the Continent. There is a strong indication of fraud on a very large scale . . . fraud, drugs, well . . . who knows what else?'

'Have you questioned Mr Valenti?'

'Ah.' The policeman tapped his pencil on his book. 'If only we could! Have *you* any idea where he is?'

'I thought he was on his yacht in the Bahamas.'

'Yes, a very convenient address, a yacht,' the Inspector said thoughtfully. 'We have found his yacht, but not him. And something tells me that neither you, nor ourselves, will see Mr Valenti again, certainly for a very long time, perhaps never.'

'Do you think he's dead?' Judith suddenly got up and, turning her back on those in the room, walked to the window where she looked out on to the strangely empty grounds. How odd they seemed without people wandering round. Then, suddenly, in her mind's eye she saw that lovely red setter Taggert bounding through the woods . . . of course, she should have known. There were a lot of things she should have known, or guessed, but it was too late now.

'We don't think he's dead, madam, but we can't be sure. In the sort of world in which people like him move anything can happen. However, my guess is that Mr Valenti is very much alive, but lying low.

'He was a very clever man, adept at covering his tracks. He used you and Sir Matthew Jenner, whom we have also interviewed, as a very convenient way to launder through Jenner Securities the considerable profits he made from his illegal activities. By the time they got to an English bank no one knew where they had come from, but we had a very shrewd idea.'

'How did you know all this?' Judith interrupted a narrative which she suspected the man from the Yard was enjoying.

'We have our sources,' he replied with a mysterious air. 'We acted, in the first place, on information received. And, once we began to dig, our suspicions were aroused. The casino was a very interesting venture. Not like "Prynne's" at all. Why? We began to investigate Mr Valenti very carefully.

'We now know that he introduced two of his men as workers in the kitchens. You probably wouldn't even know their names, but this morning they were arrested. Friends of his who came to gamble in the casino served as the carriers for the drugs which were stored in your outhouses. Cocaine looks like packets of salt; very convenient, very ingenious. Thus this was the distribution point for a vast network that was to cover the British Isles. Yet there were surely people behind him. Although he was

very rich, they are probably richer still and they will hide
him . . . or kill him, as his son Richard was killed.'

Suddenly Judith felt faint and reached for a chair. Gentle
hands helped her into it. And, from very far away, she
could hear herself saying 'I can't believe this . . .' and a
voice saying regretfully, softly, in her ear:

'It's a pity, Miss Prynne, that a lady such as yourself
should ever have become involved with a person like
Valenti. It's a great, great pity.'

And his sigh seemed full of sincerity.

When Marcel appeared later in the day he completely took
charge. Judith was resting, aware of the sound of doors
banging and voices raised as the police almost took the
place apart. They went into every room and looked behind
every cupboard, under every bed, beneath every
floorboard.

Judith had been set up by an unscrupulous man who had
pretended to love her.

She and Marcel had very little to say to each other when
they met. They knew that would come later. She was aware
of his support, his strength, even his love. Suddenly,
compared to the massive integrity that was Marcel, Leo
seemed a weakling.

The following day Michael arrived to drive her to
Cornwall and she left at about noon. The senior detectives
had departed, but a number of men stayed behind, and
outside the kitchen door were black plastic sacks full of
debris, as if the builders had moved in again.

As they drove down the drive Judith gazed stonily
ahead. She doubted if she would ever return to Aylestone.

They were quite well on their way when Mikie said:

'Shall you miss him, Mum?'

'I shan't miss him, but I shall never forget him. I may
yet find myself in the Old Bailey charged with being an
accessory.'

'Dad doesn't think so.' Mikie reached over and tenderly put a hand on her arm. 'Dad had a long conversation with the Inspector. He knows you were set up.'

'I wonder when Leo decided to use me?' Judith murmured in a faint voice. She still didn't feel at all well. It would take months, maybe years, to get over the shock.

'I think Leo did love you, Mum. I often saw you with him. He couldn't have planned this all those years ago.'

'The police seemed to think someone was behind him. Maybe they told him to do it.'

'I think Leo loved you,' Mikie insisted again. 'I didn't like him, but I think his affection for you was genuine. Pauline does too.'

Judith looked with some astonishment at her son who was scarcely out of his teens, yet who was speaking to her with the wisdom of a much older man.

'Thank you, darling, for saying that.' She returned the pressure of his hand. 'I've been a very silly woman. Your father was always right. He knew. But for him Leo and I would have been married. God knows where I'd be now.'

'You're here, Mum, and you're going home,' Mikie said gently as they reached the main trunk road that would take them to Cornwall.

'Home? Do you already think of Dragon's Reach as home?'

'We all do. We like it. Pauline is there and Aunt Moira is coming down tomorrow. The place is filled with flowers and messages. People love you, Mum. As for the rest, the public will soon forget. They have very short memories.'

'Let's hope so,' Judith said and, leaning back in her seat, let her body relax, her tired eyes close at last. Already, in her mind's eye, she could glimpse the calm expanse of sea, the gulls wheeling in round the bay and that beautiful place waiting for her on the cliffs.

It seemed like home already.

Epilogue

1989

Through the trees it was possible to see the outline of the house that had enjoyed such spectacular, if brief, notoriety.

The gates were fastened by a long, strong chain and at one time a patrol car used to pass by every few hours to make sure there were no intruders.

But people soon forget and, as the months and then the years went by, it became a place of dereliction, an objective for vandals who used to go up to it just to throw stones through the windows. Gradually it grew derelict.

The seasons passed, summer came and went; then it was autumn, winter, spring and summer once again. But the house still had the sad, forgotten look of an old friend who has suffered repeated rejection.

People had tried and tried again; but it had failed, and now it was associated with shame and failure.

In time the Prynne family, in their new home at Dragon's Reach, recovered from the rumpus. In the world of instant global communication, scandal and humiliation are scarcely even a nine days' wonder. The Prynne hotels were so successful that they were only marginally affected when the shares dropped on the Stock Exchange. There is so much other news to feed the public's relentless appetite that events fade, names are forgotten and legends disappear. If asked about the shadowy figure behind it all it is probable that few would even remember the name Valenti.

Now, after the passage of years, a new chain was placed on the rusty gate yet, through the trees, the old house looked just the same: windowless, crumbling, but still proud.

On the other side of those old stone walls, however, it

was a shell but, on the outside gate, a large sign in bold green with black letters proclaimed:

FREEHOLD SITE TO BE SOLD FOR DEVELOPMENT

So pass the glories of the world.